A LIADEN UNIVERSE®
CONSTELLATION
✧ Volume 4 ✧

D0250226

A LIADEN UNIVERSE®
CONSTELLATION
✧ Volume 4 ✧

SHARON LEE &
STEVE MILLER

Copyright © 2019 by Sharon Lee and Steve Miller

"Street Cred" © 2017 by Sharon Lee and Steve Miller (First published in *Change Management: Adventures in the Liaden Universe® Number 23*, Pinbeam Books, February 2017); "Due Diligence" © 2017 by Sharon Lee and Steve Miller (First published in *Due Diligence: Adventures in the Liaden Universe® Number 24*, Pinbeam Books, July 2017); "Friend of a Friend" © 2016 by Sharon Lee and Steve Miller (First published in *Sleeping with the Enemy: Adventures in the Liaden Universe® Number 22*, Pinbeam Books, July 2016); "Cutting Corners" © 2017 by Sharon Lee and Steve Miller (First published on Baen.com, April 2017); "Block Party" © 2017 by Sharon Lee and Steve Miller (First published on Baen.com, December 2017); "Degrees of Separation" © 2018 by Sharon Lee and Steve Miller (First published in *Degrees of Separation: Adventures in the Liaden Universe® Number 27*, Pinbeam Books, January 2018); "Excerpts from Two Lives" © 2018 by Sharon Lee and Steve Miller (First published in *Star Destroyers*, Baen Books, March 2018); and "Revolutionists" © 2018 by Sharon Lee and Steve Miller (First published in *Razor's Edge*, Zombies Need Brains, June 2018).

A Baen Books Original

Baen Publishing Enterprises
P.O. Box 1403
Riverdale, NY 10471
www.baen.com

ISBN: 978-1-4814-8404-6

Cover art by Sam Kennedy

First Baen printing, June 2019

Distributed by Simon & Schuster
1230 Avenue of the Americas
New York, NY 10020

Printed in the United States of America

10 9 8 7 6 5 4 3 2 1

✧Contents✧

A LIADEN UNIVERSE®
CONSTELLATION
✧ Volume 4 ✧

✧ Foreword ✧

AS PREDICTED,
LIADEN UNIVERSE® CONSTELLATION
NUMBER FOUR

IN THE GENERAL RUN OF READERS there's an expectation that SF writers are all about prediction. In that case, we're doing it right. Back in June of 2014 we made a prediction about the future, and truth told we were pretty sure it would happen.

We—that is Sharon Lee and Steve Miller, authors of the Liaden Universe®—predicted that eventually you, or someone very much like you, would be holding this book in hand. Right. We predicted the advent of *Liaden Universe® Constellation Number Four* and here you are, listener in the forest, proof that our prediction was accurate.

Understand that we had good cause to predict this book. People were reading our novels, of which there were already more in train, and our publisher, Baen, had been coming to us—still comes to us in fact!—with a request that we turn in a shorter work in support of each new novel. The editors at Baen add that story to the free monthly offerings at Baen.com and—*voila*, over time there builds up a backlog of Liaden stories that may not have been seen by you, our constant reader, on account of them only being featured in electronic format.

The "in support of" story at one per novel would take a long time to accumulate into a hundred thousand word plus collection, and clearly we wrote the foreword to the third *Liaden Universe® Constellation* just four years ago. We've been lucky in our work, since our Baen editors have also asked us to write stories for several anthologies. We're also lucky in our work because other anthologists have requested stories from us—some specifically asking for Liaden material. Since we have far more Liaden story ideas than we've outlined, much less written, each opportunity to aim at a specific deadline with a specific story concept helps us cross a "you know what would make an interesting story" off the list we've been accumulating for decades.

There, you see, is the area we have trouble predicting—*which* story idea will be asked for strongly enough or often enough that we have to start work on it, which will fit an anthology theme perfectly. "Balance of Trade," the short story, became *Balance of Trade* the novel after a cascade of requests, and several stories in other *Constellation* volumes grew out of a simple, but oft-asked question, such as, "What happened to the taxi driver?" from Cheever McFarland's first stop under Korval's roof.

Thanks for reading the stories here, and thanks for helping editors and other readers ask for more of our work. Whether this is your first read or your thirteenth, we hope you'll keep your eyes on our *Liaden Universe® Constellation*s as a good way to keep up with the characters who people our stories.

Oh yes, about predictions . . .

Are we predicting the eventual appearance of a fifth *Liaden Universe® Constellation*?

Well . . . what we know for sure is that we're still writing.

So! Watch the skies!

Sharon Lee and Steve Miller
Cat Farm and Confusion Factory
August 2018

✧ Street Cred ✧

JUST LIKE IN REAL LIFE, the people who populate the Liaden Universe® have to live with the consequences of their actions; in many cases they've built the situations they're in not through the machinations of their authors, but out of their own necessities. "Street Cred" takes place on Surebleak after Korval's relocation; and it takes a look at what happens when the Rule of Contract meets the Rule of Justice on a back world where everyone is armed, or should be.

✧✧✧✧

VAL CON YOS'PHELIUM leaned back in his chair and sighed.

It was his day to address such business as demanded attention from Delm Korval, while Miri his lifemate minded the Road Boss's office in Surebleak Port, answering what questions and concerns as citizens might have regarding the Port Road and its keeping.

The Surebleak Port Road having only recently acquired a Boss, they were yet an object of curiosity, and the office on-port was busy enough. It might be, later, that the presence of the Boss her-or-himself could be dispensed with, in favor of a proxy. He could find it in himself to hope so. His thoughts lately had been turning to ships, and lifts, the simplicity of Jump, and the charms of planets which were not Surebleak, Clan Korval's new home.

He was a pilot from a long line of pilots, trained as a scout, and far better suited to flying courier than to administration. It would be . . . a pity if he were never to lift again.

Which was, of course, boredom speaking, or self-pity. Or, more likely, an aversion to duty. Courier pilot had *never* been his destiny; and he would fly again, soon enough. But first, Surebleak required finer sorting; and Korval needed to find its feet on their strange new homeworld.

Which meant, among other matters, revisioning Clan Korval.

The bonds of kinship were as strong as they had been in his lifetime, though the individual clan members numbered so few that it seemed they must, eventually, marry into another situation, in order to survive. In fact, such an offer had only recently been made to him, as the Delm Genetic. He had . . . *not quite* said no, which was only prudence. Now was not a time to close doors suddenly found open, nor for relying too heavily upon the wisdoms of the past.

More pressing than kin-ties at the moment, however, were the clan's finances.

Clan Korval did business under half-a-dozen trade names, and while it was true that they remained a force in the markets, it was also true that they were now a *lesser* force. Formal banishment from Liad, their previous homeworld, had cost them trade partners, allies, and goodwill. It had been expensive to remove all of their goods, and themselves, to Surebleak; nor was their new home port nearly so conveniently situated as their former address.

Shan yos'Galan, the clan's master trader, was off-planet even now, seeking to establish a new main route, and coincidentally, reverse Korval's faltering finances. No small task—perhaps, indeed, an impossible task—but when Val Con had tried to express his regret at placing such a burden upon Shan's knees, his *cha'leket* had laughed aloud.

"You've asked me to develop new outlets, negotiate partnerships, build viable routes, and earn us a profit! Tell me, *denubia*, what is it that you think master traders *do?*"

So. Shan was off-planet even now, doing those things that master traders did, for the good of clan and kin.

In the meantime, Shan's delm wrestled with various knotty

problems of their own, such as Korval's relationship with Liaden society: specifically, the Liaden Council of Clans.

As part of the Contract of Banishment, the Council, speaking for all Liaden clans, had agreed that expulsion from the planet would constitute full and complete Balance for Korval's crimes against the homeworld. The contract had stipulated that there would be no personal Balances launched against individual members of the clan, or against Korval entire.

The Council of Clans had agreed to this; and each one of its member delms had signed the contract, which included a guarantee that they would educate the members of their clans regarding the contract, and its terms, and make it clear that no further Balance was appropriate.

Unfortunately, it seemed that the delms, or the Council, had not been as assiduous in education as they might have been. Balance had been brought against one of Korval, in violation of the terms of the contract. Young Quin had escaped harm, though the person who had sought to Balance the death of her heir had sustained a wound to her shoulder.

And all involved were fortunate that the attempt had not met with success.

Failure though it had been, it had also been against the terms of the contract, which stipulated that any breach, or seeming breach, be met with a formal inquiry.

Therefore, Korval's *qe'andra*, Ms. dea'Gauss, had contacted her firm's headquarters on Liad. The formal inquiry had been drafted by the senior partners there, and reviewed by the Accountant's Guild's protocol committee. The *qe'andra*, and Korval, wished to know if the Council was aware of the violation, and, now that it had been informed, what its next step would be.

Instead of immediately taking up this rather straightforward matter, the Council had—not tabled it. No, the Council had not even entered the inquiry into the agenda.

That they would refuse to even discuss the matter; that they risked offending the Accountant's Guild, one of the most powerful on Liad . . .

These things were not comforting to the delm of a small clan seeking to establish itself upon a new homeworld.

Korval yet had friends on Liad; if they had not, those on the Council who had wished to see Korval Themselves executed for crimes against the homeworld, and Clan Korval's assets—including its surviving members—distributed among the remaining clans at Council, would have prevailed.

That banishment had been the final Balance spoke directly to Korval's *melant'i* and its place in Liaden history.

In retrospect, had the Council indeed made a formal ruling against the Contract of Banishment, Val Con was certain that he would have been in receipt of a dozen or more pinbeams warning that he and his were now targets.

No such pinbeams had arrived, which led one, rather inescapably, to the conclusion that there was something more subtle, and perhaps more deadly, underway.

He had written letters to a few staunch allies, and to his mother's sister, the delm of Mizel. His sister Nova had written to Korval's old friend and ally, Lady yo'Lanna.

Unsurprisingly, to those who knew her, Lady yo'Lanna had replied first, and Nova had only this morning forwarded that answer to him.

The news . . . was mixed.

"The Administrative Board of the Council of Clans," wrote Lady yo'Lanna, *"recently published a Point of Order, directing the standing committee of* qe'andra *to study the question of whether the Contract of Banishment remains binding upon it, now that one of the parties has ceased to exist.*

"Well, of course, they're idiots, and so I said to Justus when he mentioned it to me. Even if the Delm of Korval has seen fit to dissolve the clan—which I trust they have not—the standard paragraph regarding heirs, assigns, and direct descendants is present in the Contract of Banishment.

"In light of your letter, and the unfortunate attempt to Balance against Quin—one enters entirely into Pat Rin's feelings on that head, I assure you!—I can only suppose that the whole purpose of this so-

*called study is to open Korval to such mischief as may be brought
against it by aggrieved persons. The longer the study goes on, the
weaker the contract becomes, even if the committee eventually returns
the opinion that both parties still exist.*

*"One wonders, in fact, what keeps them so long at the matter? An
hour, out of respect for the past* melant'i *of the Administrative Board,
ought to have been enough to have produced the rational answer in
the approved form.*

*"Be assured that I shall make further inquiries, dear Lady Nova,
and will write again when I have more information. In the meanwhile,
please guard yourself closely. I really must travel to Surebleak some
day soon. My grandson does not wish to move the clan's seat, nor do
I think that he ought to do so, but a bored old woman who has outlived
her lifemate and her nearest friends may perhaps be forgiven a bit of
wistful wanderlust.*

*"Please recall me to Korval Themselves, and to Kareen, as well as
to your delightful siblings. Maelin and Wal Ter desire, also, to be
recalled to Syl Vor, and to assure him of their continued regard. They
ask, respectfully of course, that he be permitted to visit. If you think it
wise,* yo'Lanna *would naturally care for him as one of our own.*

"I remain your friend and ally,

"Ilthiria yo'Lanna Clan Justus"

Val Con reached for the cup sitting by the screen; found it empty,
and sighed. Had Korval still been seated upon Liad—

But, of course, matters would have fallen out very differently,
after the strike which had neutralized the Department of Interior's
headquarters under Liad's capital city, if Korval had remained
unbanished.

In fact, they *were* exiles; Clan Korval had been written out of the
Book of Clans kept by the Council.

However, contrary to what seemed to be a growing belief in
larger Liaden society, and in direct opposition to what was set forth
in the *Code of Proper Conduct*, being written out of the Book of
Clans did not constitute the dissolution of a clan. The Book was an
administrative tool, used by the Council to track its membership.

The formalized kin-group which was recognized as a *clan* could only be dissolved by the action of the delm—which he and Miri, as Lady yo'Lanna had correctly supposed, *had not* taken.

Clan Korval existed: it stood by its charter; it sheltered and protected its members; supplied itself; negotiated new contracts, and honored its existing agreements. Thus, the *qe'andras'* most basic definition of a viable clan was satisfied.

The business entity known as *Clan Korval* likewise kept its contracts, paid its bills, invoiced its clients, nurtured its partnerships, and supported its allies. Such was the complexity of trade, that it would require far more than the word of a mere delm to dissolve *that* web. It would require a team of *qe'andra*-specialists a dozen years and more, so he very much feared, to shut down the *business* of Korval.

Clearly then, Clan Korval existed, across several spectra of reality. To suggest otherwise was, as Lady yo'Lanna had so eloquently proposed, idiotic.

The Council of Clans—*someone* on the Council of Clans, or, indeed, someone from the Department of the Interior, which had appointed itself Korval's exterminator, and which was known to have infiltrated the Council—*someone* wished to place Korval in increased peril.

And, sadly, the one resource Korval was lately richest in—

Was enemies.

· · · ·⋄· · · ·

"I WISH YOU wouldn't keep doing this," Miri said. "At least take back-up."

They were in the breakfast parlor, sharing the morning meal before parting for the day—she to the delm's office, and he, first, to the city, thence to duty at the Road Boss's office.

"Taking back-up will invalidate the results," he answered. This was not a new argument—in fact, it was so well-worn it was no longer an argument at all, merely a restating of their relative positions.

"I take back-up when I go down to the city, and the port," Miri said, which was her usual second move; however, she then tipped her head and produced a vary.

"Guess you think I'm soft."

He grinned, and raised his tea cup in salute.

"Yes; it is entirely possible that a mercenary captain who is twice a Hero is too soft for Surebleak's streets."

She shook her head, refusing to let him lighten the mood.

"Streets ain't as hard as they was, but that don't mean they're a walk in the park. One man, dressed up-scale, and walking by himself, is just asking to have his pocket picked, or his head broke. There's folks'll kill you for the jacket, never mind the boots."

"Am I clumsy?" he asked her, with interest.

She picked up a vegetable muffin, and glared at him, which gave pause. One wondered what had happened to bring heat back into the game.

"Anybody can make a mistake, Val Con," she said, sternly.

"That is very true; I have myself made a rather appalling number. But, Miri—"

"And," she interrupted; "it ain't no use bringing in how the Delm of Korval had an obligation to walk the Low Port, back on Liad, because, in case you ain't noticed, we're not on Liad, anymore."

He put his cup down, and reached across the small table to put his hand over hers.

"I was going to say that, I am the sixth member of the strike team. My function is to remain in sight, thereby encouraging any watchers to believe that there will be no strike at all."

"You can *be seen* with back-up," she said; "and it's less easy to pick you up for a chat."

"True," he said, gently. "However, I don't think they'll risk that just yet, do you?"

She closed her eyes, and took a hard breath.

"Miri, I am careful," he said earnestly. "I *will be* careful."

He tasted her distress, and regretted that he was the cause. But, surely, she knew that he dared not risk Nelirikk or Tommy Lee or Diglon, or any other innocent to be taken up by—

She sighed.

"It's your nose to get broke," she said, withdrawing her hand and picking up her coffee cup.

"I just hope I ain't in your head when it happens. Pain *hurts*."

• • •✧• • •

IT WAS HER TURN to be delm-for-the-day, so she walked him out the side door, where the car and Nelirikk waited to take him into the city. Then, this being one of those days that seemed to him to be good for tempting the Luck, he'd be dropped off at Pat Rin's house for a catch-up meeting before walking down to the port.

Alone.

She might've hugged him harder than usual. He might've done the same.

"See you tonight, Boss," she said, stepping back.

"Until soon, *cha'trez*," he answered, and turned away.

She watched until the car disappeared around the curve in the drive, before going back inside.

In the delm's office, she drew herself a cup of coffee from the pot, sat behind the big desk, put the mug to one side, and tapped up the screen.

Plenty of mail in the delm's queue.

Miri took a deep breath and dove in.

• • •✧• • •

THE SEASON, so he'd been told, was early autumn, which meant that winter was coming. The wind seemed to think that it had already arrived.

Val Con turned the collar of the leather jacket up around his ears, and tucked his hands into warm, fur-lined pockets.

Space leather turned the chill, as it would also turn a pellet, or a knife, or a stone. A pilot's second defense, her jacket, the first being her two strong legs, which were best used to run from trouble.

That, at least, was what young pilots were taught at the knees of their elders.

It was to be supposed, therefore, that elder pilots as a breed possessed a sense of humor. Or perhaps they merely hoped that one day a new sort of pilot would arise; a generation that was prudent, above being rash.

If the latter, their optimism had not yet been rewarded, as every pilot in Val Con's rather large acquaintanceship was reckless to a fault, though always with very good reason. It was to be most earnestly wished, then, that the elders found themselves fulfilled by their humor.

He had just left Pat Rin, who had been wonderfully plain on the subject of Val Con's wandering the city streets alone. It was not the first time he had expressed his opinion on this, though it had been, thus far, the most scathing. Plain speaking was of course permitted between kin, though one normally spoke with rather more restraint to one's delm.

Well, there. Pat Rin was a pilot.

The fact that both Miri and Pat Rin had chosen to be more than usually forceful on the topic of back-up, *today*, did give one pause. He was not a fool, after all, to discount good advice given by those who held his continued survival close to their hearts.

Perhaps, he should reconsider his strategy. In fact, he *would* do so. For this morning, however, he was committed. Best to finish as he had begun.

The wind gusted, enclosing him in a brief swirl of grit. He put his head down, and heard a shout from the alley to his left.

• • •✧• • •

THE REPORT from the *Qe'andra* Recruitment Committee, aka the Storefront *Qe'andra* Project, was encouraging, if you liked your encouragement laced with sheer terror.

One more 'prentice'd been accepted by the Liaden *qe'andra* who'd set up shop on Surebleak, bringing the total to four.

This newest one'd been a cornerman for Penn Kalhoon, back in the Bad Old Days, and Miri could see he was a good choice just by the quoted street cred: *fast and fair fixer*. Jorish Hufstead was used to thinking on his feet, he parsed complicated situations quickly, and he had the personal charisma necessary to make his solutions stick.

The Board of Advisors had been impressed with all that experience, like they should've been. What they didn't like so much was that Jorish couldn't read Terran, much less Liaden. Still, they'd agreed to a probation period, since Ms. kaz'Ineo, the Liaden pro, had a shipload of *melant'i* in her own right, and she was convinced he'd do fine, with a little work in the basics from the Liaden side of things.

Miri sighed and reached for her coffee mug. Change, and more change, and suddenly, everything'd be different.

All you could hope for, really, was that it'd be better, too.

· · ·✧· · ·

THE ALLEY was less than a block long, ending in a noisome courtyard where two men were beating a third, with fists, feet and knees.

Val Con took cover behind a row of trash compactors, and surveyed the situation.

The third man had managed to stay out of the hands of his attackers, and seemed no stranger to fisticuffs. His problem lay in the fact that his two attackers were at least as skilled as he, and—they had him boxed against the wall.

Unless there was a diversion, or a rescue, it was only a matter of time before he would fall, and very likely be killed.

A diversion, thought Val Con, could easily be arranged.

He threw the compactor lid in a low, flat trajectory that struck the leg of the attacker on the right, knocking him sideways, off-balance, arms flailing. His partner spun, seeking the source of the threat—and fell as the victim lunged forward and landed a solid blow to the side of his head, before turning to deal with the one remaining.

Val Con waited no longer. It had not been his plan to become involved in the altercation itself, only to even the odds. Mission accomplished, he slipped out from his hiding place and ran, quick and silent, back up the alley . . .

. . . and very nearly into the arms of three persons blocking the way to the street. Two held pellet guns; the third showed a knife.

Val Con dove forward into a somersault, heard the sound of pellet-fire passing uncomfortably near, and snapped into a flip, boots striking the nearest gunman in the arm. There was a snap, a scream, a curse—and he was rolling again, pellets hitting the alley's 'crete surface. He twisted to his feet, reaching for the gun on his belt—

Someone shouted behind him, he half-turned, and saw the three late combatants surging forward, apparently now united in purpose. One was carrying the trash compactor's lid, which he skimmed across the alley's floor. Sparks jumped along its passage, but it was scarcely a threat.

A pellet whined, too close to his ear, he ducked, hopped over the thrown lid—and landed awkwardly, a stone rolling under the heel of his boot.

Several shots came from the front-guard, who were closing, now that reinforcements were to hand. He felt something strike the jacket, as he lost his footing entirely and hit the alley floor, rolling.

∙ ∙ ∙✧∙ ∙ ∙

MIRI was halfway across the office, mug in hand, when her ankle twisted, and she went down, rolling, gasping with the delayed realization that she'd taken a hit high in the chest. The familiar office space blurred, and for a split second she saw a crowded street, a confusion of bodies—and lost it even as she felt her fist connect with something that gave with a satisfying crack.

"Miri!" Jeeves said sharply from the ceiling. "Do you require aid?"

"Not me," she lay flat on the rug, not trusting the ankle just yet. "Val Con—call McFarland, and the Watch. Six on one in Timber Alley, off Blair Road. Val Con's down, but he's still fighting."

∙ ∙ ∙✧∙ ∙ ∙

HIS HEAD HURT, and his chest; his hands, and his ankle. His pride—that hurt, too, possibly more than all the rest—though he hadn't bothered mentioning this to the medic.

Instead, Val Con had allowed himself to be treated; his hands wrapped, and the scalp wound staunched. The bruises on his chest each marked a pellet the jacket had stopped. His ankle, said the medic, wrapping it in a cold-pack, was possibly sprained, though it had not swollen so much that the boot had needed to be cut off.

That was fortunate; it was his favorite pair of boots.

While the medic worked, Val Con had answered such questions as had been put by the officer of the Watch. When those were done, and the woman had gone away, the medic told him to lie down and rest.

He had therefore stretched out, carefully, on the treatment

couch, closed his eyes, and began a breathing sequence, which would—

"Ain't asleep, are you?"

The voice was familiar to him—Cheever McFarland, his cousin Pat Rin's—that was to say, Boss Conrad's—head of security, who had arrived first on the scene of the . . . *stupid* situation he had gotten himself into. McFarland's handling of the matter had been efficient, and effective. When the Watch arrived, some minutes behind him, six neatly trussed people wearing 'bleaker motley had been waiting for them.

And one bruised, bleeding, and chagrined Liaden.

Who now opened one eye and looked up into McFarland's broad face.

"I am not sleeping. Tell me, *were* those people all local?"

"Well, now, that's what I wanted to talk to you about, particularly. They're so local, they're on first names with the Watch and Medic Svenz."

"It was opportunistic? They were waiting for anyone who came down the alley?"

"Be a long wait, most 'bleakers not being stupid enough to go *toward* a shout for help. Outworlders got less sense, so it still might've been worth the trouble, but no, as it turns out, and according to Pan and Ruthie, independently, they was looking for you, specific."

He extended a long arm, snagged a chair, pulled it close to the couch and sat down.

"Not curious as to why?"

Val Con sighed.

"I am told it is equally likely that I will be killed for my jacket as for my boots."

McFarland tipped his head, his face taking on a thoughtful cast, as if he gave the question serious consideration.

"Maybe a little more likely for the jacket. Them boots are kinda small for your average 'bleaker, and they don't look like they'd be good in the snow."

"Thank you, Mr. McFarland. Your insights are always welcome."

The big man threw back his head and laughed.

"Sounded *just* like Boss Conrad, right there, and no mistake!"

"I hear that the family resemblance is strong," Val Con said sourly. "Indeed, the boss and I could be brothers."

Cheever, still grinning, shook his head.

"Could be, at that. In the meantime, you got reason to thank me that he ain't here himself to read you the riot act, after he just got through telling you all over again how you're gonna have to take on a couple 'hands, and let the street know you're a Boss."

Val Con sighed.

"Indeed, I am grateful for your intervention. I believe that Miri will soon arrive with a song in the same key."

McFarland's grin faded a little.

"Yeah, you're on your own there. No percentage in gettin' between a man and his wife."

"Mr. McFarland, are you *afraid* of Miri?"

"Respectful, say. Now, listen up. The reason this crowd of do-no-goods set up their little play for you is—you got a price on your head, Boss. It's out on the street that there's two cantra in it for anybody who retires the Road Boss."

Val Con sat up, which did nothing good for his headache. He reached out and grabbed the big man's wrist.

"The Road Boss?" he repeated. "Is the target *the Road Boss*, Mr. McFarland, or is it Boss Conrad's little brother?"

McFarland blinked, then his mouth tightened.

"Gotcha. Word from Pan *and* Ruthie was the Road Boss. I'll check it."

"Thank you, Mr. McFarland."

"Shoulda thought of it, myself. The Road Boss is you *and* her."

"Yes, though some might consider it to be me *or* her."

"Right."

He levered himself out of the chair, and nodded.

"I'll get on that. Your lady oughta be here pretty soon to take you on up the house."

"Yes—Mr. McFarland, one more thing, if I may?"

"Yeah?"

"Who is offering this bounty?"

"Well, there the story goes a little off-center. Pan says it's Andy Mack set the price, which is plain and fancy nonsense. I'll check it, naturally, but he even *told it* like it was a lie. Might be he was threatened with mayhem, did he tell."

He shrugged.

"Whichever. Ruthie, now—Ruthie's brighter and gutsier—and *she* says it's somebody named Festina—which the Watch seemed to make sense of. They're sending somebody along to talk to her."

"Is there a reason for Festina to wish the Road Boss dead?"

"Well, that's what's funny. Way I get it, Festina brokers jobs, and takes a piece of the action."

"So, there is some *other* person who wishes the Road Boss to be retired, and who has engaged Festina's services."

"That's it. The Watch is looking to get the name of her client."

"Ah. Please keep me informed."

"Will do. You rest, now."

He turned away. Val Con began to ease back down onto the couch—and paused on one elbow, as his ears caught the sound of familiar footsteps in the hall.

"'Afternoon, Miri," McFarland said, just outside the door to the room.

"Hi, Cheever," his lifemate said. "He's awake?"

"Yeah."

She would, of course, *know* that he was awake, but it was what one said, to be polite. To seem to be like the vast number of others, who would never know the peculiar joy of a true lifemating. Val Con came gently back into a sitting position and folded his wrapped hands on his lap.

He heard Cheever McFarland's footsteps receding.

Miri's footsteps grew closer; shadows moved at the door, and she entered, Nelirikk at her back. The big man stopped just inside the door, facing the hallway. Miri continued across the room, walking deliberately.

Her face was neutral, much like the song of her that he heard in the back of his head. She sat down in the chair Cheever McFarland had lately vacated, and considered him out of calm grey eyes.

"You look a little rugged," she said eventually.

"Doubtless so. They have not offered me a mirror. However, I find that I am in complete agreement with you, Miri."

"Really. 'bout what, exactly?"

He smiled, feeling sore facial muscles protest.

"Pain hurts."

• • •✧• • •

A SOFT CHIME sounded in his ear, growing steadily louder. Val Con opened his eyes with a sigh that was not entirely pleasure in the absence of pain. He swung his legs over the side of the autodoc, which satisfied the chime, and sat there, listening to Miri's song inside his head.

To his very great relief, she had not chosen to engage with him on the drive home, while he was yet off-balance, and she stood between fear and care.

Now, though . . .

Ah, yes. *Now*, she was in a fine, high, temper, and no mistake.

Well, and who could blame her? Certainly not her erring lifemate, who had thus far turned his face from both common-sense and her legitimate concerns, showing the flimsiest of excuses as his reasons.

Excuses that he had been allowed, just so long as he could support himself. Having failed most notably in that endeavor, and having also, to his shame, frightened her, he could expect a *splendid* row in his very immediate future.

She would want the truth, to which no one had a better right, and he would look the veriest lunatic, did he tell it to her.

And yet, he told himself kindly, *she had known you for a lunatic when she married you.*

There was, indeed, that.

And if he did not soon go to meet the tempest, he thought, gauging the impatience that was growing beside her anger, the tempest would assuredly come to him.

He slid to his feet and reached for the clean clothes that were neatly folded on the table beside the doc.

Best not to go ungirded into the fray.

* * *◇* * *

MIRI had taken a shower, and dressed—house clothes, a comfortable sweater and loose pants. The conversation she was going to have with Val Con—the conversation she shouldn't have let him dodge *for months* . . . It wasn't likely to be pleasant. She hated pushing him into a corner—*insisting*, but dammit, he *could have* been killed this morning, just as easy as stumbling on a stone. The jacket wasn't armor; space leather could be breached, and a shot to the head . . .

No, she told herself, taking a deep breath. *Easy, Robertson; that didn't happen.*

He *hadn't* gotten himself killed, not today. He'd been lucky—well, of course he'd been lucky. Came with the turf. Only sometimes, *the Luck*, like the family called it, wasn't real neat.

And sometimes it failed.

Another deep breath.

She'd felt him wake up out of the healing session, though he didn't seem to be in any hurry to get himself up to their suite. Not that she blamed him. He wasn't a dummy, despite today's evidence; he'd know he was in hot water, and he'd know she was done being easy on him.

Still, she thought, he could stir himself to hurry *a little*, so they could get this over with. She took a step toward the door. Stopped.

No. She was *not* going to him.

She turned, walked across the room, opened the sliding glass door and stepped out onto the balcony.

Let the man have a few minutes to collect his thoughts, she told herself, looking out over the inner garden.

Some of the flowers were still in bloom—the Tree's influence, both Val Con *and* the gardener swore. She wasn't inclined to argue; as far as she'd been able to determine, Korval's Tree lived to tinker: plants, micro-climates, cats, human beings—it didn't particularly matter *what*, only that whatever it *was* presented a challenge.

She crossed her arms on top of the railing and deliberately took a breath, drawing the warm—call it *less chilly*—scented air deep into her lungs.

Closing her eyes, she brought the Scout's Rainbow to mind and worked through it more slowly than she was wont to do, seeking a balance between fear, anger, and what you might call necessity.

The air at her elbow moved; the railing shifted oh-so-slightly, as if someone else had come to lean next to her.

She opened her eyes, looking down at the garden, and the stone pathway all but overgrown with unruly greenery.

"So," she said, soft enough she might've been asking herself, "you ready to work with me on this?"

He sighed, and she tensed for another excuse.

"Yes," he said, sounding wry, and tired, and rueful.

She turned her head to look at him, and met his eyes, green, steady, and very serious. The last of her anger drained away.

"Good," she said, and pushed away from the rail.

"Come on inside; we'll have a glass of wine and talk about it."

* * *✧* * *

"KNEW IT WAS A BAD JOB when y'took it," Festina said, as she locked the door behind her, and slid the switch up on the loomerlamp. Slowly, light melted the shadows; a chair came up outta the dim, covered over with a fluffy blanket. Next to it, handy, was a cook-box, and under that was a cooler. Books on the table by the other side, anna 'mergency firestone right there in the center of the floor.

Cozy 'nough nest; and certain better'n the Watch's idee of overnight lodgins. Watch was lookin for her, natural-nough. Wasn't a force knowed to man'd keep Ruthie shutup. Pan, he'd lie, good boy that he was, but he'd never got the knack on it, though it was a hard thing to say 'bout her own blood.

So, anywhose. It was a couple days down in the den, which weren't so bad. Things'd die down; Watch'd get other worries; she'd gawn home and open back up for bidness.

Been a stupid thing, anywho, that job, she told herself, as she made sure o'the locks—*good* locks, all coded and modern, none o'your mechanicals with the spin dials all it needed was a wise way wit'a bolt cutter to solve . . .

So—stupid thing, takin' that job. Road Boss—you dint wanna retire the Road Boss. Not really, you dint, though on the face, it looked good for bidness.

She sat down in the chair, opened the cooler and pulled out a brew.

Problem was right there—what usetabe good for bidness . . . maybe wasn't anymore. Boss Conrad's sweep, the knockin' down o'the tollbooths, the openin' up o'the Road, all the way up an' down the whole of it—

Couldn't really argue any of those things was *bad* for bidness. You looked close, you saw them changes might be *good* for bidness. Early days, big changes made, bigger changes comin'—it could go either way, with all that in the air. You wanted to be careful of it, somethin' so big an' wibbly-wobbly. You dint wanna go breakin' what wasn't quite taken shape yet. Had to trust to it, though it went 'gainst the grain—*had* to trust the Bosses knew what they was aimin' at, and that it'd be more worse'n better if they missed.

"Shouldna taken the damn job," she muttered, cracking the seal and sipping the brew. "Couldn't turn away from the money, that was it. Slush f'brains, Festina Newark, that's what you got—slush f'brains."

Well, and it *was* always about the money for her. Two cantra—you dint turn down that kinda cash, not anybody she'd ever met. Not that anybody she'd ever met had ever really been offered that kinda cash . . .

So, anyways.

She leaned back in the chair and sipped.

They'd had 'er sign a paper—that was your Liadens for you, crazy 'bout their papers. Paper said she'd keep on tryin' 'til the Road Boss—that bein' him *or* her, either one, 'cording to what was writ—was dead an proved. Festina figured the client, they'd thought one without the other was good as both dead. Herself, personally, she thought maybe one without t'other was more snow'n anybody could shovel, but it weren't her place, to be showin' the client their errors.

No help for it. Much as it'd hurt, she'd have to refund the money. Less the starter fee, 'course, girl hadda eat, and she'd paid out a little lite upfront to the six of 'em, so's to put some fire in their stoves.

Refund the money, that was it, tear up the paper . . .

An' don't be stupid again, Festina, she told herself sternly. You're too old a woman to be makin' that kinda mistake.

She sighed and sipped—and then froze, staring.

There came another knock at the door.

* * * ✦ * * *

THE ROAD BOSS wasn't exactly doing a lot of business this morning. Despite the minutes of past meetings and the agendas for coming meetings all lined up neat on her screen and ready for review, Miri'd twice caught herself nodding off. That was the thing about sitting in an office all day. The home office was at least *at home*. She could take a break, walk in the garden—even go down to the gym for a quick dance of *menfri'at*, or a swim in the pool.

The Road Boss's office, well—say it was big enough to do the job, and not much room built in for anything more expansive than behind-the-desk calisthenics.

After she'd found her head heavy again, she snapped to her feet, crossed the tiny space, and jerked open the door.

Nelirikk spun 'round in his chair, his reactions a little less quick than normal, too. She grinned.

"Captain?"

"I'm up for a walk," she said. "Clear the cobwebs out. It's either that or lock the door and put down for a nap."

Her aide considered her.

"A run around the port with a full battle pack?" he suggested.

"I'm too old for that," she told him. "But you do what you like. Let's put up the back in half-hour sign and see if we can make it to Mack's and back."

"The distance, easily," Nelirikk said, fishing the appropriate sign out of its bin, and looming to his feet. "But if Colonel Mack wants to talk . . ."

Miri laughed.

"Be there all day, easy. So we'll go down the portmaster's office. C'mon."

She opened the door, and stepped out into the day, knowing he was right behind her; took a deep breath of crisp-to-the-point-of-crunchy air, sighed—

And spun, going low by instinct, grabbing the leading arm before she properly saw it, pivoting, then falling, as her assailant got a boot around her knee, yanking the leg out from under, and they both went down on the tarmac, hard.

Miri kicked, and twisted, got one arm free and up, just as metal gleamed in the edge of her eye. She grabbed the wrist and kicked again, hard, pitching them over with her on top, banging the wrist against the 'crete until the knife flew away and a hoarse voice gasped into her ear.

"Good, now, Boss you gotta listen. I'm inna lotta trouble and I need your help."

• • •✧• • •

"SO," Miri said, "they didn't let you tear up the paper and walk?"

"Worse'n that," said the rangy woman with the black eye, and the field-wrapped wrist. She was holding a cup of coffee in her undamaged hand.

Miri closed her eyes. The woman had given her name as Tina Newark— "Festina's the formal, named after my four-times grandma, never could figure out why"—and it was bad enough she'd agreed to take a job getting the Road Boss—one or the other, the client hadn't been picky, which—retired. Even worse, she'd taken the job from a pair of Liadens, who'd of course insisted on a contract, all right and proper, which o'course Festina had signed, because they were dangling two shiny cantra pieces in front of her eyes like candy, and 'sides, anything written down could be written out.

"What's worse?" she asked Festina now.

"Well, they said they saw I needed more incentive to get the job done, and so they'd bailed Pan—that's my nephew, all the family I got left—outta the Whosegow, and was giving him hospitality—that's what they called it, *hospitality*, until it happens the terms is met."

That sounded a little edgier than you'd expect from your plain vanilla Solcintra street Liaden, Miri thought. Could be the DOI'd decided to use local talent—wouldn't be the first time, in fact.

Either or any way, though, it had to be taken off at the knees and *now*, before they lost Tina's boy, or any other sort-of innocent bystander.

"You don't happen to have that contract on you?" she asked.

Festina grinned, and nodded.

"Right jacket pocket, Boss. I can ease it out, nice and slow, or your mountain there can do it for us."

"Beautiful," Miri said. "Help Ms. Newark get that paper out of her pocket, please."

"Yes, Captain."

He leaned in, as Miri reached over to the desk and picked up the comm.

. . . ✧ . . .

"THE FORM is unobjectionable," Ms. kaz'Ineo murmured, putting the contract on the desk before her, and squaring it up precisely. "The conditions are . . . somewhat stern, even allowing for the natural grief of kin. On Liad, the second party's *qe'andra* would have sought softer terms."

She turned her head toward the stocky grey-haired customer leaning against the wall of Miri's office.

"Your opinion, Apprentice Jorish?"

"Well, ma'am," he said slowly; "you an' me been talking about Balance, and how the best contracts strike fair between the needs of both sides—"

She raised a hand.

"*Fair* is inexact, I think," she murmured.

"Could be it is, ma'am," he said agreeably. "What I'm thinking, though, is about this sternness you was notin'. What I heard was rage and black bitterness. The folks wrote this thing wanted *revenge*, not Balance."

Ms. kaz'Ineo considered him, her head tipped to one side.

"I believe that I understand you," she said after a moment. "While a contract is not necessarily an instrument of Balance—you will remind me to revisit the concept and place of Balance with you; we seem to have taken a wrong turning."

"Yes'm; not the first time, is it?" he said cheerfully.

She smiled slightly.

"No, indeed, it is not. Nor will it be the last. I am, however, confident that we shall navigate these differences, Apprentice Jorish, as we learn, each from the other.

"For the present moment, allow me to state that contracts are written to provide advantage. The best contracts provide advantage to all members in the agreement. This is not so much Balance as it is mutual profit. While it might be that a contract will be written in order *to effect* a Balance, you are correct in your conjecture that it ought not promote active harm. This contract . . ."

She touched the small, squared pile before her.

"The payoff of this contract is anguish and loss. No one profits—not even the originators. I admit to some surprise, that it has come from the offices of ber'Lyn and her'With, a reputable firm."

She paused, staring again at her little space of nothing.

"Would you have written that paper, ma'am," asked Jorish, "if they'd come to you?"

Ms. kaz'Ineo blinked.

"A provocative question, Apprentice Jorish. It grieves me to say that—I am not certain. One becomes so busy; it is far too simple a thing, merely to follow the forms, and fail to look beyond them.

"No, I cannot say that I would not have written it. Certainly, had it come to me from the hands of a client, I would have negotiated, and sought softeners. It would not have occurred to me to counsel my client to withdraw. The belief, among *qe'andra*, is that all is negotiable. We are not accustomed to thinking in such terms as a contract that ought never to have been written."

She inclined her head.

"Thank you, Apprentice Jorish."

"Thank *you*, ma'am."

"So," said Miri. "What do you advise?"

The *qe'andra* shook her head.

"I cannot advise. However ill-conceived, the contract has been written; it was presented to the second party, who signed it, thereby signaling her agreement to all terms. We might, on Liad, were the difficulties noted beyond the form, as they have been here, have convened a committee, but, here—?"

She looked again at her 'prentice.

"Is there some native protocol, Apprentice Jorish, which addresses such matters?"

He grinned.

"You mean besides me getting my crew together and going against their crew, knuckles-to-knuckles?"

"We would prefer not to fuel a riot, yes. Also, there is the question of the young man's safety."

She inhaled sharply, and looked to Miri, eyes narrowed.

"In fact, I may be of some use as a negotiator. There is no provision in this contract which requires the holding of a valuable, or a kinsman, as surety for delivery."

Miri considered her.

"You can get the kid out safe, you think?"

To her credit, Ms. kaz'Ineo hesitated.

"There are no certainties in life. However, I believe that the odds of removing the young person from his current situation are with us. They may be misguided, but it would seem that—"

She flipped the contract over to the signature page.

"Geastera vin'Daza Clan Kinth and Tor Ish tez'Oty Clan Yrbaiela wish to follow proper form, and to see their complaint honorably retired. They wished there to be no opportunity, *within the form*, for error.

"I believe that it may be possible that the taking of the young person into their care was a rash move which they are even now regretting. They need only to be shown how to come back into proper alignment."

She looked aside.

"Apprentice Jorish—your opinion, please."

"I think you got the straight of it, ma'am. They got rattled, an' let scared, mad, an' tired, push 'em into a power move. Good chances they even knew it was a bad move when they made it, but now they don't know how to give it back without looking weak—losing face, that would be, ma'am. All's we gotta do is show 'em how to unkink that bit, and Pan'll be back home in plenty o'time for supper. But—"

He hesitated.

"Yes, Apprentice Jorish? You have another consideration?"

"Well, only, ma'am, it's all good, getting young Pan back onto the street—leastwise 'til the Watch picks him up for whatever he'll bungle next—no offense meant, Tina, but that boy's got two left feet an' ten thumbs."

"No argument, here," Festina Newark said equably. "But he's everything in this cold world I got to call kin."

"That's right," said Jorish Hufstead. "Ain't nobody can't say he's a good boy at heart, but here's what I'm thinkin', ma'am—"

He turned back to his boss.

"We can get the boy outta this particular snow drift, but that leaves the paper itself. Plainly said, ma'am, that's a bad paper—an' if you can't say it, I will—that never oughta been made. No profit to anybody that I can see comes with retiring the Road Boss. Planet's just getting out of a considerable drift of our own, and we need the Road Boss just zackly as much as we need Boss Conrad and his Council."

"I agree, Apprentice Jorish," Ms. kaz'Ineo said in her cool Liaden voice. "However, the contract is properly formed—"

"No'm, all respect and honor—it ain't," interrupted Jorish. "If these—people—got a grudge 'gainst the Boss here, and need 'er dead for to be satisfied, where's the sense pushing Tina, or one of her pool, to do the job? It's personal, is what it is, an' if was mine to judge right there from m'corner, I'd be tellin' 'em to settle it that way.

"So, I'm thinking—ma'am, ain't there *any* way to call that paper void?"

Ms. kaz'Ineo pressed her lips together.

"We have Jumped into uncharted space, my friend," she said. "How is it said here? Ah. We are in the belly of the blizzard. On Liad, even a committee would not *break* the contract, or cause it to be unwritten. It is not done. There is—"

She moved one tiny, precise hand.

"There is no precedent."

She paused, hand still suspended, and looked to Hufstead.

"Your passion does you credit, Apprentice. However, it is the role of the *qe'andra* to remain objective, and marshal resources for the best good of the client."

Miri stirred.

"I think we can handle the wider issue of the contract," she said.

"First things first, though. If these folks—vin'Daza and tez'Oty—are as committed to proper behavior as it seems they might be, then we'll be able to locate where they're lodging, and send 'round a note. Tell 'em that Tina here took the contract to her *qe'andra*, and the expert opinion is there's been a breach. Set up an appointment, so the breach can be mended, soonest. Serious thing, breach of contract."

"That is correct," said Ms. kaz'Ineo composedly.

"Good. That's the first bit, then. Cut the boy loose before somebody makes another mistake, and things get serious."

"I will be pleased to call this meeting."

"Hold on," Tina Newark said. "If she's workin' for me, I need to know how much this is gonna cost."

Ms. kaz'Ineo turned her head and awarded Festina a broad, Terran smile.

"Because you provide both my apprentice and myself with this valuable . . . *learning experience,* we will preside over the discussion and reparation *gratis.*"

"That's *no charge*, Tina," Jorish said helpfully.

"I know what it means," she told him, and gave Ms. kaz'Ineo a nod.

"Thank'ee. Much appreciated."

"Good, then," Miri said briskly. She stood up.

"Jorish, you got a minute for me while Tina gives Ms. kaz'Ineo her contact info?"

"Sure thing, Boss," he said promptly, and followed her out into the reception room.

* * * ✧ * * *

"INDEED, we admit; it was an error, and a breach in the conditions set forth in the contract."

Geastera vin'Daza Clan Kinth was a straight-backed, fit woman, who fell into the age group Miri thought of as "old enough to make her own mistakes." Her face wasn't quite Liaden-smooth; almost, her expression could have been said to err on the side of haughtiness. High Liaden, with its precise chilly phrasing, suited her.

Tor Ish tez'Oty Clan Yrbaiela, sitting at her left, seemed younger, and tireder. So tired, in fact, that the usual, infuriating Liaden *sangfroid* was showing a little frazzle at the edges.

In the little waiting room behind Ms. kaz'Ineo's office, Miri sighed.

"Boy's outta his pay-grade," she said softly.

Beside her, Val Con shook his head.

"They are neither one at ease," he answered, his eyes on the screen. He was frowning at tiny tells that were as good as screams to a trained muscle-reader.

"Miri, will you, please, step away from this?"

She reached out and put her hand over his.

"It's gotta be both of us," she said. "We talked it out."

"Indeed we did," he answered, soft voice edgy with anger. "And I am a fool for agreeing to anything like."

"Well, maybe so," she said judiciously. "But you know how they say—once you eliminate all the safe and sane solutions, the one that's left, no matter how crazy, is the one that's gonna work."

"*That*, my lady, is a shameless distortion."

"Information received was that the local custom is physical; that demonstration carries the point more clearly than argument," vin'Daza was continuing. "And thus our error was made. We regret our actions, and will, indeed, be pleased to see the young person returned to the proper care of his kinswoman."

Festina had taken her role as kin and independent business person serious. She'd dressed up real nice in a pair of good dark slacks, and a white shirt under a snowflake-knit red sweater. There was even jewelry—a couple gold and titanium necklaces 'round her neck, and a ring too glittery to be real on her left hand. Miri didn't know if she'd thought of it her own self, or taken some advice from Ms. kaz'Ineo, but, whichever, it played well.

The two Liadens were dressed down, which Miri took to mean they'd found that looking too pretty on the street was an invitation to get relieved of extra baggage.

"We would be grateful to the *qe'andra*," said tez'Oty, stolidly, "for her advice on proper recompense for our error."

"Ah," Val Con breathed. "They learn. *Recompense*, not Balance."

Festina stirred, and Jorish leaned forward in his chair to wave Pan, who'd been standing tight against the wall behind the two Liadens—across the room to his aunt. He got there quick as he could while moving quiet, and sagged into the chair at Festina's side. She reached out and patted his knee without taking her eyes off Ms. kaz'Ineo.

"Recompense in this instance may be made by the payment of our fee," Ms. kaz'Ineo said, and Festina's head whipped 'round fast to stare at her. Ms. kaz'Ineo declined to make eye contact.

vin'Daza inclined her head.

"Certainly, *qe'andra*."

"Excellent. Ms. Newark, I am certain that you and your kinsman are anxious to catch up after so long a separation."

"Yes, ma'am, that we are," said Festina rising right on cue. She bowed—not a Liaden bow, but what was coming to be the common Surebleak general politeness bow—a more or less seventy degree angle from the waist, with the arms straight down at the sides, and a quick glance at the floor before making eye contact again, and coming tall again.

"Thank you for your care," she said, and gave young Pan a glare out of the side of her eye 'til he bowed, too, and produced a mumbled, "Thank you, ma'am. Mr. Hufstead, sir."

"It is a pleasure to serve," Ms. kaz'Ineo assured them.

"Taxi's waiting at the door. You go on home now and rest up," Jorish Hufstead said. "Pan, you take good care of your Aunt Tina; she was that worried 'bout you."

"Yes, sir," said Pan, and by way of maybe proving that he was as good as his word, he turned, opened the hall door, and stood back, one hand hovering near Festina's elbow as she walked out.

The door closed.

vin'Daza and tez'Oty exchanged a glance. tez'Oty cleared his throat.

"Your fee, Ms.—" he began—and stopped with a blink when Ms. kaz'Ineo raised her hand.

"If you please, I would like to speak with you further regarding this instrument which you caused to be written, and brought to Surebleak for implementation." She put her hand atop the single file adorning the top of her desk.

vin'Daza chose to bristle.

"The contract was written by ber'Lyn and her'With. Surely you will not say that *their* work is suspect!"

"Indeed, no," said Ms. kaz'Ineo. "Their work is, as I would expect, unexceptional. However, there have been errors of . . . implementation, shall we say? It has surely come to your attention that Surebleak is not Liad—indeed, you said so yourself, Ms. vin'Daza. You said that you were aware of Surebleak local custom of using force to carry a point. *Might makes right* in the local vernacular, an unfortunate aspect of Surebleak's most recent past which we are attempting to refine into something more nuanced and less perilous."

She paused to glance at Jorish Hufstead. He met her eyes with a frank little smile that she mirrored exactly, before turning back to the audience.

"When I say *we*, I of course mean the accountancy professionals of both Surebleak and Liad. We are forming teams, such as you see here, and attempting to craft a new protocol for a mixed society."

tez'Oty looked somewhere between flabbergasted and horrified. vin'Daza kept control of her face, but the hand resting on her knee curled into a loose fist.

"In keeping with this goal of crafting a new protocol, and also to assist you in forwarding the goal of your contract, I will now turn this meeting over to my colleague, Mr. Jorish Hufstead. Mr. Hufstead was for many years an arbiter of custom, a servant of the common good, and a dispenser of justice. He was employed by Boss Penn Kalhoon in this capacity, which is locally known as *cornerman*, because cases were heard and justice dispensed at a particular, known corner location. All and any could apply to Mr. Hufstead for the gift of his expertise, which was known as both rapid and balanced, far outside of his own territory."

"The contract," began vin'Daza . . .

"Right," said Jorish easily, leaning forward slightly on his elbows.

"That contract of yours is the problem. Now, Ms. kaz'Ineo, she tells me that's some fine work, in form and flavor, an' all them sorta things that find favor with folks back in your territory. I gotta tell you, I appreciate that. Ain't nothing happier to the eye than something's done just right; I know it for myself. So, we're all agreed there."

He paused, glanced down at the table, and back up, catching tez'Oty's eye and holding it.

"Where we ain't agreed on is that this is a valid contract—"

vin'Daza stiffened. Hufstead held up a hand, palm out.

"—on Surebleak," he finished. "Now, just hear me out, all right?"

He didn't wait for a response, just rolled on, still keeping tez'Oty's eyes with his.

"'Way I see it, first problem with this contract here isn't on Surebleak, it's on Liad. I read that guarantee from your very own council of bosses there in Solcintra City, and it says that—once they're moved off-world, and their name written outta the membership book—the family that's settled here under the name of Clan Korval, they ain't got a target painted on 'em no more, and they don't owe nobody on Liad one thing else."

He paused, and glanced at vin'Daza.

"What's that I hear them pilots say down the pub? *The ship lifts, an' all debts are paid?*"

vin'Daza took a breath and inclined her head about a millimeter.

"I am familiar with the concept," she said, sounding a little breathless.

"However," tez'Oty said, sounding suddenly heated; "the Council of Clans made that guarantee for itself, and for the clans. There has been personal loss sustained—in the case of Geastera and myself—insupportable loss! The Council cannot forbid a just Balance!"

Jorish frowned slightly, and glanced down at the table, like he was taking counsel there, then looked up and met tez'Oty's eyes.

"Y'know, I think that's *zackly* what the Council's contract was meant to say. But, that's actually a side issue, 'cause, see, what you just said? *Personal loss. Just Balance.*"

He flipped a disdainful hand in the direction of the contract sitting neat and innocent in the center of the table.

"Sleet, you don't need no contract to settle up personal loss—not here on Surebleak, you don't. You got something personal to settle—that's personal. Anybody can unnerstan that.

"But, see, *personal* don't mean you pay Festina to do your work for you. You got a *personal* grudge, or a *personal* need to be Boss, or a personal loss that needs answerin', well—you settle that . . . *personal.*"

Miri stood up, and shook out her lace. They'd gone with Liaden day-wear for this, and it was a good thing they hadn't decided on formal clothes, which woulda upstaged their complainants. This way, they were nice and symmetric; respectful, but not boastful.

"Guess our cue's coming up," she said, looking into Val Con's face. He was outright grim; the pattern of him inside her head edged with scarlet lines of worry.

"Hey."

She leaned into him, and he hugged her close.

"I can take a strike for both," he murmured, and she returned the hug just as tight, before she stepped away, looked up into his face and said, "No."

"And how shall we take this *personal* action?" vin'Daza demanded on the screen.

Jorish gave her a grin.

"Now, I'm glad you asked that question. Gives me new hope for makin' this transition work for everybody when I see that willingness to embrace our custom. So—y'unnerstan, this kinda thing comes up a lot on Surebleak, and how I took to handling it on the corner was to ask whoever'd come out that day to stand back and make room. Then I'd ask if the party-or-parties of the first part—today that's you and Mr. taz'Oty—if they got their own knifes, and if they do to show 'em to me now."

"Knifes," repeated taz'Oty. "I have of course a gun, but—"

Jorish raised a hand again.

"No need to 'pologize for your personal choice of protective weapon, sir. I know most prefer their gun. For the purpose of this bidness, here, though, us cornermen found out knifes was the best weapon, and it got codified, see?

"So, no worries. I got two right here for you."

He pushed back, rose, slid two blades out of his jacket pocket, and leaned over to put them, handles toward Liadens, on the far side of the table.

Miri blinked, and felt Val Con's hand on her shoulder.

They were ugly, those blades, one step up from meat cleavers; street knives, that was what, without finesse or honor to burden them.

"Well, *cha'trez*?"

"Pretty well," she said, though her voice was breathy in her own ears. "They'll do the job, all right."

"Indeed," he answered.

"Now," Jorish was saying. "That one on the right there, that was Boss Kalhoon's loaner, for when somebody wanted to get personal with him about who really oughta be Boss. That other one, that's the one I used to loan out, as part o'my duty."

He straightened, and looked to Ms. kaz'Ineo, sitting still and calm, with her hands folded in front of her.

"Ma'am, this is gonna get messy—nature of the thing, really. I shoulda thought. Might be best, we take this outside, 'steada—"

"Carpets can be cleaned, Mr. Hufstead. Surely, we do not wish our clients' private business to be spread about the streets."

"Right you are," he said, and turned back to the Liadens, who were sitting like they'd been quick frozen.

"What you each wanna do is choose a knife, get yourselfs stood up an' centered. I'll just shift these chairs outta the way—more'n enough room for what we got today, just a personal settlin' up like we are . . ."

vin'Daza got herself in hand first. She picked up Penn's loaner, and stood holding it like she knew what she was doing. That was good, Miri thought; amateurs would only make more of a mess.

tez'Oty picked up the remaining knife, reluctant, but competent.

"Right, then," said Jorish. "You just wanna turn to face the door, 'cause it'll be opening in just a sec."

"That's us," said Miri, and stepped forward.

The doorway wasn't quite wide enough to let them through side-by-side, which would've been the most correct, *melant'i*-wise. Val

Con managed to slip in between her and the knob, and so be the first in the room, which was aggravating, but, according to the book, *next* most correct, *melant'i*-wise, with him being Delm Genetic and all. She was just half-a-step to the rear, stopping right beside him when they'd cleared the threshold, so it all came out right.

Nobody said anything. vin'Daza and tez'Oty both looked like somebody'd smacked 'em across the head with a board.

"These the folks caused you irreparable personal harm and loss?" Jorish asked, quietly.

Surprisingly, it was tez'Oty who spoke.

"My *cha'leket* died, as a result of the strike they ordered against Solcintra."

"Right, then. Ms. vin'Daza?"

"My lover, also dead as a result of Korval's strike from orbit."

"Well, then. Seems like we got symmetry. There's two of you; there's two o'them. Have at whenever you're ready."

Miri was watching tez'Oty; he actually paled, his chest lifting in a gasp as his eyes widened.

"We are supposed to kill them?" he demanded, not taking his eyes off her.

"Well, it's what you was wantin' Festina to have done for you, wasn't it? This way, you cut out the middleman; make sure the job gets done right."

There was more silence, before vin'Daza said, starkly, "This is a trick to rob us of Balance."

"No," Miri said. "No trick."

She raised her hands, palm out, and looked directly into tez'Oty's eyes.

"I'm sorry," she said, and shook her head when he flinched. "I was born on Surebleak; it's what we say. *I'm sorry* for your loss, and for my part in bringing it to you. No explanation of our intention, or measure of our success, can possibly count more than the life of your *cha'leket*, and I surely don't expect that you'll ever forgive me."

She lowered her hands, though she still made eye contact.

"I, too," Val Con said from her side, and his voice was rougher than polite Liaden discourse allowed. "I, too, regret. There is not a day nor a night that passes, when I do not regret. Necessity is a cold comrade, and takes no care for lives, or joy."

Silence, growing longer.

tez'Oty moved his eyes first.

"I accept your—apology," he said, and turned blindly to one side, fumbling the knife onto the table.

"Do you expect me to believe," vin'Daza said to Val Con, "that you will stand there and allow me to cut your throat?"

"No," he said, matter-of-fact, now. "Neither of us believes that. I am trained in hand-to-hand; I know very well how to disarm an opponent armed with a knife and a desire to end me. Also, while my life has no more value, objectively, than your life, or your lover's, I have work, and purpose. I can, alive, improve the universe in some few small ways, and therefore bring it closer to the ideal of Balance."

He took a breath, and turned his hands palm up.

"If it were me with a dead lover, a knife in my hand, and a decision to make, I would take into account that a cut throat is a quick death, while a lifetime of regret may come more near to matching your own pain."

Silence, then a turn to place the knife on the table with a small, decisive *snick*.

"Live then," she said harshly, "and regret."

"*Qe'andra*," she said, over her shoulder.

"Yes, Ms. vin'Daza. May I serve you?"

"You will write the appropriate paper. When it is ready, please send it to our lodgings so that we may sign. We will, of course, pay your fee. Please do this quickly, as we intend to leave this terrible world within the next two days, if we have to walk away."

"I understand," said Ms. kaz'Ineo.

• • •◇• • •

IT WAS SNOWING. Outside the breakfast parlor's window there was only a rippling sheet of white. The Road Boss's office was closed for weather, as were all other non-essential businesses.

That was the new Surebleak, Miri reflected, staring out the window, half-hypnotized by the blizzard. The old Surebleak, there hadn't been any such thing as closing for weather. What would be the sense in that? Only thing Surebleak could be said to *have* was weather.

"Good morning, *cha'trez*." Val Con slipped into the chair she'd put next to her, so they could go snowblind together. "I hope I have not kept you waiting long."

"Just long enough to have my first cup of coffee," she told him, with a smile, showing him the empty cup. "Perfect timing."

"I agree."

"What was the emergency?"

"Not so much an emergency," he said. "Nova merely wished to be certain that I had seen Lady yo'Lanna's most recent letter. Shall you like more coffee? A cheese roll, perhaps?"

"Yes, thank you," she said, though she still had to control the twitch that said *he* shouldn't be waiting on *her*. It was getting easier. Another twenty years or so, she'd have it completely under control.

When fresh coffee and tea and a plate of various breakfast edibles was on the table between them, she brought the letter back up.

"Lot of good gossip?"

"Lady yo'Lanna's letters are always a rich resource," he murmured, his eyes on the white-filled window. "Much of it will require closer study, as we now live so far removed from society, but the bits which are immediately comprehensible would seem to be that the Council of Clans has issued a new statement to its member-delms regarding the state of the entity known as Clan Korval, seated on Surebleak.

"It would seem that this entity has been forgiven all and any damages it might have caused to the planet of Liad, or disruption it may have perpetuated upon the common good. Further, if any individual persons feel that they are owed Balance in the matter of those actions which the entity Clan Korval brought against Liad, they are to apply to the Grievance Committee at ber'Lyn and her'With."

Miri blinked.

"That's—quite a come-about," she commented.

"As you say. It is well to reflect what outrage may accomplish, when turned toward the common good."

"What's the next bit?" Miri asked, after her cup was empty again, and the breakfast plate, too.

"Hmm?"

He pulled his gaze from the window with an obvious effort.

"Ah, Lady yo'Lanna. She plans a visit. In fact, she expects to be with us within the season, as she has commissioned a Scout at leave to bring her to us."

Miri eyed him.

"Us?"

He turned his head to smile at her.

"Us." He extended a finger to trace the line of her cheek.

"Only think, *cha'trez*; we shall shortly be in a position to learn from a master."

"I don't think I can possibly keep up."

"Nonsense, you are merely fatigued with staring out at all this weather."

"You got something better to do?"

He smiled into her eyes.

"Why, yes; I do."

✧ Due Diligence ✧

IN A UNIVERSE where one wrong brush with the law can ruin your life and bad manners can get you killed, the question of who you accept as a bed partner—and why—can have a certain piquant challenge to it. The challenge becomes more difficult when you're from one of the most important clans in the galaxy, and need something very special, indeed.

✧✧✧✧

I

"FOR ATTACHMENT to a criminal endeavor designed to disrupt the operations of this port, evidenced by signed papers recovered, Fer Gun pen'Uldra is fined two cantra, to be assessed from future earnings. Should there be no such earnings within one Standard Year, the amount will be deducted from Fer Gun pen'Uldra's accrued Guild dues, and his name shall be struck from the rolls."

That was steep, that was, Fer Gun thought, his belly tight and his breath coming short and shallow. Two *cantra*? Still, he was a Jump pilot—a damned good Jump pilot, as he needn't say himself, since the record supported him—he might be able to find a berth—

"In addition," Solcintra Pilots Guild Master continued, "Fer Gun pen'Uldra's license to pilot is suspended for one Standard year. After

39

such time, he shall be eligible for reinstatement when a pilot in good standing testifies on behalf of Fer Gun pen'Uldra before the Guild, and guarantees his good behavior as a pilot for the following Standard Year."

It was as if a fist had slammed into his belly. For a moment, he couldn't see; couldn't breathe. They were taking his license! He was—a two cantra fine, *and* his license suspended? How—

"Fer Gun pen'Uldra," said the guildmaster. "Do you have anything further to say?"

Say? What could he say? That it hadn't been his signature on the damned paper? Of course, it had been his signature. That he hadn't any notion what his cousin Jai Kob had in mind to do on—or to— Solcintra Port? That he was a pilot, that was all and everything he'd ever wanted to be? His cousins did their business; *his* was to fly them where business called.

He managed a breath.

"No, sir." His voice was firm, if subdued. "Nothing further to say."

The guildmaster looked to the port proctor standing at the corner of the table. The proctor stepped to Fer Gun's side, her face impassive.

"Fer Gun pen'Uldra, relinquish your license to the Pilots Guild. When the terms are met, it will be returned to you."

There was black at the edges of his vision. His license. Turn over his license to this blank-faced flunky? He would die before he did anything so daft! For a moment, indeed, he thought he would turn over his fist and make a run—

But that was no good, he told himself. The Guild would blacklist the license, then, and he'd be in worse case than he stood right now. So.

"It's in the jacket," he told the proctor and his voice was nowhere near steady, now. "Inside right breast pocket."

"Understood," she answered, and watched while he slid his hand inside his jacket, and fingered the card—his license to fly—out of the hidden pocket, and offered it to her between two fingers.

She received it without comment, and returned to her place at the corner of the table.

The guildmaster inclined his head.

"Fer Gun pen'Uldra, you may go."

. . . ◇ . . .

WELL, and he'd gone—of course he had. An overnight in the holding cell had been plenty enough for him. It might fairly be said that having no place to go was a superior situation.

Out on the port, he paused to get his bearings, acutely aware of the absence of his flight card. Not that it had weighed so much, but knowing it was gone created an imbalance in the fit of his jacket.

He took a breath, then another, ignoring the rumbling in his stomach. They hadn't fed him in the holding cell. They might have done, if he had asked, but it hadn't occurred to him to ask them for anything.

What he wanted now was *Lady Graz*, though Jai Kob's welcome for a wingless pilot was not likely to be warm. His value had been in his license. Remove that single value and he was only the dim-witted singleton, dependent on Telrune's charity. It was entirely possible that his cousins would leave him here, once they found his situation.

Fer Gun squared his shoulders.

Well, then. They need not *know* his situation. It was his business, wasn't it? Oh, he would definitely cite the two-cantra fine at Jai Kob, so he would! But the loss of his ticket . . .

It came to him that his skill had not been taken from him. He was still a pilot, and a damned good one, wherever his license reposed. Granted, he could not record his flight-time, and he would therefore not advance in the Guild.

But, he could still pilot a spaceship.

Jai Kob need not know that Fer Gun had lost his license.

He had his bearings, now, and turned east, toward the edge-yard where they'd brought the *Lady* down, and locked her. His stomach complained as he moved into a quick walk. He ignored it.

. . . ◇ . . .

"OH," said the dockman wisely, when Fer Gun arrived at the office, to find the board listing only three ships. "You've come about the quick-hire, have you? You're only a half-day too late. They meant *quick*, they did, and they weren't particular, either. Took the first good card that walked in the door."

Fer Gun stared at him.

"*Lady Graz*," he said slowly, to be certain he understood; "she's lifted?"

"That's right," the dockman said. "Regular pilot walked out soon as they hit port. Found a better opportunity, I'll wager. That knife cuts both ways, though, on Solcintra. The owners didn't have any trouble at all, hiring new."

"Thank you," Fer Gun said, feeling the absence of his license like a blade through his heart. He took a breath.

"Is there somewhere nearby where I might . . . buy a beer?"

* * * ◇ * * *

TEETERING on the edge of the Low Port, the bar was called Wingman's Folly, and the beer was cheap for a reason. The few coins in his pocket might even, Fer Gun thought, stretch to a bowl of soup, though if the food were equal to the quality of the beer . . .

Wingless and broke, near enough; and Jai Kob had set it up; had deliberately schemed to remove the idiot cousin.

And that, Fer Gun told himself, taking a cautious sip of his so-called beer, was what came of asking questions. They had not been deep questions; they had not been questions inappropriate to a pilot, though they had touched—lightly!—on the business Jai Kob conducted, with Cousin Vin Dyr's able assistance.

Two questions, and he had rendered himself a liability, abandoned to the mercies of the port proctors and the Guild, without money, without kin, without contacts, his only means of making a living residing by now in a safe at Guild Headquarters . . .

Jai Kob might not have known that they would take his license, Fer Gun told himself. And, in truth, Jai Kob's knowledge of the universe was not in his queue of immediate worries. Those included finding some sort of food, a bed, and work.

Work ought to be possible, he told himself, nursing his beer. He was strong; he had a good head for numbers. He could take orders—gods, couldn't he just! In any wise, he *could* work, and he would work. The important thing was not to slip over the line from Mid-

Port to Low. He was accounted good in a fight, but he had no illusions regarding the odds of near-term survival on Low Port for a single, partnerless pilot, wearing spaceleather and a good pair of boots.

The thing then was to go right when he left the Wingman—up to Mid-Port, Low Port at his back. He'd ask at the docks and the warehouses, first. Long-term would be good, but day-labor would do. The first priorities were to feed himself, and find that bed . . .

"More beer, Pilot?"

The barkeep was young and pretty, and it passed through Fer Gun's mind that he might, if he were clever, flirt his way into a bed for a night—or even several.

The idea hung there for a moment, before he rejected it. What could a lad—even a pretty lad who doubtless commanded pretty tips?—earn in such a place, situated as it was? Enough to feed and shelter himself, *and* a hungry pilot, too?

"No more beer, I thank you," he said, putting more of his coins than he ought on the bar.

"Come again, Pilot," the 'keeper said, and swept away to tend the other custom.

Fer Gun slid off his stool, and headed for the door, standing back as it swung open, then stepping forward.

"Going so soon?" A woman's voice spoke very nearly in his ear. "I thought you might share a glass with me."

The mode was Comrade, the voice unfamiliar. As was the face, when he turned to look at her.

The first thing he noticed was her height—taller than he was, which wasn't usual. She wore a Jump pilot's jacket, scarred and soft with wear. Her hair was blonde, pulled back into a knot at her nape; her face sharp; her eyes blue. Not a beauty, though she could pass. There was something about her drew and held the eye. She was also, he saw on third look, older than he was. Considerably so.

"Pilot," he said, giving her Comrade, because were not all pilots comrades? "Pilot, I do not know you."

"And I do not know you!" she said with a broad grin. "That is why we ought to drink a glass together, and perhaps share a small meal. They put together a very edible cheese plate here, for which I vouch."

He hesitated, which was pure madness. If the blonde pilot had a fancy for a younger bedmate, then she was the answer to tonight's problem, at least.

And if she were a thief, or part of a wolf pack, she would, he thought with a certain amount of irony, shortly be very disappointed in him.

So.

"Thank you," he said, inclining his head.

"Excellent—here!" She guided him to a table well-back from the door, and Fer Gun marked how those at the bar kept their backs to the room, while those at table did not look up. "Sit—sit!" said his new comrade. "I will order."

She threw a hand in the air. The pretty 'tender looked up as if he had heard the gesture, ducked out from behind the bar, and walked briskly toward their table.

"Service, Pilot?" he asked.

She smiled at him, and bespoke a bottle, two glasses and a "nuncheon plate," to share between comrades.

The boy bowed, and left them, whereupon the blonde pilot flowed bonelessly into the chair across from him and folded her hands on the tabletop.

"My name is Chi," she said, with an informality that might yet equally come from a pilot shopping a bedmate, or a wolf casing a mark.

"My name is Fer Gun," he answered, matching her tone.

"In fact your name is Fer Gun pen'Uldra," she said calmly. "I have a proposition to put before you."

"No!" he snapped, shoving the chair back—and freezing on the way to his feet, staring down at her hand on his wrist.

"Will you not even hear it?" she asked.

Her grip was firm, but not painful. It was, in fact, very nearly a comrade's touch. He raised his eyes to meet hers, finding a sort of amused kindness in her face.

"I will not go grey—or dark," he growled.

"All honor to you," she said lightly. "My proposal is nothing to tarnish your *melant'i*."

She paused, brows contracting somewhat.

"There are those who might argue the point, but I think they need not concern us."

"Let me go," he said, though he could have easily broken her grip.

She did so on the instant, and inclined her head.

"Forgive me."

He took a breath, thinking he would rise and leave her, after all— but here came the 'tender, bearing a full tray. The plate came down between them; the bottle went to the fair-haired pilot, and the glasses, too.

Fer Gun's stomach loudly reminded him of the recent abuses visited upon it—and was it not Balance, to eat the pilot's food and drink her wine, while he listened to her proposal?

"Thank you," she said to 'tender, and poured the wine, offering Fer Gun the first glass.

He waited until she had poured her own, inclined his head and sipped, finding the wine far superior to the beer. Apparently, Pilot Chi had deep pockets, which would account for her thinking she might order all to her liking.

"Eat," she said, and reached to the plate herself.

He did the same, and at his stomach's prompting twice more before he recalled that he was in company, and folded his arms on the tabletop.

"In its simplest form," Pilot Chi murmured, "my proposition is this: I require a child."

Fer Gun did not choke, but it was a near thing. He studied his comrade's arresting face, and found no hint of mockery, or madness, only a clear-eyed earnestness.

"Why not go to Festival?" he asked.

"A reasonable question. I seek to avoid notoriety . . ."

She paused, and again there was that quizzical, and slightly self-mocking expression.

"*Additional* notoriety. And, sadly, Festival-get will not answer my purpose, though it would seem, as you say, the simplest solution.

The child must arrive properly by contract, above reproach and unexceptional in the eyes of the world. Also, I fear that I require a pilot to stand father, and I see from your records that you are a very fine pilot, indeed."

He blinked.

"My records? How did you see my records?"

"Ah. I have access to the Guild files."

He took a breath.

"That must be expensive," he said, trying to match her tone of calm nonchalance.

"Not at all."

She plucked a tidbit from the tray, and popped it into her mouth.

Fer Gun took a breath.

"If you've seen my records, you have seen that I am convicted of crimes against the port, and have had my wings clipped for it. I may fly again when I produce two cantra to pay my fine, and also a witness to my reformed character."

"Yes. Your cousins are very clever, are they not?"

He considered her.

"If you're looking for brains in addition to reactions, you'll want to shop elsewhere."

"No, I do not allow you to be stupid, merely naive. Naivety may be mended."

A sip of wine, and a glint of blue eyes. Fer Gun ate another bit of cheese, and a round of bread, washed down with a careful sip of wine.

Putting his glass aside, he leaned toward Pilot Chi.

"Clan Telrune is outworld, and Low House. We're scoundrels, in a word, and, so I learn, there is not even honor among kinsmen."

"If it comes to that, my own clan not infrequently throws out rogues. We do better by our kin than Telrune would seem to do, but, then, we are much poorer in cousins. I do not wish to rush you, Pilot, but may I know if you find my proposal of any interest?"

He sipped his wine, considering.

In well-ordered clans, as even he knew, he would at this juncture place the matter in the hands of his delm. As Telrune was nothing like well-ordered, and there being no gain to the clan in breeding him, the last pen'Uldra, he supposed he might make his own decision in the case. After all, the proposed child would remain with Pilot Chi, and burden Telrune not at all. Unlike himself, who was, as Aunt Jezmin often said, nothing more than another mouth to feed, useless as all his Line had been, and luck he'd been born able to least to think with his fingers, since his brain was only a hindrance to him.

There might, perhaps, be something in the business for Telrune, should Pilot Chi prove to be of a clan useful to the delm's on-going schemes. But the truth was that Telrune's focus *was* scheming. He had never, in Fer Gun's memory, negotiated a contract for alliance— or for any other thing. Mostly, his kin allied as suited themselves; babies were born, and came into the House haphazard, though Telrune did, often, remember to record their names.

In the case of the proposal before him . . . he found himself largely neutral. The issue would be no concern of his. And if it came to the pilot herself, his proposed contract-wife, she looked likely to give good sport in bed. There was that tendency to order all to her own satisfaction, but he was accustomed to have someone else do his thinking for him, now wasn't he?

And among orderly Houses, he thought, his wine glass arrested on its way to his lips, as he suddenly recalled a custom he had never truly learned . . . In proper clans, contract-spouses were given a payout, once the conditions of the contract were met. It might be that Pilot Chi represented the manner in which he might pay his fine. Also, it would fall to Pilot Chi's clan to feed him, and clothe him, and shelter him during the term of the contract. In that free year, then, he might order his affairs, make contacts, find work . . .

"I am prepared," Pilot Chi said quietly, "to be generous."

He stared at her.

"To Telrune?"

That drew a smile.

"To yourself, though of course Telrune must be accommodated in such a way that the contract does not reflect badly upon the child."

"That's an extra-size lot of respectability you're wanting," he pointed out. "I *did say* we're scoundrels."

"You did. But I've no objection to scoundrels, being one myself. What I *must* have is the seeming of propriety. We will do the thing properly, for the sake of the child, who must be able to deal from a solid foundation."

She picked up the bottle and refreshed their glasses.

"What do you think, Pilot?"

He sipped his wine, and *did* think, for a wonder and a novelty, before meeting her eyes once more.

"I think," he said slowly, "that I will need to know who you are, Pilot. You have the key to my life, but I know nothing of you."

"Fairly said."

She seemed to square her shoulders under the worn leather, and met his eyes firmly.

"I am Chi yos'Phelium Clan Korval."

The floor bucked, and he nearly lost his glass.

Korval.

Everything was illuminated by her name: access to the Guild database, her need of a pilot-father; the necessity of proper adherence to the forms.

"Surely," he managed, his voice breathless in his own ears, "you can do better, Pilot."

She laughed at that and held her hand out to him.

"Do you now? I think that you and I will get on extremely."

He looked from her face to that hand, slim and strong. She was a clever woman; she was older and more experienced than he; it was, he reminded himself, an opportunity.

"I think so, too," he said. And met her hand.

II

PETRELLA YOS'GALAN came to the end of the file, flipped to the photo, sighed, and spun the chair so that she faced her twin, leaning with arms crossed against the corner of the desk.

"Well," she said, "he's not in the common way."

Chi half-laughed.

"No, he's barely tamed; and now that he's learnt to distrust kin, he's well on the way to ruination." She tipped her head.

"Wine?"

"Of your kindness."

Chi straightened out of her lean, and crossed the room. Petrella looked once more at the flat-pic on her screen.

A young man, rangy and rough, with unruly dark hair tangled 'round a fierce, bony face. The eyes alone would slay dozens, black as space and hard as obsidian.

Yet, among all this ferocity, there was a hint of sweetness 'round the mouth; a barely perceptible softness in the jutting chin. Not ruined yet, she thought, but wary as a cat, and dangerous.

Chi was of course fully capable, but it had never been her habit to bed dangerously.

A breath of air alerted her, and she moved her eyes from the screen to her sister's face, and received the wine from her hand.

Silently, they lifted their glasses, and drank in unison. Chi sighed.

"His piloting record—" she began . . .

"Is astonishing," Petrella finished. They were identical twins from a clan which had given many to the *dramliz* over the generations. Often, they did not even need to speak aloud. More often, they finished each other's thoughts seamlessly.

"But is it enough?" Chi asked the question Petrella had not.

She leaned over and touched the screen, calling up the boy's record.

"Won a scholarship to Anlingdin, despite the deplorable condition of his House," she murmured. "Graduated early from an accelerated course; 'prenticed on a Looper for the long-side, and mastered Jump before he came twenty-four."

"Whereupon his delm called him home, and his troubles began." Petrella sighed this time. "You *might* have found someone more convenable, you know."

"And young Fer Gun?"

Petrella hesitated.

"Mistress Toonapple often has need of pilots, and she is, so we hear, accounted a fair Boss."

Chi raised her eyebrows.

"Are you advising me to place a pilot into Juntavas hands, Sister?" she asked.

Petrella felt a twinge of shame before her twin shook her head.

"Even if that is your advice, it won't answer. The child himself tells me that he will not fly grey—and never dark."

"*Does* he?"

Petrella tipped her head.

"That is . . . promising," she murmured.

"You might say it," Chi agreed, and half-raised her glass.

"There's more, if you'll have it."

"I must," Petrella assured her, "have everything."

"Yes, well. His cousins set him up beautifully, with that contract in hand, and his signature there for all to see. He must have become inconvenient for them, do you think? Perhaps he began asking questions. Jai Kob cho'Fadria—the elder cousin—is something more than a mere scoundrel; the other cousin—Vin Dyr—killed a man in a bar brawl on an outworld, and the proctors bought off."

"So the cousins wanted young Fer Gun out of the way," Petrella said, and raised her eyes to meet Chi's gaze. "Or dead."

"We can do better than either for him, I think," her sister said, and raised her glass.

"As for finding someone more convenable . . ." she continued . . . "the sole Line on the homeworld which always produces a pilot is yos'Galan, and we have crossed lines too recently for that match, even if Sae Zar was willing."

Petrella snorted.

"The mother's twin bedding the halfling nephew. Yes, propriety would be satisfied by that."

"It does become problematical. Young Fer Gun, on the other hand, will offend no one."

"He will offend *every*one," Petrella corrected.

She sipped her wine, thoughtfully.

"Which comes to the same thing, I suppose."

Chi lifted her glass in ironic salute.

Petrella reached to the screen and tapped up Pilot pen'Uldra's picture once more.

"The Code teaches us," she said slowly, her eyes on that space-cold gaze; "that a contract ought benefit both parties. What benefit comes to this boy by making contract with Korval? You will of course stand hostage to his wings, which for him will count for much. But, I wonder, is that enough? He is unpolished. He is, forgive me, not merely Low House, but, as he himself said to you, affiliated with a House composed entirely of rogues and petty thieves. To raise him up, even just for the length of the contract, into the brangle and spite the High Houses . . . He may survive it—he looks a hardy lad—but he will not thrive. He will make errors, possibly errors that will follow him for the rest of his life, and even if not—"

She paused, considering the tattered remnants of sweetness in the hard young face.

"Even if not," she finished, as Chi was silent; "he will mind it, and it will cost him."

She glanced up into her sister's grave eyes.

"It will cost him," she repeated.

Chi inclined her head.

"I agree," she said, her voice as grave as her eyes. "The child cannot thrive in alt, and I will not ask it of him. I intend due diligence, and a careful Balance."

She sipped her wine.

"We may easily, I think, manage the signing, and an afternoon meal."

Petrella frowned slightly.

"Guests chosen from allies and aspirants," she said slowly. "A luncheon, rather than a dinner. Bold he may be, but we do not wish to try his mettle at a full formal affair."

"Precisely. I have it in mind to place him in Ilthiria's hands—though, perhaps her brother would answer better . . ."

"A collaboration might serve best of all," Petrella said, tipping her head slightly. "Give him enough polish and manner to manage the necessaries—if he's a clever boy and keeps modestly quiet . . . Stay! Allow him to be overawed by his good fortune, and sweetly shy. That should play well."

"My thoughts, yes. So, that Jump is made."

"But what then?" demanded Petrella. "Will you keep the child locked in his rooms? He's a pilot, and very nearly feral. He won't care to be confined."

"Certainly he would not! No, I have in mind to take him off-planet. Korval can afford to be generous. *I* can afford to be generous. How then a business arrangement, negotiated separately from the marriage contract, in which he becomes provisional captain of that small-trader we had been discussing last week? We shall do a tour, and I will introduce him to those who will be useful to him, returning to Liad in time to appease propriety in the matter of the child's arrival. After, the pilot will be released to his rightful business. We might easily steer likely crew, and a trader, in his direction."

She paused, frowning.

"I suppose I will need to retain a share. Small enough not to encumber him; large enough to deter any plans his House might nurture to wrest the enterprise away from the child and repurpose it for their own use."

She moved her shoulders.

"dea'Gauss will contrive."

Petrella sipped her wine, inspecting the thing from all sides. Finally, she put her glass on the desk with a decisive click.

"It will answer. Especially as I have already made arrangements to keep to Liad for the term of my own marriage, through the child's birth."

"And thus may stand in my place, should urgent business of the clan arise. Yes. I believe it *will* answer—if you are satisfied now, Sister, that the scheme will more likely benefit the child than harm him?"

"It is more than generous," Petrella said, with feeling. "I very much hope that it will result in a new pilot for yos'Phelium."

"If it does not," said Chi, rising and putting her glass next to Petrella's on the desk, "there will be your own child to take up the Ring when the time comes. Have we not already determined that yos'Galan, at least, breeds true?"

"Yes, but yos'Galan has no ambition to rise to delm," Petrella said quellingly.

"I understand. However, if yos'Galan produces a pilot and yos'Phelium does not, we will need to rearrange ambitions, as well as expectations."

She stretched.

"I'm away to dea'Gauss, and possibly yo'Lanna. Have you any errands I might dispatch for you in the city?"

"Thank you, no—no, stay! Where is Pilot pen'Uldra at the moment?"

"At the Pilot's Rest in Mid-Port. I hope to have him in less perilous conditions soon. Ilthiria may take him, once dea'Gauss has drafted the marriage lines."

"Assuming Justus agrees," said Petrella, and Chi laughed.

"Whenever has Ilthiria's lifemate stood against her?"

"There is that," Petrella said, and stood to open her arms.

Her sister stepped into the embrace, and then stepped away.

"Until soon, Sister," she said.

"Until soon."

Petrella sighed, carried the wine glasses over to the buffet, and came back to her desk, frowning.

Something . . . there was something she was missing. Not Echieta, world of thieves that it was.

Not Telrune, certainly.

Not—was it the boy's *name*?

pen'Uldra.

She sat down at the desk, frowning.

pen'Uldra.

There had been . . . *surely* there had been . . .

She reached to the screen, and called up the *Encyclopedia of Trade*.

pen'Uldra, now . . .

III

FER GUN PEN'ULDRA sat in the little sunroom that had become his favorite corner at Glavda Empri. He had been the guest of Lady yo'Lanna long enough now that it no longer seemed . . . very strange that the house—the structure—had its own name, as if it were a ship or some other nobler thing than a place to sleep and sup.

Though to be sure, Glavda Empri housed many, entertained more, and was older itself than Clan Telrune. Mayhap it had earned its own name.

He shook out his ruffles and settled himself in the chair. Go back twelve days and he could have said with perfect truth that he had never worn ruffles in his life. Now, he possessed several shirts—made to his own size!—in various colors, each of them showing lace at cuff and collar. In the usual way of things, so he had lately learned, a gentleman did not wear lace in the daytime, or, unless expecting visitors, in the privacy of his own parlor.

But, said Lady yo'Lanna, he had so short a time to learn the way of them, that it must be ruffles and full dress coat throughout the day.

He feared that he would never learn the way of ruffles, though he had marked that there had been less corrections to his manner over the last two days. Perhaps he had gained some proficiency, after all.

That, he thought was more likely than the possibility that Lady yo'Lanna had given him up as a hopeless case. After a *relumma* in her care, he had *her* measure at least—and she was not a woman who accepted defeat. Also, she was Chi yos'Phelium's especial friend; and she had promised that she would deliver an unexceptionable spouse-elect to the signing.

So it was that he had language lessons, and deportment lessons, and dancing lessons. He was given several fat chapters of the Code to sleep-learn, that he might discuss them with his hostess over mid-morning tea, and so fix them in his mind.

It was, he admitted, gazing out over the garden that seemed to have no outward boundary, an unusual and demanding curriculum. He had never been an avid scholar; even at Anlingdin he had cared for nothing beyond his piloting lessons, deeming the rest of his courses distractions from the real business he had come to learn.

And, atop his new clothes, and his new manner, he had also achieved grooming. Nothing would make his hair amenable and smooth, but the barber summoned by Lady yo'Lanna had clipped the thick stuff short on the sides, and swept it away from his face, while leaving the crown and back longer, so that it almost *seemed* his own hair, though shockingly free of elf-locks.

Even Lady yo'Lanna had been pleased with the results. At least, he supposed that, "Yes, I thought that you would dress well," conveyed pleasure.

Of all the persons he had met over this twelve-day, and there had been a surprising number of them, he had seen his wife-to-be only once, and that in company with a very worthy city-man who had been introduced as "Mr. dea'Gauss, my man of business. He will be writing the contracts."

They had then gotten immediately down to details, presented with perfect clarity by Mr. dea'Gauss: In return for his service to Korval, Fer Gun pen'Uldra Clan Telrune would receive a sum of five cantra, to be delivered to his hand on-signing. His daily expenses and reasonable others, for the duration of the contract, would be borne by Clan Korval. Should eighteen months elapse and best efforts had not resulted in a child, the contract would be considered ended, and he would receive the remainder of his fee. Clan Telrune would receive a sum totaling his expected earnings as a first class pilot for the term of the contract, payable to them when the contract was complete. Telrune, dea'Gauss assured him, had accepted those terms, without question, which Fer Gun doubted not at all. The marriage-portion was free money to Telrune, and only a fool would turn it down, or endanger its arrival by scheming for more.

So, the marriage contract.

There had been a second contract, much more complex, and he had understood that it would likely not be complete before the marriage was made.

That contract . . . he smiled in anticipation, and did not allow himself to consider that she would withhold it, once she had him married. He had, he told himself, already agreed to the marriage; there had been no necessity to offer—

"Ah, I thought I might find you here," Lady yo'Lanna said briskly, startling him out of what he supposed must have been a doze.

"It's quite the most pleasant room in the house, isn't it?" she continued, coming 'round to sit in the chair across from him. She had a courier envelope in one hand and a pen in the other.

"You will be glad to see this, I warrant, Pilot," she said, offering the envelope and the pen. "I am told that this is the draft of the marriage lines for your review. If all is well, you are to initial it in the place indicated and return it to dea'Gauss."

He opened the envelope; somewhat dismayed by the number of pages. Still, he knew from experience that paperwork was complicated, even when the agreement was simple.

There was a bright green clip on the next-to-last page. He flipped the packet open to the spot, turning to place it on the chair-side table, as he uncapped the pen and—

"Stop this instant!" Lady yo'Lanna said sharply.

He blinked, and turned his head to look at her, pen poised over paper.

"Have you read that contract?" she demanded.

"No," he admitted. "But we spoke—myself, and Pilot Chi, and *Qe'andra* dea'Gauss. All agreed what ought to be in it."

"And so you will sign it blind?" she demanded. "How do you know that there is not a paragraph in that contract which states, should you indeed provide a pilot to Korval, that you will be kept at stud for the next twelve years?"

He stared at her.

"Pilot Chi—" he began.

She held up a hand, freezing the words in his throat.

"Chi yos'Phelium is my dearest and oldest friend. She is also Korval. Chi certainly would do no such thing. But Korval is a very different matter. *She* will do what she must for the clan. And you will do well to remember, young Fer Gun, that it is *Korval* who produced the basis of that draft, after the three of you had your discussions."

Fer Gun took a breath. His stomach, he noted distantly, was . . . unsettled.

"You will sit there, and you will read that contract, word by word, and line by line," Lady yo'Lanna told him. "I will not permit you to sully *my melant'i* by doing otherwise." She rose, and looked down her nose at him.

"You will do well to take it as a life-lesson, Pilot pen'Uldra: *Always* read the contract. Always *understand* the contract. I will return here in an hour, and I will expect to be told the terms of that document. If you should have questions, or find that there are provisions you do not understand, make a note of them so that you may inquire either of our clan's *qe'andra*, or another of your choosing."

Fer Gun swallowed.

"Yes, ma'am," he said. There was no other possible answer.

Lady yo'Lanna inclined her head.

"I will send tea," she said, and left him.

IV

"YOU MUST ADMIT," said an overly cheerful voice just beyond the dressing room where Fer Gun stood, staring at the stranger in the mirror and wishing very much to be anywhere else.

"What do I have to admit?" he asked, around a queasy stomach.

Lady yo'Lanna's brother, Lord ter'Meulen, had taken an active part in Fer Gun's education. Where the lady was incisive and inclined to scold, her brother was light-speaking, unflappable, and unserious. Well. That was the impression he wished to give, at least. Fer Gun was fairly certain that, in the extremely unlikely event that he was seen to pose a threat, he would find his lordship wearing a very different face.

As Fer Gun was no threat, and ter'Meulen well aware of it, the face he saw was amused and a little sardonic. His lordship was every bit as informative as his sister, though of a slightly different flavor. If the lady's preferred topic was form, her brother's was function.

"You have to admit," his lordship said now, strolling into the dressing room, "that Chi has an eye for a well-looking man. Ilthiria doubted that you would clean up more than passably well, but look at you! You might be the *nadelm* of some off-world High House."

"Or I might be a wingless pilot from a clan so low neither Korval nor Guayar can see us on a clear day."

ter'Meulen's eyebrows rose slightly.

"Dismay gives you an edge, I see. Take my advice and keep your knives close. Soft words, and few, will win this day for you. If Korval had decided upon full formal, and all the High and high Mid-Houses in attendance, then, my child, you would have needed all the knives in your arsenal, and all that I could lend you."

Lady yo'Lanna had very carefully explained to him that the event surrounding the signing of the lines was small, scarcely more than tea with friends. Which, he conceded, it might well seem to one who had known the attendees for all of her life. For him—well, he was the two-headed calf, as Jai Kob would have it; an oddity with only one thing to recommend him.

He turned to face Lord ter'Meulen, letting the reflection of the stranger in his fine clothes and jewels slide out of sight.

"Why does Korval make the signing public at all?" he asked, a question that had only lately occurred to him, as all of his informants had simply spoken of the signing and the luncheon as an accomplished fact. "It is only a contract marriage, after all. We might sign the lines in *Qe'andra* dea'Gauss' office."

"Ah, has no one bothered to tell you?" asked ter'Meulen. "That was ill-done of us. We are well-versed in the reasons, but they are far from a universal interest."

He walked over to the bureau, where someone had left a tray holding six glasses and a pitcher.

"Cold mint tea?" he asked. "It will settle your stomach." He poured a glass, and inclined his head. "And mine."

That must have been meant as a jest, Fer Gun thought. *ter'Meulen* wasn't about to be married before of a room full of strangers, all of whom would see through the fine feathers he had been lent, to the molting magpie beneath.

"Truly," ter'Meulen said, turning to look at him. "The tea will do you good."

"Thank you, then," Fer Gun said with ill grace, and moved forward to receive the glass. "She had told me that she needs a child who will grow to be a pilot, as the elder child has proven unfit, but—"

Lord ter'Meulen raised his hand, his face in the moment very nearly stern.

"The elder child is brilliant, and convenable, and an asset to her House. Merely, she is not a pilot, and Korval House law states that the delm must be a pilot."

Fer Gun felt his face heat. He bowed.

"I meant no insult to the lady. Forgive my awkward tongue."

His lordship awarded him a broad smile, all displeasure vanished.

"There! *That* is the mode—sweet and soft-spoken. Now, the answer to your question is this: yos'Phelium is the delm's Line. As Kareen cannot stand *nadelm*, and Chi unwisely placed all of her coins on that one cast of the dice, she must now scramble for an heir. And she must do so as publicly as possible, to put to rest any rumor that this second child's claim is illegitimate."

Fer Gun had a sip of tea, which was pleasantly cool in a parched mouth.

"She had said that Festival-get would not serve her purpose," he recalled.

"The least attractive solution, though it may yet be brought to the board, should Korval wish to fill the nurseries against need. That, of course, is Korval's decision."

ter'Meulen sipped from his glass.

"There is another child. Sae Zar yos'Galan is a pilot and so might be delm, but he is yos'Galan's heir, and will be the clan's master trader, in his time. There are no more children behind him, either. So we come to the current solution, which is that yos'Galan will contract-wed—that happy event has already taken place—and yos'Phelium also. This will produce two children—the nadelm and an extra. The best outcome is that both children will prove to be pilots. The lesser, but acceptable, outcome is that one will be a pilot, and so Korval will have a delm. If neither child is a pilot . . ."

His lordship shrugged.

"But, why is Korval so few?" Fer Gun blurted, recalling Telrune's house, overfull with cousins, and never lacking for babies.

ter'Meulen sipped his tea, and put the glass aside.

"That is a question best put to Chi. I can recite facts, but you will want reasons, and those I cannot give you." He cocked his head.

"Finish your tea, child. It's time we were off."

• • •✧• • •

CHI TOOK ONE LAST LOOK around the contract room. The flowers twined prettily up the bed posts, their fragrance subtly scenting the room. Light flowed sweetly into the room from the wide window that overlooked the inner garden.

Of course, she ought to have used the contract room overlooking the formal gardens at the front of the house, but the inner garden was, in her opinion, a pleasanter prospect, and smaller, which might, perhaps, comfort a boy who had been accustomed to limited sight-lines even before he had taken to ships.

The contract-room having proved itself agreeable, Chi crossed to the door in the right-hand wall, opened it and stepped into the room that would be occupied by Fer Gun pen'Uldra for the small time that he would actually be residing in the house. After the business of the contract-room was completed, he would retire here, to sleep, or pursue what other activities might beguile him. Again, she had attempted to make it agreeable to the sensibilities of a boy of humble means. There was a comfortably worn sofa and a well-broken-in chair near the fireplace, and a modest offering of real bound books on the shelves. Over near the window was the desk, the screen useful for either entertainment or work. She had also had a scanner placed on the desk, so he might listen to the business of the port.

The kitchenette was reasonably well supplied with wine and tea and small foods, such as one might wish for of an evening while one sat with a book, or an afternoon snack in front of a work screen.

The sleeping room was adequate without being opulent. There was a soft rug underfoot, and a sky-window over the bed. An extremely modest jewel box, sufficient to accommodate the lad's extremely modest jewels, sat atop a plain, six-drawer dresser. There were clothes in the closet—not very many, and tailored as simply as could be managed while still preserving elegance and style.

It would, she decided, do. Indeed, it would have to do. And, after all, the lad had spent a *relumma* in one of Glavda Empri's guesting suites. Perhaps he had acquired a taste for elegance.

She returned to the contract room, being careful to close the door to the spouse's quarters firmly behind her, and opened the door in the left-hand wall.

This would be her apartment while the contract was in force; not very much more luxurious than its opposite on the other side of the contract room. After all, they would not be on Liad above a day or two before removing to *Comet* and lifting in pursuit of their new-signed business venture.

She owned herself to be looking forward to the small introductory trip. Liad became tiresome after a while, with its *melant'i* games and intrigues. The challenges of piloting, and even of establishing a base-line for a new route to be run by a new captain, were charmingly straightforward, and even refreshing, by comparison.

A glance at the small clock on the bookshelf told her that it was closing in on the hour.

She would soon be wanted downstairs. The guests would have arrived by now, received by Petrella; and Bal Dyn ter'Meulen would be arriving soon, her spouse-to-be in hand.

She tarried a moment, yet, considering that spouse-to-be. A rough lad, scantily tutored. She did not expect that he had been given any bed-lessons beyond what had been learned from such lovers as he may have had. And, truly, it scarcely mattered if he merely lay there and left all the details to her. The point of the exercise being, not an enjoyment of art, or of each other, but simple, even coarse, biology.

A child, of her body. A pilot, if the genes aligned, to lead the next generation of Korval.

And, if yos'Phelium had played out at last, then best to *let* the Line die, and leave yos'Galan free to marry another Line less likely to draw catastrophe upon it and all its workings.

The small clock chimed the hour.

Chi yos'Phelium sighed lightly, squared her shoulders, and took herself downstairs to be married.

• • •✧• • •

KAREEN met her at door to the small gather-room, all proper and smooth-faced. Chi did not sigh. Kareen was inclined to the opinion that Korval clan law was outmoded and required revision to bring it into modern times. She was further of the opinion that adhering to a protocol made in a previous universe during a time of war and strife did active harm to a clan residing in a time and universe of relative peace and prosperity.

She was not, as Chi had admitted, entirely wrong in either of those assessments. However, there was a contract to keep, and to that, once shown the terms, not even Kareen had an answer.

"Mother." Her eldest bowed and offered an arm, which Chi took gently.

"Daughter," she answered. "I am grateful for your guidance."

It was only partly a joke; she *was* grateful that Kareen had agreed to be her support at the signing—and not merely because it would involve her personally, and perhaps reconcile her to the inevitable.

If she did not actively frown, nor did Kareen smile; she merely stepped across the threshold and into the room.

The clamor of voices softened somewhat as they entered, and not a few pair of eyes followed them on their way to the small dais, where her sister waited.

"You are just in time," Petrella said, leaning close to kiss her cheek.

"So long as I am not late," she answered, and allowed Kareen to assist her onto the stage.

She took up her position behind the table, to the left of the portfolio and the pens, Kareen standing one step to the rear and the right.

Those who had watched her progress turned back to their

interrupted conversations. The sound of voices swelled—and all at once went silent.

Bal Dyn ter'Meulen, whose instincts *never* failed him, paused on the threshold, head up, face calm, and allowed the room to look their fill, not of him . . .

. . . but of the young man on his arm.

Oh, thought Chi, looking as well—Ilthiria, whose instincts perhaps surpassed even her brother's, had risen above all of her past perfections in the dressing of the spouse.

A dark blue coat with a deep nap that showed subtle pinpoints of silver when the boy moved. A white shirt, modestly ruffled down the front, as pure as a child's honor. The ruffles at his wrists were deep, falling softly over hands that were no strangers to hard labor; a ring set with a dark blue stone flashed shyly on his right hand, and the dark trousers accentuated long, shapely legs.

He was not, Chi thought, considering the guests, anything like what had been expected. They had expected outworld manners, graceless, if not crude, but this—finely dressed and haughty, like a dagger in a velvet sheath—took them back a step. He stood straight and utterly cool, his arm linked with that of his escort, his face composed and even cold; eyes like black diamonds glittering beneath heavy dark lashes.

Very likely the child was terrified, Chi thought, but if so, those gathered were not to know it. Indeed, she thought, watching the pair of them approach the stage unimpeded, as one after another stepped aside to let them pass—Indeed, it would seem that Fer Gun pen'Uldra's whole purpose was to deny those gathered the spectacle of his fear.

There was not the least bit of awkwardness at the dais, and Fer Gun took his place, unhurried and deliberate, behind the table, at the right of the portfolio and pen, while Bal Dyn stood one step behind and to the right, witness to the proceedings.

The crowd parted once more, and Mr. dea'Gauss stepped forward. He walked up to, but did not mount, the dais, and turned to face those gathered.

"We are here to witness the signing of the contract of

engenderment made between Chi yos'Phelium Clan Korval and Fer Gun pen'Uldra Clan Telrune, with the child coming to Clan Korval."

You might have heard a speck of dust fall onto the floor; it seemed that no one in the room dared breathe.

"We begin," said Mr. dea'Gauss gravely. "Fer Gun pen'Uldra Clan Telrune, please affix your name to the contract."

• • •✧• • •

"LADY YOS'GALAN, a moment of your time, if you please."

Petrella turned to consider the society page editor for the Gazette, Finlee as'Barta.

"Certainly, ma'am," she said, watching out of the corner of her eye as Chi maneuvered her contract-husband toward a knot of stalwart friends of Korval. "How may I assist you?"

"I would value some insight into who, precisely, Fer Gun pen'Uldra Clan Telrune is," Editor as'Barta said crisply.

Petrella raised an eyebrow.

"Surely, the Book of Clans . . ."

"I have, I assure you, perused the Book of Clans. It reveals to me that Clan Telrune is seated upon Echieta, a world which appears to exist to offer repairs to ships in . . . reduced circumstances. It is, perhaps, an unsavory world; nor does Clan Telrune appear to stand high among the Clans seated there."

"Alas, there are many such worlds, and stations, as Echieta, which pursue their lives as they find best, away from the luminous oversight of the homeworld," Petrella said, perhaps not as gently as she might have done. Indeed, the editor's lips parted. Petrella raised her hand, and spoke on.

"Your question, however, has to do with the personal history of yos'Phelium's contracted spouse. Fer Gun pen'Uldra is the grandson and only surviving heir of Arl Fed pen'Uldra, who had been for many years an influence in the so-called Divers Trade Association. He served two terms as one of the twelve seated commissioners—six Liaden, and six Terran—and served also for many years as one of the twenty-four ombudsmen, as well as standing Thirteenth—the tie-breaking vote—for three cycles of the council.

"At one time, Arl Fed pen'Uldra owned, with his lifemate, a fleet of four small traders."

Finlee as'Barta stared at her.

"I would ask for documentation, as the Book of Clans has failed me."

"The information is largely found in the trade histories. It will be my pleasure to send the cites to you."

"I thank you. One does wonder what became of the tradeships, the grandfather, and the spouse's parents."

"The tale turns bitter, I fear," Petrella said. "This information will of course be included in the cites. In short, the success of the Divers Trade Association made its members targets of pirates and other unsavory persons. Captain pen'Uldra lost his ships, his lifemate, and his children. With the one grandchild remaining to him not yet a Standard old, he sought refuge with his cousins in Clan Telrune, the better to hide the child from those who would murder him for his birthright. Captain pen'Uldra died very soon after going to ground on Echieta, and the child, now yos'Phelium's spouse, was raised by Telrune."

"A touching history," Editor as'Barta murmured. "Pilot pen'Uldra is fortunate that Korval was aware of his circumstances. Of course, he is a pilot to behold?"

"By all accounts, he is," Petrella acknowledged.

"Which must of course, Korval being Korval, carry all before it."

Editor as'Barta turned to survey Chi and her spouse, who were receiving congratulations from Azia pel'Otra Clan Elarnt, a solid trading family long affiliated with Korval in general and yos'Galan in particular.

"Quite young, too," as'Barta said, which was merely spite, "and one assumes, easily guided."

"That has not been my experience of the pilot," Petrella answered sweetly.

"I must excuse myself," she added. "Be assured that I will send the cites to you this evening."

She bowed, and as'Barta did, and Petrella walked away, seething, to greet the other guests.

IT WAS DONE.

Well, no, Fer Gun corrected himself; the signing and the reception, and the displaying of manners only recently learned to persons he had never thought to meet, even if he had known of their existence—*that* was done. He hoped he did not flatter himself, to think that it had been done, if not well, at least credibly.

He had found it . . . astonishingly easy to fall into Lord ter'Meulen's suggested mode of soft-voiced modesty, and allow his spouse to carry all before her. It was entirely possible that he had learned some important and interesting things during his tour of the gather-room on Chi yos'Phelium's arm. His grandfather had told him that information was a coin with limited value, until it was paired with another, like, coin.

His grandfather had said other things, too, most of them doubtful, if not outright daft. But the importance of holding on to scraps of information until all the pieces came together to form a quilt—*that* Fer Gun had found to be apt. Trader Yinzatch aboard *Selich*, where he'd hired on directly after school—Trader Yinzatch held to a similar understanding of data and its relationships, and had in addition been a wizard in matching edges. It had been an education to watch the trader at work, even for a pilot.

For now, though . . .

For now, he was at liberty, having been shown to the apartment which was to be his during the time he guested in Korval's house—another named as if it were a ship: Jelaza Kazone.

They were pleasant rooms, much less grand than those he had lived in at Glavda Empri, which was, he admitted to himself, a relief.

He took some moments to explore, after he had removed his loaned finery, and placed the ring and earrings into the plain box atop the dresser. He frowned on finding several rings, and earrings, a handful of jeweled pins, and glittering chains in the box when he opened it. He took a breath, to cool the flicker of temper. The contract, he reminded himself, stipulated that he might be required to attend several more gathers in support of his spouse. It would not show well on her, if he appeared each time in the same coat—which was why there were six made in his size hanging in the closet. It would show equally ill on her, if he repeated today's jewels—or wore those which were his in truth—a pair of silver earrings set with ruby, which his grandfather had told him had belonged to his mother, and a silver bracelet which had, according to grandfather, belonged to his mother's mother.

After he had explored the apartment, he looked in the tiny kitchen. He had eaten little at the luncheon, and only sipped the wine, feeling the need to have such wits as he owned well about him. Nor had he done justice to the breakfast he had been offered at Glavda Empri.

He ought, he reasoned, be hungry; it had been a long day and difficult, and by no means over yet. A perusal of the various small foods and vintages in the kitchen, however, failed to turn up anything that tempted, and in the end he drew a glass of cold water, and went to stand in the window and look down at a tangle of vegetation through which a slender walk could barely be seen.

He knew little about growing things or gardens. The disorder of this one appealed to him, though, and he was drawn to the colors of the many flowers.

He glanced upward, but the angle of the window foiled any sighting of Korval's Tree, the top of which he could see quite clearly from his rooms at Glavda Empri.

After a time, his water finished, he left the window, and glanced to the bookcase, not so that he might know which titles were available to him, but that he might see the small clock set on one of the shelves.

His stomach tightened, and his chest cramped. In an hour, he was to meet his wife in the contract-room, there to perform such duties as had been laid out in the contract.

Deliberately, he closed his eyes, and ran one of the mental exercises which were taught to pilots, to ensure that their minds were clear and their energy levels high.

His breathing smoothed; his muscles relaxed.

Yes, he told himself, that's more the mode; it's a risky flight, but you'll do well so long as you mind your board.

Well.

With another glance at the clock, he went to ready himself for duty.

• • •◇• • •

HE ARRIVED in the contract room early, so not to keep his wife waiting—which was respectful, according to the sections of Code Lady yo'Lanna had him Learn, and then discussed with him over the morning meal, in order to set the material in his mind.

Respectful it may have been, but it did nothing for his nerves to be alone with the ornate bed, a living vine growing up the posts and across the headboard, the flowers nodding heavily and giving up their scent to the room.

He regretted now, his failure to eat; he had wanted to keep a clear head, but the flowers would have him muddled before ever the business was well underway.

Stepping away from the bed, he opened the window, filling his lungs with cool air lightly scented with loam and green growing things and flowers of a . . . less complex nature.

He leaned closer into the window, closed his eyes—and snapped upright, eyes open, as he heard a door open.

Chi yos'Phelium, his contracted wife, glided silently toward him on naked feet. She wore, as he did, a long silk robe, belted at the waist. His robe was black, painted red flowers extending from his left shoulder, across his chest, down, and all around the hem. Her robe was green, patterned with small blue birds—or small blue dragons—and the belt was tied loosely, indeed.

He swallowed, hard, and recalled himself, a bare *relumma* in the past, rough and angry in a low port bar, thinking that *certainly* he would bed the elder pilot, if she was prepared to buy herself some fun, and maybe he would keep her on his string, too, since he'd had no other means to eat.

That Fer Gun pen'Uldra, he thought now, had been an idiot. A swaggering port-tough who had no idea of *real* danger.

This Fer Gun pen'Uldra, contracted to give the fine elder pilot before him a child . . . recognized every one of his failings in an instant; his lack of finesse or any other bed-skill, save, perhaps, endurance, and even that, he thought, as she crossed the room like a tigress, might fall before her.

She was good to look upon, too. *Elder pilot*, indeed, he sneered at his past idiot self. Oh, she was older than he was, in years, in guile, in polish. She might undertake to teach him his own name, and he would learn from her lesson. He was not her match—not near her match, in any thing—and it was far more likely that she would have kept a brash pilot on her string for exactly so long as she had use for him, had their first meeting gone as he had predicted, and cast him away with nothing when she was done.

The green robe clung to every line of her long, strong frame. The skin revealed by the loosened knot was pure gold, and so smooth his fingers, still rough despite Lady yo'Lanna's lotions, would surely catch and scratch her.

She came to stand beside him, and turned her face to the window, smiling into the soft breeze.

"The inner court at this hour is splendid, is it not?" she said in the comfortable mode of Comrade.

"The breeze is refreshing," he offered in turn, marking the unsteadiness in his own voice.

"That it is," she said, apparently noting nothing amiss.

She stepped slightly away from the window, turning so that they faced each other.

"I have a gift for you," she said; "may I give it?"

His victory was that he did not look immediately at what the robe revealed, but kept his eyes on hers.

"I . . . have no gift for you," he said, around a feeling of strong dismay. The giving of contract-room gifts had not been among those customs he had Learned. Had he given offense already? Perhaps it might soothe the feelings of his past self, that at least it had not been for his performance in bed.

"There is no reason why you should have any gift for me, other than yourself," Chi yos'Phelium was saying, with a smile. "It is a whim—I fear that you will find me whimsical."

She paused, head tipped to one side.

"May I give the gift?"

He drew a breath, seeking calm, and managed to meet her smile with one of his own.

"Yes, please."

"Excellent."

She raised the hand she had kept slightly behind her; he took the card from between slim fingers—and only just managed to swallow a curse.

"My license!" he said, staring at her.

She raised her eyebrows.

"Is the gift inept?"

He drew a breath, folding his hand around the card in sudden fear that she might snatch it back. Whimsical, indeed.

"The gift is appreciated," he said choosing his words with as much care as he was able. "But, Pilot—I was to have stood, wingless, a year. At the end of our contract, you had promised to come with me to the Guild and speak for my good name. That," he concluded, somewhat breathlessly, "was the agreement."

"Well, so it was," she said. "But you will need your license and your wings if we are to take our partnership forward in the matter of the small trader, and so I said to the Guild Master. He was much struck."

She bought your card back for you, Fer Gun told himself. Gods alive, she *bribed* the guildmaster. He ought to have cared, indeed, the risk of it chilled him, but very nearly all of his thought was for the license in his hand, which he would not relinquish again for anything he could name.

"We also reviewed the matter which had brought you to the attention of the port proctors and so the Guild," Chi said, turning toward the small table that held a pitcher of wine and a plate of cheeses and small breads.

Fer Gun swallowed.

"And?" he said.

Her eyebrows rose again.

"Why, the guildmaster agreed that your cousins are very clever. Will you have wine?"

He blinked. That was twice she had commented on the

cleverness of his cousins. There was something there, and he too thick-headed to see it—and the lady had asked him a question.

"Wine," he said careful again. "I would prefer not. The flowers . . ."

The flowers were making him queasy, and his head was beginning to ache with their stench. If he was to do her any good at all this night . . .

"Ah."

She inclined her head.

"They are rather insistent, are they not?" she said and walked past him to push the window wide.

Pausing there, she looked down into the garden, then turned again to face him.

"I should like to go for a walk in the garden," she said. "It is my habit of an evening, and I have not had an opportunity, amid all the brangle and the bowing. How if you put your ticket safely away, and accompany me? It is a very fine garden, despite its disreputable habit."

"I—" he stammered to a halt. "What does one wear, to ramble through a garden at night?"

She glanced down at herself, and then to him.

"These will do," she said. "Will you come?"

"Yes," he said, and bowed. "I will only be a moment."

IT WAS MUCH PLEASANTER in the garden than inside, Chi thought; and the lad—she stopped herself. She needed to stop thinking of him in quite that way. Yes, she could give him a dozen years or more—yet he was a man grown, who held a Jump pilot's license, and had managed, against considerable odds to the contrary, to survive his childhood, the death of his sole protector, and the particular attentions of his so-clever cousins.

Thrust into a game the rules of which he could not hope to master, yet he had managed to keep himself in good order, without exposing vulnerability or weakness to those who might be expected to exploit such things. He had *learnt* the lessons he had been set to, and Ilthiria had not spared him, for either his youth or his upbringing.

"Who cares for all of these?" he asked now.

She glanced over to him—very nearly, he matched her own height, a novelty of its own—and moved her shoulders.

"In theory, I do," she said, wry in the face of his earnestness. "In truth, there is Master Gardner Byneta with whom I confer, and who will occasionally allow me to weed out a planting, but does not, I fear, quite trust me with a landscape knife."

He frowned at her.

"You were a Scout, Lady yo'Lanna told me."

"Oh, indeed. A captain of Scouts, as it came about, and to the astonishment of everyone, including myself."

"Then you're surely safe with a landscape knife," he pursued.

She grinned.

"As you know and I know. However, those who recall the days when one was scarcely safe with a rubber ball, and liable to stab one's own hand with a butter knife . . ."

She smiled, inviting him to acknowledge the joke, and after a moment had the pleasure of seeing a smile that actually reached those space-black eyes, and very nearly thawed them.

"In any case, it is Master Byneta who cares for the garden, as I do not dare go against her wishes."

The path they were following all but disappeared beneath an overgrown bank of viburnum. She stepped ahead of him, slipping her hand into his as she passed. She felt his fingers twitch in shock, but he did not withdraw, and she tugged him after her, around the path's last curve, and into the Tree Court.

She paused at the very end of the path to allow him to see what it was he approached. His hand, she kept firmly in hers and he did not withdraw, nor even seem to know that they were linked.

Herself, she felt the Tree's regard focus upon her, and a greenly sense of welcome. Excellent, her throw had not gone awry.

"Korval's Tree," she said, quietly, to her husband. "My favorite place in all the inner garden."

"It is less grown over, here," Fer Gun said, soft-voiced, as if he sensed something sleeping, and did not wish to wake it. "But . . . more wild."

"That would be the Tree's influence," she said. "It likes its comfort, be certain of that, and makes certain that all and everything in this court is arranged to its best liking. Come, let us introduce you."

She stepped forward, walking carefully over the surface roots, the grass cool and damp against naked feet. He came willingly, still with his hand in hers.

"You would introduce me to a . . . tree?" Fer Gun asked, when they had achieved the trunk and she had placed her hand palm first against the rough, warm bark.

"It likes to meet people," Chi told him. "There are not many new faces come to speak with it in the Tree Court, and it does not itself, you know, travel very well."

She heard a chuckle, then, and pleasant hearing it was, low and honestly amused.

"I can see that travel might present problems," he said. "What am I to do? Bow?"

"Indeed not. Merely put your hand, so, against the trunk, and let us see what will happen."

* * * ⋄ * *

THE GARDEN BREEZE brought immediate relief to his aching head and queasy stomach. He considered the plants that grudgingly allowed their passage along the stone walk with grateful benevolence. It occurred to him that he had not been at ease—truly at ease—since he had been picked up by the port proctors for holding a piece of paper for his cousin Jai Kob, and thereby lost his wings.

And hadn't the ship spun three hundred sixty degrees on its axis, when that event, which had been the low point of his life, was now revealed to be his most fortunate moment?

The path narrowed again, and Chi stepped ahead of him, light-foot. He felt a warm hand slip 'round his, caught his breath—and let it out in a sigh.

Hand-clasped, he followed her 'round a pile of living green very nearly as tall as he was, which had put forth round blue flowers easily as big as his head.

On the other side of the bush, the path vanished, and he came to rest next to his wife on the edge of what looked to be a public park, the grass short and well-tended, and the space open. Roses rioted on edge of the clearing and to the right there was a bench placed before them. In the center of the clearing, though, was an enormous trunk. He craned his head back, and sighted along it.

Korval's Tree.

"You would introduce me to a tree?" he asked, though, really, the notion scarcely seemed out of the way, given the presence of the Tree. He was conscious of Chi's hand in his, and of the fact that the breeze in this enclosed place was slightly brisker than out in the wider garden. Wisps of blonde hair had been teased out of the loose knot at Chi's nape, and he was suddenly taken with the notion of sliding his hands into her hair, becoming complicit in its disorder; and placing his lips against the soft skin of her throat.

Her hand tightened 'round his and she led him forward, to the very Tree itself.

"What shall I do?" he asked her. "Bow?"

"Indeed not. Merely put your hand, so, against the trunk, and let us see what happens."

He did as she said, pressing his unencumbered hand flat against the bark.

It was rough, and surprisingly warm. He felt a wave of—of happiness?—crash into and through him, and he was so delighted that he threw back his head and laughed aloud.

He heard Chi laugh, also, through the racket of happiness, and felt her hand still warm in his. From somewhere, he heard the sound of leaves snapping, and, obedient to the prompting of the joyful presence all about, he stepped back, and raised his free hand, palm up.

Next to him, Chi had done the same, and they each caught a round, green . . . seed pod, he thought . . . at the same instant.

The uproaring welcome faded, leaving him buoyed with anticipation, he turned, to see her eyes sparkling; the loosened tendrils of her hair moving softly about her face, scandalously stroking cheeks and brow and . . .

He swallowed and brought the pod up.

"What is this?"

"This," she announced, sounding as breathlessly delighted as he felt, "is a rare treat indeed! I wager you have never had the like. Here—"

She held her hand up, showing him the pod on her palm. Perhaps she blew on it. Perhaps she had squeezed it when she'd caught it.

In any case, the pod merely . . . fell open, revealing a nut nestled in each quarter.

"We eat them," she said, and without further explanation, slipped a portion of nut into her mouth.

He looked down at his hand, to find that his pod, too, had fallen open, and the aroma of the nuts made him realize all his hunger at once.

He all but snatched up the first piece, managing not to cram it into his mouth. It was—he had never . . .

It was perfect.

He ate the second piece, and it, too, was perfection; as was the third.

The fourth . . . he hesitated, and looked into her brilliant blue eyes.

"This," he said, holding it toward her; "is yours."

She smiled and raised her hand.

"And this," she murmured, "is yours."

She stepped forward, and he did, each lifting the treat to the other's lips. Warmth filled him, and surety; his loins were beyond warm, and he stepped forward again, or she did. He thrust his fingers into the silly knot, freeing silken strands for the breeze to make merry with, as he bent to press his mouth to the base of her throat, feeling her fingers tracing down his chest, and his robe—her robe . . . Gods, she felt so good.

She made a soft growling sound, and pulled his head down to her breast.

* * * ✧ * *

SOME TIME LATER, they lay together at the base of the Tree, the grass as soft as any mattress while they learned each other, and learned themselves, and cried out in joyous release.

Chi woke . . . later, to find the Tree park filled with a gentle glow, and a blanket of leaves cast over them like a quilt. Fer Gun lay with his head on her breast, and she was of no mind to move him, or to rise and go into the house.

She settled her chin atop his head, closed her eyes. Above them, the wind moved through the leaves in a lullaby.

Chi went back to sleep.

V

THE GOOD SHIP *Comet*, out of Chonselta, Liad, belied her name somewhat, erring on the side of dependable and everyday, rather than on flash and glitter. She was patient with two pilots who continually tried her, teasing out her strengths and her limits; unapologetic when they confirmed that she was not a scout ship, for they had also found that she was not a garbage scow. A working small trader, that was all and everything that she claimed to be, and that was, in fact, exactly what she was.

Pilot Fer Gun pen'Uldra proved to be something other than Chi had anticipated, given his scores, his Guild test ratings, and his speed. Oh, he was everything that was quick and knowing at the board—that she had expected. But she had not expected Fer Gun pen'Uldra to be patient with the limits of so pedestrian a vessel. She had, in fact, rather thought that he would chafe under those limits, perhaps show a bit of temper, and even some disdain for work-a-day *Comet*, so far beneath his abilities.

Instead, he fair crooned over her, and gave her fulsome praise when she held her line and refused to be intimidated by the demands of an extended run at the top of her range.

"She won't let us down, this lady," he told Chi. They had finally gotten done with testing and trying and got themselves on the way to Mondaw. *Comet* had gone into Jump with nary a complaint nor a bobble, all boards green and steady.

"She has heart," Chi agreed.

They were in the galley, sharing a celebratory cup of tea. Fer Gun was having a bowl of soup, too, while Chi contented herself with some salted crackers.

"We won't be picking up anything at Mondaw?" asked Fer Gun. "The whole reason is to meet this Vigro Welsh?"

"We are running podless, with two pilots the whole crew," Chi pointed out. "How much cargo can we take?"

"Small packages, and courier work," he said, lifting a shoulder. "Ships don't fly for free."

That was spacer economics, and true, so far as it went. Chi sipped her tea.

"We may find some small thing which needs to travel in our direction, but you will recall that the primary purpose of this trip, Captain pen'Uldra, is to introduce you to those firms and contacts with whom you will be working, once this ship is fully crewed and wearing her pods."

As he was still frowning, she added.

"Korval funds this tour as part of the cost of doing business."

"True enough, though it goes against the weave," he said, finishing his soup and rising to put the bowl in the washer. "Would you like more tea? Or something a little more to eat than two crackers?"

"By the time I am done here," she told him with dignity, "I will have had *three* crackers. And yes, I would like it if you would warm my tea."

He did so, and stood looking down at her. He was, she thought, much more suited to a ship than to Liad. It had been a wanton cruelty, to conspire so carefully to rob him of his wings. Though there always remained the possibility that the cousins had expected him to succumb to Low Port. She sighed, lightly. One would so treasure an opportunity to speak with the cousins.

Still . . .

"What are you thinking?" Fer Gun asked her. "Will Mondaw be a problem?"

That was a nicely reasoned leap, and phrased so that she need only answer one query.

"Mondaw ought to be nothing like a problem," she said, truthfully. "You have the files for review, do you not?"

He laughed.

"Do I not!" he repeated. "And I will set myself to reviewing them, again, I swear. In the meanwhile, you might have a nap."

She did *try* not to glare at him.

"Am I a fragile flower, Pilot?"

He traded her a stare for her glare. Those black eyes produced an admirable stare, indeed.

"The pilot requires the copilot to be able," he said. "You're tired. Even I can see that."

Chi bit back a sharp retort. After all, he was correct—she *was* tired, and would be the better for a rest. And he was twice correct to remind her of the progression of responsibilities, though she had learnt them before she could walk; there was a teaching rhyme that her nurse had sung to her.

The pilot being correct on both counts, she smiled up into those black, black eyes.

"I will, in fact, nap," she told him. "That is an excellent idea, Pilot."

· · · ✧ · · ·

VIGRO WELSH was plain-spoken and hearty, and Monday something very like him. Fer Gun felt a cautious optimism. When this plan—this partnership—had first been proposed, he had had his doubts. Who would not have had doubts, partnered with Korval? *Comet* herself had been a reassurance—a ship in the common way, accustomed to the common work of ships, and nothing of the glittering luxury of Liad about her.

In the same way Vigro Welsh was reassuring—a merchant, who dealt in everyday wares, and presented no airs. He was comfortable in a matter-of-fact way that drew Fer Gun's envy. Where Glavda Empri, Jelaza Kazone, and Trealla Fantrol had discomforted and distressed him, Vigro Welsh's office and—nameless!—home was not only appealing, but seemed . . . attainable in a way that Chi's house would never be, for the likes of Fer Gun pen'Uldra.

There had been a tour of the warehouses, and introductions to various others of the Welsh network. The merchant's initial instinct had been to speak to Chi.

"Captain pen'Uldra will be regularly on the route," Chi said. "He will naturally be taking on a trader and crew. This stop is to make you known to each other, and so the captain may provide *Comet*'s trader-to-be with current introductions."

That had set the merchant straight, and Fer Gun had found himself the center of a very sharp attention, indeed.

He was pleased to believe, at the end of the tour, after they had shared dinner at a local restaurant that was also in the network, that Vigro Welsh would not find himself embarrassed to be associated with Captain pen'Uldra and *Comet*. That left an unaccustomed warmth, which still buoyed him when they returned to the ship.

Once they were in and sealed, the two of them sat in the galley over wine, and talked through what they had seen, and he had learned, and considered those questions that he had.

When the debrief was done, he would have gone to his own quarters, but Chi had put her hand on his arm and smiled in that way that made his breath short and his blood warm. He had gone with her, therefore, and pleased he was to have done so.

. . . ✧ . . .

IT WAS NEXT SHIFT that trouble struck, though he thought nothing about it at the time. He'd risen, checked the comm, and the screens.

No messages for them on the overnight, but the screens showed a package sitting just over the line of their dock. A smallish package, easily carried in the courier hold, and it was such a common thing that he thought nothing of opening the hatch and walking out to pick it up.

He scanned it, naturally—he wasn't a *fool*, after all—and was on his way down the hall when the storm hatch snapped shut almost on his nose.

"What is that in your hand, Pilot?" Chi asked him over the intercom, her voice calm.

"A package," he said agreeably.

"Had we arranged for a package?" Chi asked, and it came to him, then, that her voice was not so much calm as *constrained*.

He frowned, suddenly and forcibly reminded of the studies she had had him make regarding lading slips, documents of transfer, the proper order and style of sign-offs.

"Had we," Chi asked again, "arranged for a package?"

"You know that we hadn't," he told her curtly. "I thought it had gotten kicked in."

There was a small silence, before she repeated, "Kicked in?"

A hasty, belated scan of the package showed no documentation, no bills, no stamps; none of the things that—that an *honest* package ought to have, leaving aside the detail that an honest package would have been openly delivered and signed for by the ship.

"When I was piloting for my cousins," he said, telling her the truth, no matter how badly it reflected on him. He had learned that: you told Chi yos'Phelium the truth, as plainly and as quickly as possible.

"When I was piloting for my cousins, it often happened that a package or a pallet was kicked inside our line, and was taken aboard as our rightful cargo." He hesitated, then finished the tale out, feeling an *utter* fool.

"We didn't have so much to do with lading slips, and tax stamps, and suchlike."

Silence for the count of twelve. He could feel the ice filling the corridor and wondered if he'd freeze to death, or if she'd only evacuate the air from the hallway.

"I am calling the port proctors," she said at last. "You will meet them on our dock and you will give that package to them. There will be questions; there may be forms to fill out. You will be everything that is convenable and forthright with the proctors, do you understand me, *Pilot*?"

The proctors. It fell on him, the memory of the proctors, the binders, the standing before Solcintra port security, and the Pilots Guild Master. The demand that he give over his license into the Guild's safekeeping . . .

It was on the edge of his tongue, then, to beg her to evacuate the air.

"The proctors are on their way," Chi said.

She would leave him here, gods, and he could scarcely blame her.

However her means, she had redeemed his wings, and he repaid her with arrant stupidity.

He took a breath, and made sure his legs were steady enough to bear him before he bowed, in full sight of the camera—the bow of deep regret—before he turned toward the hatch and his doom.

· · ·◇· · ·

"EIGHTH ONE this port-week," the elder of the two proctors said, who was clearly displeased, but not, it seemed, at him.

Her partner finished scanning the package, produced a scan-proof bag from one of the many pouches on his belt and sealed the package inside.

"Inert," he said. "Like all the rest."

"And like all the rest, it will doubtless flash-bang when it's opened," the elder said. She looked to Fer Gun and bowed slightly.

"Our apologies, Pilot. This prank has been on-going. So far no harm has come of it, because the ships that dock at Mondaw are honest ships, and call the proctors immediately. We will need to take your statement, and we request a copy of your dock surveillance records. Perhaps we'll get lucky this time, and see a shadow."

For a moment, Fer Gun thought his knees would give beneath his weight. A prank; an on-going prank, and he nothing more than its latest victim. The ship had behaved correctly, and the proctors had been called.

He wasn't going to be arrested, again. His license would remain in his pocket.

There would still be Chi yos'Phelium to deal with when this was over, but if she struck him dead on the spot for idiocy unbecoming a sentient, still, he would die a pilot.

"Certainly," he said to the proctors. "We will be pleased to share our records."

"Thank you, Pilot," the elder proctor said, and produced a note-taker from her belt. "Now, if you'll just tell me what happened, we'll add your testimony to the file."

· · ·◇· · ·

THE CHILD was exhausted, Chi thought. Not surprising, really; terror did drain one's resources.

Now, he sat at the table in the galley, nursing his tea, and clearly waiting for doom to fall.

She sat across from him, and leaned her chin on her hand.

"I amend my opinion," she said, and smiled slightly when his eyes flew up to meet hers.

"Which opinion would that be?" he asked, his voice rough. "That in fact I am not naive, but stupid beyond redemption?"

Well. Here was angst. She had forgotten, almost, how very young he was.

"It was somewhat stupid to bring an undocumented package onto this ship," she said conversationally. "Though you were not so stupid that you failed to scan it. Habit is compelling, and we are all victims of our education. You have now, I believe, received an alternate education, and one that you will not soon forget. So, no, I have not changed my opinion of your abilities or potential."

"What then?" he asked, his voice less rough, and his face showing some ease.

"Well, I had been in the habit, as you know, of considering your cousins to be clever. I think now that they are not so much clever as very lucky. Did they never cheat anyone on the grey-fees?"

He blinked, and straightened somewhat in his chair.

"I was the pilot; not part of the dockside arrangements. Jai Kob had his contacts." He paused as if considering the matter fairly. "He also had Vin Dyr. Very few make progress against Vin Dyr."

"I see. They are then common port-toughs, with an amount of low cunning, but they are not, necessarily, clever. That is a fair judgment, I think, and I have no shame in altering my opinion of them. Now."

He winced slightly, and she smiled.

"I had been under the impression that you had known who your grandfather was. That may have been an error."

"Grandfather?" He frowned.

"My grandfather was old and ill and unsteady in his head. He came to rest at Telrune because no one else of his kin would take him."

"Ah," she said, and took a breath against a hot breath of anger.

"I will send some information to your screen," she said, rising. "We have several hours until lift, which should be sufficient for you to make yourself familiar with the data."

He rose, and bowed contrition.

"I will," he said, "try to . . . improve your opinion of me, Pilot."

"There's a worthy goal," she said lightly, and left him.

VI

THEY HAD SET UP their table on the hiring side of the Trade Hall on Dameeth, and had seen a suitably brisk business. There were some, so it seemed to Fer Gun, who altered their course to avoid when they saw the "Tree-and-Dragon Affiliate" card. That was well enough, in his opinion. It was no small thing, as he knew, to partner with Clan Korval. Such a partnership was more likely than not to change one's life, which was all very well for those like Fer Gun pen'Uldra, whose situation could only be changed for the better. Those who were satisfied with their lives, though—they did well to plot a course wide of Korval.

They had given five data-sticks, and collected three for review, which they would most assuredly do that evening on return to the ship. He had a favorite among the three, an elder trader with a steady air. Traveling with Chi yos'Phelium had taught him the value of a steady and knowledgeable elder. A new captain on a new route certainly would need all the steadiness and experience he could amass.

He scanned the room. It was edging toward the end of the day, and the hall was thinning. Those crewing the tables at either side of them were packing up to leave, their conversation all about dinner, and a glass or two of wine to aid the process of decision.

Indeed, he was on the edge of suggesting to Chi that they remove to review what they had collected, when a movement at the entrance to the hall drew his eye.

A trader had entered, walking with purpose down the line of hiring tables. She was tall, and wide-shouldered; her hair a smooth and glossy brown. Her clothes were respectable without being ostentatious, as had a few of the early applicants. Her single jewel was a garnet ring—which told the universe that she was a full Trader.

She paused at a table five up from theirs and spoke to the hiring crew. A Terran crew as it happened, and it seemed to him that she spoke that language easily, switching seamlessly to Trade when one of those behind the table put a question to her thus.

There seemed some interest on both sides, and, indeed, she did leave a stick with them before taking her leave and moving once more down the row.

She was near enough now that he could see her face—round, and amiable, and pale. Terran herself, then, he thought, with a sharp stab of regret. That might not be so well. The two Terrans they had spoken to on the day had been capable enough in their own language, which he was in the process of Learning, himself, but utterly at a loss in Liaden, and neither proficient in hand-talk.

She passed on, and raised her eyes to look past those who were done for the day, and read the sign on their table.

Her eyes were the color of the Tree's leaves, seen through morning mist. They widened somewhat, and he expected her to pass them by.

She surprised him, however, and quickened her pace until she stood before their table.

She bowed the bow of introduction, and straightened to address them, her face smooth and properly Liaden.

"Pilots. I am Karil Danac-Joenz, Trader, lately serving aboard *Argost*. I am interested in learning your requirements. Perhaps we might benefit each other."

Gods, her Liaden was better than his. Fer Gun managed to keep his countenance, though it took him too long to find his voice, and Chi spoke first, in Terran.

"Trader Danac-Joenz, well-met. We offer a new route which will require fine-tuning, a new captain and crew, and an older small trader. Are you up for a challenge?"

The trader grinned, in that moment utterly Terran.

"Pilot, if I weren't a fool for challenge, I wouldn't have become a trader, over all the objections of my family, who wanted a calm life for me."

Chi inclined her head, and spoke next in Trade.

"You are under contract. When will you be at liberty?"

"My contract with *Argost* expires in two months Standard. The captain has a standing arrangement with an affiliated Line, and an appropriate trader has just recently finished out his contract. As matters stand at the moment, I will be set down at Boert'ani Station. That may be adjusted, of course."

"It is possible that our interests may align," Chi said, back into Liaden, but less formal, closer to his own most comfortable dialect. "May we offer a key?"

"I receive your key with pleasure," Karil Danac-Joenz said, her dock-side bearing an odd Terran inflection, but perfectly intelligible to his ear. "May I offer my own key?"

Chi glanced to him, and back to the trader.

"I am Chi yos'Phelium, representing Korval's interests in this set-up period. This—" she half-bowed in his direction— "is Captain Fer Gun pen'Uldra, who will be regular on the route."

Trader Danac-Joenz turned to him and bowed.

"Captain—" the Liaden word.

"Trader," he answered, in his poor Terran. "I am pleased to accept your key."

She put it on the table before him with dispatch—Liaden manners, again. She had handed her key directly to the Terran recruiter, five tables up.

He inclined his head, and on a hunch added the hand-sign for *well-met*.

"I'm pleased to meet you, too," she said her fluid Terran, her fingers answering *well-met*, with just the right emphasis to convey, also, *agreed*.

· · · ◇ · · ·

THE THREE RESUMES they had gathered were surely worthy, Chi thought, watching the crowd thin. Since she had the benefit of Petrella's notes, she knew to a whisker precisely *how* worthy. One at least would serve *Comet* well and honorably, though the raising up of a new captain might try her somewhat.

It would do, she thought, if nothing else presented, and the hour for presenting was growing late. They might take another day here at Dameeth—the schedule was that loose—to see if something more promising arrived on the morrow. On the other hand, there was no certainty that tomorrow would produce any more interesting choices.

She felt Fer Gun shift in the chair next to her. He was about to suggest that they strike their table and retire to the ship, to study what they had gained. Not an unreasonable suggestion, yet something other than the weight of her belly kept her in her own seat, waiting—

There was a stir at the doorway, and a trader, short for a Terran, tall for a Liaden, moved down the line of tables, deliberately, scanning each in turn. She strolled past the two big-ship tables, with a Terran smile and a nod, and paused at the table which represented the Lazarus Line, which had a long-Loop in need of a trader.

That conversation went well, sticks were exchanged, and the trader moved on, past the empty table, and that being dismantled. She raised her head, read their sign, and glanced to Fer Gun.

Her eyes widened; her lips parted slightly.

Well, now; this was interesting.

The trader stepped forward and introduced herself, and Chi drew a careful breath. She recognized the name, from Petrella's notes.

Interesting; nearly an original. Contracted three years to Argost, and has achieved wonders, despite the limits placed upon her. Possibly Korval will want her, after she's tempered a bit more.

Tempering, thought Chi. Surely it would do the trader no harm, if Korval took active part in her tempering?

Fer Gun had lost the use of his tongue, she noted; first contact was hers to make.

She smiled, therefore, wide and Terran.

"Trader Danac-Joenz," she said cheerfully; "well-met."

VII

"**STATION MASTER** assigns us inner ring twelfth quadrant."

"Got it," Fer Gun answered.

Copilot was riding comm, which is how they had worked out the board between them. In addition, she had a good eye for a likely berth, and the in-ring at twelve was about as likely as they could get, coming in to Boert'ani Station.

Their pick-up here was personnel, in particular, Trader Karil Danac-Joenz.

He was still . . . not entirely certain how Karil Danac-Joenz had come to be their first choice for *Comet*'s trader. She was young, she was Terran—well, she had been born into the Terran population on a world that supposed itself Liaden, and was therefore what Chi was pleased to call cross-cultured. She was well-spoken in three languages and in hand-talk, was Trader Danac-Joenz. He had *liked* her, but—the last seven months had taught him the value of having an older and more experienced crewmate to draw upon. And thus he had settled upon Trader Losan vey'Norember, experienced, sober, and very able to advise a new and, despite all his best efforts, ever-to-remain-foolish pilot-captain.

Chi, however, had seen benefit in Trader Danac-Joenz's ease in two cultures, and presented as uniquely useful that the trader held both a five-year trade key from TerraTrade *and* wore the garnet of a Liaden trader.

It had been Chi's opinion that a new route wanted youth and flexibility.

"Old heads tend to be hard heads," she said. "A young captain and a young trader grow together into a team, plan routes and expansions between them; get to know each other's minds. Where you'll want older heads, if I may be so bold, Captain Fer Gun, will be on your copilot and your engineer. And if it were up to me, I'd hire general crew with multiple areas of expertise, rather than just muscle, but you'll suit yourself, of course."

He valued Chi's opinion, and so set himself to compare the resumes of both contenders.

And in the records, he saw Chi's point. The elder trader was surely elder, her list of accomplishments, as one might expect, many times longer than that of the younger trader. But the list of her contacts had been static for years, and the rate of gain for new was ... slow. Very slow, indeed.

Trader Danac-Joenz, on the other hand, *had* to develop markets and contacts precisely because she *was* new. Further, those markets she had developed remained with her, even as she added to her contacts and expanded her areas of expertise.

And that was how Karil Danac-Joenz had come to receive their offer first, and had accepted it on the spot.

It had been, Fer Gun told himself, his decision, based on Chi's recommendations. Chi's experience.

He only hoped it worked out as she had foretold.

He would, Fer Gun thought, sending a glance over to second chair, miss his copilot, her bossy ways and her encyclopedic knowledge of ships, trade routes, goods, and human persons. More, he would miss her humor, and her patience, and her generosity in bed—oh, he had learned much, this trip, and not merely the ship, and the names of those to whom she introduced him as her business partner, and proper business manners. She had said at the start that she would be generous, and she had more than kept her promise.

Boert'ani Station was their next-to-last stop. Take on the trader, that was one thing; take on a small cargo bound for Lytaxin.

Chi had kin at Lytaxin, and she was under some obligation to show them her belly. That weighed on her, as even he could see; weighed on her enough that he had broached the notion of arranging for another ship to take Lytaxin's small cargo, so she might spare herself at least that burden of propriety.

She had smiled, and kissed his cheek, as if they were true kin and not merely contracted.

"But you know, it must be done. *All* the forms must be observed for this child; and if I make any misstep, it must be in the direction of Too High."

That was just *melant'i* games and High House spite, so far as he'd been able to determine, which had made him glad to be so insignificant, and sorry that she must bear with such nonsense, when she must have a care for the babe on his own account. Surely, this had been no good time for her to take up the frustrating hobby of polishing rough pilots, but she had never stinted him.

Navcomp pinged, and he looked to his boards to find that the approach to their berth had arrived from the station master's office.

"Course received," he said quietly, fingers moving; "locked in."

He glanced over to the second board.

"End of shift, Pilot?" he asked—a broad hint; "I'll take her in."

"Glutton," Chi said cheerfully. She rose, carefully, though without strain, from her chair. They kept ship's gravity a trifle light so that there would *be* no strain; that had been his idea. She had noticed, of course—Chi yos'Phelium noticed *everything*—but beyond a raised eyebrow had made no comment, which he took to mean light grav might remain.

"Tea, Captain?" she asked him. "A board-snack?"

"Both would be welcome," he said. "I thank you."

"Copilot's duty," she said lightly.

That was proper enough. Still, he might have felt a pang, that she was required to perform such small tasks for him, had she not regaled him with tales of her time as a Scout, and confessed that this trip to establish him had benefit to her, as well.

"Far better for me to be here, where things are so much more straightforward and sensible, than negotiating the gathers, and the *melant'i* games, and turning the attempted strikes against Kareen, poor child."

Kareen, had not, he thought, cared much for him. Not that she hadn't a full pod of good reasons to dislike him, not least because he was the instrument by which she would be denied what ought to have been her proper place in her clan. Having been the less-than-able among his own kin, he felt a sympathy for Kareen, but possessed nowhere near the address necessary to express such a thing to her.

And, really, they were not *that* much alike, when he thought more deeply upon it. He was a barely-lettered pilot from a clan which was no higher than it should be, his failing a lack of imagination in the matter of extortion.

Kareen, on the other hand, was a brilliant scholar, gifted in the field of social science, valuable to her clan as he was not—would never be. It was merely that she was not a pilot, and so, by Korval's own law, she could not stand delm.

"Well," Chi had said, one evening as they lay together in bed, sated and in a mood to tell over history. "It is a difficulty with charters made so long ago. We ought, perhaps, to modernize ourselves, but we have obligations every bit as ancient, and so we abide."

She had smiled as he recalled it, wistfully, and murmured.

"Perhaps someday there will be no reason for the delm of Korval to be a master-class pilot. But that day will not, I think, dawn within my lifetime."

The child they had made, then, had best *be* a pilot, capable of mastering Jump at the very least, else Clan Korval would undergo a change—a small change, so it would seem on its face. yos'Galan would ascend to the primary Line, and yos'Phelium would fall into the subordinate place.

It was plain to him . . . say it was plain to him *now*, having had his eyes opened somewhat to nuance by close association with the most complicated mind he had yet met—that the possibility of yos'Phelium failing troubled her.

"Those who came before you ought to have seen the clan-house full of pilots," he said to her, which was surely an impertinence, but she had merely given him a wry smile.

"We were more plentiful before we became embroiled in intemperate politics, and three of our delms came mad—two with the notion that yos'Phelium's connection to the old universe made us a blight upon this one, and far better that the Line died out."

"Do you hold with that?" he asked, not believing it of her.

"How can I believe us to be utterly evil?" she answered, whimsical as she was when she did not care to answer a question too closely. "And, you know, it is not the loss of precedence which I care for, but that we will lose our wings. From the very first, we were pilots, and to fail of being pilots, ever again—perhaps it *were* best that the Line die out."

That had been too melancholy for pillow-talk, and he had set himself to bring her into a happier frame of mind, which he flattered himself he had done.

And he hoped, that for once in his life, he had been apt.

The proximity sensor beeped at him, then, and he looked to his screens, fingers already moving across the board, making minute adjustments, dancing with the station, and made a wager with himself that he would dock her tight on the first attempt.

* * * ✧ * * *

HE WON HIS WAGER handsomely, sliding into dock with no slightest bobble. He refused station air, and the list of dockside services. Station would know that they were short-dockers, Chi not having been likely to have omitted that detail in negotiating their space. Still, he supposed they had to ask, on the chance that the PIC was an idiot, or the ship had a surplus of funds. Their bad luck that the pilot had lately graduated from idiot to half-wit, and ship's funds were adequate for the necessities, without running to luxury.

Details settled, he opened the port directory, meaning to place a call to cor'Wellin Warehousing, and arrange delivery of the cargo bound for Lytaxin.

Before he could open an outgoing line, though, the comm lit green—call incoming.

He touched the switch.

"*Comet.*"

"Good spin, *Comet*," said a light, cheerful voice, speaking Liaden in the mode between comrades, "this is Karil Danac-Joenz. Do I speak with Pilot pen'Uldra?"

"Trader, you do," he said, meeting her in Comrade. "I hope you are well."

"Well, but bored—you cannot imagine how much!" she told him. "The market here is dismal and the trade floors—as Boert'ani Station acts as my host, I will say only that the trade floors are bland in the extreme. There. We need never speak of it again."

His lips twitched.

"Will you come aboard, then? I warn you that we are also bland, sitting at dock as we do."

"But that is an affliction which will soon be remedied, will it not?" she said, and before he could answer, swept on, "Yes, Pilot, I would very much like to come aboard. May I? Soon?"

"Yes," he said. "What is your direction? I have a delivery to arrange, but then I will come for you. Have you much luggage?"

There was a small pause, as if he had surprised the trader.

"Pilot, thank you. I am at the Spinside Hyatt, and can be at your hatch within the hour. As to luggage, I assure you that I require no assistance."

He hesitated, but Boert'ani was rated safe, after all, and surely a trader must be dock-wise.

"Come, then, and welcome," he told her. "We will expect you."

"Excellent! Until soon."

"Until soon," he answered, but the light had already gone out.

Well, then. On to the next task. He located cor'Wellin in the port directory and placed his call.

"This is Fer Gun pen'Uldra," he told the man who answered; "small trader *Comet*. I wish to arrange delivery of our cargo, hold number CW9844."

The warehouseman's face changed. Perhaps it was dismay. He held his hands up to the screen.

"My apologies, Pilot, but you must come to us. Your cargo has been damaged. You will want to inspect it before taking delivery."

"Damaged? What kind of damage?"

The man licked his lips.

"I cannot say, Pilot. It will be best for you to come yourself, perform an inspection and file a damage report, if you deem it necessary."

Fer Gun glared at the warehouseman. The warehouseman simply stared back at him.

"I will be there within the hour," he said curtly, and cut the connection.

He had hoped to let Chi sleep her fill; and now he would have to wake her for board-duty—another irritation.

Well, it couldn't be helped.

He rose, and crossed the bridge to the main hall—

A bell rang.

Fer Gun frowned—then his face cleared. Trader Danac-Joenz had arrived. Perhaps he could let Chi sleep after all.

He turned left, down the access hall, glanced at the screen, and verified that the tall woman with the amiable face, pretty brown hair braided down her back today was, indeed, Karil Danac-Joenz—and cycled the hatch.

* * * ✧ * * *

CHI WAS IN THE COPILOT'S CHAIR when they came onto the bridge, having stopped on the way from the hatch to stow the trader's meager luggage in her quarters.

Fer Gun swallowed a curse.

"Pilot," Chi said agreeably. "Hello, Trader; well-met."

"Pilot." Trader Danac-Joenz bowed. "It's good to be aboard."

"It's good to have you," Chi assured her, then turned a sapient eye to him.

"What's amiss, Fer Gun?"

He sighed.

"The warehouse lets me know that the cargo for Lytaxin is damaged. They won't deliver until I've gone to the warehouse, inspected the damage and filled out some paperwork. I had hoped to let you rest. In fact, why not rest again? The trader will stand comm."

He saw Chi look aside, and followed her gaze. Karil Danac-Joenz was frowning slightly.

"Yes?" Chi murmured. "Do not hesitate to share your thoughts, Trader. You will find it a plain-spoken ship."

A subtle grin briefly illuminated the trader's face before she turned to Fer Gun.

"Unless Pilot yos'Phelium's need is dire, I think the ship is better served if I go with you to the warehouse," she said. "I am something of an expert on cargo, and on the sorts of damage cargo might reasonably receive."

She paused, not quite a hesitation, and bowed slightly.

"I am also an expert on paperwork having to do with cargo." She gave him a whimsical look. "My master insisted that I learn it all, no matter how tedious, and well it was that he did—the garnet exams are nearly all about paperwork."

It was his decision. Chi could have said, "That would be the best use of resources, Pilot." She *didn't* say it, but he heard it inside his head, just as clearly as if she had. And, yes, he told himself grumpily, it *was* the best use of available resources.

"Well, then," he said, bowing lightly; "are you ready now, Trader?"

She returned the bow.

"Yes, let us go now. It's a lovely day for a walk."

. . . ⟡ . . .

"I AM HERE," Fer Gun told the clerk behind the counter, "to inspect cargo that was damaged. Lot Number CW9844, on hold for *Comet.*"

She glanced down, presumably at a screen set below the counter, and looked up again, face stiff.

"Lot CW9844 is being held in the inspection bay. Down this hall, Pilots, to the end. There is a door."

"We will require the presence of a warehouse representative," Trader Danac-Joenz said. "We were told there would be paperwork."

The clerk took a breath.

"Someone will be waiting for you in the inspection bay."

There was a momentary hesitation, as if the trader had weighed this answer and found it wanting. Then, she inclined her head, and turned to him.

"After you, Pilot."

. . . ⟡ . . .

THE HALL was short, and oddly unpeopled. Fer Gun hesitated, and glanced at his trader.

"Do you have a weapon?"

She met his eyes.

"Will I need one?"

"I don't know," he admitted, and moved a hand, fingers flickering in the sign for *bad feeling*. "You won't wait in the hall, I suppose."

She laughed.

"Already, we are beginning to know each other! No, Pilot; I will *not* wait in the hall, but I will cover your off-side."

Well, that was fair enough, he owned; and, by the look of her face, it was the trader's best offer.

"To my right, then," he said, and lengthened his stride, so he was first through the door.

The bay was bright-lit, which he hadn't expected; and there was the pallet, in the center of the light, looking remarkably unscathed. He cleared the door for his back-up—six strides beyond the door—and stopped, looking to the right of the cargo, where the light had thrown shadows.

"Jai Kob," he said, finding the first cousin easy enough, leaning against a pod-lift, just at the edge of the shadow.

A longer look brought him the second, deeper in the dimness, crouching on his heels.

"Vin Dyr," he added, and over his shoulder— "My cousins."

"Is that the contract-wife?" Jai Kob asked, strolling forward, his hands tucked comfortably into his belt. He gave the trader an appraising glance, and looked back to Fer Gun, frowning.

"Withholding yourself, Gunny? Or just inept?"

"I was told," Fer Gun said, watching out of the side of his eye as Vin Dyr straightened to his feet. "That my cargo was damaged, and required an inspection, with a paper filed. Working for the warehouse, Cousin?"

Jai Kob laughed, and Vin Dyr drifted closer to the light. Fer Gun felt the trader's attention shift in that direction.

"The cargo's well-enough, so far as my inspection goes," Jai Kob said. "Given the terms of the contract you're under, we thought it best to meet you in private. *Is* that the contract-wife?"

"No," said Trader Danac-Joenz.

"Good," Jai Kob said. "That's good."

He stepped closer, his hands slipping out of his belt. There was a packet in his off-hand, which he lifted slightly to show Fer Gun.

"The damage call was only a prank, Gunny—just a joke between kin. But it's true enough that you've papers to sign."

Fer Gun felt his stomach clench. Papers. Often enough, he'd had papers to sign, since the day he came halfling; his grandfather gone, and what care he had coming from his clever older cousins.

The very same older cousins who had given him papers to sign at Solcintra Port, scheming to strip his wings away, and likely long-ago murdered in the Low Port, if Chi yos'Phelium's iron whim hadn't settled on him.

"What papers?" he asked Jai Kob. "Agreeing to an extra fee for the release of the pod?"

Jai Kob looked hurt, which meant nothing. Jai Kob could assume any expression or attitude the moment wanted.

"Are we pod-pirates, Gunny?" he asked and swept on before Fer Gun could answer, which was just as well. "No, we've only this paper here that needs your signature. You remember the quarterlies. Well, it's past time for the next."

He remembered the quarterlies, so he did. The very first one signed at his cousins' direction barely three days after his grandfather's death. He hadn't read that one. Jai Kob had assured him there was no need; Jai Kob had read it, after all, and had found everything in order.

"What's that about the marriage contract?" he asked, then.

"Didn't they tell you, Gunny? Korval was paying Telrune a handsome sum for your . . . abilities, but just the smallest taste up-front, and all the rest on completion, contingent on no kin contacting you during the marriage."

"So you've just breached the terms," Fer Gun pointed out. "Telrune will like that you've snatched cantra out of his fingers."

"The little cousin's gotten sharp," Vin Dyr said dryly, stepping fully into the light.

Jai Kob shook his head.

"Who's to know it, unless you tattle, and then Telrune will know right enough who to blame. But, here, Gunny, I can see you're in no mood to play. Just sign the paper, we'll be off, and you can take delivery of your cargo."

Fer Gun took a deep breath, teetering on the edge of choice. Sign the paper and Jai Kob released the cargo in good order. Refuse to sign the paper, and the cargo would not survive the next hour, no matter how good his cousin's humor appeared.

To allow Korval's cargo to be destroyed because he had grown squeamish about his cousins. Was that even a choice?

It occurred to him then that there was a *third* choice.

"Trader Danac-Joenz," he heard himself say calmly; "of your kindness."

"Certainly, Captain."

She stepped forward and held out her hand for the packet.

Jai Kob took a step back, glaring.

"What's this, Gunny?"

"This is the ship's trader," Fer Gun said. "I brought her to deal with the paperwork for the damaged cargo."

"This is between cousins," Jai Kob protested. "It's not for anyone to look at and blab around the docksides."

"Sir." Trader Danac-Joenz sounded halfway between angry and amused. "I am, in fact, *Comet*'s trader. I assure you—I know how to treat confidential business. If you would care to step up the hall to the office, I will call up my references for you."

Jai Kob stared, frozen in place. Vin Dyr shifted, boots grating on the floor as he adjusted his balance, his hand moving toward the place where he kept his hideaway. Fer Gun stepped to the side, and waved the trader forward, putting her and Jai Kob into the same frame.

It was still a risk, Vin Dyr being more than a fair shot, but he wouldn't take the snap-shot now, just to see what would happen, not with Jai Kob so near.

At least, Fer Gun hoped so.

"The trader will review the paperwork," he said; "to be certain that everything is in order. Surely, Cousin, you don't want to risk Telrune's anger on a faulty instrument."

"*Faulty instrument*," Vin Dyr repeated, not quite under his breath. "The child has airs."

Fer Gun ignored him.

"Will you be able to work here, Trader? Or will the warehouse office be better?"

"This is perfectly adequate," she assured him. "This light is particularly good. Now, if the gentleman will relinquish the packet . . . ?"

For a moment, Fer Gun thought that Jai Kob would do no such thing. It was possible that Jai Kob thought so, too.

Then, he took one step forward—and placed the packet into the trader's outstretched hand.

"Thank you," she said with complete composure.

And broke the seal.

• • •✧• • •

"THE THIRD PARAGRAPH references the terms of a previous contract, dated some dozen Standards back," Trader Danac-Joenz murmured, "which would appear to be the foundation for the rest of this currently proposed document."

She looked up from the papers and gave Fer Gun a bright, candid glance.

"You have that contract among your records, of course, Captain. Will it be available to the ship's system?"

Fer Gun felt his stomach clench, as in the back of his mind, he heard Lady yo'Lanna scolding him: *Read the contract; understand the contract; keep a copy of the contract for future consultation.*

"My cousins have been in the habit of keeping my paperwork for me," he told the trader, and waited for the scorn to fill her eyes.

Instead, her eyes narrowed, and if there was any emotion on her face, he would have said it was anger.

"I see. Naturally, you would have been very young when the foundation document was made, and it would have been natural for elder kin to hold the files. They ought, of course, to have transferred the records to you when you came of age, but such things often slip the mind.

"Happily, we can regularize the situation now."

She turned to Jai Kob.

"If you will kindly bring forth those records, sir, I may continue my work. Thus far, the contract you offer appears . . . promising. But we must, as I am certain you understand, have the foundation document. Indeed, it ought to have been appended to this paper—but again, it is so very easy for such details to slip the mind."

Boot soles grated against a gritty floor.

Fer Gun turned sharply toward Vin Dyr, his hand dropping to the gun on his belt.

His cousin twitched—and raised both hands, showing them empty.

"The foundation document," Jai Kob was saying in the quick, light voice he used when he was lying. "Certainly, Trader; how foolish of me to have forgotten! There is, in fact, a copy in the ship's files. Unfortunately, with Fer Gun under contract, we have no third to leave on-board while Vin Dyr and I attend business. It will require only an hour to go to the ship and bring back the complete files for you to peruse. If you would care to wait here? Or—of course! The Trade Bar. We will meet you there, in an hour, if that will suffice you?"

Fer Gun kept his warning behind his teeth. Korval's cargo, he reminded himself; that was the important thing here: To recover the cargo intact.

"Certainly," Trader Danac-Joenz said cordially. "An hour, in the Trade Bar. We will be much more comfortable there, and will have access to the library, should there be need."

"Excellent," Jai Kob said. He extended a hand to the trader, for the contract. She merely looked at him.

"I will keep this, of your kindness," she said, "and continue my review. I know that your time is valuable."

"Just so," said Jai Kob, and bowed.

"Trader," he said. "Gunny." He glanced aside.

"Come along, Cousin," he said to Vin Dyr, who needed no such urging. Walking briskly, they were through the door—and gone.

"What are the odds," Trader Danac-Joenz said, lightly, her eyes on the door, "that they will come back in an hour, with or without those documents?"

"No odds, Trader. Next we hear, they'll be casting off without having filed with the station master."

She nodded, reached to her belt, and pulled out a portcomm.

"Ship's name?" she murmured, thumbing the call button.

"*Lady Graz.*"

"Thank you." She tipped her head.

"Pilot yos'Phelium, this is Karil Danac-Joenz. We have a situation," she said crisply. "Can you—or Korval—hold the ship *Lady Graz* at dock?"

VIII

CHI SAT IN THE COPILOT'S CHAIR. She had the surveillance camera feeding screen three, though she expected no trouble on their own dock. Frowning, she examined that thought.

No, she decided, the trouble, whatever shape it took, would be with the cargo. Well that Fer Gun hadn't gone alone. Well—well, indeed—that Karil Danac-Joenz was far removed from being a fool. She was encouraged on that front, very much so.

She glanced at the clock. An hour gone, and no word from either. That could be good news. Or bad news. Or no news at all.

"You're as jumpy as a cat with one kitten," she growled at herself—and snapped forward when the comm pinged.

"*Comet,*" she snapped, and frowned slightly at Karil Danac-Joenz's voice.

"Not even Korval holds ships at a whim," she said. "We need a reason that will compel the station master."

"It will have to be piracy, Pilot. Pilot pen'Uldra's cousins met us at the warehouse, wishing for him to sign a document. *Very much* wishing for him to sign a document, and desperate enough for it that they were holding our cargo ransom.

"My reading of this document leads me to believe that they have been cheating Pilot pen'Uldra of the profits of his birth-right since before he came of age. The present scheme is to transfer the ship wholly to them, and to strip him of all his assets."

Chi closed her eyes and counted to one hundred forty-four. How one did *long* to speak, personally and alone, with the cousins.

"Do you have the document?" Chi asked, keeping her voice calm.

"I have the new document," the trader said. "The case would be stronger, with the entire series in hand." She paused. "Pilot pen'Uldra's cousins have said that they are going back to their ship to retrieve those, and will meet us at the Trade Bar inside of an hour."

Chi gave a sharp laugh.

"Yes, exactly. You see why it must be piracy?"

"I do, indeed. Where are you and Fer Gun now?"

"At the warehouse."

"Come home," Chi said. "Leave the damned cargo. Until we have a chance to order a comprehensive scan, it is compromised, and it is not coming anywhere near this ship."

"Yes, Pilot. Agreed."

"Good. I'll call the station master, and file our complaint."

* * ✧ * *

"**THANK YOU,** Pilot; we're on our way."

The trader thumbed off the unit, and looked at Fer Gun.

"Your copilot requests that we return to the ship."

"The cargo?"

"We're to treat it as compromised and a danger to the ship."

He almost smiled at that. Trust Chi yos'Phelium to protect the ship.

"Right," he said, and jerked his head toward the door. "Let's go."

Together they exited the inspection bay.

He stopped at the office to let the clerk know that the cargo was to remain isolated until it had been thoroughly inspected by a third party. She pushed him to leave a deposit for the space, he said curtly that he would do so when the inspection was complete, and in the meantime, he expected the bay to be placed under seal.

Possibly, he was too rough. Her face paled somewhat and she lowered her eyes.

"Of course, Pilot."

They were well away from the warehouse when the trader's comm pinged.

"Yes," she said, putting the unit to her ear. She listened, and nodded, Terran-wise.

"Thank you. Yes, we'll go at once."

The comm vanished, and the trader turned to him.

"*Lady Graz* has been locked down, pending a formal filing of piracy."

He looked at her.

"That means . . . ?"

"It means," she said, "that you must go to the station master's office and sign some paperwork."

He stiffened, and caught his breath when he felt her hand on his.

"We'll both go, of course, and read the papers together."

Fer Gun managed a smile.

"Of course," he said. "My thanks, Trader."

"If we're going to be working together, I think I ought to be Karil," she said, still keeping a hold on his hand, as she turned them back to the station master's office.

"In that wise, I will be Fer Gun," he answered, and traded her, smile for smile.

IX

WELL, AND IT CAME TO LIGHT, once all of the documents were found and accessed, that the first paper he had signed for Jai Kob, giving him free use of the ship *Lady Graz*, which had been left to Fer Gun by his grandfather—that paper had not been regular, at all, since Fer Gun had been too young to sign such a thing.

The second paper gave Jai Kob access to the accounts Grandfather had left to Fer Gun, himself, and also immortalized Fer Gun's agreement to pay for any repairs and upgrades required to *Lady Graz* from his own funds.

That, too, was irregular, having been presented to the still-grieving Fer Gun barely two days after the paper which had stolen away his ship.

At the last, it was a matter for *Qe'andra* dea'Gauss to sort out, which was done. Jai Kob and Vin Dyr had been fined, blacklisted, stripped of all licenses, and placed on an ore boat as working crew, their wages limited to berth and meals. Eventually, they would arrive home, and Telrune would deal with them . . . not kindly, as Fer Gun saw it. They had lost the ship, the money, Telrune's portion of the marriage settlement, and exposed themselves to discovery and punishment. He could not predict what further penalty the delm might place upon his cousins, but he doubted it would be pleasant.

In the meanwhile, there was work to be done—he had two ships now, though *Lady* was in need of upgrading, as well as new licenses and registrations. A deal was closed with Korval's Chonselta Yard for the refurbs, which would take up the year of *Comet*'s first real run; and another with *Qe'andra* dea'Gauss for the applications and the purges and the clear new record.

He'd taken crew on for *Comet*; and Karil had emerged from several hours closeted with Chi's sister, the master trader, with an amended route, a goods list, and a thick notebook full of contacts.

There remained one more duty to perform, as per the contract, and he was there at the early hour of the morning Chi's son had chosen to make his entrance into the world. He stood witness as the child was born, and examined, and pronounced fit. And he remained there when the room was cleared of Healer and medic and the Council's eyes. At her invitation, he sat on the edge of the bed, covering her hand with his, and smiled at the boy with his sharp black eyes, and his black hair, already rumpled and unruly.

"When do you lift?" she asked him.

"Tomorrow morning," he answered. "We can file an amendment, if you have need of me."

She smiled at that.

"I see no reason for such desperate measures as that," she murmured, still half-drowsy with whatever the Healer had done.

"Then, tomorrow morning, we're away; and returning to Liad in a year, to outfit the *Lady* and see her crewed."

"Come and see me, Pilot, when you're back again," she said, and he squeezed her hand lightly.

"I must, after all; you'll want an accounting of the ship's business."

"Which you may and shall file with dea'Gauss," she said with a faint smile. "Come to me anyway."

"I will," he promised.

She closed her eyes, then. The boy—Daav yos'Phelium—stared at him for another minute from knowing dark eyes, before he, too, slipped away into sleep.

Epilogue

DAAV AND ER THOM were having a game of tag back and forth across the Tree Court. At least Chi supposed it to be tag, though she conceded the possibility that it was some other game of their own devising, the rules of which she was not meant to know.

In any case, it involved a great deal of running around, and shouting, and dodging behind bushes in order to lie in wait, and leaping out at one's brother, whereupon there was laughter on both sides, and a bound once more into action.

There had also been what she allowed to be only the most necessary amount of rolling about in the grass, and at least one unfortunate encounter with the gloan roses, which had taken, so she believed, no permanent damage. The scratches, she had declared minor, and the game was therefore rejoined.

She . . . was supposed to be reading the agenda and briefing documents for the next meeting of the Council of Clans. Indeed, the material lay on the bench beside her, though she had not even glanced at them, finding the play of her sons—of her son and Petrella's—to be far more compelling.

They made a striking pair, grass-stained and perspiring as they were. The eldest, Er Thom, Petrella's lad, was already a beauty, with gilt hair and violet eyes surrounded by dark gold lashes. He looked, in fact, quite a lot like Petrella, and thus very much like his foster-mother, Chi.

By contrast, Daav was lean and vulpine, a changeling, with his dark hair, dark eyes, and marked brows. It was well that she had made her pregnancy and his birth a matter of very public record, indeed. Looking at him, even if he could be persuaded for five minutes to stand still, never mind remaining clean, unrumpled, and with his hair combed—even then, he could scarce be taken for one of Korval, never mind the delm-to-be.

Well, and it was too soon, yet, to know if Daav would in fact be delm. If not, the Ring would fall to Er Thom. And however it went, Korval would have at his side his brother, who had been given exactly the same education, shared the same history, and stood always as a valuable and beloved ally.

"Catch me!" Daav cried, and bolted for the Tree, rounding the enormous trunk with nary a stumble, despite the plentiful surface roots waiting to catch the feet of the unwary.

Er Thom flew after him, every bit as nimble, and vanished on the far side of the Tree.

She felt it then—say it was a small flutter in the air, or a puff of pleasure at seeing an old friend. She turned her head so that she could see the path, and here he came, tall, and lean, and . . . somewhat less wolfish than when first she had seen him.

The leather jacket hugged shoulders that had filled out; shoulders that wore the easy weights of success and satisfaction. The dark hair was tidy, if still over-long; the face fuller at cheek and jaw.

He raised a hand as he left the path. She smiled and moved the unread papers beneath the bench.

"Fer Gun," she said. "Well-met."

"Well-met," he answered and settled next to her with the ease of an old friend. "We came in early and I thought I'd call before we're swamped tomorrow with business."

"Is Karil with you?" she asked, already knowing that she was not.

"Not today, though she hopes to see you before we lift again," he said, and turned his head sharply at the whoop from behind the Tree and the sudden appearance of two small bodies, running flat out toward the rose bank again.

"They're in fine fettle," Fer Gun said, and gave her a sideways glance. "I do regret that mode, you know. There was no reason he should look like me when he had you as a model."

"Well, there is something to be said for contrariness," she said comfortably. "It's a family trait, after all."

His wide mouth softened into a smile, and he leaned back as Daav flung his arms out, shouted, "Zooooom!" and banked hard, only brushing the flowers, and flew back toward the tree, trailing rose petals.

"Here's a bit of news you'll enjoy," Fer Gun said. "We were approached by Telrune regarding an accounting owed the clan."

"Were you? How did that go?"

He moved his shoulders.

"Karil sent a copy of our incorporation as a Family, and the contact information for our *qe'andra*."

Another slight shrug.

"We received in return a rather curt letter stating that it would have been good form, had I contacted Telrune to *formally sever* my connection with the clan. I'm properly put into my place."

Chi laughed.

"I see that you are. And the children?"

"Telrune has no claim on our children," Fer Gun said sternly. His voice softened as he added, "If they tried to lay such a claim, they would have to go through Karil."

"Daunting, for bolder hearts than Telrune, if I may be forgiven for speaking so of your clan."

"Not my clan, haven't you been listening? We're Family Uldra-Joenz, incorporated on Fetzer's World."

"Fer Gun!" a young voice yelled, and here came Daav pelting across the grass, Er Thom a fleet shadow at his side.

Fer Gun came to his feet in a rush, swooping the lean body up, spinning as he held the boy over his head.

Daav shouted with laughter, and collapsed flat on his back in the grass when he was let down so Er Thom could have his turn.

"Well, my sons," said Chi, when the merriment had somewhat abated. "I believe it is time the two of you bowed to the necessity of baths, and study. You may join me for Prime on the east patio, unless you have other obligations."

"We have no other obligations," Er Thom said gravely. "Thank you, Mother."

"Will Fer Gun stay for Prime?" Daav wanted to know.

"Not today," Fer Gun answered. "Maybe your mother won't be too busy to have me and my lady back, sometime before we're set to lift again."

"We will arrange a time," Chi said, standing, and waving the boys toward the path. "Make your bows, now."

They did, very prettily, if briefly, before breaking to race for the path.

"Bathe!" Chi called after them, and bent to retrieve her paperwork.

"I don't know," Fer Gun said, as they followed the boys at a more sedate pace; "if I ever properly thanked you for all of the good things you brought into my life. In fact, you *saved* my life." He paused, and took a breath, before meeting her eyes.

"I don't know that there *is* any *proper* thanks for such gifts. Notice that I say gifts, because there is no hope I can bring us into Balance."

There came a shriek of laughter from the path ahead, and he raised his eyebrows.

Chi smiled.

"We are perfectly in Balance, my friend," tucking her hand into his arm and increasing their leisurely pace somewhat.

"Let us speak no more about it."

✧ Friend of a Friend ✧

FRIENDSHIP among free-spirited Surebleakers is far different than it is among rule-bound Liadens, whose melant'i *must always be observed, and in some cases preserved. Imagine, then, the potential for miscommunication when a 'bleaker's best friend was born and bred on Liad and a stranger decides to take advantage of that relationship.*

✧✧✧✧

TWO YOUNG MEN, much of an age, but unalike in almost everything else, save having a good head for numbers, and a facility with the Sticks, walked down-Port toward the Emerald Casino.

They made a pretty picture—one tall and fair and lissome; the other supple and dark and golden-skinned. The fair lad wore a blue jacket, to set off his eyes. The dark one wore leather, and had a bag slung over his shoulder.

"So you'll be back in a Surebleak week?" the fair one asked, ending what had been a rather long pause between them.

His companion gave him an approving nod.

"That's very good, doing the conversions in your head on the fly."

"I've been practicing," Villy said. "I'll keep it up, too. By the time you're back, I'll be able to do a four-level conversion in my head!"

"Here's a bold assertion! Will books be all of your lovers, until I am returned to your arms?"

Villy considered him out of suspicious blue eyes.

"*That* sounds like a play-quote," he said.

"Discovered!"

Quin gave a small, on-the-stride bow of acknowledgment—for which he would have been severely reprimanded had he been observed by his protocol tutor—or, twelve times worse!—his grandmother.

"It is a play-quote, yes. If you like, I'll find a tape and we may watch it together."

"Would I? Like it, I mean."

That was a serious question, and Quin gave it the consideration it deserved.

"You might well. It's a classic *melant'i* play, and I had to study it, and write papers on it, and view several productions, from the first recorded to the most modern, which is why I have the phrase so apt, you see. But—yes, I think you might find it useful, and interesting, too. Especially the sword fight."

"Sword fight?"

"The most diverting thing imaginable, and quite harrowing, despite you know it's all mummery."

"Okay, then, I'm provisionally interested. If I get bored, though, I'll make you speed through to the sword fight."

"Fair enough."

The casino was in sight; they would part in another few minutes. Villy was bound for the Sticks table and his shift as dealer. Quin was for Korval's yard, *Galandasti*, and Pilot Tess Lucien, who was to sit his second, who had undoubtedly arrived early, and would therefore believe that he was late . . .

"What will you do," he asked, "while I am away?"

Villy looked arch.

"Jealous, honey? I'll keep busy, don't you worry. And books won't be half of it."

Quin laughed, Villy grinned, and stepped close to drop a kiss on Quin's cheek.

"You fly safe now, handsome," he said, huskily, and slipped away to join a group of the casino's morning workers, calling out to Cassie to wait for him.

Quin shook his head, his cheek burning where Villy's lips had brushed. For Liadens, such a salutation was given between kin, or lifemates, or—perhaps—long-time lovers.

For Villy, a kiss on the cheek denoted casual affection. Or, as Villy himself had it, "I kiss all my friends."

Yes, well. Local custom. It was Quin's part to step away from the custom—and Villy, too—if he was offended.

Which, truth told, he was not.

Surely, his grandmother was correct when she deplored the state of his *melant'i*.

His father had nothing to say regarding Quin's friendship with the best Sticks dealer the Emerald employed. In fact, he and Villy had met over the Sticks table, and the relationship had been firmly fixed before Quin discovered that Villy was also one of the company of *hetaerana* attached to Ms. Audrey's house of delights.

Quin had been tutored in the protocols of pleasure, though circumstances had not granted him much opportunity to refine his knowledge. From observation, however, it would seem that Terrans and Liadens approached bed-sport on vastly different trajectories, and merely being among the number of Villy's *friends* meant receiving casual kisses on the street. A Liaden *hetaera* would blush to presume so far on the *melant'i* of even a frequent partner-in-joy.

And, again . . . local custom.

"We will all need to be Scouts, if we mean to settle here," Quin had said to Grandfather Luken, who had only laughed.

"But we *have* settled here, boy-dear! Never fear, your grandmother will find us a way to a new Code. In the meanwhile, your father is not *quite* an idiot, as you know, nor are his fellow Bosses. They teach and learn in equal measure. What remains for us is to be slow to take offense, and to cultivate the *melant'i* of a little child."

Children—*little* children—were understood to stand within the *melant'i* of their clan. Their own *melant'i* was . . . flexible and open, and very specifically did not pursue Balance. It was tradition, to give a child upon their twelfth Name Day a Small Debt Book, in which entries were made by the child, and reviewed with a clan elder. On the fourteenth Name Day, a private Debt Book was given, and it was considered at that point that the child was competent to take up the keeping of their own *melant'i*, and Balances.

On consideration, Quin thought that Luken might have the right of it.

He also thought that most of the Liadens who had followed Korval to Surebleak were not . . . capable of accepting the *melant'i* of a little child. Most especially if it also meant tolerating insults from Terrans.

It really was too bad that Father hadn't chosen a civilized world to subjugate to Korval's purpose.

Quin threaded his way through the ships sleeping in Korval's yard. There, just ahead, was *Galandasti*, and, as he had feared, there also was Pilot Lucien, her long self disposed down half-a-dozen gantry steps, from the tread where she leaned her elbows, to the stair where her boots rested.

"Well, there you are! I was starting to wonder if you wanted to fly today, after all."

He felt his ears warm, and his temper rise—which was nonsense; hadn't he known how it would be? The good pilot was always early; he, by extension, was always late.

"I think we can make up the time," he said evenly, for, in addition to being annoying, Pilot Lucien was a master pilot, in charge of observing him, and of registering his flight time with the Guild.

"I have the package. If you will do me the honor of ascending and waking the board, I will do the walkaround."

Pilot Lucien's hair fell in jagged points to her jawbone, the ends were dyed silver and purple; the rest was dull black. The silver and purple distracted as she tipped her head, and looked at him through narrowed eyes.

"Did the walkaround while I was waiting," she said.

Quin's temper flared again. Really, did she think he was a fool?

He took a breath and calmed himself. Of course, it was a test. This whole flight would be a test. There would doubtless, therefore, be many instances in which his temper was tried.

Best, then, to practice patience.

He produced a smile for the pilot.

"Thank you. I am accustomed to doing a walkaround myself; it soothes me and prepares my mind for the lift. I doubt that the ship will take harm from having the eyes of two pilots upon it."

She shrugged and came to her feet.

"Suit yourself," she said shortly, and went up the gantry, her boots clanging on each stair.

Teeth grit, Quin ducked under the gantry to begin the Pilot's Pre-Lift Visual Inspection, precisely as outlined in the handbook.

* * * ◇ * * *

"BUSY NIGHT?" Cassie asked him three days later, when they were again on the early shift together.

Villy liked Cassie. She didn't mind about his other job, like some of the crew did; just treated it like . . . well . . . another job.

"Not busy at all," he said ruefully, "so I got the idea to study, and *that* turned into *late*."

"Didn't you remember you had the early shift here?"

"I remembered, all right! I can't tell you how many times I said to myself, *Villim, cut it off, you gotta work early tomorrow!* Didn't do a bit of good!"

Cassie laughed.

"What're you studying that's so absorbing?"

"Communication," Villy said, oversimplifying wildly. "We're getting a lot of new clients who ain't—aren't—from Surebleak, just like we get here at the casino. I'm studying up on what's comfortable, and what's not, and bows—that's useful here, too . . ."

Cassie's smile had faded into something serious-looking.

"That's pretty smart," she said, which it was, and Villy would've felt proud of thinking of it, but he hadn't—not exactly. He'd only said out something that he'd been thinking, about not feeling like he was offering everything he could to the new custom, because he didn't know the rules. He didn't have any idea beyond his own frustration, really; it'd been Quin who identified the problem and figured out a way to maybe deal with it.

"Do you think you could lend me the tapes, when you're done

with them?" Cassie asked, waving her card at the clock. "Or maybe we could study together? I'd really like to get a handle on them bows. For starters."

Well, no, he couldn't lend the tapes. For one thing, they weren't tapes; they were lessons Quin had archived from his school. He'd been a tutor, so he'd been able to give Villy a passcode to access the basic lessons. Supplemental data and tests and stuff were only available to Quin's code.

Anyway, nothing he could share with Cassie.

He stepped up and waved his badge. The clock beeped acceptance, and he stepped over to where Cassie was waiting for him.

"You know what we should do?" he said brightly.

"What's that?" Cassie said, and he appreciated it that she didn't smirk or wink or make a joke.

Villy paused, briefly having no idea what he was going to say, then heard himself speak up.

"We oughta ask Beny to organize a class. Then we could all learn together, and . . ."

He stopped because Cassie was staring at him.

"What?"

"That's brilliant. Villy, that's *brilliant!*"

"Well, it's not. I mean, I was so focused on how to do better at my other job, I didn't even think about us here, until you asked me what I was studying. Then it all sort of clicked."

He gave her a smile. It was one of his professional smiles: two parts shy and one part mischief, and she smiled back, the muscles in her face and shoulders relaxing.

There, he thought, pleased; that's better.

"I'll talk to Beny on my first break," he offered. Cassie shook her head.

"I'm covering for Joon this morning, upstairs. I'll be seeing him right off and I'll mention your idea to him."

"It's your idea as much as it's mine!" he said, but Cassie only smiled and waggled her fingers at him in good-bye, turning toward the stairs.

Villy sighed, and headed for the Sticks table.

• • • ◈ • • •

THE CASINO was bustling but not overcrowded, which was usual for the morning shift. Most of the players were late-nighters, still at the tables, with a smattering of the regulars who stopped in on their way to work to drop a coin in one of the machines, or roll a round of dice. Pretty soon, they'd get the night-workers comin' in, ready maybe for some longer play at the wheel, or the card tables.

Or the Sticks.

All in all, Villy kept tolerably busy until it was time for his mid-morning break. Sonit came to relieve him as the last players left the table, both of them considerably lighter in the pocketbook. Villy's knees were shaking some, and his forehead was damp. The House had won, fair. The House nearly always won, though Boss Conrad, who owned the Emerald, said the Sticks were an honest game of skill, more like cards than like dicing—or the wheel. The House was *expected* to win against most comers 'cause the Sticks dealer was an experienced and skilled player.

This time, though . . . The players had insisted on playing three-way, with the House taking a full part. Usually, Villy only played single players. Playing against two—well, he'd done it before, but it was uncommon *and* nerve-wracking.

He'd demonstrated his skill, though, and the House'd won, though he'd gotten a bad jolt when he'd thought the orange stick was gonna roll off the table . . .

"Everything okay?" Sonit asked.

"Yeah. Just finished up a three-way is all."

Sonit whistled.

"Better you'n me. Gwon and getcher coffee. I'll stand here an' just sorta glare and scare 'em all away."

That wasn't a joke. Sonit wasn't anything more than a good enough Sticks dealer, and not much of a player, but he *was* big and intimidating, and his frown was almost a physical shove in the chest. A player had to have a death-wish to approach the Sticks table while Sonit was presiding.

"I'll be back soon," Villy said.

Sonit grinned broadly, which made him look even more savage than his frown. Villy shook his head, and held up his hands.

"I'm going," he said. "Don't hurt me."

"Like I could lay a hand on you," Sonit said, his grin softening into a really attractive smile. "Git."

Villy got.

. . . ✧ . . .

HE WAS AT HIS USUAL TABLE in the break room, overlooking the floor, coffee and a cookie to keep him comfortable. He enjoyed looking down on the playing floor, seeing all the stations laid out like a map, and the players moving between them like leaves ahead of a snow wind. Lately, he'd taken to studying different styles of walking, and thinking about what each style told about the walker, or their culture. He'd shown Quin the game, one day when he was working the casino backroom, and they'd met for lunch.

Quin had been interested—and good, too, which wasn't a surprise. Quin had fast eyes and if he wasn't the sharpest knife in the drawer, he'd do 'til something fatal came along.

Villy took a bite out of his cookie and washed it down with hot coffee.

The locals, they kinda scuffed along the floor—that was from having to walk on ice and snow most of the time. You didn't want to slip and fall, so you sorta half-skated along. Liadens walked tall and broad, for all they was skinny and short—world-bound Liadens, anyhow. Off-world Terrans walked with knees slightly bent, and hands away from their body, like they might have to grab something fast to keep from falling, which made sense, 'cause most of the off-world Terrans were spacers. And it was kind of funny, 'til you thought about it, that the space-faring Liadens—the pilots and the crewfolk—they walked like the Terrans: soft in the knees and ready to snatch a grab-bar.

Scouts now, they walked soft, and sort of swayed, like every muscle was loose. Their heads hardly moved, despite which, they saw *every*thing. Quin said it was because Scouts had quick eyes, and quicker ears.

Mercs—Terran *or* Liaden—marched tall, looking left-then-right, footsteps falling firm enough that when a group of them went through the casino, you could feel 'em hit, even 'way up in control.

Security—well, there was Security now in the shapes of Big Haz and Tolly. Haz, she walked like a Scout, quiet and loose, and eyes moving. Tolly . . . Tolly was a puzzle. Sometimes, he walked Surebleak, sometimes he walked spacer. Other times—just for a step or two, and you had to be watching sharp to catch it—*sometimes* he walked like a hunter cat, muscles oiled and chin up, like he was scenting lunch nearby.

Right now, he was pure 'bleaker, leaning on the bar and talking with Herb. Haz stood tall beside him and a little behind, like she always did, alert to the room, and just as relaxed as if she had eyes in the back of her—

"Hey, Villy."

A chair scraped as Beny, the day-side crew boss, slid in across the table.

"Hey," Villy said. "Cassie talk to you?"

"'S'why I'm here. That's a good idea you had about the seminar. We all got the basic training when we were hired on, but you're right; it's time to go to the next level. We don't just got spacers and locals; we got people who expect the comforts of home. So, anyhow, I just wanted to tell you—I ran it by Mr. Conrad, and he's gonna hire us a *protocol master*—prolly be a Scout, he said—and we'll have lessons in how to be a little easier on Liaden eyes. Mr. Conrad, he was firm that he didn't want us to cross over into looking too Liaden for our core clientele, but we still got room to bend. It was smart of you to notice."

"I didn't know I'd noticed 'til I was talking with Cassie," Villy said, dunking his cookie in his coffee.

"Right, right. She said that, too. Now, here, I know your break's just about over, so I'll get done and leave you to finish up."

Beny reached into his vest pocket and pulled out an envelope. He put it on the table, and pushed it toward Villy.

"What's that?"

"Don't you read the sign by the clock? Anybody comes up with an idea about how to make the casino run better, or increase profit, gets a reward if Mr. Conrad accepts the idea. Mr. Conrad accepted the idea, and you get fifty cash. Pretty good, huh?"

Fifty cash was a nice bit of money, but—

"I didn't earn that."

"Says so on the wall. Gwon and read it when you punch back in. Which you better start thinking about." Beny got up, leaving the envelope behind him.

"Good thinkin', Villy," he said, and left.

Alone, Villy finished his cookie and coffee while staring at the envelope.

Fifty cash for saying they ought to learn how to bow better? That was like . . . free money.

On the other hand, he thought, pushing back his chair and coming to his feet, there wasn't anything wrong with free money.

Was there?

He sighed sharply, grabbed the envelope and shoved it into an inner pocket of his vest.

• • •✧• • •

IT WAS COMING UP on shift-change, and Villy was looking forward to going home and having a nap before he had to get ready for his other job. He'd just finished watching Margit Pince lose her day-pay on a solo Sticks fall. Once a week, she lost a day's pay at his table, and he really wished she wouldn't. Couldn't talk her out of it, though; not his job. His job was to suppose she could afford the loss, and to witness the play to be sure it was fairly done. He wished she'd give up the Sticks, but there wasn't any sign she was going to, anytime soon. She considered them a challenge, and she was determined to beat them—which she wouldn't, anytime soon, in Villy's professional judgment. Unfortunately, she'd gotten—*a little*—better, which only encouraged her to continue to play.

Honestly, Margit was one of the few downsides of the casino job. His gran used to say that grown-ups chose for themselfs, and Margit was a grown-up. So. He took a deep breath and settled himself. Not his problem; he'd done his job.

There not being anybody looking to step up and take Margit's place at the table, Villy started to straighten the drawer, so the dealer next-shift could just open right up. He collected the tokens into their bag, and updated the tally sheet; lined the wrapped and sealed bundles up: twenty-fours all together at the top, thirty-sixes beneath; eighteen stick bundles tucked in their own compartment down the length of the drawer.

The bigger bundles were standard offers at Liaden casinos. The bundle of eighteen—called Quick Sticks—was a Surebleak variation, offered only at the Emerald casino, and approved by no less a gamester than Pat Rin yos'Phelium.

Pat Rin yos'Phelium, that was Boss Conrad's real, Liaden name. Not many people knew that, though it was right there to be figured out, by those who paid attention.

Most people, though, they didn't pay attention, though it ought've been plain that, if Boss Conrad and the Road Boss were brothers, and the Road Boss didn't make no secret of his name being Val Con yos'Phelium, that Boss Conrad's real name ought at least to have *yos'Phelium* in it somewhere.

Even though it wasn't true that the bosses were brothers—he'd asked Quin, who'd said they were cousins, though it was true that Quin's father—that being Pat Rin—was the older of the two.

"Likely they decided it was simpler for those not familiar with Liaden Lines to understand them as brothers, and such a simplification did no damage to their *melant'i*."

Quin'd been lying on his side on Villy's bed, his head propped on his hand. He'd paused for a second, staring hard at nothing, which meant he was weighing something in his mind.

"There was the matter of the two Rings, also . . ." he said, quiet, like he was talking to himself before he said, louder and firmer, "Yes, I think they decided for simplicity."

He'd smiled at Villy.

"After all, I agreed to have had a younger brother, for much the same reasons. It does me no harm to honor the memory of a boy who had placed himself under my father's protection. Had he survived, we might well have been declared foster-brothers. That being so, why should I not agree with what is already widely known?"

That bidness—about Quin's younger brother—that was about Jonni, who'd been a kid in Boss Conrad's house, and gotten in the middle of a firefight. The story'd gone out on the street that Jonni'd been the Boss's own son, which Villy'd known wasn't true. Jonni's ma'd worked for Ms. Audrey. She never did say who was his father; might've been she hadn't known. Or that she had, and thought her boy'd be better off without 'im.

Villy'd tried to 'splain that, once, to somebody who knew the street story, and who didn't care to believe anything else. That had kinda cured him of ever trying to 'splain it again.

Well, no wonder the bosses just accepted what the street said; they might as well save their breath for—

Something moved in the corner of his eye. He looked up from the drawer, smiling slightly and impersonally at the Liaden woman approaching the table. She wasn't wearing leather, but she walked like a spacer, with some merc mixed in.

"Buy a bundle, ma'am? We have Solcintran Sticks in packets of twenty-four and thirty-six. Or, if you're pressed for time, we also offer the local eighteen-stick variation."

"Thank you," she said.

She smiled at him. Some of the world-bound Liadens were trying to learn to smile at Terrans, having heard that Terrans liked to be smiled at. Their efforts usually ran from faintly unsettling to painful.

This was the first smile Villy'd gotten from a Liaden that was outright terrifying.

He swallowed and bowed his head, like he was welcoming her, but it was really to hide his face. His foot twitched toward the panic switch on the floor under the table, but he stopped it just short of connecting.

"I believe," the Liaden said, "that you are a companion to Quin yos'Phelium, as I am myself. I wonder if you might tell me his direction."

That was off; his mouth tasted sour, that's how *off* it was. Sure, him and Quin were friends, but there wasn't no reason for this stranger to know, or care about it, once she'd come to know it. Quin's father *owned* the Emerald, didn't he? And if she was one of Quin's friends, wouldn't she *know* that?

He took a breath, thought about the panic switch again, and decided it was better not to make a fuss. That being so, he got his professional smile into place and looked up to meet her eyes.

"I can't talk about that here," he said. "My *melant'i's* Sticks dealer, right now."

She blinked—he'd surprised her—and inclined her head.

"Of course," she said, polite enough; "I understand. Good-day to you."

She turned and walked away, giving off that mixed vibe of merc and spacer.

Villy let out the breath he'd been holding, and closed his eyes.

When he opened them again, Sara was on his side of the table, tally-sheet in hand.

"Time to go home, hon!" she said cheerfully.

He gave her a grin, though it felt a little uncertain on his mouth.

"Already? I was having so much fun, I thought I'd do a double."

"Nope, nope. My turn to have some fun. You've had enough."

"Right, then," Villy said. He patted her arm, and scooted out from behind the table.

Going across the floor to the stairs, he kept an eye out for the woman who'd wanted Quin's *direction*. He didn't see her, which might've meant she'd left—or maybe she'd smartened up and asked one of the Security Team to take her to the Boss.

Either way, it wasn't none of his bidness. He just hoped he'd never see her again.

* * * ✧ * * *

VILLY WOKE UP from his nap in plenty of time to eat dinner and get ready for his regular date with Bradish Faw.

Bradish was one of his favorite dates, and not just because he brought a platter of pastries every week to share out among the whole crew, and a special treat, tied up in colored cellophane with a big bow, for Villy himself. No, he liked Bradish because the baker was genuinely kind, and because no date was exactly the same as all the others. Sometimes, Bradish would bring a book and ask Villy to read to him, sometimes he'd bring a music tape, sometimes he would bring a toy or something special he wanted—or wanted Villy—to wear.

Tonight, Bradish hugged him, then held him at arm's length, looking him up and down.

"You been worryin'?" he asked severely.

"Studying," Villy answered with a smile. "Does it show?"

"I saw it, din't I? Nothin' wrong with studyin', but you don't wanna lose your looks over it."

He released Villy and looked around the room, his eye lighting on the low table with the toys laid out, and the oil on its warming tile.

"Oil nice and warm?" he asked.

"Ought to be. I'll check it while you make yourself comfy."

"No, you get comfy, and I'll check it. I ain't give you a massage in too long."

Dates went the way the client said they did, within limits set out in the House Rules—that was a House Rule, too. Villy slipped his robe off, stretched out on his stomach, and put his head down on his crossed arms. He heard the sound of Bradish getting undressed, and raised his head again.

"Want me to help you with that, honey?" he asked, husky and suggestive.

"You just stay right there," Bradish told him, "where I can 'preciate the view."

There was some more rustling, then a gentle clink which was probably the oil bottle being lifted off the tile. The bed gave when Bradish knelt beside him, and Villy shivered when warm, knowing hands stroked his back and sides.

"Beautiful," Bradish said, moving his hands away. "Let's get you relaxed."

The hands were back, oiled this time, strong fingers finding the knots in his shoulders and the tight places along his spine and patiently smoothing them away.

Villy sighed—and sighed again, as his muscles loosened. Over his head, his date laughed softly.

"You melt like butter on a griddle," he murmured, his breath warm in Villy's ear. He shivered obligingly, and Bradish returned to the massage.

When he was thoroughly oiled, utterly melted, and almost half-asleep, Bradish leaned over him, murmuring in his ear. Villy lifted his head; Bradish gently pushed it back down onto his arms.

"You just stay like you are. I'll take care of everything," he whispered.

* * * ✧ * * *

SOME WHILE LATER, Bradish having left for home, the sheets changed and hygiene observed, Villy went downstairs. Bidness'd been light the last few days. Even though he was still feeling languorous and drifty, he really ought to take another date tonight, if there was anybody waiting in the parlor for company. In the event that there was, he was wearing fluid dark pants, and a see-through white shirt. The new rug in the downstairs hall felt nice under his bare toes as he headed for the parlor.

"Hey, Villy," Jade said as he paused by the desk beside the parlor door. Jade was on reception tonight, keeping track of requests, who went upstairs with who, and how long they were logged for.

"Hey, sweetie," he said, smiling at her. "Anybody lonely in the parlor?"

"Nothing to worry you, if there are. You been reserved. Paid cash upfront, too, for a whole two hours."

Villy blinked. Two hours was pretty rich. Then he realized that it had to be one of his pilots, back on-port and looking for company. He didn't wince, though vigorous pilot exercise wasn't quite what he wanted after Bradish's treatment. But, two hours paid up full wasn't something he could afford to pitch aside just because he wasn't feeling athletic.

"I'll just get a cup of coffee first," he said to Jade. "What his name, my date?"

Jade shook her head.

"The lady said her name was Desa ven'Zel. Liaden—well, with that name, what else?—and she asked for you, specific."

Villy felt a cold breath of air down the back of his thin shirt. Suddenly, he was a lot more awake.

"Lemme see the screen," he said, and Jade obligingly spun it around to him.

There were four clients in the parlor. Three streeters were talking with Nan, Vera, and Si, for values of talking that involved lap-cuddles and nuzzling. The fourth client sat in the chair nearest the fireplace, hands folded on her knee, pensive gaze directed to the hearth stone.

Villy spun the screen back to Jade, wide awake now.

"Who's bouncing?" he asked.

"Patsy."

"Buzz her and ask her to meet me at the coffeepot."

"You're not taking the date?"

Villy shook his head, emphatically.

Jade didn't frown, but she did say, "I need something to put in the log."

"Not safe," Villy said, which wasn't something you put down in the log lightly. *Not safe*, meant that Ms. Audrey would never open to this particular client again.

"I'll buzz Patsy," Jade said. "Go get your coffee, Villy; you look green."

• • • ✧ • • •

"**. . . AT THE CASINO.** She said she was a friend of Quin's, like I was, and wanted me to tell her where to find him. I—something felt off, is all, an' I brushed her off, told her my *melant'i* didn't let me talk right then."

"Took that, did she?" Patsy asked. She was leaning against the wall by the buffet, watching him drink his coffee.

Villy nodded.

"Took it. Shift went over 'bout then. I looked out for her on the floor when I left. Didn't see her and figured somebody smarter'n me'd sent her up to the Boss."

Patsy nodded.

"Shoulda been the way it went, if it was *Quin* she was after," she said in her deep, quiet voice. "Her comin' here, after *you*, again—

either she *didn't* get her answer from the Boss, or she *did*, and took a fancy to you, separate from that bidness."

Villy's stomach cramped. He held his coffee cup in icy hands and looked up at Patsy.

"I don't want to talk to her," he said. "She scares me."

She eyed him.

"Considering the people I've seen who *don't* scare you, that's pretty tellin'. Quiet a minute, now; I gotta think this out."

Patsy stared up into the corner of the room. Villy felt his stomach sink. Nothing good could come outta Patsy's thinking about this. Dammit, there wasn't anything to think *about*! It was open and shut; he had the right to refuse any client he considered was dangerous—that was in the Rules a couple times, put down in different ways.

"Where *is* Quin?" Patsy asked abruptly

"Off-world making a delivery," Villy told her, and put his cup down, still half-full of coffee. Patsy had thought something out and he was pretty sure he wasn't going to like whatever she'd decided on.

"So," she said pensively, "we got this Liaden woman asking the Sticks dealer does he know where's the Boss's son? Even if she's a friend, she still might not know anything more particular about where he is, past *Surebleak*. Still an' all, why ask the Sticks dealer? Why *not* ask the Boss—or McFarland, if the Boss was too busy to talk?"

Villy didn't answer; the questions weren't for him; they were to help Patsy fix her reasoning. She was working her way up to something, and he didn't like the direction she was tending toward.

"Patsy, *I don't wanna* talk to her."

Her eyes focused on him; she gave him a smile and patted his shoulder.

"I know you don't, sweetie. Stick here just another sec. I gotta check something with Jade."

She left, walking fast. Villy considered going up to his room, but Patsy was perfectly capable of getting Ms. Audrey to order him to come out and do what he was told.

He sighed, looked at the coffee cup he'd put down—and didn't pick it up again. Which was a good thing, because here came Patsy back again, her face firm and professional.

"Okay," she said briskly. "Your date's starting to get impatient."

"I said I didn't want the date," Villy said, as patient as he could. "Jade can tell her that, and give the deposit back."

"Well, she might've done that," Patsy said, as one being fair, "'cept I butted in and told her you'd be right down." She held up a hand to stop him squawking, so he just shook his head.

"Look, this—whatever *this* is—bears on the Boss's household. She might *be* a friend—though McFarland didn't know anything 'bout nobody looking for Quin today. From t'other side, she might *not* be a friend, which fits with the pieces we got. Either side, it's Boss Conrad's to solve. McFarland'll be here inside ten minutes. All you hafta do is keep her in the parlor 'til he gets here and takes her in hand."

"Give her money back and set her out on the street. Cheever can take 'er up there," Villy said, knowing it wasn't going to go that way. Patsy's mind was made up, and, well, sleet—what was ten minutes? He could talk that long in his sleep.

"No, now, you're not thinkin'. We don't want to put ourselfs in the way of Balance, now, do we? Because we're nice, sensible people who don't wanna get shot today, or to get put on a list to get shot five years down the road when we're least expecting it, because we interfered where we shouldn't've. So, if this lady wants Quin, and Quin ain't here, then the very best thing we can do is get her into the hands of Quin's dad—and Quin's dad's 'hand—who'll know zackly what to do with her, and how to do it."

Put that way—well, he *was* thinking now, if he hadn't been, before. He didn't believe for a minute that Desa ven'Zel was any friend of Quin's. That didn't mean they didn't know each other, anyhow, and maybe *did* have bidness—Liaden bidness—to do together. Either way, Patsy was right; they didn't want to tangle themselves—and maybe the whole of Ms. Audrey's house, too—in any Liaden Balances.

Villy sighed, quietly. He knew what Patsy wanted him to do, and if it had been anyone else—well, sleet, it was what he *did do*, a lot of the time, if somebody was upset, or rambunctious—*get Villy*, that's what they said, and he'd come and get 'em all settled down. That was all this was, really, soothe the lady's impatience, and keep her busy talking 'til Cheever came and took her in hand.

"All right. But I don't want her in my room."

Patsy smiled at him.

"You don't worry about that; she's not going anywhere outside that parlor. Just all you gotta do is talk to her 'til McFarland gets here," she said soothingly. "I'll be watching the whole time. If she tries to hurt you, I'm there. Promise."

"Even if it means she puts you down on her list?"

"Sweetie, you're more important to me than any Liaden's shit list. I started living on borrowed time a year or two before you was borned."

He took a breath. *All you gotta do is talk to her*, he told himself. *Give 'er an on-the-house drink and ask after what she likes and how she likes it. Keep her from killing Jade*—that was an uncomfortable thought, but he didn't doubt the aptness of it. He looked at Patsy.

"Time for Jade's coffee break, maybe," he said.

Patsy narrowed her eyes.

"I think you're right," she said, with hardly a pause to think on it. "I'll relieve her while you go in to see your date."

"Right," Villy said.

He breathed in, and breathed out, which he pretended calmed his stomach, and headed for the parlor, stride loose and face languid.

• • • ✧ • • •

"I HAVE BEEN WAITING FOR YOU," she said, rising as he came into the room.

Villy looked around the room; the three couples had apparently moved upstairs, and he was alone in the parlor with the Liaden woman—Desa ven'Zel—who was at least not smiling. Her face wasn't really doing much of anything; it was like she'd painted it over with clear glue. If her greeting was a complaint, you couldn't read it in her expression, or in her eyes.

Villy gave a little smile of his own.

"I didn't know you were waiting, honey," he said, carefully

avoiding anything that sounded like an apology. "I'd've been down sooner, if I had."

"I made an appointment," she said. "The person at the desk was to have told you."

"Well, but my last date went over," Villy said, improvising; "and I didn't check my messages right away, after I was alone." He gave her another smile, purely professional, and made a show of looking her over and liking what he saw.

"There's no reason for us to fight. I'm here now, and we can get to know each other." He moved over to the refreshments table, wondering how many minutes he'd used up outta Patsy's ten. His nerves said it'd been a year since he'd come into the parlor, but his head was arguing for under two minutes.

"What would you like to drink?" he asked over his shoulder.

"I would like nothing to drink," she said sternly. "I desire to go to your rooms. There are . . ." She hesitated, and he turned to look at her, which was a mistake, because it encouraged her to smile.

"There are . . . *very special things* that I wish you to do for me."

Villy managed to suppress his shudder, and smiled back.

"I'm looking forward to that," he said. "But the first thing we gotta do is sit down and talk a little bit about the House Rules. The very first House Rule is that we have to talk about 'em with all our new dates, so there's no misunderstandings or . . . *unwanted* surprises. This is a house of pleasure," he said, warming slightly to his topic; "we don't want any . . . mistakes."

The smile had slipped off of her mouth, leaving it hard and straight. He thought he saw impatience in the set of her face, but she bowed her head nice enough.

"Indeed, all should be informed of the House Rules," she murmured. "Mistakes are very costly, as I'm sure your Ms. Audrey would agree." She raised her chin. "For the drink, is there wine?"

"Sure there is," he said heartily, knowing that what he had on offer wasn't anything close to the beverage she'd expect. "I've got lorinberry wine, dandyweed wine, and soran wine right here, all nice and cold."

She considered him out of narrowed eyes.

"Soran wine is sweet?" she asked finally.

"Sweet as love," he assured her.

"I will have that."

"Good choice. Why don't you take a seat and get comfy while I pour for us?"

• • •✧• • •

HE'D HOPED she'd go back to the single chair she'd been sitting in, absent his specific invitation to get comfy on one of the couches. The hope was dashed when he turned, glasses in hand, to find her curled into the corner of the softest, and least easily escaped couch Ms. Audrey owned.

She smiled, and patted the cushion beside her.

He crossed the room, frantically wondering how long it had been *now*, handed her a glass and settled in beside her.

She lifted her glass, by which he knew she meant to offer a toast. He lifted his glass in imitation.

"To successful endeavors," she said, which sounded a little strange for a toast from a client to a host in a whorehouse. Villy raised his glass in answer.

"Successful endeavors," he murmured, and sipped.

The wine was icy, and so sweet the inside of his mouth puckered for a moment. Even Desa ven'Zel seemed momentarily speechless.

Villy took a breath.

"A question," his so-called date said.

"Sure."

"Is this time that we linger over the rules deducted from the amount I placed upon deposit?"

Worried about her money, was she? Villy guessed he didn't blame her. He gave her a reassuring smile and reached over to pat her knee, which was the last thing he wanted to do, but, under other circumstances, was the thing *he would have done*. It was like patting a rock, except that a rock couldn't narrow its eyes. And she wanted him to do *very special things* to her? When snowballs got up and danced a jig, she did.

He sipped his wine and got his hand back without making it seem like he couldn't let go of her soon enough; and smiled again.

"The talk and the drink's on the house," he told her, which was true for every new client. "The clock won't start ticking on that deposit until we close the door on our bedroom."

"That is well," she said, and leaned forward to put a hand on his thigh.

That was a surprise, and what was more of a surprise was that she kept it there. Her fingers were cold through the thin pants, and her grip was hard and impersonal. Away in another part of the house, he could just make out voices. The doorman was sending visitors down to the overflow parlor. That meant Ms. Audrey knew what was going on, and approved it. The House was making sure him and his date weren't disturbed.

"So," she said, and her fingers tightened until it *hurt*. He drew a sharp breath, looked into her eyes, and gasped again at her smile.

"Tell me the rules, Villy Butler."

She leaned back into her corner then, taking her hand with her. He'd have a bruise for sure, and—

Where the *sleet* was Cheever McFarland? Villy thought, in a sudden spike of raw terror.

He took a breath and pushed it out of his head, pushed *all of it* out of his head. For the length of the date, he concentrated on the date. He pretended—only it wasn't pretend, not zackly—that the date was the most important thing in his life. The *only* thing in his life. That was the way it worked. Let yourself get distracted and the date noticed. Even if they didn't know *what* they'd noticed, they wouldn't ask for Villy again . . .

"The Rules," he said, smiling into her eyes. "Since you want me to do *really special things*, let's talk about those Rules."

He had a sip of his wine, still holding her eyes with his, though he didn't want anything else, except to look away.

"There's no cutting, no flogging, no carving, no burning— nothing that draws blood, or does harm, is what I'm saying. There's no choking, no crushing, and nothing that breaks bones.

"Bondage, spanking, rough play—all allowed under the Rules; rough as you like it, without crossing the lines we just talked about.

"Before we go to a room, host and guest each picks a quit-word.

That's everybody, no matter what. Even if all you wanna do is take a nap together."

He smiled at her then, in such a way as to suggest that a nap was at the bottom of a long list of activities he wanted to share with her.

"The quit-word—if you say yours or I say mine, that's the signal for everything to *stop*. The person who used their word tells out what happened to make them wanna quit, and the session's done."

"Does the patron receive a refund for time unused?" his date asked him. Woman was tight with her money.

"Ms. Audrey decides," he said.

She nodded, and leaned over, supple as a snake.

"I am told that Terrans . . . like this," she said, holding his eyes with hers. "Is it so?"

She stroked the back of her fingers very lightly down the side of his face. Villy shuddered, he couldn't help it. He hoped she'd think it was desire, and managed not to pull away, and *where* was McFarland?

Desa ven'Zel smiled, and gripped him by the chin, fingers tightening.

"The Rules . . ." he whispered, and he thought for a moment that she was going to *laugh*, and if she did, the sound of it would kill him outright.

"The Rules," she murmured, instead, her fingers holding his chin in a grip that was just next to painful. "The House seeks to maximize its profit, and minimize its expense. Therefore, it limits accidents, which are, as we have agreed, expensive."

She released his chin, trailing her fingers down his throat and his chest, where the shirt was open, and rested her palm flat on his abdomen.

"You are very pretty," she said, which he'd heard before. But he'd never heard it said like it was an insult. "Do you bring the House much profit?"

"Sweetie . . ." He wanted her hand *off* of him, dammit; he wanted out of here; he wanted a shower—two showers!

"Sweetie," he said again, hearing his voice wobble; "that ain't polite to ask."

"Is it not?"

Her eyebrows rose, but she didn't take her hand away.

"I will remember. Are there more Rules, or may we go to your room, now?"

There were more Rules, all right, including that he could tell the bouncer he considered a client unsafe, and *refuse the date*. Better not tell her that one, though. Thundering blizzards, how did Quin *know* this woman?

"One more," he said, and dragged up what he hoped she'd take for the smile of a man just managing to keep his arousal in check, rather than a man who was scared outta his mind.

"You wanna take that hand back, before something . . . goes off."

The look she gave him might've melted lead, but she took her hand away.

"Since you're a lady who's careful with her money, I gotta tell you this—sometimes a visit'll go a little over-time, and if it does, the House expects to be paid for the extra time. I try to make sure that we'll wind up on time, but sometimes, everything's clicking along, and neither one wants to stop while it's good. If you *do* wanna stop at the end of your reserved time, we'll tell the desk before we go up. They'll send somebody to open the door, in case we don't hear the timer."

"I understand. Come."

She stood, putting her cup on the side table as she did.

"Come?" He looked up at her. "There's more Rules."

"You will relate them later, or you will instruct me if I have inadvertently offended the House."

Damn. He *didn't* want her in his room. He *didn't* want to be alone with her any more. He wanted—

He raised his hand.

"You wanted me to do special things, you said. Can you tell me some details?"

She looked down at him, her face completely expressionless.

"I will tell you what you are to do for me when we are together in your room."

"Well, see . . . I don't have all the special toys in my room. If you want something I don't have, I'd have to call down to get it sent up. It'd save time—and money—if we just—"

She moved, almost as fast as Quin, grabbed his arm and *yanked him* to his feet. The glass flew out of his hand, wine spilling out in an arc—

"Hey!"

"We are going to your room now," she said. "I have been patient long enough."

He planted his feet, but, honestly, he didn't think he could take her, and Patsy ought to—

"Where's my girl Jade?" A big voice demanded from the hallway.

"Three times a week I come here, and she's always waiting for me, with a big smile on her face. I 'spect to see her when I come in, 'less she's upstairs changin' into that *red dress* for me. No, no, I'll just take a looksee into the parlor, that's all. Might be somebody looking for some extra-big fun."

Villy heard a light step, and a big shadow came across the door.

"There you are!" yelled Cheever McFarland, and swung a long arm out to gather Villy in by the shoulders and tug him into a bear hug.

His captive arm—but she let him go, and turned all the way 'round to stare at Ms. Natesa, who was standing in the doorway to the back hall, gun steady in her hand, and her face closed and cold and somehow *still* more alive than his date's . . .

McFarland swung him behind his broad back— "Stay behind me, boy."—and *his* gun was out, too. Desa ven'Zel glanced at him over her shoulder, not looking particularly threatened, or the least little bit scared.

"You will come with us," Ms. Natesa said.

The other woman turned again to face her.

"I regret," she said—and gasped sharply.

McFarland swore and jumped forward, going down on one knee and catching her before she met the rug.

"Poison," he said, without looking up. He holstered his gun, and put a hand on her chest as she stiffened, making a sound like a kitten mewling, then collapsed, completely boneless.

"Dammit."

"Indeed."

Ms. Natesa slid her gun away, and came into the room.

"Villy, are you hurt?"

"No ma'am, just scareder than I ever been in my life."

"I regret that," she said, and paused, as if she heard the echo of Desa ven'Zel's last words.

"I am sorry that it took us so long to arrive. We needed to be certain that she was acting alone. You were very clever to keep her here in the parlor."

"She was getting ready to carry me up to my room," Villy said.

"Yes, we heard."

Cheever McFarland rose, Desa ven'Zel in his arms, and put her gently down on the sofa. Villy bit his lip, and looked over his shoulder gratefully as Ms. Audrey swept into the room.

She paused at his side, taking the situation in with one encompassing glance.

"I didn't hear a shot," she said, maybe to Ms. Natesa.

"She poisoned herself. We have learned that some of the operatives are equipped with this ability."

Audrey sighed, and turned to Villy.

"You all right, honey?"

"Yes, ma'am."

She gave him a close look.

"Just scared blue. Well. You and me and Patsy and Mr. McFarland'll are gonna sit down, go over this and figure out how we could've handled it better. But not tonight. Tonight, I want you to take a drop and go to sleep."

He didn't usually take the sleeping drops, but he had a strong suspicion he wouldn't be doing any sleeping, unless he did. At least he didn't have the early shift at the Emerald tomorrow.

"Yes, ma'am," he said to Ms. Audrey, and she gave him another sharp look.

"I asked Teddy to keep you company tonight, all right?"

Teddy was old enough to be Villy's mother, he guessed. She was round and sharp-tongued and encompassing. He'd sleep good tonight, if Teddy was holding him, even without the drug.

Ms. Audrey must've seen that thought cross his face, 'cause she nodded, and said, "The drop too, Villy."

"Yes, ma'am," he said for a third time, and turned at another step in the hall, which was Teddy.

"Come on, honey," she said, opening her arms. "Let's get you comfy."

He nodded—and turned back to Ms. Audrey.

"I'm sorry about the wine on the new carpet," he said, wincing as he saw the red arc slashing through the field of pretty, pale flowers.

"Never you mind it," Ms. Audrey told him. "Mr. Luken tells me that rug's got a surface that'll repel anything. Just wipe it with a rag, he says. We'll test that in just a minute. Now, go to bed, Villy."

"Yes," he said, and nodded at the room. "Ms. Natesa. Mr. McFarland. Thank you."

Then he let himself be tucked under Teddy's arm and guided out of the parlor.

✧ Cutting Corners ✧

BEESLADY *is a yard tug in a space station's orbit, a far cry from a* *Jump ship. Therny Chirs, cargo master on* Fringe Ranger, *never heard of* Beeslady *until a jammed cargo lift rapidly changes his perspective on the future.*

✧✧✧✧

"THERNY, you awake up there?"

That was Gwiver, his supposed assistant, and emergency back-up, just like in the rule book, with the exception that "assistant" and "emergency back-up" were supposed to be two separate bodies. Any wise, it was a silly question, even given Gwiver's standards, since he'd seen Therny Chirs squeeze his long and lanky self into the pallet lift's maintenance bay a ship's hour ago, and it wasn't like there were two ways out.

An hour he'd been working on the double-dorfle-damned thing, not in the Cargo Master's job description, not by a long Jump, it wasn't. Ought to have a real mechanic at the job. Mechanic? Engineer! He slanted a look at the several pieces of metal that weren't supposed to come loose from the main housing. Horrifying as that discovery had been, it really wasn't surprising, of its type. Not having a proper mechanic on-board—just one more way that the line cut corners, and saved itself, so the story went, a goodly amount of money.

Therny Chirs shook his head, only half at himself and his jerry-rigged repair, then he punched the button that, in theory, cycled the lift door to full-open.

This time, for eighteen wonders, the door did open. To a point.

Chirs's helmeted head was pressing against the putative ceiling of the bin and his eyes a hands-width above deck level. He could, this time, actually see out, onto the dock, the slight breeze going past his ears letting him know that the ship's proper over-pressure was functioning, at least.

He watched as several pairs of legs passed close, pushing a cart, probably cutting corners across what was marked out as their private work area. Out on the dock's main way, half a dozen pilots, arms and mouths in motion as was usually the case with pilots in a group, strode by with a will. Probably coming from the bar, or maybe from the regional cruise ship taking up four gates at once and making the working ships crowd hard into the rest of Codrescu Station's ramps.

In the wake of the pilots came a smaller figure, small enough that Chirs's tiny window on the dock drew its attention. He thought it was a child, even as it bent closer and he saw its eyes—as knowing as any of the pilots, those eyes, and looking at him with interest. It came closer, the shadows shifting over the oddly-shaped face—

He felt shock then, the eyes having fooled him, for his auditor was not a child, after all, but a . . . creature, with a fur-covered face, and—

"Hevelin!" shouted a voice.

The . . . creature turned, there was the sound of running steps, a pair of legs rapidly coming into Chirs's view, and a large pair of hands scooping the creature up, and away.

"Shoulda taken you right back to the garden!" The voice said, the tone somewhere between scolding and laughter. "Don't you gimme that sad—"

A loud BEEP BEEP BEEP drowned out the voice. The half-open hatch rumbled, the readout on his belt chimed, all telling the same story. Safety auto-close had kicked in.

The view went away, the breeze stopped. Therny Chirs did not swear.

"Therny, are you up there?" That was Gwiver, again. "Did I hear something working?"

He took a careful breath.

"Yeah, it was working, It's not working right now, though. I'm . . ."

"Chirs, we got to make up some time here, you know. Get it moving!"

That was *not* Gwiver. *That* was the captain himself, the line's representative, and therefore the author of this particular set of problems.

Fringe Ranger should have had a major refit done five Standards ago. When Therny Chirs came aboard as Cargo Master, three Standard Years back, he'd been promised that the ship was in line for refit in two Standards. They'd promised other things, too, like apprentices for cargo master Chirs to train, who would then be promoted to cargo masters of their own ships, while more 'prentices came to the *Ranger* to learn. *That* had been the hook for Therny Chirs: Teaching. Students . . .

All dust and ice. Instead of doing anything they'd promised, or even following their own damn' rule book, they kept saving the wrong credits and insisting that you got profit out of cutting corners, instead of good maintenance, full crews, training up the next generation, and delivering goods on time . . .

"Chirs, we're almost on schedule. You're supposed to start unloading in three hours. You've got another half-hour to—"

He took a deep, deep breath, and let it, carefully, out.

"Captain Jad, this one can't be hurried," he said, just stating facts. "It ought to be fixed if you expect to be carrying break freight handled through a cargo tube. *Fixed*, Captain, or maybe replaced entire."

"Replaced, at Codrescu Station's prices?" the captain said, outraged. "Just get it working!"

And *that* was the break point on the pullion screw, so there was no use crying about it or pushing past it. Down. . . .

He took a *particular* breath, counted himself lucky he knew that relaxation technique, and moved things so *down* was possible.

It was shimmy, and bend, and back, and back, and watch the

head, and pull the tub of tools around with him and down, and not drop them on the captain's deserving head.

"My suggestion, Captain, is that you show an engineer what I've got here. I'm two hours past regulation shift end and that puts me in the redzone for safety—my light's been flashing like a pulsar for the last hour! Just you—and an engineer—look at this!"

The final four feet wasn't that bad, except that Captain Jad had no sense of self-preservation and had almost managed to get his shoulder shlagged by the tool tub anyway. Chirs was the skinniest man on the ship, but not weak, and that was a bonus for sure for the captain whose hat still had a place to sit.

Chirs pulled the work helmet off once the tub was settled safe, meaning the sweat was free to run down his neck now.

He pushed the dupe button, watched the amber lights flash three times, and pulled the duplicate chip out of the helmet control bar and tried to hand it to the captain, but ended up giving it to Gwiver since the captain was sucking on his trucafe like he did when he got nervous. Damnnity well *ought* to be nervous!

"Take a look. And here, I brought 'em out because there was no way I was going to be able to put them back on."

Gwiver took them, too, after managing to hand off the recording to the captain.

"There's metal missing, sir. There's grooves in things that oughtn't be touching anything, sir. There's a spot of something that's flaking and several things that are bent. I've been measuring and checking and . . . I'm done with this until it gets *fixed*, sir."

Probably he'd been overdoing the *sir*, Chirs realized, but if worse came to worser and the captain put him on warning he had a lot of stuff to go against a complaint. In fact, for back-up, he slipped a chip he owned into the slot, duped it while the captain watched him, and shoved that down into his personal work-wallet.

"The Cargo Master reports and certifies to the best of his abilities that the inner lift assembly is out of true and that he will not utilize it for any purpose until it is repaired by a technician fully pedigreed to fix and certify it right."

"We've got to move that . . ."

Chirs pulled a 'sorb sheet out of his pocket, and wiped his forehead. He nodded, rubbed his hair down past his ear, and threw a pilot's *I can do it if we have to* hand-sign at the mechanism, at the captain, at Gwiver . . .

"When I come back on duty we can do an eval. That's ten hours, regulation, before I can come back on duty. There's a way to do it— open hold—with a rent-boat. It'll take losing some air, and you'll have to cut grav, but the ship will let me peel it out of there pretty quick as long as you get the pod-packs tethered and secured ahead of time. Gwiver can do that while I take my break."

"Open hold. That's pilot work, Chirs."

"Yessir, and that's why the line hired me, wasn't it? I got a secure Pilot Third and you don't have to void any of the contracts by having outside haulers involved. I'm good for it. That lift's not good, and that's a fact."

"I hear your suggestion, Chirs. I'll take it under advisement if we can't get the lift going while you're on break. I'll note the cargo master's scheduling issues for later discussion."

The glare was so cold it was hot, but Chirs strode away, wondering if he could recall where his Third Class certificates were.

. . . ✧ . . .

HE LOST A LITTLE BIT OF HEAT on his way across to the station, official IDs and records to hand, found right where he'd thought they should be. Doubts about things—*Fringe Ranger* was making him doubt what he was doing more each docking.

He was a very good cargo master all the time and just about a decent warehouse-grade in-system pilot, on an average day. He knew it and the Pilots Guild knew it . . . and his certificates were perhaps, maybe, just a little, on the wrong side of the reup date. With luck, he could point to the routes they'd been on and sweet talk the rules and get this part done.

It would be a long walk from here to Skaller Three if he couldn't.

. . . ✧ . . .

THE PILOTS GUILD OFFICE was bigger than he'd expected, given the overall size of the station. It was crowded, and it was also noisy. His plea went to the first person who recognized what he was saying. Not that his Trade-talk wasn't good, but an on-going lament from someone claiming a stolen first class license and jacket had a couple of people's attention, and there was some other ruckus to be heard through an open door to another room, some of it the lilting sound of Liadens speaking at speed. Doubtful ID seemed to be the gist of the situation, and he guessed he wasn't supposed to know about it.

"Pilot, you have a date issue here . . ."

He'd caught the attention of a uniformed woman hurrying past the desk, who'd listened to him, looked at his info, and looked at him, suspiciously. Her name tag read *Sterna* and her rating was . . . First Class Provisional. A Jump pilot.

He nodded.

"I'm on *Fringe Ranger.*" He jerked his head in the general direction of the docks, "and they don't give me much time to . . ."

She looked up; her mouth was borderline grim . . .

"So why haven't you taken this to Second?" she asked. "You've had ten years."

He grimaced, tucked his annoyance away where it wouldn't show—it was a good question, after all. Not really her business but . . . there, straight was the best answer.

"No time for hobbies, Pilot. Started in with cargo twenty Standards ago—just exactly what I wanted to do. The third class, that was an afterthought; it'd be useful to me, in my work. Hard to carve out the time, truth said, but I did get it, and I was right—real useful to have."

She blinked, then, grudgingly, smiled.

"There's a reminder for me. Not everybody wants to be a master pilot!"

She waved at the noise around them.

"Here's our problem. You showed up here in the Guild Office in person. If you'd filed from your ship, I could've given you a flight-length extension, so you could get your cargo settled. Since you came in, that means a re-test to fresh up the ticket."

She frowned, her nose wrinkling slightly.

"You're not looking for up-grade?"

He shook his head, and she nodded.

"You'd never know it, with all this drama going on, but we've got the resources available right now to do your physical, and the sim. Take a few hours. Then we'll see what the boss wants to do about a ship-test. How's that?"

It was fair, Chirs thought. More than fair, from her point of view. Unfortunately, he doubted Captain Jad would waste a day, waiting for his cargo master to freshen up his pilot's license.

"I was hoping to be able to rent a local to do some transfer that's come up . . ." he said, omitting the potentially troublesome news that the ship at the dock couldn't open the main internal hold.

Sterna sighed a real sigh then.

"Oh, dreamer, dreamer, dreamer. Codrescu Guild Hall is hosting the annual members meeting. You'll have noticed we're a little pilot-heavy, and they're all here on business. I doubt you could hire much more than a hand cart and a part-time handler right now."

Chirs sighed, and turned his hands palm up.

"Right," Sterna said. "Sometimes the route flies you.

"Let's see what we can do about your first problem, then we'll know what we can do about the second. Can't always cut corners, Pilot."

• • •✧• • •

HE'D DONE WELL ENOUGH on the sim tests to see that he could pass a live-board test—*and* to see that he was rusty and ought to get more ship time. But there, the line's officers had been promising ship time, too . . .

Chirs shook his head. Past was past. Right now, he needed to focus on the fact that, despite all the unruliness caused by pilots with too much off-board business to do, Sterna had managed to put together a live-board test for him.

"We've got a local switch-tug that can use some side-work, but isn't certified for the higher class ships. We'll give you a testing key and the captain will let you get your two hours in—enough for you to pick up another couple years of cert. You in?"

"I'm in," he said.

. . .◇. . .

THE SWITCH-TUG was called *Beeslady*, under the command of owner and Third Class Pilot Giodana Govans. She'd clearly been purpose-built to handle one project—now long done—then sold off to the scrap-yard, where she was duly bought and unscrapped by someone with more guts than gudgeons.

She was a serviceable ship, solid to Chirs's eye, but rough. There'd been no need to blast clean the welds and joins, so they hadn't been; the work was thorough though, and the nameplate was neatly done in Terran and transliterated into both Trade and Liaden. The call letters were clear, the lights bright and accurately timed. A surprising array of antennas spider-webbed the hull.

Inside, the control deck *was* the tiny ship's whole; two seats in front of the surprising dual control panel—one standard and one indecipherably custom—a berth to the left of the controls with a combination head and shower beside it, a galley of sorts to the right. He'd seen cabins with more room than this, and Captain Govans apparently lived aboard! That sense of a homeplace was reinforced with the scent of—must be coffeetoot, baked breads, and spiced yeast quite at odds with the transparent overhead canopy and front ports showing cold stars as gleaming as the ceramics of the station's outer panels.

"We gets you some credit here, Mister Pilot. *Beeslady* done this kind of work for a bunch of folks, been thirty years and some."

The pilot—captain that would be—was small, skinnier than him, and barefoot when he was introduced at the freight gate. Her hair was short and colorless and her uniform the soft sheen of old cloth, long used. For all that she was Terran her diction was her own . . .

"Cargo master, good job that to be, and knowin' what a pilot knows, that's bonus for all an eny, I betcha, ain't it?"

He'd agreed and she pointed him to the seat—

"In luck, that's you are. 'at seat got less than ten hours in it, ought'n be fine and dandy—saved for two years for it! Sit, make it fit, and then we get you to stand up and start the test with a sit down. I don't go easy on no one—this place out here's nowhere to be easy 'boutn. We're quick and tidy; I got all standard latchlocks and we'll have you test a couple, like you're 'sposed to. Don' worry—if you're up to it, you're fine."

He sat, found the seat a high end fit and wondered if was one of those things that were said to have dropped out of a hold. . . .

"Mr. Chirs, here we go. Sit and do."

He'd seen the outside of the ship and the first fifteen minutes were taken up with checking gauges and comm lines, being sure of clearances, and he'd done that all in sim not two hours before so he was fresh. The pilot sat at her board and he saw that she wore it more than sat at it; there were pedals and switches in odd places and once away from the station's light artificial gravity she clearly fit it perfectly. His own seat was comfortable, and the two screens good.

"First mission is to take us out to Yard Three; it's netted so you gotta look sharp. Mind the cross-traffic; keep a special close eye on *Flingwagon* down there on the cruise docks."

Flingwagon was tied tight and going nowhere; the cross traffic consisted of a couple space-suited figures attached to an antenna rig and a two person jitney. The netting, now, that was a new one to him, but the little ship's manual controls were relaxing to operate after the broken lift work on his own ship, and he entered the area with no problems, the markers obvious and with plenty of clearance.

Captain Govans had him rotate the ship, pull it to a dock, leave the dock and rotate it again, lock to centered mass of metal stanchions, every bit of it copied to his test-key.

"Now take us out twice as fast, and go high on the station so the rotation's under you, spinward."

Not as easy as it sounded; the net looked more like a tunnel at this speed, and he had to spin the ship and . . .

"That's the slow way, but it'll do. We're looking for doin' at all 'stead of best 'fficient, 'specially in the nets. Gotta know *Beeslady* got no big meteor shield, so we won't bounce if you hit 'em."

He mentally allowed that she was right—all he wanted was the certificate. He listened in to the port chatter, some of it aimed good-naturedly at *Beeslady*.

"Hey '*Lady*, you running in your sleep?" And . . . "Hain't the way you showed it to me, slowship . . ." "Gonna take you a long time to Jump Point that way, ain't it?"

"*Beeslady* going to Codrescu azimuth, Pilot Third Class Chirs is PIC."

He'd switched that to a broader band than he ought maybe, but no one said anything and they all knew what he was doing.

After a few seconds, the chatter started again.

"You take care o'that ship, PIC Chirs—she still owes me a tow and a tug," and "That'll do it, put some guy half her age in there and it'll slow the whole yard down . . ." and "Don't need amateurs in my space, Govans!"

The captain was quick over more chatter: "Don' mind dem; most don mean nothin' and some think dey're better 'n dey are, as you kin hear. So's everhead else hearnin' too!"

Instructions then:

"Twenny clicks above station, then you gonna come down back along to the main arms and follow in over *Flingwagon* at 'spection speed and level, be so kind, headin' hub to out."

"That's pretty close, I'll need to . . ."

"You told 'em you're PIC, and so less'n I pop the switch das da plan I know. You do what you need, I do what I need."

And so what he did was rotate the craft when he'd hit the theoretical spot above the station. Next was to contact station Ops with the plan he'd been given, and with that go-ahead "You have any problem, you defer, PIC—*Beeslady*'s good close in but we don't know you. Proceed."

"Fumfingers! Dint have no need to tell you dat—we doin' fine."

Govans muttered and he realized she wasn't duplicating his screens now, instead, she was watching where he was supposed to go and . . .

"*Flingwagon*, PIC Chirs here on *Beeslady*, I'm on a recert test and need to do a flyby. Kindly keep your RF and shield low and I'll do the same . . ."

He glanced away from his screen, saw Govans nodding in the near dark of her seat, "Thas good, boy, thas how . . ."

"No permission here, *Beeslady*! Stay away. This is a passenger ship! You've got to stay fifteen seconds away and . . ."

"Docked!" Chirs knew those regs and once docked the distance regs were the same as for the station—maintain way as posted . . .

"Hold steady, boy! Steady steady steady steady steady on that course. . . ."

Steady was easy enough—the craft was tiny and nimble to manual controls, with the cruise ship glowing in dock light in the artificial below. This side of the ship was a nearly blank wall of hatches, antennas, and working rigs that the passengers would never see.

"Das stupid! Shootin' plastic whipline in a place this crowded."

Whipline was high tension restraint, printed with a bias that let it curl into a neat bundle when released but capable of being made into polarized nets and containment units. It was often used as a guideline to snake goods or tools across short gaps but had to be watched since it was invisible to most radar. Because of that bias to curl it could foul equipment and because of the high tension and near invisibility, it could slice a non-hardened spacesuit to pieces.

Nothing showed on his screen, but on the captain's screen there were four bright lines . . .

"Gonna go where we was goin,' just twenny-fi meters ta port. '*Lady*'ll go where you point her, so point her good. I got good visual on this, and we're recording, 'cause of the test here, and so . . ."

Chirs muttered under his breath and Govans laughed out loud.

"We alweys is right dere, duckin' the big shots. Too bad we ain't got a really big boat in here right now—hardly get eny, so I guess he's figuring he's the big mass in da' orbit. Listen at 'em plainin' left and . . . sumbith! Half speed and ten meters off tha' deck, now!"

The ether was full of complaints from *Flingwagon*, with the bridge, security, and hospitality all chiming in, but Chirs ignored the complaints in favor of live orders and his own screen. Govans's screen now . . .

He dared not look at it again, one glance showing bright tangles and tiny bunched pods almost as bright; and there, space-suited figures with no beacons.

Chirs eased the throttle even more, felt the response in his guts as the little craft responded neatly. Even his sensors were showing

minute reflections this close—it was like they were flying beneath a
flock of ghostly birds.

"Hazard!"

Govans did something and he had an overlay on his screen of
whatever she saw.

Indeed, hazard. A jumpship would never have made it, but the
warning was sufficient for him to slow to walking pace and weave
through a knot of strings and wires moving slowly away from the
docks. The ship twanged once, twice, three times but he steadied
the heading automatically. The hazard had vanished again from his
screen, but there, some bits of wire flapped at the front screens and
flipped across the canopy. Then they were past *Flingwagon*, the rest
of the arm brightly lit by open ship bays.

"*Beeslady*," he said into the mic, "hazard nearport, hazard
nearport. We've been struck by debris and are returning to dock for
inspection."

"Sorry, Captain, I didn't mean to . . ."

"Hush dat, boy. Take us in an' I'll sign for you, sure."

· · ◇· · ·

CHIRS SAT CLOSE TO DOZING in an inner office, momentarily
forgotten in the rush of the guild office gone on alert. There were
two screens here, no doubt sharing external feeds with the station,
and every third view on one showed a twin of his initial sighting of
Flingwagon, except now there were traveling lights and numerous
small craft about—whatever the station could raise to study the issue
and clear the whipline.

The other screen was quieter, showing Borjoan's Repair and
Salvage's scaffold rig nearly enclosing *Beeslady* and beyond,
accidentally in view, *Fringe Ranger*, no activity at all but the normal
dock lights.

An intern brought him a meal and lots of real coffee, and
Guildmaster Peltzer himself stopped by to shake his hand, promising
to quickly sort everything out, and not keep him overlong . . .

The doze had deepened into sleep. He knew this because he was
dreaming about the creature with the wise eyes that he'd seen on
Ranger's dock, only that morning . . .

Here and now, in the dream, the creature was helping itself to the local vita-greens Chirs'd left untouched, all the while studying Chirs as if he'd been talking in his sleep. There seemed to be a matter of credentials to solve. He tried to explain that he had gotten that straightened around, but he was distracted by a flurry of pictures.

Pictures of faces.

Captain Govans he knew, and Sterna, and Guildmaster Peltzer, and the intern—Jon had been the name on his badge.

A man with a lean pirate's face and black eyes like ice picks was a stranger, as was the sandy-haired woman beside him. A woman with slanted blue eyes, and green hair; a child's liberally freckled face; a grey-haired man with an augmented eye; a—

Why was he dreaming the faces of strangers? Chirs wondered, and in the wondering woke up. Standing on the chair next to him, murbling over the greens with clear satisfaction was the creature from the docks.

He sat up fast as the door to his little private space opened.

"Oh, I'm sorry!" Sterna said. "Is Hevelin bothering you? Besides eating your dinner, I mean." She bent forward to address the creature.

"You have perfectly good fresh greens in your own garden!" she said sternly. "You don't have to steal from Pilot Chirs!"

There was a protest that Chirs felt more than heard, regarding both the greens and an exciting new friend.

"I don't eat much grass, myself," he told Sterna. "If he likes it, he can have it." He frowned. "Seems he just said it was good."

She laughed, lightly.

"Did he show you faces?"

He blinked.

"I thought that was a dream."

"It might have seemed like that," she allowed. "Especially if you're not used to talking with a norbear."

"Don't think I've ever . . . encountered a norbear, previously."

"Well, you have now. It's a pretty small club. I've only met two. Hevelin . . . travels with Guildmaster Peltzer, and helps him with guild business. They've been together for ten Standards, since back when the guildmaster rode circuit."

She sighed and shook her head.

"I wish I could figure out how he opens the doors. On the other hand, Hevelin more or less gets what he wants."

Chirs had the feeling that Captain Govans's face had come back to view, then faded into another, similar face, accompanying a sense of sadness.

"Yes, he was on *Beeslady*," said Sterna. "But he's new here, Hevelin. This isn't his regular route. He wouldn't have met Marg Addy—she lived here her whole life!"

The sense of sadness pervaded the room, radiating from the nearly expression-free face of the norbear.

"Yes, it is sad. I really don't think Pilot Chirs has met many of your friends. Now, I need his attention; maybe you can talk to him later."

Petulance? That was the feeling Chirs had as the norbear reached over, patted him on the knee, and jumped down, taking care to gather up the greens in their packing and carry them away with him, through the open door.

Chirs reached for the coffee mug and found enough to chug before it slurped empty. The room certainly felt as empty as the cup, now that the norbear was gone.

"So, Pilot, I personally ran your route in sim, and talked to Captain Govans. Here's your new docs, and a five year all ports certification, with a ten year rider—so if you come through again we'll recert up to that limit as long as your medical's good."

He received his credentials gingerly, as if there might have been an error.

"Me aborting to the dock, that didn't get me in trouble?"

She shook her head, Terran-style.

"Not here, it didn't. You ran most of the route and played the anomaly perfectly. No issue there at all."

His relief echoed through the room. Not only did he sigh, he felt as if the relief was palpable, affecting the pilot as much as him. He watched her face, feeling there was something more she was going to say about how glad *she* was.

Instead she turned toward the still-open door and snapped her fingers.

"Hevelin, if you're going to listen at doors I'm going to put you in the garden alone for a week!"

The doorway seemed abruptly full of blustering norbear, but the thing was only pocket high. How could it—he—

Sterna laughed. The norbear sidled a half step into the room, shrinking his bluster, and radiating self-satisfaction.

"How is he doing—whatever it is he's doing? I feel like—"

She smiled down at him.

"He's an empath—all norbears are empaths. He can feel your emotions, and manipulate them, a little. He also collects—connections between people."

He found himself smiling up at her.

"The catalog of faces."

"Right."

Chirs looked to the norbear.

"He can manipulate emotions, you said. Does he always get his way?"

"No, he doesn't. But that's the problem. Some planets have banned them outright, some even send out hunters. Afraid they'll take over. A little too much getting their way and they're seen as dangerous."

She paused. He—wanted to stay in the chair and talk with her more, but—well, she had work to do, with all those pilots on-station, and the meeting. And he—needed to get back to his ship.

He put his hands on the arms of the chair, sent a last glance at the screens—and froze.

Beeslady had moved. She was clearly between the pod mounts now, engaging the pressure panels on *Fringe Ranger*'s hull. Exactly the idea that had gotten him into this long day that ended with empaths, good company, and a fresh ticket . . .

"What's going on?" he asked Sterna.

"*Beeslady* is moving those loads that were stuck—turns out there's no one on station certified to work on those lifts. Captain Jad was raising a stink, I'm afraid, and says he can't wait three weeks to get out of here."

"Three weeks?" he did quick math, though, and saw the chance of Jad paying for a technician at express rates was slim to none.

"Actually, I think that's twenty-four days, going by Eylot's week. We're going to have an inquest, you see, and it'll take at least that long for everything to be put together. So Jad's worked out a deal to get his cargo off."

A chill went down his back about the same time the norbear pulled on Chirs 'knee and managed to climb onto his lap.

"I really ought to be out there. I'm cargo master! I'll . . ."

Hevelin was a nearly immovable weight on his lap now. Sterna sighed.

"I'm afraid not, Pilot. That inquest, that's about smuggling, you see. You're the principal witness. You'll have to stay."

. . . . ◇ . . .

THE INQUEST had been a joke, with no one being held entirely responsible: clearly that much effort would have taken more than one person, clearly the purser had not rigged all of those whipline ejectors nor connected those multi-kilos of super grade *vya*, nor fronted an operation of a scale that must have had multiple ships waiting, hidden in the confusion of ships at dock for the members' meeting.

A fine was imposed, and paid off. In due time, *Flingwagon* departed the station; the probable couriers for the *vya* no doubt slipping away, still covered by the crowd.

The hospitality of the pilots had *not* been a joke. They'd let him bunk in an unused pilot's ready room, feeding him, and treating him as well as they did the first class and master pilots, for all of his lowly third class status. Several of the advanced pilots expressed appreciation for his run, the sim being available on station, and almost everyone sympathized with the slow grind of officialdom.

He'd managed, after several days, to relax. Yes, in effect he *had* quit *Fringe Ranger* when he'd walked out, if that's how the captain wanted it. Yes, he'd been paid full rate for the voyage, anyway; more than one new friend pointed out—the ship hadn't been safe. He was better off of it.

He had in his pocket a pilots' guild chit good for one trip somewhere, practically anywhere, he wanted to go.

Probably that chit would stay in his pocket; it had no end date, after all.

Today, though, he would be gathering his effects and heading down to Eylot for the in-person interview of a job application he'd made. Anlingdin Academy was expanding, and they'd wanted an experienced cargo master to teach a few courses. Apparently the fact that he spoke formal and colloquial planetary Terran was good, even if he wasn't exactly from this region.

He heard a low voice, not amplified by Hevelin's assistance. Hevelin had finally agreed to stay in the garden of a night.

"Therny, are you awake?"

He was still deciding the answer to that when Pilot Sterna asked again, this time with a nip of his ear included. Well, she was off today, too, for a year-long run. She was provisional First Class, after all, flying for the leather jacket and all the glory of a Jump pilot.

And he? He was going to teach, after all.

He turned over, slowly, and she sighed.

"The pilot wakes," she acknowledged. "Let us perform a preflight check. No cutting corners."

✧ Block Party ✧

BLOCK PARTY came about because Baen editor Tony Daniel asked the authors for a winter holiday story for Baen.com and we discovered that there weren't too many year-end-equivalent holidays shared between Terrans and Liadens. On the other hand, one place where Terrans and Liadens are seen in a collision of culture is Surebleak, and there we found a story of a shared holiday.

✧✧✧✧

THE LIGHTS WERE ON at the Wayhouse, which was still enough of a novelty that Algaina paused after she'd unlocked the shop door to look at it. Wasn't many got up as early in the day as she did, an' the Wayhouse . . . well, it was a wayhouse, wasn't it? Always had been, back to when the Gilmour Agency ran Surebleak. Wasn't meant but to give a newbie on the street someplace in outta the snow to sleep while they got themselves sorted an' settled.

This new batch of folks'd been in maybe four, five days, an' every morning, when Gaina opened the shop, there was the light. Made her feel a kinda warm pleasureableness, that she wasn't awake alone in the dark.

Well.

She shook herself and turned back to the shop, her thoughts still half on the Wayhouse. According to the neighbors, there were at least four kids living there, but not one of 'em come in to her shop for sweets. Might be they was shy. She wondered if she oughta take a plate o'cookies up, whatever was left over, when the shop closed. Introduce herself. Find out who was awake so early, every day, and what they did in the dark hours.

* * * ✧ * * *

ALGAINA WAS IN THE BACK, getting the batch of sparemint cookies outta the oven, when she heard the bell on the front door ring out, which would be Luzeal, comin' in for her hot 'toot and warm roll before headin' down to Boss Conrad's territory an' the archive project. Luzee was always her first customer, ever since the first day she opened up.

"Be right out!" she called. "Got somethin' I want you to taste."

Wasn't no answer from the front room, which was typical; Luzee needed a cup o'toot to make her civilized.

Algaina closed the oven door, and stepped back into the shop, sliding the tray onto the counter, and looking 'round.

It wasn't Luzee who was her first customer this morning; it was Roe Yingling, who wasn't zackly a stranger—she let him run a ticket, after all—but nowhere near a reg'lar.

Algaina wasn't that fond of Roe, but he was a neighbor, and aside from having loud opinions at inconvenient times, he didn't stint the street.

"Mornin'," she said, giving him a nod. He'd already drawn himself a cup and was sipping it gingerly, wanting the warmth against the cold, but not wanting to burn his tongue. "You're up early."

He nodded around a sip from the cup.

"Word on the street's they're hiring over Boss Kalhoon's territory, long-term labor. Gonna go over an' see what I can get."

"Hadn't heard that," Algaina said; "good luck with it."

"Need it all, an' then some," Roe said, leaning over the pot and topping off his cup. "Body's gotta be quick if they wanna grab a job before a newbie gets it."

That was Roe's biggest and most frequent complaint, right there, Algaina knew. Not that there'd been that much work, the way things'd been fixed before Boss Conrad showed up to sort Surebleak out, which it—and they—surely had needed. Breaking up the old ways hadn't made work so much as it made time and room for 'bleakers to be able to roll up their sleeves and get on with what needed doin'.

The newbies, they'd followed the Boss to Surebleak, and they were a point of contention. So far's Algaina knew or saw, they was just as willing to work as any 'bleaker, an' somewhat more'n others. They come in with off-world skills, certain enough, but they wasn't 'bleakers. They didn't know what work needed done before that other piece o'work could get done, or necessarily how the weather played in—stuff that 'bleakers knew by instinct. Mostly, the work was team-based, 'bleaker and newbie, and plenty too much for everybody.

Still, there was a certain class of streeter, of which Roe Yingling was one, who wanted to have it that the newbies was taking work away from them, an' there wasn't nothing could convince 'em otherwise.

All of which was worth hopin' that Roe got work today.

"You better get movin'," Algaina said. "Early worker 'presses the boss."

Roe nodded at her.

"Zackly what I'm thinkin'. Need a couple rolls to have in m'pocket for lunch," he said. "What was that you wanted me to taste?"

Well, she hadn't wanted Roe tastin' her sparemint, she'd wanted Luzee. Still, she'd said the words and he'd heard 'em—an' it couldn't hurt to have another opinion.

"Here go," she said, holding out the tray. "Take one o'them and let me know what you think. Something new I'm thinking about adding in."

He took a cookie—not quite the biggest—and bit into it, eyes, narrowed.

While he was chewing, she got his two rolls, and wrapped 'em up in paper against the probable condition of the inside of his coat pocket. He took another bite, and was ruminatin' over it, when the bell rang, and a kid scooted in, let the door bang closed behind her—and stopped, big-eyed, and shivering, taking stock.

Algaina considered her: Too young to be out by herself before the sun was up. She was wearing a good warm sweater, pants and boots, but no coat or hat. Her hair was reddish brown and hung in long tangles down below her shoulders.

"Sleet," muttered Roe, not nearly quiet enough for a kid's ears to miss; "it's one a *them.*"

Algaina frowned at him, but he was staring at the kid, cold as she was, an' tryin' to decide if she liked where she found herself.

Of a sudden, a big grin lit up her thin face. She rushed up to the counter, dodging under Roe's elbow, and addressed herself at length to Algaina in a high, sweet voice.

Algaina frowned and held up a hand.

"Slow down, now, missy. My ears ain't as young as your tongue."

The girl frowned, reddish brows drawing together 'til there was a crease 'tween 'em, her head tipped to one side. Finally, she raised her right hand palm out, like Algaina had raised hers, and said, "Slow down."

"That's right," Algaina told her with a nod. "Now whyn't you tell me what you just said—slow enough so I can hear it."

"Goomorn," the girl said obediently; "beyou manake—baneken— *cookies!*"

The last word came out as a triumphant shout, like it was the only one she was sure of, thought Algaina. On the other hand, if you only had one word, it was pretty smart to be sure it paid out profits right away.

"That's right," she said. "I bake cookies. You want one?"

"You gonna feed it?" Roe asked, still not botherin' to keep his voice down.

Algaina glared at him.

"Feedin' you, ain't I?"

He opened his mouth, and she shook her finger at him.

"You finish that cookie, Roe Yingling, and get yourself goin' or you'll miss all the good jobs!"

He blinked—and shoved the rest of his cookie into his mouth.

Algaina turned back to the kid. Out from the Wayhouse, sure enough. Looked like somebody at home'd moved their eyes for a half-second, and she decided to go splorin'. Algaina's kid had done the same when he'd been what she guessed was this one's age. Scared her to death, so it had, until she found him wandering the street, or a neighbor brought him back.

Best thing to do, really, was to keep her 'til whoever was prolly already looking for her came by.

So.

Algaina bent forward some and caught her eye.

"You want a cookie?" she asked again.

The girl blinked.

"Cookie," she asserted.

"Comin' right up," Algaina said, and chose a nice big sparemint from the tray. She held it down across the counter. "You try that and tell me how you like it."

The girl took the cookie from her hand with a solemn little bow, and bit into it, her eyes squinched in concentration.

"Gaina," Roe began, low-voiced.

"Later," Algaina told him.

Roe took a hard breath, an amount of stubborn coming into his face, and who knows what he might've said next, except the bell rang again, and in come a boy wearing an oversized flannel shirt over a high-neck sweater, good tough pants, and worn-in boots, carrying a bright red coat over one arm. He caught the door, and eased it closed, the while his eyes were on the kid.

"Elaytha."

She spun on a heel, and threw up her arms, nibbled cookie still in one hand.

"Donnnee!" she cried, rushing toward him.

He didn't bend down to take her hug, nor even smiled, just stood there with his arms folded, and a frown on his face.

She stopped, arms falling to her sides, cookie still gripped tight.

"Elaytha," he said again, and held out the coat. "It is cold. You wear this when you go out. Also, you frightened your sister."

His voice was level; his accent marked, but understandable.

The response to this was a burst of words as musical as they were unintelligible—which was cut off by a sharp movement of the boy—no, Algaina thought; *not* a boy. A man grown, only a little short and scrawny, like *they* was.

"In Terran, Elaytha," he said, still in that stern, solemn voice. "We speak Terran here."

"Pah," the girl said, comprehensively. She advanced upon her—brother, at a guess, Algaina thought—cookie extended.

"You try that," she said, her inflection and accent Algaina's own; "and tell me how you like it."

"Yes, very well." He took the cookie, and thrust the coat forward. "You will put this coat on," he said sternly. "*Now*, Elaytha."

She sighed from the soles of her boots, but she took the coat and shoved first one arm, then the other into the sleeves.

"Seal it," her brother—Donnie—said in that same tone.

Another sigh, but she bent her head, and began to work on the fastenings.

He watched her for a moment to be sure she was in earnest, then raised his head to meet Algaina's eyes. His were dark brown, like his hair.

"We watch her," he said, in his careful Terran; "but she is very quick."

She grinned at him.

"I remember what it was like, raising my boy," she said. "Yours looks like another handful."

He tipped his head, eyes narrowing, then nodded slightly.

"A handful. Indeed. I am happy that she came no further, and hope you will forgive this disturbance of your peace."

"No disturbing done. Bakery's open for bidness. I'm glad she come inside. It's cold this morning, even for born streeters like us." She nodded at Roe, who hissed lightly, and turned away to pick up the wrapped rolls.

"Thanks, Gaina," he said. "On my ticket, right?"

"Right," she told him, and watched him push past the girl and the man without a nod or a glance, goin' out the door into the lightening day.

"You have a taste of that cookie and lemme know what you

think," Algaina said brightly, to take attention away from Roe bein' so rude. "New recipe; just trying it out the first time."

Donnie gave her a particular look, and a nod.

"I am honored," he said, and took a bite, chewing as solemnly as the child.

"Donnnee," Elaytha said.

He held up a hand, and closed his eyes.

After a moment, he opened his eyes.

"The texture," he said slowly. "It wants some—" He frowned, looked down at the kid, and held out what was left of the cookie. She took it and had it gone in two bites.

"It wants—" he said again, and stopped with a sigh.

"Your forgiveness; I have not the word. I will demonstrate. Elaytha, make your bow to the baker."

She turned and did so, smiling sunnily, the red coat meant for a taller, wider child. Like her brother's shirt had been made for somebody Terran sized.

Straightening, she added a rapid sentence, that Gaina guessed was some order of thank you.

"You're welcome," she said. "You come again, anytime you like. But you don't get no cookies unless you're wearing your coat, unnerstan me?"

She pouted, damn if she didn't, but answered, "I nnerstan."

"Good," she said, and turned her head, eye drawn by a movement.

Donnie was making his own bow.

"Thank you," he said. "I will demonstrate. For the moment, we are wanted at home." He held out a hand.

"Come, Elaytha."

She took his hand. They turned to the door—and paused, as it opened to admit Luzeal.

"'Morning," she said, giving the two of them a nod and a smile before passing on. "Gaina, I'm starving! Got any mint rolls?"

"When don't I got mint rolls?" she asked, as Donnie and Elaytha exited the shop. "Got something else, too—want you to give it a try."

LUZEE WAS CARRYING a three-ring binder under one arm like she'd taken to doin' ever since the call came out from the Lady and the Perfessor for old records, old letters, old books—all and anything.

Luzeal's family, they'd been in the way of managing the Office of the Boss, 'way back when the Agency was still on-world, and the Boss—the really big Boss, who oversaw it all—was called The Chairman. Even though they'd left her just like they left everybody, Luzeal's great-grandma'd organized a rescue operation, and moved all The Chairman's papers, and files, and memory sticks and, well— everything, down the basement of their own house, so it'd all be safe.

Which, Algaina admitted, it had been, all this time. Safe as houses, like they said. Safer'n most people'd been, includin' Luzee's grandma, who'd got herself retired by standin' in front of The Chairman's front door and tellin' the mob of Low Grades they couldn't come in.

Luzeal headed right for the hot-pot. She drank the first cup down straight, just like every morning, and brought the second over to the little table in the corner, so her and Algaina could talk while one et her breakfast and t'other minded the oven.

Algaina set the roll out on a plate, and ducked into the back to take the next batch out. More rolls, this was; rolls was the best she could do, not havin' a mother-of-bread, like grandpa'd wrote about in his card file. That was all right; her rolls were good an' hot for breakfast, and she was best at making cookies and simple sweets. Sometimes, though . . . she shook her head as she brought the tray out into the shop.

Just as good to wish for flowers in a blizzard, Algaina, she told herself.

Luzee had broken her roll in half, and was busy at breakfast. Algaina slid the fresh tray into the case, then went down to the end of the counter to pour herself a cup of 'toot.

"Was that the Wayhousers, just now leaving?" Luzee asked.

"Couple of 'em, anyhow. Little girl give 'er sister the slip an' gone splorin'. Big brother come lookin' for 'er. Too bad it was Roe Yingling in here when they come."

Luzee frowned.

"He didn't get ugly with a kid?"

"He coulda been less rude, but nothin' past talking too loud."

Luzeal sighed, and picked up her cup.

"He's a neighbor, but *sleet*, I wish that man would learn not to say everything jumps into his head."

"Day that happens, I'll make a cake for the whole street," Algaina said, and nodded at the binder on the table. Most of Luzee's binders had seen work, but this one looked downright *rough*. There were bits o'paper hanging out the edges, including a strip of ragged red cloth, and its edges were banged up like somebody'd thrown it up against a wall—or a head—more times than twice.

"Looks like that one's seen some fun," Algaina said.

"This?" Luzee put her hand on the old binder. "Now, this is the Human Resources manual, all the rules about how the company and the employees was s'posed to act in just about every situation you can think of, an' a couple more you can't. Got lists, pay grades, holidays, memos—I 'spect the Lady's gonna be real glad to get the one—I was up all night reading it and more'n half a mind not to let it go!"

"Agency's long gone," Algaina pointed out. "An' I'm not sure we need a rule book that don't say, right up at Number One: Don't desert your people to die, f'all you ever knew or cared."

There was a small silence while Luzee finished her roll.

"Actually," she said, putting her hands around her mug and meeting Algaina's eye. "It does say that. There's a whole evac procedure. They coulda done it—they *coulda* took everybody offa here, there wasn't no disaster nor any reason they had to make hard decisions. They was *s'posed* to've took everybody."

Algaina stared at her.

"Why?" she asked. "Why'd they leave us? My grandad always said there wasn't room . . ."

"Turns out," Luzee said; "there's room, and then there's *room*."

She took a long swallow from her mug and pushed back from

the table, heading for the hot-pot. Algaina picked up one of the sparemint cookies and bit into it, chewing slowly, trying to figure out what Donnie Wayhouse had found missing . . .

"What they did," Luzee said, coming back to put the mug on the table, "was a *cost-benefit analysis*. And it come out that it was more . . . well, *fiscally responsible*'s bidness-talk for it. Means they figured it'd be cheaper to leave everybody below Grade Six right here on Surebleak, and declare a loss on the equipment. Woulda put 'em in the red for years, an' given 'em a disadvantage with Corporate, if they'd brung all of us away."

She took a hard breath, and put her hand on the beat-up binder. "It's all in here—the original policies, and notes and the votes from the meetin's that rescinded 'em. Dates, names . . ."

She shook her head.

"That's what made me decide the Lady needs this more'n I do."

Names and dates. The way Luzeal told it, the Surebleak Historical Search and Archival Liberry din't think there was nothin' better'n names and dates.

"What're those?" Luzee asked, nodding down at the sparemint cookies.

"Hermits. Had the receipt in my granddad's box, but couldn't never get raisins, is what they're called. Always wondered what they'd taste like—the raisins and the cookies. Yesterday, I was at market, and freeze me if there weren't a whole bin o'raisins just come in."

She grinned.

"Couldn't just let 'em set there, could I?"

"Not you!" Luzee said, grinning back. "That what you want me to taste?"

"If you got time. Try one and see what you think."

Luzee chewed thoughtfully.

"S'good," she said eventually. "Crunchy. You gonna be able to do these reg'lar?"

"I'll talk to the grocer next time I'm in; see what we can and can't do. I got a couple receipts in that box wantin' raisins. I'll look 'em out. In the meanwhile, we'll find does anybody else like 'em."

"Hard to think anybody wouldn't," Luzee said, finishing hers and eyeing the tray.

Algaina handed her another cookie.

"Thank'ee. I tell you what, Gaina—you oughta take that box down to the archive."

"That box is my livelihood! 'sides what's a buncha receipts gonna tell the Lady—or anybody else?"

"Well, this one right here'd tell 'em raisins used to be usual 'nough they got put in cookies—more'n one kind of cookie—and here you never seen 'em your whole life until just now—nor me, neither!"

"Still—giving away my receipts! I don't got 'em all by heart, now do I?"

"See, now, if you tell 'em you're bringing a *working document,* they'll make a copy and give you the original back. You take 'em in a plate o'these cookies and tell 'em how they was last made in your grandad's day, they'll see the importance o'them receipts."

"Anyways, it's what I'm planning on doin' with this book here."

"You want a copy of all the old rules the old bosses voted out when they wasn't convenient? For what?"

"Well, I ain't finished reading it, for one! For t'other, there's maybe things in here we could adapt for the Surebleak Code, like the Lady talks about. It was the *Human Resources* manual, after all, an' far's I know 'bleakers and newbies is all human."

A bell pinged in the back, and Algaina went to bring out the next batch. When she came back out, Luzee'd finished her coffeetoot, an' was pulling her hat down over her ears.

"Gotta get goin'. You wanna take that box to the archive, I'll come with you, whenever you decide."

"I'll think about it," Algaina said, and watched her out the door.

* * * ✧ * * *

KEVAN had a nightmare again.

Don Eyr woke him, and sat at his bedside, holding his hand until he stopped shaking, and answered the questions that kept *him* awake most nights; answered them to soothe and heal. Not lies; he did not lie to the children, and less so to a comrade. But where there were no facts, *there* a heart might build light and airy palaces of hope.

So, for Kevan, and for himself, he answered—no, there had not yet been word from Serana; not from Ail Den nor Cisco nor Fireyn. Yes, it was worrisome. But only recall how confused and dangerous it had been in Low Port when Korval's mercenaries arrived.

So four of their house's defenders had gone to show the mercs the alleys and back ways, that they might flank the approaching forces and deny them Low Port.

Don Eyr might have been with them—Jax Ton and Kevan, too. They had the right, and just as much knowledge of the streets as the others. But head of house security—Serana herself—had counted them off; three to go with her to guide the mercs; three to keep the children safe.

Serana had more lives than a cat; she said it herself, and certainly she had survived—they had *both* survived—desperate situations before they had arrived in Low Port, and became the defenders of youth.

Surely, Serana was alive. *Was well*. Don Eyr did not accept a universe in which these things were not facts.

No more than Kevan might come to terms with a universe that lacked the living presence of Ail Den.

And so, in that small space of uncertainty, where the truth was not yet known, they had each built a palace of hope.

Kevan was nodding off, his grip softening; Don Eyr heard a soft step behind and turned his head as Ashti came to his side, holding a cup of tea and a book.

"I'll stay with him," she said, the low light waking sparks of red along her cropped hair.

He slipped his hand free, and stood, flexing his fingers, looking down at the boy.

Ashti put her hand on his arm.

"Sleep, Don Eyr," she murmured. "We need you."

Not for much longer would they two, at least, need him, he thought, though he did not say so to her. She and Kevan were old enough, able enough; the younger ones trusted them. He might leave, and have no fear for any of them—but he would not leave.

Not yet; not while there still remained some hope that Serana, and the others, would find them.

He left Kevan in Ashti's care, but he did not seek his own bed.

Instead, he walked through the crowded rooms, checking on each sleeper, straightening merc-issue blankets, picking up fallen pillows, smoothing the hair of those who moved uneasily on their narrow cots; and once stopping to murmur a few words in Liaden.

Their daytime language might now be Terran, but Liaden was the language of home, no matter how little they had been cherished there, and it soothed the fretful back to sleep.

Satisfied that all was well with the children, he descended to the kitchen, where he found the teapot warm and a cup set by. He smiled, recognizing Ashti's hand, and poured himself a cup, which he carried to the window.

The street was a short one, sparsely lit by what a daylight inspection had revealed to be self-adhesive emergency dims. One might wonder who had put them up, and who replaced them, but in that Surebleak was like the Low Port: Someone had taken up the task, for reasons known to themselves, which might or might not have anything to do with the common good.

Halfway down the street, a brighter light flared, and he stepped back against the wall before his laggard brain realized that it was not muzzle-flare, but only the light coming on in the sweet bake shop.

He sighed and shook his head. This place . . .

The unit commander charged with seeing them to safety had chosen to interpret her orders liberally, the children having quickly become favorites, and the mercs having no opinion of Low Port. Thus, their eventual arrival at Surebleak, deemed a *damned sight safer'n where we found you. No offense. Sir.* The mercs had seen them generously provisioned, and brought them to the attention of the proper civilian authorities, who took their application and the character reference provided by the unit commander, settled them into transitional housing, and located a 'prenticeship for Jax Ton.

Don Eyr sighed. He was, indeed, grateful to the mercs for their care, which had included putting messages through their internal networks, for Ail Den, Cisco, Fireyn, and Serana.

He closed his eyes, and sipped his tea, deliberately turning his thoughts toward the future.

They would need to find larger quarters within three local months. That was the limit of the local authority's charity, and more generosity than Liad had shown any one of them. He hoped to hear of opportunities, when Jax Ton came to them for his *day off.*

For now, then, they were well-fixed. Locating a more suitable establishment and employment were high on the list of things to be done. The most urgent item on that list, however, was Elaytha.

Elaytha had been theirs from a babe, pulled from a pile of wreckage that had once been an apartment house; the only survivor of the collapse. She had been odd from the first, and remained odd as she grew. Her mind was good; she could read, and cipher, and follow directions. She could speak—Liaden, Terran, and Trade— though she preferred her own tongue, which she shared with no one else they had ever found. She was sweet-natured, and her ability to mime was nothing short of astonishing.

She also had a tendency to wander, heedless of hour or weather, and was afflicted with odd terrors. Lately, she had achieved a horror of food, and would cower away from a bowl of cereal as if from an assassin.

Perhaps worse, she had since arriving in this place, become convinced that there were . . . *shintai*, as it was said in her tongue, which he understood to be akin to ghosts, upon the street, who required her care. The others tried to dismiss it as play, but, if so, it was like no other play in which she had previously indulged.

Ashti suggested that Elaytha was merely framing the strangeness of their new situation in her own terms. For himself, he feared that she was delusional.

Don Eyr left the window to pour himself another cup of tea.

Elaytha needed a Healer, he thought, carefully.

On Liad, that thought would not have been possible. In Low Port, the situation would have been hopeless. The Healers did not administer to the clanless.

He could not have said why he thought the Healers who had come to Surebleak might deal differently, unless it was merely that,

Surebleak had dealt them a hand, when Liad had refused even to sell them a deck.

He would ask Jax Ton to also find them information regarding the Healers of Surebleak. He sighed. Perhaps, instead, he ought to send one of the elder children to bear Jax Ton company, and to find the answers to all of Don Eyr's questions . . .

He carried his tea back to the window. The sky was brightening; the emergency lights a fading reflection. Down the street, the window of the sweet-bake shop blazed like a sun, which brought to mind the fact that he had not fulfilled his promise to the baker. One needed to deal fairly with one's neighbors. Neighbors were important, for those who had neither kin nor clan to shield them.

Ashti would scold him for not going back to bed, but, truly, baking was every bit as restful as sleep. Moreso, now that he slept alone.

Turning away from the windows, he set the tea cup aside, and began to assemble his ingredients.

* * * ✧ * * *

THE BELL RANG while she was in the back, and Algaina called over her shoulder.

"Make yourself at home; just gotta get this batch in the oven!"

There was no answer, but Luzeal was prolly more'n half-asleep still, at this hour. Algaina glanced at the clock. It was some early for Luzee, but—sleet, it was early for *her*, if it come to that. It'd been one of them nights where bad memories come slipping into your sleep, pretending like they was dreams.

Just as good—better—to be baking, than laying flat in the bed staring up the ceiling, and afraid to close your eyes. So, she'd gotten dressed and come downstairs, started the oven up and pulled a recipe out from the old box without looking at it.

Turned out it was a cake she hadn't made but once before, on account it was so fussy. Well, good. Fussy was just what she needed.

She slid the pans in, closed the oven and set the timer.

Wiping her hands on her apron, she stepped out into the shop.

"You're early for the rolls—" she started to tell Luzeal . . .

'Cept it wasn't Luzeal in the shop at this early hour of the day.

Standin' all solemn right in front of the counter was the little girl from yesterday—Elaytha. Her hair'd been combed and braided, and her red coat was buttoned up against the cold. She was holding a covered plate in two ungloved hands, and smiling to beat the sun.

Just behind her was an older girl, with a good knit cap pulled down over her ears, hands tucked into the pockets of her short jacket—no gloves there, either, Algaina was willing to say. Well, that was easy 'nough to fix. She had the kids' old gloves an' mittens that they'd outgrown. Might as well they got some use. If you didn't look out for your neighbors, who'd look out for you?

"You coulda set that down, got yourselfs a cup of something hot," she said now, looking from one to the other of 'em.

"That's what *make yourself at home* means."

She looked pointedly at the younger girl, who opened her wide eyes even wider.

"We will remember," the older girl said, her voice unexpectedly deep. "We are grateful for the information."

"You're welcome," Algaina said, gruffer than she meant to. She cleared her throat. "Either one of you want a cup of something hot?"

She nodded at the hot pot, steam gently rising from its spout.

"Thank you," the older kid said politely, "but not this time. We are to deliver Don Eyr's cookies. They come with this message."

She gave the younger girl a slight nudge with her foot.

"Try it!" that one said, loudly, holding the plate high; "and tell him what you think!"

"That is correct, Elaytha. Well done."

Algaina took the plate and set it in the center of the counter.

"I'm obliged," she said. "I ain't got anything out yet, but if you—"

"Thank you, no," the older girl said, with a small bow. She held out her hand.

"Come, Elaytha."

"Yes!" said the child, and that quick they were gone, the bell ringing over the closed door.

Algaina shook her head, and lifted the towel from the plate. A warm breath of spice delighted her nose, and she smiled as she picked up one of the dainty little rectangles, and bit into it carefully.

Still warm, and it fair melted in the mouth, soft and sweet, with just a bite of something tangy on the back of the tongue.

She had another bite, analyzing the taste, working out the spices, wondering how he'd gotten it so *soft* . . .

The bell jangled, jerking her out of her reverie. She opened her eyes as Luzeal stepped into the shop, shaking her head from the cold.

"Mornin'," she said, moving over to the hot pot.

"Mornin'," Algaina answered. She pushed the plate down the counter.

"Try one o' those and tell me what you think."

Luzee picked up a cookie and bit into it, eyebrows rising.

"'Nother new receipt outta the box?" she asked.

"This," said Algaina, "is what Donnie Wayhouse thinks those cookies I made yesterday oughta be." She took another bite; sighed.

"He had a bite o'one of mine, and I asked him to tell me what he thought—and he *did* think something, but he run outta words. Promised to send a demonstration."

She nodded at the half-cookie still in Luzee hand.

"That's his demo, right there."

Luzee took another bite, pure satisfaction on her face.

"I tell you what, Gaina," she said. "You know I don't like to meddle in other people's bidness—" That just wasn't so, but let it go; they all meddled in each other's bidness, that's how the street had stayed more or less peaceful, even in the baddest of the bad ol' days.

"I'm thinking you'd do worse'n go partners with that boy, if he don't got other work. Be good for both of you."

"We're thinking along the same lines," Algaina assured her, picking up another of the dark, soft cookies. "I'll return his plate proper after I close up this afternoon. Can't hurt to ask, can it?"

"Not one bit," said Luzee, and reached for another cookie.

* * * ✧ * * *

IT WAS SNOWING, but only enough to make an old woman wish she'd remembered put on her flap-hat, 'stead of the one that just covered the top of her head.

She knocked on the door of the Wayhouse.

It snowed a little more before the door opened, and she looked down into a pair of bright blue eyes under a shock of bright red hair.

"Yes?" the kid said. "Please say what you want."

Well, that was one way to answer the door, Algaina thought. Right to the point, anyhoot.

"I'd like to see Donnie," she said, and hefted the plate she was carrying covered over with the same cloth. "Wanna return his plate."

L'il Red took a bit to chew that over, then stepped briskly back and raised a hand to wave her in.

She crossed into the tiny hall, and stood to one side so the kid could shut the door and throw a series of bolts.

"This way," was her next instruction, and off the kid went, turning right into the hallway, and Algaina barely able to keep up.

It wasn't a long hall, but they passed four kids, and then a couple, three more on the stairway before the one she was following cut right again, through a swing-door and into a cramped, too-warm kitchen.

There were another two kids at the stove—older kids, Algaina thought, though none of 'em was tall enough to look like anything but a kid to her.

Not even the one standing at the table, working with a spoon in one hand and something else in the other, a plate set before him, and a couple small bowls.

"Donnie, there's a lady," the red-haired mite said, and turned to look up at her.

"Here you are, lady."

And was gone.

Donnie looked 'round from his work, eyebrows lifting slightly on seeing her, his face a study in unsmiling politeness.

"Baker Algaina. It is good to see you. Did the cookies please?"

"The cookies more than pleased, which is something I'd like to talk with you about, when you're less busy. In the meanwhile, I brung your plate back, with a little something to say thank you . . ."

She glanced around. There didn't seem to be any room on the work table. There didn't seem to be any room, anywhere. Every surface was full, and there were kids underfoot, and . . .

"Kevan," Donnie murmured, and one of the kids at the stove turned, gave her a frank smile, and slid the plate out of her hands.

"I'll take care of that," he said, and his Terran was good—not 'bleaker, but not sounding half-learned, neither. "Thanks very much, Miz—?"

"Now, no Miz called for. I'm Algaina from the bake shop down the street, like your brother here says."

Dark eyes flicked to Donnie, back to her.

"Miz Algaina, then. Thank you; we always appreciate something extra with dinner." He turned back to the stove, uncovering the plate, and showing it to his partner there.

Dinner, she thought. They was cooking dinner, with all these pots 'n pans. Dinner for—

"How many kids you got here?" she asked Donnie, before she had a chance to work out if that was the kind of question he was likely to answer.

Turns out, it wasn't.

His eyelids flickered.

"Some few," he said quietly. "If you do not . . . mind, we may talk now." Another quick glance at her before he said over his shoulder.

"Velix, take Miz Algaina's coat and hat to dry. Cal Dir, bring her a cup of tea. Ashti—"

A stool appeared even as her coat and hat were whisked away to hang on a peg near the stove, and steam that smelled like flowers rising from the mug that was put in her hand.

She took a careful sip, just enough to discover that the tea tasted like the steam. Then, she put both hands around the mug, and watched Donnie make another one of . . . whatever it was it was he was making.

Flowers, birds, leaves . . . all somehow fashioned from one scoop of whatever was in the bowls, and him working with a spoon.

He put the latest creation—a fish—on the plate with the others, and she sighed in mingled pleasure and frustration, which caused her host to look straight at her.

"There is a problem? The tea does not please? We have—"

She held up a hand.

"The tea's wonderful, thank you. It's only—I just watched you make that, and I can't figure out how you did it."

He smiled then—she could tell more by the way the corners of his eyes crinkled up than from his mouth curving, and it come to her then that Donnie wasn't as young as she'd taken him, even on second look. In fact, now she was close, she could see there were some few threads of silver mixed in the dark brown hair, and lines worn in 'round his eyes and mouth.

Still might be the older brother, she thought, at least to some of the kids. An' he wasn't gonna tell her nothin' about 'em at all. Well, she thought, taking a sip of tea, why should he? He didn't know anything 'bout her; and the kids had to come first.

'Course they did.

"Once you have made a few dozen, it comes without thought," he was saying. "These are *chernubia*. Small sweets, to have with mid-morning tea, after the first work of the day is done."

She watched him make two big wings connected at the center; she didn't think it was a bird. Something from his home, prolly. Way she'd heard it, there were a lot of things on his homeworld that never'd quite made it to Surebleak, nor weren't likely to ever arrive.

"I tell you what," she started, and then stopped, turning on her stool to discover the reason for the sudden ruckus out in the hall.

The mob in the kitchen shifted, one kid going out the door with a big bowl held in both hands, calling out what might've been names. She'd scarcely cleared the room when another took her place—older, though younger still than Donnie. This one was wearing a tool-belt and a couple shirts, Surebleak style, heavy over lighter, and a knit cap on his head.

"Jax Ton!" Kevan called from the stove. "I don't think we made enough food!"

"All is well, little brother; I will be satisfied with your dinner, only."

That was greeted with laughter, and a little one came running into the room, arms working, yelling, "Jax Ton! Jax Ton!"

"Kae Nor!" the newcomer called back, and swooped the kid up into his arms, spinning in the tight space like he had the whole street to dance in. The child screamed with laughter; and was still laughing as he was transferred to another pair of arms, to be toted out of the kitchen.

"Jax Ton," Donnie said quietly, and here he was, slipped in close, right between her stool and the table, like it was all the room anybody needed.

"Don Eyr," he said, quietly, and paused, his eye drawn to the plate of fanciful shapes.

"*Chernubia* in cheese and vegetables?" he asked. "I do not think this is one of your better ideas, brother."

"Elaytha has become afraid of her dinner," Donnie—no, Algaina corrected herself, *Don Eyr* said levelly.

Jax Ton looked solemn.

"Badly?"

"Very badly."

"Will this cast work, do you think?"

"It is all that I *can* think," Don Eyr said, sounding suddenly weary. They'd forgotten she was there, Algaina thought, and sat very still while they talked family around her.

"I am happy you came tonight," Don Eyr continued. "She needs a Healer. Can you find if they will they see her at the hall here?"

"They see Terrans at the hall here," Jax Ton said. "They *train* Terrans at the hall here. I will take her with me when I go back to work."

"We cannot leave her alone among strangers . . ."

"Which is why Kevan will accompany us. He will bide with her, and I will join them after the boss is done with me. They will neither be bereft."

Don Eyr took a breath, sighed it out.

"The cost?"

"If the child needs a Healer, that is where we begin. We do not count cost against need." Jax Ton extended a hand and gripped the other's shoulder. "So you yourself taught us."

Don Eyr half-laughed.

"Did I? A poor influence on soft minds, I fear."

"Never that," said Jax Ton.

He removed his hand, and seemed to see her for the first time.

"My apology," he said. "I—"

"Jax Ton, this is Miz Algaina from the sweet bake shop. Our neighbor."

"Ah!" Jax Ton smiled like he'd been born on Surebleak. "Welcome, neighbor. I am Jax Ton tel'Ofong—or Jack O'Fong, according to my boss."

"Pleasure," Algaina assured him. "You live here, too?"

"I am 'prenticed to Electrician Varn Jilzink, in Boss Torin's territory. It is too far to travel every day, but I come home here for my day off."

"It's good to be with family," she said.

"That is truth," Jax Ton said solemnly, and turned back to his brother, who was holding out a plate full of fanciful shapes.

"Do you think that you might try?"

"Of course, I will try, though it likely means I will have to eat a carrot *chernubia* myself."

"The carrot *chernubia* are very good," Don Eyr told him gravely.

"Everything you bake is very good. Where is she?"

"Upstairs. In the tent."

Jax Ton's smile faded somewhat.

"Ah, is she? Well, as I said—I will try. Miz Algaina, I hope we will meet again soon."

He was gone, bearing the plate, and it came to Algaina that the kitchen was empty now, save for herself and Don Eyr. There were still voices to be heard, but down the hall, in another part of the house.

"Well." Don Eyr turned to her. "Now, at last we may address your topic."

"I don't wanna be keeping you from your supper," she said, "so I'll be quick. I'd like it if you made cookies like you sent down to me this morning, an' some of those *shernoobias*—sweet ones at first, then we'll try and see if the veggies'll sell—"

There was the smile again—easy to see now she knew what to look for.

"I figure the split to be seventy for you, thirty for me. I buy flours and other supplies wholesale, you can buy from me at my cost, if that'll suit. Anything special you need . . ."

She let it run off and waited, taking a sip of her tea, which had gone cold, but was still tasty.

"I will like that," Don Eyr said slowly. "When do you wish the first baking, and how many?"

Algaina smiled, and leaned forward.

"Okay," she said. "Now, here's what I'm thinking . . ."

• • •◇• • •

DON EYR had gotten up early, to see Jax Ton and Kevan and Elaytha on their way, with two pails packed with food and *chernubia*. Elaytha had been so excited to be going with Jax Ton that she scarcely had time to give him a hug. It pained him to let her go, but that was foolish. Jax Ton and Kevan would keep her safe, both knew her moods and her foibles, and Kevan understood—or seemed to—a good deal of the language she had created for her own use.

He hoped the Healers would see her.

He hoped the Healers would effect wonders.

He hoped . . .

Well.

In the end, it was good that he had the baking to do; it kept him aside of worry, even as he was reminded of other days—better days—when he was up early to bake for the shop in Low Port, and Serana would slip in, cat-foot, to make tea, and sit on a stool to watch him. The early morning had been their time, when they reaffirmed their bond, and their curious orbit, each around the other.

He had expected her to leave, many times over the years.

Serana had a warrior's heart; she had been born a hero, fashioned for feats of valor. Caring for children—for gormless bakers—wasted her.

And yet, she had stayed . . .

. . . until that moment when her skills were at last called for, and she had not hesitated to take the lead.

He took out the first batch of spice bars, and slipped the second into the oven. He had a brief moment of nostalgia for his ovens, then shook his head. What was, was. This oven, this kitchen, was perfectly adequate for the baking of a few batches of sweet things.

At . . . home, he had made loaves, cheese rolls, protein muffins—sweet things—those, too. But it had been the bread that drew customers in, and provided the household income.

He had spoken of bread to Miz Algaina. Her kitchen was also too small to accommodate large baking, nor, she confided, did she have the knack of yeast things.

He had the knack, but his bread-heart was lost in the shambles of Low Port, with his ovens, and the library, and the homey things they had amassed over the years. Algaina had spoken of a larger house at the far end of the street, beyond the gate. It had been part of the former boss's estate. There were ovens, she said, and quarters above that were more spacious than those of the Wayhouse.

They might, so he understood, petition the Council of Bosses Circuit Rider to relocate to this other house. He would have to show that the property would be put to "use and profit," so it was even more important that this venture with Algaina prove successful.

He also understood that the granting of the petition would go easier, if he secured the support of the rest of the neighbors—and here, too, Algaina had offered her aid. All the street came into her shop, and she would talk about the idea. It would also be useful, she said, if he worked the counter a couple hours every day to show the world his face.

This made sense, and was something he could easily accommodate. Without the shop, now that they were settled again, together, he found himself with few duties. The elder children taught and cared for those who were younger, with any disputes brought to Ashti, who now stood as his second. It would be good, to have work, and to meet their new neighbors.

The timer chimed, and he removed the second batch of spice bars from the oven.

While they cooled, he looked in the coldbox where the *chernubia* prettily adorned their plates. He glanced at the clock and did a quick calculation. Yes, he did have time to make a batch of quick cheese rolls—not real bread, but satisfying enough. Perhaps Algaina's customers—his new neighbors—would find them pleasant.

• • •✧• • •

WELL, that might not've been the best decision she'd ever made in her life, Algaina thought, but it'd sure do for now.

She waved day's done to Don Eyr and Velix, and locked the door behind them. He'd taken to bringing one of the kids with him on-shift, so the neighbors would get to know all of them.

Don Eyr taught her his way with the hermits—spice cookies, according to him—so that baking came back into her shop, while he continued to provide *chernubia*, and day-rolls. She'd shown him the receipt for flaky pastries, and the sorry result of her efforts. He took it away and brought back a plate of buttery crescents so light she feared they'd float out the door and into the sky.

An' more than his baking improved the shop. He'd brought in two more hot-pots, each with a different kind of tea—one fruity and light, and the other grey and energizing. Her pride was piqued at that, and she ordered in a better grade of coffeetoot, for them that had the preference.

Luzee saw that people wanted to linger over their sweet and their cup, so her and Binni Bodyne went together to get some old tables from down the cellars up into the street, then wheedled a hand o'kids, including one of the Wayhousers, to scrub 'em clean.

Erb Fliar come down to see what all the commotion was about, went back inside his place, an' a half-hour later reappeared, holding a bolt of red-and-white checkerboard cloth.

Well, Pan Jonderitz knew just what to do with that, din't he just? An' while he was doin' that, Luzee organized *another* hand o'kids to clean the windows and wash the walls, and by the time it was all done . . . din't it just look fine?

Better'n the place lookin' fine, and bidness bein' up, Don Eyr was making a good impression on the neighbors, and the kids were, too.

The best sign she saw, though, was the afternoon she walked to the door to close up for the day, and there was a confusion of kids running 'round the street, armed with snowballs—street kids, Wayhouse kids—all of 'em shouting with laughter.

The only oil on the ice was Roe Yingling.

If he came into the shop while Don Eyr was on counter, he turned on his heel and left. He quizzed her on each roll, cookie, and cupcake to find which'd been made by *them* and flatly refused to try any of it—even when a sample was offered for free, which was just unheard of.

Worse, he didn't see any reason why *they* should move into the old catering house. If *they* needed more space, *they* could find some other street to live on. Sleet, they oughta buy their own damn place up on a hill somewhere; everybody knew the newbies was rich. Look at the Road Boss, bringing his own damn *house* with him, on account of nothing on Surebleak was good enough!

Well, fine, *they* could do what *they* wanted—somewhere else. Chairman Court hadn't asked for 'em, Chairman Court didn't need 'em, Chairman Court was better off without 'em—and *that*, by sleet, was exactly what he was gonna tell the council's circuit rider, next time she was by.

Algaina shook her head.

Roe was only one voice, after all, she told herself. There was still the whole rest of the street who liked Don Eyr and his kids just fine. All they had to do was say so.

Everything would be fine.

· · ·✧· · ·

THE HOUSE was noisy when he and Velix entered, having done their shift at Algaina's shop. Not merely noisy, thought Don Eyr, stopping with his hand on the lock, head tipped to one side—jubilant.

He stood, listening, Velix at his side, until one voice rose above all the others Velix was off, running down the hall toward the gather-room, shouting, "Fireyn!"

Hope flared in his breast, so fiercely he could scarcely breathe, yet somehow his feet were moving, not quite Velix's headlong flight, but quickly enough that he was in the room before his heart had settled; sweeping in, gripping an arm, wringing a hand, taking in the familiar faces of his kindred-in-arms, those who guarded the children with him—

"Ail Den," he murmured; "Cisco. Fireyn—"

He stopped, searching faces gone suddenly still. It was Fireyn who gripped his hand, and Ail Den who caught him 'round the shoulders, even as he whispered—

"Serana?"

"No," Cisco said, voice rough, his face thinner, worn, and wet. "Old friend, no. We were separated. We searched, we checked; the mercs counted out their wounded, and the dead . . . Serana . . ."

"We lost her," Fireyn finished. "We had hoped . . . she was already with you . . ."

He took a hard breath, ears roaring; an edge of darkness to his vision. All three of them closed 'round him in a comrade's embrace, while he gasped, trembling, and saw . . .

. . . the bright palace of his hopes crumble beneath the weight of truth. Crumble, flicker, and die.

* * * ⟡ * * *

"SO, THAT INFLATABLE TENT we found in the cellar when we went down to get the tables?" Binder cuddled against her chest, Luzee was talking to the crowd pushed in as tight at they could be, some sitting at tables, some standing 'round the walls.

"Well, that tent was special made for the year-end block party. I got all the information right here!" She raised the binder over her head and shook it like a bell.

"Happens that The Chairman threw a party for all the Grade Six an' belows, at the end of the fiscal year. It was s'posed to increase morale and team-buildin'. I showed this to the Lady and to the Perfessor, and they both said that one of the things that pulls people together is a shared holiday. They was wonderin' if us here on Chairman Court wouldn't like to follow the directions in this Human Relations manual, and throw a block party. The Bosses'll be invited, to see how it works out, and might be next year, Surebleak entire'll have a block party, and . . ."

Algaina went into the back and pulled out a tray of cookies. Spice cookies, they were. She'd made an extra batch for the meetin', which was good, because there wasn't nobody, always exceptin' Roe Yingling, who didn't like the spice cookies.

But it was also a bad thing, because they reminded her of Don Eyr . . . who hadn't been in to the shop for more'n a week, which was bad enough. Worse was the notion that he wasn't baking, neither.

"Don Eyr is . . . ill," Ashti had told her. "He will come again when he is able. In the meanwhile, two of us will come to you every day, to give you rest, as we have been doing. We do not wish to stint a neighbor."

Stint a neighbor? Algaina thought, and—

"How sick is he? Can he bake?"

"He . . ." Ashti had closed her eyes and taken a deep breath. "I regret, not at the moment. None of us has his touch with *chernubia* or the other small sweets. We may continue to provide rolls; several of us are proficient."

"Rolls, yes; that would be good—people like the cheese rolls. But—I don't want to meddle—should he see a medic? Or I could come and take a look—"

"Our medic has rejoined us," Ashti said. "She is watching Don Eyr very closely."

She'd managed a smile then, shaky, but true.

"He is dear to all of us, as to you. We will not lose him."

• • •✧• • •

HE OUGHT TO STAND, he thought, for the dozen dozenth time that day. He ought to leave this room, and be sure that all, and everyone, was well. The children needed—but no.

Ail Den, and Cisco, and Fireyn were home. The children had no further need of him. He was free to leave, to strike out again alone, as he had wished so often to do, when they had first come into Low Port, on a day-job.

Day-job. What use was he on a day-job? But, there, his delm had called him home, the least of the clan's children, to fulfill a debt owed to Clan Arba. The terms of settlement required an agent of Clan Serat to hold himself ready at all times to fulfill those tasks Arba required of him.

Serana had come with him; his bodyguard, as she explained herself, which Arba found to be a very fine joke, and so it had been the two of them, sent down to clear a newly-inherited parcel in the Low Port.

Clear it of *debris*.

They had not understood the nature of the *debris* until they arrived at the corner they were to clear.

Eight children and one barely past halfling; their leader, who had promised them safety, and, judging by his grip on the piece of pipe he had chosen for a weapon, was prepared to die for his word.

Together, the three of them cleared the area. He and Serana, they had thought they would establish the children safely, give their protector advice, and such small funds as they held between them— a few days spent, only that.

They had been fools.

Over time, they had gathered to themselves, to their service, other fools, and so the children were kept safe.

Serana had died, to ensure their safety, and he—

He heard the door open; raised his head, and took a breath. It was Ashti, perhaps, come to tempt his appetite, or—

"Donnee?" came a high, sweet voice, followed by Elaytha herself, unruly hair braided; cheeks plump; eyes wide and bright.

"Ah, *shintai*. Donnee *zabastra kai*."

"Elaytha," he murmured. "Welcome home, child."

"Welcome home," she repeated in a tired, flat voice, and climbed into his lap, putting her arms around his neck, and leaning her forehead against his.

"Donnee is filled with light," she said, in a voice he did not recognize. "*Shintai goventa*."

• • • ✧ • • •

JAX TON WAS IN THE KITCHEN, eating soup. Velix, at the stove, immediately filled another bowl, brought it to the table with a mug of tea, and slipped away, leaving them alone.

"Ail Den told me," Jax Ton said softly, rising. "*Al'bresh venat'i*, brother."

They embraced, cheek to damp cheek.

"The child is a Healer?" Don Eyr asked, when they sat again to the soup.

"The child *will be* a Healer," Jax Ton corrected him. "She shows some early ability, which, while unusual, is no cause for alarm. She has received instruction in controlling her gift, and also in its best use."

He cocked his head.

"I would say that, so far, her training has been adequate."

"Indeed. However—trained in best use, young as she is?"

"As I understand it, once a gift has manifested, it cannot be denied. So, yes. As young as she is."

He spooned soup; looked up.

"The Healers will want her back with them for a full evaluation and training on her twelfth name day. In the meanwhile, they have Healed her of most, if not all, of her terrors. My challenge lately has been to feed her *enough*."

Don Eyr smiled.

"They did not Heal her of talking nonsense."

Jax Ton moved his shoulders.

"It is, according to the Healers, not an affliction; it causes her no distress; and creates no impediments for her in daily life."

"Ah," said Don Eyr, and pushed his empty bowl aside.

"What other news do you bring me?"

"Boss Jilzink's associate has taken Kevan to 'prentice. He will learn the art of resource reclamation from Esser Kane, who has several teams working for him, and sees in Kevan a future leader of a new team. Master Kane is well and favorably known to the Employment Office. Kevan will tell you all, when he comes home on his day off."

"Soon, we will be scattered all over Surebleak," Don Eyr said, not without dismay.

"Children grow up," Jax Ton said, and reached to catch his shoulder in an affectionate embrace. "This is what you set yourself to do, brother, and I will tell you that there is not a morning that I wake in which I do not thank the gods, should they exist, that it was you and Serana who came that day. I had promised to keep them safe, but you—you kept my honor for me."

"You do me too much—"

"That is not possible," Jax Ton said firmly, letting him go.

"I have one more piece of news, which may not be so delightful as I had hoped, as Ashti informs me that you have given over baking."

Don Eyr looked at him.

"Perhaps I shall begin again, if the news is of interest."

"Well, then, I bring it forward at once! There is a baker in Boss Conrad's territory, with an established shop, who is interested in adding Liaden delicacies to her offerings. I may have shared one or two of your *chernubia* with her. If you would be willing to provide these to her, non-exclusively, she will pay you a percentage of the profit, and will seal the contract with a portion of her mother-of-bread."

· · ·◇· · ·

THE BLOCK PARTY hadn't been much of a spense to The Chairman, Algaina thought grumpily. Management provided the tent, and some prizes, and—all right, bought the beer and the desserts. Most everything else, though, was made and brought by the guests. Eating each other's food and trading receipts was s'posed to be good for morale and team-building.

There were games set out in Luzeal's binder, and a timeline of how things were s'posed to go. F'rinstance, there was a space o'time put aside where everybody said what their best accomplishment had been in the last year. An' another space o'time when the year's just-borns were called by name.

An' a space o'time right at the beginning of the party where everybody stood in a circle, and said outloud the names of those who'd died during the year.

Algaina'd made a batch of almost everything in grandpa's receipt book, and had the neighbor kids moving them out of the shop the second the tables went up inside the tent. For drinks, Erb Fliar'd promised to put out tea, 'toot, juice, an' beer—*light* beer, he'd added. No sense anybody getting stupid.

Algaina was pulling on her bright green sweater, which was too good to wear in the bake shop, when the bell over the door rang.

She turned around, and there was Ashti, and Elaytha, and Jax

Ton, and Velix, all carrying a tray of *chernubia*, each one looking different.

She looked at Jax Ton.

"He's better?"

"Better, yes." Jax Ton smiled and nodded at Elaytha. "He said to tell you that the *chernubia* on that tray are made from carrot, and kale, and cheese."

She laughed, in equal parts relief and fun.

"Well, that's just fine. You come with me and we'll get them set up in the tent." She looked at each of them, sharply, in turn.

"You're all comin' to the party, now?"

"Yes," Ashti said. "All of us are coming to the party. We are sent ahead with the trays."

"Good," said Algaina, and added, believing it for the first time since Luzeal had decided on having a block party; "it's gonna be fun."

• • • ◇ • •

DON EYR CLOSED THE SACK, and crossed the kitchen for his coat. The others had gone ahead, leaving him to pack his contribution to the shared meal alone.

His offering—his personal offering—to the goodwill of their neighbors was bread—a small loaf for each. He had also made a loaf—one loaf only—of Serana's favorite: a crusty, chewy round, with a dense, nutty crumb.

Coat on, he shouldered the sack and left the wayhouse. It was snowing, densely, diffusing the tent's glow into an iridescent fog.

The street was filled with the sound of voices, and laughter, and for a moment, he stood, frozen in the snow, every nerve in his body marking Serana's absence.

A deep breath; a memory of the light Elaytha had given him. Serana was here, because he was here; her memory, as her life, a benediction.

Centered, he walked the short distance down the street, then out of the snow, into the bright warmth of the tent.

"I ain't sitting here with them!"

Roe Yingling's voice soared over the pleased chatter of those gathered.

"They invaded our planet! They took our jobs! They ain't really people! Sure, they want a party, let 'em have their own party, and let us real 'bleakers alone!"

Carefully, Don Eyr put the sack down on the table by the door, and moved across the room, toward the man confronting Jax Ton, with Ail Den and Cisco flanking him, and the others spread behind.

"Roe," that was Luzeal, moving between the angry man and the children. "These are our neighbors. They don't stint the street, an' nor do you, nor anybody here! We're neighbors, we depend on each other."

The man threw his hand out, pointing at Elaytha, who had stepped out from behind Jax Ton.

"It ain't bad enough that they don't belong here, but they're broken, too! That one can't even talk!"

That brought a hush, shortly broken by a quiet voice.

"I can talk," Elaytha told him, evading Jax Ton's hand, and walking forward until she stood before the man in all his anger. She glanced at Don Eyr as he arrived, near enough to kick the man's legs out from under him, if he dared try to—

Elaytha smiled and looked up at Roe Yingling.

"You can be more happy," she said. "You don't need to be angry. You don't need to always want to be mad."

"Why you—" Roe Yingling began—and stopped, a perplexed look on his face.

"What do you know about what I want?" he said, at a somewhat lesser volume. "Newbie can't know what I want. Strangers can't . . . How can I tell you what I want?"

"Don't you want to be more happy? You came to the party to be more happy. Have a *chernubia*, or a cookie. What do you want? Which?"

The crowd closed, listening. Elaytha leaned toward him, hands in a gentle gesture of request, eyes locked on his.

"What I want is . . ."

It seemed to Don Eyr as if he swayed.

"Roe?"

A woman came out of the crowd, glanced at Elaytha, and took the man's hand.

"I'm sorry, missy," she began; "he's a good man, but sometimes he don't think before—"

"What I want is," he tried again, his face losing tension, "is a *reason* to be happy. Can you understand that?"

Ashti stepped around Jax Ton, bearing a tray of *chernubia*. She paused at Elaytha's side.

"A reason, yes," Elaytha said. "Please, take a sweet. Be happy with the day. Be happy with your neighbors. You will feel better—"

Don Eyr felt that last strike hard against his chest; the child was performing a Healing, here and now? He held his breath as she plucked a flower from the tray, and offered it to the man on upraised palm.

"This is very good, made by my brother. Please, take it. Be pleased with it. Do not be mad at everything, and you will not hurt so much! Look, we have a party. The neighbors have a party. Better is now. For your friends, be happy."

He stared down into her face, then, like a man in a dream, he took the *chernubia* from her hand, and ate it. A long sigh escaped him; there was no other sound in the room.

"Roe?" his wife asked, putting her hand on his arm. She looked down at Elaytha, eyes wide, and Don Eyr tensed, even as Luzeal stepped up, taking each by an elbow, and turning them toward a table at the side of the room, where two children were watching, eyes wide.

"She's right, Marie," Roe Yingling said suddenly. He stopped and looked around the tent as if he had just woken to the realization of the gathering.

"She's right," he said, more loudly. "I don't *hurt* . . ."

"Well, who could hurt," Luzeal said practically, "with one of them good sweet things inside you? Now, you just come on over here and have a sit-down, Roe Yingling . . ."

In the back corner of the tent, someone said something, and someone else laughed. Don Eyr felt a small hand slide into his, and looked down into Elaytha's smile.

"Will that last?" he asked her.

She frowned slightly.

"Maybe?" she said, and moved her shoulders. "*Kai zabastra, kai?*"

A sound, then, of quiet engines, and someone near the entrance called out that the Bosses were here.

Most people moved further into the tent, finding chairs and tables. Luzeal and Algaina were heading for the entrance—the hosts, Don Eyr understood, coming to greet the Bosses.

He stepped back to let them pass, and Algaina reached out to catch his free hand.

"You, too!" she said; so he and Elaytha joined the reception line, just as a dark haired man—Boss Conrad himself, he heard someone whisper, loudly—stepped into the tent, shaking the snow from his hat. He paused, turning back to the entrance, one hand extended to the woman who followed, leaning heavily on a crutch, snow dusting her cropped red hair like sugar.

She paused, just short of the Boss's hand, and threw out the arm unencumbered by the crutch, but Don Eyr was already moving.

He caught her in an embrace perhaps too fierce. She was thin, so thin, and the crutch . . .

"I said I would come back to you," she whispered roughly into his ear.

"Even a cat comes to her last life," he answered. "Cisco, Fireyn, Ail Den—they lost you in the fighting; the mercs had no records."

"All true. But not dead. Quite."

"I'm a fool," he answered, and, even softer, "What happened?"

"I will tell you everything, my small. But, for tonight—you must introduce me to our neighbors."

✧ Degrees of Separation ✧

DEGREES OF SEPARATION happened because, once we'd written Block Party at Tony Daniel's request, we looked at each other and said, "Well, fine, but, really who are these people?" We'd known someone had to have done what they did, but once the story box opened, we discovered that bakers can be choosers.

✧✧✧✧

ONE

Liad

IN THE PORT CITY of Solcintra, on a certain day in the third *relumma* of the year called *Phantione*, a boy was delivered to the delm of Clan Serat, who did not want him.

Serat had a son; Serat had a nadelm, twelve years and more the infant's elder. Furthermore, Serat maintained a regular household, and had no need of a second in the delm's line. Most especially *not* the child of a sister who had failed both Line and Clan.

Still, to refuse the boy—Don Eyr, as he had been named, exactly the name of the previous delm of Serat—would be to invite scandal, and Serat did not indulge in scandal. He was, therefore, given a place in the empty nursery, and thereafter forgotten by the delm, his uncle, and unregarded by his cousin, who was away at school.

He was *not* forgotten by the household staff, nor by the clan's *qe'andra*. These persons were after all paid to tend the interests and the business of the individuals who together were Clan Serat. The delm having issued no instruction other than, "Take it away, and see it trained," in the case of his sister's child, Don Eyr received all the benefits and education which naturally accrued to a son of Serat.

Save the affection of kin.

The boy himself did not notice his lacks, for he was well-regarded, even loved, by staff.

His nurse was inclined to be gentle with an isolated child, and collaborated with the House's *qe'andra* in the matter of his education. He had a quick intelligence, did Don Eyr, an artist's eye, and a susceptible heart. Very like his mother, said Mr. dea'Bon, the *qe'andra*, who had served the House since the days of the current delm's father. She ought never have been sent to mind the outworld business; her talents had better been used at home, administering the clan. Well, well. Delm's Wisdom, of course; doubtless he had his reasons, for the best good of the clan.

The boy Don Eyr early showed an interest in baking, and the pastry cook took him into her kitchen to show him the way of cookies, and tea tarts. When he mastered those, she taught him filled pastries, and cheese rolls.

The day he came to the notice of his cousin, the nadelm, he was removing a loaf from the oven in the back bakery, under the supervision of the kitchen cat, and Mrs. ban'Teli, the pastry cook. He had a wing of flour on one cheek, his hair was neatly, though unfashionably, cut, his hands quiet and certain. He wore a white apron adorned with various splashes, over white pants and a white shirt with the sleeves rolled, showing forearms already well-muscled.

"The nadelm, younger," his companion murmured, rising and bowing to his honor.

The lad lifted his eyes briefly from his task, and gave a civil nod.

"Cousin," he said, gravely—and set the pan he had just removed onto a cooling stone, before turning to the work-table, and picking up another pan, which he slid carefully into the maw of the oven.

The nadelm had only lately come from school, and was not so much accustomed to having his rank recognized. In his estimation, the lad had been perfectly civil, given that he had work in hand. Therefore, he waited patiently until the pan was settled, and the oven sealed.

"I wonder," he said, once these things were done and the boy turned back to face him. "I wonder if you might not have an hour to spend with me, Cousin. I feel that we should know each other better."

Don Eyr's gaze shifted toward the oven, doubtless thinking of the pan so recently deposited there. Mrs. ban'Teli stirred.

"I will stand for the loaf, young master, unless you think me unworthy."

A smile adorned the grave face, and the nadelm was able to make the judgment that Don Eyr was a pleasant looking child, in a modest sort of way.

"Yes, of course I think you unworthy!" he said with full good humor. "I suppose you will even turn out the first loaf when it is cool without my asking that you do so!"

"I might at that," the old woman said with a smile. She nodded to him, her voice taking on the brisk tones of an aunt, or a nurse.

"Take off your apron, wipe your face, and attend your cousin, child. I was baking bread before either of you were born."

The nadelm found himself a little put out by this familiarity from a servant. Don Eyr, however, merely said yes, pulled off his apron, wiped his face and stepped forward.

"Where shall we go, Cousin?"

· · ·◇· · ·

IN FACT, they went into the garden, the nadelm not wishing to meet the delm just yet. He had spent much of his time away at various schools and fosterings. He did not know his father well, though he knew his delm somewhat better, and his young cousin, here—well, he knew the boy's mother had died on Ezhel'ti, where she had been sent by the previous delm to mind the clan's off-world affairs, with an eye toward increasing profit.

Instead, the clan's businesses had faltered, and finally collapsed, under her care, which his father, the delm, swore she had done a-purpose, in order to bring ruin to Serat. The question of why she might have subsequently committed suicide, if she had failed a-purpose, he waved away with wordless contempt. The woman had been disordered with envy; she had wanted nothing more than Serat's Ring, and so the former delm had sent her away, as he had sent away his own brother, who had also aspired to Serat's Ring.

The nadelm, who was no fool, and who furthermore had learned how to do research and analyze information, had discovered that there had been an adjustment in the markets very soon after Telma fer'Gasta arrived to take up her duty. Ezhel'ti had been flooded with cheap goods when its sister planet unilaterally devalued its currency. Much history had been gathered from Serat's *qe'andra*, who had of course received reports every *relumma*, as well as the occasional personal letter.

The clan's businesses had been only a small portion of those destroyed by this rapid economic readjustment, and, from the records that she had forwarded to Mr. dea'Bon, it was plain that Telma fer'Gasta had very nearly preserved Serat's holdings. It had been a close-run thing, indeed, and for a time it seemed that she would hold the line. She had navigated the rip tide, she sold and consolidated wisely, she had—but in the end, she made an error; a small error, as their *qe'andra* had it, but it had been large enough, in those times, in that place. Certainly, she knew how news of this blow to the clan's fortunes would be received. It troubled the nadelm that she had chosen to kill herself; that action speaking to a . . . disturbing understanding of her delm and her brother.

She had placed her child in the care of her long-time lover, whose babe it likely was—and no shame, there, either, so the nadelm had discovered. The lover's clan was above reproach; their *melant'i* impeccable. Which is doubtless why they had sent the child to Serat.

All that to the side, the *nadelm* spent an informative and pleasant hour with his young cousin in the gardens, parted with him amicably at the staff's entrance to the kitchens, and went immediately to seek out his father and his delm.

Serat was in the informal parlor, reading the sporting news. He looked up sharply as the nadelm entered, and put the paper aside.

"Well, sirrah? And how have you busied yourself your first day at home in the fullness of your *melant'i*?"

The nadelm paused at the wine table, poured two glasses of the canary, and brought them with him to the window nook where his father sat.

He placed one glass on the small table by his father's hand, and kept the other with him as he settled into the chair opposite.

"I busied myself by meeting with our *qe'andra*, so that I might better know how Serat is fixed—which very duty you gave to me, Father, so *do not* stare daggers."

"Eh. And how are we fixed?" Serat asked, picking up his glass and sipping.

"Well enough, so Mr. dea'Bon tells me, though we are not perhaps expanding as well as we might do to maintain our own health."

"dea'Bon's been singing that song since the day I put on Serat's Ring," his father said sourly. "There is no harm in being conservative."

"Indeed, no," the nadelm agreed, "though there may well be harm in allowing ourselves to ossify."

"Pah."

"But that," the nadelm said, "is something for us to discuss at our business meeting tomorrow." He sipped his wine.

"After the *qe'andra*, I spent a very pleasant hour in the garden, becoming acquainted with my cousin, your nephew."

"So you wasted an hour which ought better to have been used in the service of the clan?"

"Not at all," the nadelm said calmly.

It was too bad that he had found his father in one of his distempers, but, truly said, it was more and more difficult to find him elsewise. He sipped his wine, leaned to put the glass on the table, and settled again into the chair.

"The boy is one of Serat's assets, after all, Father, and you *did* charge me to learn how we are fixed." He paused; his father said nothing.

"So. I find that we are fortunate in our asset," he continued, taking care not to speak the lad's name, which would surely send his father into alt. "He is a bright lad, who has been well-taught, and who has thought about his lessons. His manners are very pretty, and his person pleases. His nature appears to be happy, and generous. Staff is devoted to him. He's young, of course, but after some finishing at a school, and a bit of society polish, I believe he will do the clan proud in the matter of alliance and—"

"Send him away!"

The nadelm blinked out of his rosy picture of the future to find his father bent stiffly forward, imperiling both glasses and table, his face rigid with anger.

"I beg your pardon?" he said, startled by this sudden change of temper. "Will you have him gone to school, sir?"

"Yes—to school, or to the devil! Staff devoted to him, is it? Scheming get! I know his game; haven't I seen it played before? Get the staff cozy in his hand, turn them against us. He thinks I don't suspect? No—send him away! He will not subvert our house with his schemes!"

The nadelm—stared. Then, he reached across the table, took up his wine glass and drank the contents in a single swallow.

"Father . . . you do comprehend that we are discussing a boy barely halfling? There is not the least bit of subterfuge. The staff love him because, frankly, sir, they have had the raising of him, and it pleases them to see him do well. If you would bring him closer to us—have the lad at the table for Prime, for the gods' love! He's too old to dine in the nursery, and he would be glad of the company. If he has fallen into error, you might teach him better."

"There's no teaching those born to deceit," Serat stated with the air of making a quote, though from which play, the nadelm could not have said. "Send him away, do you hear me? I want him out of this house by the end of the *relumma*."

"But, Father—"

Serat stood and glared down at him.

"You've done a valuable service to the house this day, worthy of a nadelm! You have found the plot before it came to fruition. We may act—we must act! See to it."

And with that, he turned and left the room, leaving the nadelm gaping in his wake.

. . .✧. . .

"SCHOOL?" Don Eyr said, frowning slightly at Mr. dea'Bon.

"Indeed, young sir. The clan would see you properly educated. The choice of institution has been left for you and I to determine between us. Now, I have on the screen a file of catalogs, sorted by primary studies. Please sit here and examine them while I pursue my other work on behalf of the House. When Mr. pak'Epron brings us our tea, we shall talk about what you have discovered.

"Is this agreeable to you?"

School, thought Don Eyr, with a quickening of interest. Mrs. ban'Teli had spoken about schools—famous schools on far-away planets.

"Yes, sir," he said to Mr. dea'Bon. "Thank you."

"There is no need to thank me, young sir. It is my pleasure to serve you."

With that, the elder gentleman moved over to the big desk and the 'counts books. Don Eyr sat at the side table and considered the catalog file. Arranged by course of study. He extended a hand, and scrolled down the list, until he came to Culinary.

He opened that catalog and took a moment to consider, eyes half-closed, attention focused inward.

Mrs. ban'Teli had spoken of many schools, as he remembered— several of them with respect.

But she had spoken of *one* with reverence.

. . .✧. . .

"I SEE," Mr. dea'Bon said, when he was presented with the list of one school which Don Eyr felt he would wish to attend.

"This is a very challenging choice," he continued, with a glance at the boy's bright face. "I wonder if you have considered all of these challenges."

"It is off-world," Don Eyr said, "so I will of course be obliged to live at school, and will not be able to help with the House's baking. But you know, Mrs. ban'Teli said to me just recently that she has been baking bread since before I was born, so I suspect she can train another boy very handily."

Mr. dea'Bon blinked, and inclined his head gravely.

"Just so. It is very nice in you, and proper, too, to think of the House first. However, I had been thinking that, in addition to going off-world to live at school, you will be required to acquire a new language—not merely Trade or even Terran—but the local planetary language. All of the classes are taught in that tongue."

"Yes," said Don Eyr, apparently not put off in the least by the prospect of not only learning a new language, but hearing nothing else from the time he rose until the time he sought his bed, every day, for . . . years.

"My tutor says that I have a good ear for languages," the boy added, perhaps sensing Mr. dea'Bon's reservations. "He also says that I have been very quick learning Terran."

Mr. dea'Bon blinked again, thinking of Delm Serat, his inclinations, and stated opinions regarding off-worlders of any kind, and most especially Terrans.

"Your tutor has been teaching you Terran?" he asked, and did not add, "Does your uncle know?"

"He is, indeed. Terran is spoken by a great many people living off-world, and, as my mother was sent off-world to mind the clan's interests, my tutor says the same may be required of me, so that it is only prudent to learn."

"I see. Well, then, you foresee no difficulties in learning yet another tongue. You realize, of course, that you will be alone, with neither clan or kin to support you—" Not that he had such support in any wise, but one could scarcely name Mrs. ban'Teli in a discussion of this sort.

"Yes, I am aware. But there will be other students, after all, and the instructors, so I won't be *alone*."

"Quite," said Mr. dea'Bon, and played his last ace.

"Let us suppose that you will be accepted into this . . . ah—*École de Cuisine*. You will have one semester to prove yourself. If you fail to be the sort of student the Institute expects, you will be sent back home."

He tapped the list of one.

"You have made no provision for a back-up," he said. "Your delm has made it clear that you will be going to school. Therefore, in respect of his wishes, you must choose at least two more schools to which you will apply."

The boy stilled; his smile faded—and returned.

"Yes, of course," he said. "A moment only, sir, of your goodness."

He leaned over the catalog, tapped two keys, and leaned back.

Mr. dea'Bon looked at the names of two more institutes of baking, and allowed that the rules of the game had been followed.

"That is well," he said. "Now, you will be required, also, to comport yourself as a Liaden gentleman, upholding the *melant'i* of Clan Serat. It will therefore be necessary for you to learn the Code and other necessary subjects, in addition to the coursework required by the school. Your tutor will work with you to build those study modules."

He paused; Don Eyr bowed.

"I understand," he said

Mr. dea'Bon did not sigh.

"That is well, then. If you permit, I will ask my heir to assist you in filing your applications."

"That is very kind in you, sir," Don Eyr said. "My thanks."

TWO

Lutetia

CAPTAIN BENOIT of the Lutetia City Watch was bored. Society parties as a class tended to be stifling on several levels. Captain Benoit preferred the night beat in the city. Best was the university district, where she could feel the cool damp breeze from the river against her face as she walked. But, truly, any of the city beats—the outside city beats—were preferable to standing against the wall like a suit of armor, to insure that Councilor Gargon's guests didn't stab each other—literally—or steal the silver, or—the worst fault of all—injure the Councilor's feelings.

In point of fact, the City Watch was not supposed to stand watch over private functions. Councilor Gargon, however, was the Patron of House Benoit, and therefore commanded such small personal services.

Fortunately, Councilor Gargon, unlike other Patrons Captain Benoit could name, possessed some modicum of restraint. House Benoit was most generally called when the Councilor was hosting a party, or giving one of her grand dinners. For the workaday world, she was satisfied with her Council-assigned bodyguards.

Tonight, the party was in the service of winning votes for the Council's scheme to route a monorail through the Old City. The Old City was protected by hundreds of years of legislation—no modern road could be built through it. That had lately become a problem because the New City had expanded, sweeping 'round the Old like a river 'round a rock. One might, of course, walk through the twisting, narrow streets of the Old City, or bicycle—but scarcely anyone did so. In main, citizens used jitneys, or rode the trains, or drove their own vehicles. They were in a hurry; it took too long to go through the Old City—and the journey around the walls was becoming almost as long, what with the knots traffic routinely tied itself into.

Councilor Gargon was, as she so often was, on the conservative side of the issue. The radicals would drive a battle-wagon into the Old City, punching a straight line through its heart, which would become a wide highway, a short route from one side of the New City to the other.

The monorail . . . found little favor among busy citizens of the New City. The monorail was seen as a ploy, an effort to forestall progress, perhaps of use to tourists, or the indolent students, but who among the busy citizens of the City had time to queue up at a monorail stop, and crawl over the ruins?

Thus, the party, and the trading and calling in of favors. Captain Benoit, who loved the Old City, tried to recruit herself with patience, but—truly, she would rather be out on her usual beat.

If you can't be where you'd rather, be happy where you are. That had been one of *Grand-père* Filepe's advisories. He had long been retired from the Watch by the time Captain Benoit had taken up her training arms, a ready source of wisdom, humor, and, often enough, irony, for the youngers of the household. He was not, of course, her genetic grandfather, nor any blood relation at all. House Benoit, like all the City Watch Houses, recruited their 'prentices from among the orphans of the city, of which there were, unfortunately, many.

House Benoit was one of eight; and second eldest of the Watch Houses. Common citizens were not, of course, trained in arms, or in combat. The arts of war were for the members of the Watch alone. All who came to Benoit, took the House's name, and training, and bore the burden of the House's honor.

There.

The caterers were bringing the desserts out to the long tables, laying down plates of *chouquettes, macarons, petit fours, éclairs.* Captain Benoit sighed. She was especially fond of sweets, and tonight's party was being catered by the *École de Cuisine,* which was justly famous for its pastries, cakes, and small delights.

Ah, here came one of the younger students, bearing a *dacquoise,* and after her another student, carrying a platter of fruit bread sliced so thin one could see through each one . . .

The guests were converging upon the table—and who could blame them? The younger student and the dark-haired youth who appeared to be the manager of catering, stood ready to assist. Others bustled about a second table, bringing out fresh pots of coffee, pitchers of cream, and little bowls of blue sugar that sparkled like fresh snow.

The younger student seemed somewhat nervous. The manager touched her arm, and she looked to him with a smile, her shoulders relaxing. Captain Benoit frowned, and brought her attention to those approaching the table.

Ah, merde, she cursed inwardly. Vertoi was here. She had not previously seen the Councilor among the guests; she must have come late. Vertoi was trouble, wherever she went; especially, she was trouble for those who had no standing, and therefore could neither resist her, nor demand justice from the Council. Vertoi being a Councilor, the common court had no call upon her; and she imposed no restraints upon herself.

Vertoi had an eye for beauty, and the younger student, now that Captain Benoit had taken a closer look, was very fine, indeed.

The catering manager took up an empty plate that moments before had held a mountain of *petit fours*, and handed it to his fair young assistant. She nodded, and left the table for the kitchen, just as Vertoi came up in the queue, her shoulders stiff and her face stormy.

Captain Benoit tensed. Vertoi was not above personally reprimanding an inferior, physically and in public, and she suddenly feared for the young manager's health.

He, however, seemed not to notice her displeasure, but leaned forward, his eyes on her face, his hands moving above the tempting sweets, discussing now the fruit bread; now the *éclairs* . . .

Vertoi turned away, leaving the manager in mid-discussion, holding an empty dessert plate. He put it behind the table, and turned to greet the next guest, his face pleasant and attentive.

She had seen him before, Captain Benoit realized. Seen him at the Institute loading bays, when dawn was scarcely a red-edge blade along the top of the walls, supervising the loading of trays onto a delivery van. In the afternoon, she had seen him, too, filling the beggars' bowls at the university district's main gates. She had noted him particularly; compact and neatly made, his movements crisp and clean. A pretty little one; and something out of the common way among the citizens of Lutetia, who tended to be tall, brown, red-haired, and rangy.

As if he had felt the weight of her regard, the manager raised his head and caught her gaze. His eyes were dark brown, like his hair. He gave her a nod, as if perhaps he recognized her, too. She returned the salute, then a drift of dessert-seekers came between them.

· · · ✧ · · ·

HE HAD SENT SYLVIE back to the Institute in the first van, with the empty plates and prep bowls. She, and the other three who went with her, would have a long few hours of clean-up in the catering kitchen, but he rather felt that she would willingly clean all night and into tomorrow, so long as she was not required to bear the attentions of Councilor Vertoi.

Don Eyr sighed. She was becoming a problem, this councilor—not merely a problem for Sylvie, who, so far as he knew, lavished all of her devotion upon a certain promising young prep cook. No, Councilor Vertoi was beginning to pose a problem for the Institute and for the affairs of the Institute. Pursuing Sylvie while she was on-duty was a serious breach of what he had learned as a boy to call *melant'i*—and which he had learned here was an insult to the dignity of the Institute, its students, and, above all, to the directors. He would of course report the incident to his adviser, as part of this evening's—well. *This morning's* debriefing. He was quite looking forward to that approaching hour, sitting cozy in Chauncey's parlor, tea in hand, and a plate of small cheese tarts set by.

Don Eyr did the final walk-through of the small prep area, finding it clean and tidy. He sighed, took off his white jacket, and folded it over one arm. Catering was not his preference. If he were ruled only by his preferences, he would be always in the kitchen, baking breads, and pastries, cakes . . . He felt his mouth twitch into a wry smile. Perhaps it was best, after all, that the directors insisted that all students learn catering, and production baking, and the other commercial aspects of their art—all of which would be useful, when he opened his own *boulangerie* . . .

Satisfied with the condition of the prep room, he signed the job off on the screen by the door, releasing copies of the invoice to Councilor Gaigon's financial agent, and to the Institute's billing office. A note would also be sent to his file, and to Chauncey's screen, so that gentleman would know when to start brewing the tea.

Don Eyr put his hand against the plate, the door to the delivery alley opened, and he stepped out into the cool, damp, and fragrant night.

The door closed behind him. Before him, the van, Keander likely already asleep in the back. Don Eyr shook his head. Keander could—and did—sleep anywhere, which might be annoying, if he did not wake willing and cheerful, eager to perform any task required of him.

He reached the van, hand extended to the door—and spun, ducking.

The move perhaps saved his life; the cudgel hit the van's door instead of his head, denting and tearing the polymer.

Don Eyr spun, saw his attacker as a looming, dark shadow between himself and the light, and launched himself low and to the right, half-remembered training rising, as he kicked the man's knee.

A grunt, a curse.

The man staggered, but he did not go down, and Don Eyr spun again, kicking the metal ashcan by the gate.

It rang loudly, though it was a vain cast. Keander could sleep through any din, though the softest whisper of his name would rouse him.

"Dodge all you like, little rat," came the man's voice, as the cudgel rose again. "Councilor Vertoi sends her regards, and a reminder to stay out of her business."

He swung again, and Don Eyr drove forward, catching the man 'round both knees and spilling him backward onto the alley.

The ash can produced another clatter as the cudgel, released from surprised fingers, struck it; and Don Eyr rolled away.

"I will kill you," the man snarled, and Don Eyr, on his knees by the service door, saw him roll clumsily, heaving himself to his knees, even as a second shadow moved in, and with one efficient move kicked those knees out from under him, and delivered a sharp blow to the back of the head.

Straightening, this one moved to the pool of light, revealing herself as the Watch Captain he had most lately seen at the councilor's party, tall and fit, with her close-cropped red hair and her light eyes.

"Are you well, *masyr*? Do you require my assistance?"

"I am well, thank you, Watch Captain," he said, hearing how breathy and uneven his voice was. "I believe I will stand."

He did so, and stood looking up at her, while she looked down at him.

"Your arrival was timely," he said.

"Yes," she agreed, and shook her head.

"That was *most* ill-advised, *masyr*. This man has been trained to fight and to inflict damage. To attempt to meet him on his own terms . . ."

"What else might I have done?" he answered, perhaps too sharply. "Stand and have my head broken?"

She was silent for a long moment, then sighed, and spread her fingers before her.

"The point is yours, but now I must ask—who taught you to fight? Is this a part of the Institute curriculum?"

He laughed.

"Certainly not! A course of self-defense was taught me, before I came here. It was years ago, my tutoring of the most basic, and—as you observe—I scarcely recalled what little I had learned."

"No, no, having taken the decision to defend yourself—you did well. A man of peace, surprised at your lawful business, and, I make no doubt, exhausted from your labors this evening. Our friend, here, he had expected an easy strike, and now he will wake in the Watch House, with a headache, a fine to pay—and an account of himself to be made to his mistress that will, I expect, be very painful for him."

She stepped back, clearing his way to the van.

"Please, be about your business, *masyr*, and I will be about mine."

"Yes," he said.

He turned, after he had opened the van's door.

"Thank you, Watch Captain."

She straightened from where she had been placing binders on the fallen attacker.

"My duty, *masyr*. Good-night to you, now. Go in peace."

"Good-night," he said, and climbed into the cab, and drove away.

• • •✧• • •

POLICEMEN AND CRIMINALS were not so very much different. So said *Grand-père* Filepe. Certainly, they tended to know the same people, to drink in the same places, to roam the same streets at very nearly the same hours.

So it was that Serana Benoit was at a table in a shady corner of a particular cafe on a small street near the river, eating her midday meal, when she heard a word, spoken in a voice she recognized.

The first word was followed by several more, forming a sentence most interesting. Serana closed her eyes, the better to hear the rest of it. The proposition was made, and, after a short pause, accepted, for the usual fee. Serana opened her eyes, and turned to signal the waiter for more wine, her glance moving incuriously over the occupants of the table to her right.

Yes, she had recognized Fritz Girard's voice; his companion was . . . Louis Leblanc. That was . . . disturbing. Unlike the hired bullies attached to the wealthy, who were used to express their masters' displeasure by way of a broken arm or a sprained head, Louis Leblanc performed exterminations. Showy, public exterminations, meant to remove a nuisance, and also to inspire potential future nuisances to rethink their life-plans.

The waiter arrived with a fresh glass, and Serana turned back to her lunch, ears straining. There came the expected haggling over price—perfunctory, really—before the two rose and left the cafe in different directions.

Serana finished her lunch, paid her bill, and returned to her beat, troubled by what she had heard.

• • •✧• • •

"THAT'S THE LAST," Don Eyr told Silvesti.

The delivery driver nodded, made the rack fast to the grid inside his truck, and jumped down to the alley floor. He was taller than Don Eyr, as who was not? His mustache was grey, though his hair was still stubbornly red. There were lines in his face, and scars on his knuckles. He worked for the distributor, and before the day broke over the city walls, all of the breads, pastries, and other fresh-baked things from the Institute's kitchens would be on offer in restaurants across the city.

"A light load this morning, my son," Silvesti commented.

"Yes; one of our bakers did not arrive for her shift. Had she allowed us to know, we would have found someone else. As it was, we were half done before her absence was noted."

He handed over the clipboard.

"Here is the distribution list. When we understood what had happened, we contacted the restaurants. Three were willing to forgo pastries today for extra tomorrow, so that the rest may have their normal share—though no extras, today."

"Understood." Silvesti took the clipboard, running a knowing blue eye down the list, before glancing up.

"You've made extra work for yourselves tomorrow," he observed, "and a baker down."

"No, we'll call in some of the promising juniors, and let them see what the production kitchen is like."

"Scare them into another trade," Silvesti said wisely.

"Perhaps. But, then, you see what a similar experience did for me."

The delivery driver laughed, and tucked the clipboard away into a capacious pocket.

"Some never learn the right lesson, eh? Until next week, my son."

Don Eyr watched the van drive out of the loading yard, filling his lungs with air damp from the river. This was when the city was quietest; very nearly still. Occasionally, there came the sound of a car moving over damp 'crete, some streets distant; or a ship's bell, far off in the middle of the river. It was not, perhaps, his favorite time of the day—there being some joy to be found in beginning the day's baking, and also the hour in which he taught the seminar . . .

Still, this early morning time was pleasant, signaling, as it did, an end to labor for a few hours, and a chance to—

A boot heel scraped against the alley's 'crete floor, and he turned, expecting to see Ameline, come out with her coffee and her smoke stick, as she often did, to sit on the edge of the loading dock to relax after her labors among the cakes.

But it was not Ameline, nor any other of the Institute.

"Watch Captain Benoit," he said, taking a certain pleasure in her tall, lean figure. She was not in uniform this evening, but dressed in leggings and a dark jacket open over a striped shirt.

"This day, only Serana Benoit," she said gently. "I hope that I did not startle you, *masyr*?"

"I had expected one of my colleagues," he answered. "My name is Don Eyr fer'Gasta. I think that our introductions the other evening were incomplete."

"Indeed, there was much about that encounter which was shabbily done," she said, walking toward him, her hands in the pockets of her jacket.

"I am here . . ." she paused, looking down at him, her face lean, and her eyes in shadow, all the light from the dock lamps tangled in her cropped red hair.

She sighed, and shook her head.

"You understand that it is *Serana Benoit*, who offers this," she said.

Melant'i. That he grasped very well. He inclined his head.

"I understand. But what is it that you offer?"

Another sigh, as if the entire business went against all the order of the universe. Her hands came out of her pockets, palms up and empty.

"I will teach you. We will build upon these long-ago basic lessons you received. A few tricks, only, you understand, but they may be made to suffice. You have become a target, *masyr*, and you had best see to your own defense."

"A target?" he repeated, looking up at her.

"Oh, yes. One does not thwart Councilor Vertoi in any of her desires. And one *certainly* does not embarrass her enforcer."

"Councilor Vertoi is not permitted to disrupt my team while we are working," he said calmly.

Serana Benoit laughed, short and sharp.

"Yes, yes, little one; you have expressed this sentiment with perfect clarity! Fritz Gerard, Councilor Vertoi, myself—none of us missed your meaning. Councilor Vertoi has done you the honor of believing you to be a serious man, and she has hired Louis LeBlanc to wait upon you."

Something was clearly expected of him, but Don Eyr could only show his palms in turn and repeat, "Louis LeBlanc?"

"Ah, I forget. You live sheltered here. Louis LeBlanc is a very bad man. He has been hired to hurt you, from which we learn that Madame the Councilor considers that you have damaged her reputation and so may show you no mercy."

Chauncey had a pet; a green-and-red bird that had learned to say certain amusing phrases. Don Eyr felt a certain kinship with the bird now, able only to repeat her own words back to her.

"No mercy? He is to strike me lightly on the head?"

Serana Benoit looked grim.

"Were you of Madame's own station, or in the employ of one of such station, Louis would have been instructed to kill you. That is mercy at Madame's level. She has, regrettably, seen that you are a catering manager, a mere minion who must be taught his proper place."

She took a breath, and added, softly.

"Louis . . . Understand me, I have seen Louis' work, and speak from the evidence of my own eyes! Louis will break all of your bones, not quickly; abuse tendons, and tear muscles. Perhaps, yes, he will strike you in the head, but I think not, for Madame will want you to *know* why you have become a cripple, and a beggar."

He stared at her, seeing truth in her face, hearing it in her voice. There were, perhaps, a number of things he might have said to her, then, but what he did say was . . .

"Come into the kitchen. There is tea—and bread and butter."

* * * ✦ * * *

HE WAS AN APT STUDENT, Don Eyr, a joy to instruct; supple and unexpectedly strong. When she mentioned this, he had laughed, which was pleasing of itself, and said that flour came in thirty-two kilogram sacks.

She could wish that several Benoit apprentices were so willing, adept, and of such a happy nature. And as much as she enjoyed teaching him, she enjoyed even more their time after practice, when they would adjourn to the little room behind the kitchen, for a simple snack of tea and bread, and talk of whatever occurred to them.

Very quickly, she was Serana, and he was Don Eyr. She told him such bits of gossip as she heard in the course of her duties, and he told her such *on-dits* as had filtered into the Institute's classrooms and kitchens. She told him somewhat of life in House Benoit, and was pleased that he enjoyed even *Grand-père*'s saltier observations.

For himself, he was the lesser child of his family, which he considered luck, indeed, as it had allowed him to pursue his talent for baking.

Yes, she enjoyed his company. Very much. Perhaps she watched him with too much appreciation; perhaps she regarded him too warmly. But she did not act on these things—he was a student, after all, clearly some years her junior, and she was his teacher.

It would not have done, and she did not need *Grand-père* to tell her so.

As for the training—apt as he was, he would never defeat Louis. The best he might do would be to surprise and disable him long enough to run to some place of safety. Whereupon the hunt would begin again. Louis might even become fond of the child, if he gave good enough sport, and one shuddered to think what *that* might come to, when he was, as he must be, at the last—caught.

Still, they trained, and two weeks along there came the news that Louis LeBlanc had been taken up by Calvin of House Fontaine, caught in the very act of threatening a citizen. Serana knew Calvin; had known him very well, indeed, when they had both been foot soldiers for their Houses. It had been some time since she had sought him out, but she had done so after that news had hit the street.

"The Common Judge gave him four weeks, non-negotiable," Calvin said, drinking the glass of wine she'd bought him. "In four weeks, plus one day, he will be on the streets again."

"Is there any likelihood of a pattern-of-behavior charge?" asked Serana.

Calvin shrugged.

"The father had said some such at first, but he's quiet now."

"Bought off?" Serana guessed, sipping her own wine.

"Or frightened off." Another shrug and quizzical glance.

"Why do you care? Even if Louis is permanently removed, another will rise to fill the void." He raised his glass, as if in salute. "There must always be a Louis; to keep the Councilors from going to war."

"It may be that a replacement Louis will enjoy his work less," Serana said, and shrugged. "One might hope."

"This is on behalf of the new lover?"

"New student," she corrected.

"So? Does Benoit agree to this?"

"No need for Benoit to agree to what I do on my off-hours," Serana said, which was not . . . precisely true. "Besides, he came from off-world, half-trained and a danger to himself and our fellow citizens. I make the streets safer by teaching him."

"A baker, I hear," said Calvin.

"You have big ears, my friend."

Calvin laughed and drank off the last of his wine.

* * * ◇ * * *

"WHEN," she asked Don Eyr as they sat together over their quiet tea. "When will you graduate?"

"Graduate?" He looked amused. "I graduated two years ago. I have completed my coursework, and taken the certification tests for master baker, pastry chef, and *commis* chef. At the moment, the Institute employs me to teach an introductory workshop in breads, and an upper level seminar in pastry. Two days, I work in the test kitchens; one day I supervise the distribution baking; and, as you know, I manage one of the catering teams."

Serana blinked, realized that she had been staring, and raised her tea cup.

Don Eyr began to butter a piece of bread.

"Soon, I will need to make other arrangements," he said. "Chauncey has been trying to entice me to stay and become faculty— to teach, you know."

"You do not wish to be a teacher?" Serana managed.

He put the butter knife aside and glanced up at her.

"In many ways, teaching is enjoyable, especially when one has an apt pupil. But, no. I want to *bake*, to feed people, and bring joy to their day. I have determined to open my own *boulangerie*."

His own bakeshop, bless the child; and she had thought him too young to understand her.

"A shop here—in the City?"

He laughed, dark eyes dancing.

"No one opens a *boulangerie* in Lutetia! What would be the point, when the Institute supplies all of the restaurants and coffee houses, and could easily supply a third again more?"

"You will leave us, then?" she persisted, which both relieved her, and filled her with a profound sadness.

He gave her a grave look.

"I think that I must, and I have a plan, you see. When I wrote to . . . my family's accountant, to inform him of my certifications, and graduation, he wrote back with information regarding certain accounts and properties which are mine, alone.

"My mother left me a property—a house and a some land—on Ezhel'ti. Those funds have, in part, been supporting me here, with the remainder being placed into an account which Mr. dea'Bon has held in trust for me. The house and the account came to me upon graduation. I have been researching Ezhel'ti, and it seems a very promising world, with two large metropolitan areas, and a scattering of smaller towns. It remains to be seen if a city or a town will suit me best, but my intention is to emigrate and open a *boulangerie*."

He gave her a small smile.

"Mr. dea'Bon is retired from my clan's business, and finds himself wishing for a little project to keep him entertained. He has offered to advise me, which is kind. Certainly, I shall have need of him."

"Indeed," she said, and put her tea cup on the tray. "It may be wise, to leave as soon as your planning allows," she said, her lips feeling stiff. "The rumor inside the Watch is that Louis LeBlanc will be off the streets for four weeks, no longer. Since it is possible for you to remove yourself from danger . . ."

"I must stay until the end of the term," he told her. "I have signed a contract."

"How long?" she asked.

"Eight weeks. But after—"

"Yes, after. I advise, make your arrangements now."

"I will," he said, as she rose.

"You are leaving?"

"I have the early Watch tomorrow," she lied. "Good-night, Don Eyr."

"Good-night," he said, and rose in his turn to open the bay door and see her out.

· · ·✧· · ·

THE PEACEFUL ROUND of weeks flowed by, each day bringing its rewards. Don Eyr had dispatched letters, received some replies, and written more letters. He and Serana had kept to their schedule of sparring and suddenly, it was the day of Louis LeBlanc's release from mandatory confinement.

He would not have said that the date weighed over-heavy on his mind, though naturally he had noted it. And truly, he did not begin to worry until he left for their usual meeting.

He arrived in the practice room before her, which was not *so* unusual. He occupied himself with warm-ups, and moved on to first-level exercises.

When he finished the set and she still had not come—*then* he began to worry. It was ridiculous, of course, to worry after Serana, who was a Watch Captain and fully able to take care of herself—and any other two dozen persons who happened to be nearby. But he worried, nonetheless. He reminded himself that she had missed their meeting on two previous occasions, and had turned up, perfectly well, if appallingly tired, at the Institute, later, wanting her tea and buttered bread—and, more than that, someone to talk to about commonplaces, and simple things. It pleased him that she came to him for comfort on those nights when her duty was a burden. But, he could not help but recall that her duty might see her maimed, or killed, much as she might laugh off that aspect of the matter.

"You will worry yourself into a shadow, little one, if you worry about me. I have more lives than a cat—*Grand-père* has said it, so you know it is true! I may be late, but always I will come back to you, eh? My word on it."

Yes, but today—today an especial danger had been released back onto the streets, and he might be assumed to be angry about his recent confinement, and seeking to wreak havoc upon those whom he judged to be most responsible.

Surely, being the sort of man he was, LeBlanc would consider Serana's friend Calvin at fault, but Serana had told him that the Commander of the Watch had decided to hold Calvin at headquarters for the first day of Louis LeBlanc's renewed liberty, and also to set a guard around the Common Judge who had sentenced him.

These were, so Serana said, temporary measures, to give LeBlanc time to work off his ill-humor, and reconnect with his usual sources.

Work, said Serana, with a certain amount of irony, seemed to exert a steadying influence over Louis LeBlanc.

Don Eyr finished his workout early, without Serana to spar with, and returned to the tea room, where he took special care with this evening's snack; her favored blend of tea; and thin slices of the crusty, chewy bread she had declared—rather surprising herself, so he thought, with amusement—the best she had ever eaten, beside which all other so-called breads were revealed as impostors. He added a dish of jam to complement the butter, and stood looking down at the tea table, wondering what he would do, if she did not come tonight.

The bell rang then, and he hurried down the hall, looking by habit at the screen—and it was Serana standing there, in her Watch uniform, her face in shadow, her posture stiff. He took a breath, and pulled the door open.

She followed him silently down to the tea-room, and stood, silent yet, just inside the door.

He turned, and saw her face clearly for the first time that evening.

"Serana, what has happened?"

She looked at him, her face haggard, eyes red, proud shoulders slumped.

"Come in."

He stepped up to her, and caught her arm, leading her to the table; saw her seated in her usual chair. Then, he crossed the room to the small cabinet, opened it, and poured red wine into a glass. He set it before her, and commanded, "Drink."

She shook herself slightly, and obeyed, downing the whole of it in two long gulps, without appreciation, or even full knowledge of what she did. No matter; it was a common vintage, and it seemed to be doing her some good. Her pale green eyes sparkled; and her shoulders came up, somewhat.

"Good," he said, and took the glass away to refill it, and to pour one for himself.

He came back to the table, and sat across from her.

"Tell me," he said.

She blinked, then, and seemed to fully see. She smiled somewhat.

"Peremptory, little one," she murmured.

"Ah, but I am a manager, and a master baker, and a blight upon the lives of my students," he told her. "Arrogance is the least of my accomplishments."

Her lips bent slightly; perhaps she thought she had smiled.

"So," she said; "I will tell you. Louis LeBlanc died today. Badly."

He blinked, taking in the uniform. Serana did not come to their meetings in her uniform. She came always as Serana Benoit; never as Watch Captain Benoit. He sipped wine to cover his shiver.

"Do you think I did this thing?" he asked.

She laughed, and it was terrible to hear.

"You? No, I do not think that."

She raised her glass and drank.

"No?" he asked. "A man in fear of his life . . ."

She slashed the air with her free hand.

"A man in fear of his life would not have *had time* to do what was done to Louis," she snarled, horror and anger in her voice. "And you, little one—you are not capable of what I saw. You are my student; I know this."

She turned her head aside, but not before he saw the tears.

He took a careful breath.

"Serana—" he began.

"Oh, understand me; I have no love for Louis LeBlanc. But the manner of his death, and the timing of it . . . It is a message, from one Councilor to another, you see; and such a message—it will be war, now, between the ruling houses, but *they* will not bleed! No, they will use us as little toy soldiers, and we will die—for what? The world will not be made better; and when the war is over, or the point is won—another will rise to become the next Louis LeBlanc. It will all be the same, only we will be fewer in the senior and novice ranks, and there will be more orphans from which to recruit replacements . . ."

There was a breathless moment, before she repeated, in a bitter whisper.

"*Replacements.*"

He was an idiot; he could think of nothing to say, to ease her. She had told him the history of House Benoit—told it lightly, as if it were a very fine joke. But, now . . .

"I am not a coward. I am not afraid to do my duty," she whispered. "But my duty is to protect the citizens, not to kill fellow Watchmen!"

He did not remember rising, or going 'round the table. He barely remembered putting his arm around her shoulders, and feeling her press her face against his side.

"Of course you are not a coward," he murmured. "You are bold and honorable. Can you not appeal—" Appeal to whom? he thought wildly. If the Councilors were at war, surely the City Council would not rule against them.

"The Common Judges?" he ventured. "Can they not issue a restraint, releasing the Watch from such orders?"

She made a sound; perhaps it was a laugh.

"Don Eyr's twisty mind works on," she murmured. "That is a particularly fine notion—and it was tried, the . . . last time the Councilors went to war. They simply ignored the order, and had those of the Watch and the judiciary who protested killed."

He closed his eyes.

"Don Eyr."

She shifted in his arms, and he stepped back, letting her go as she straightened in her chair. She caught his hand, and looked into his face.

"Don Eyr," she repeated.

"Yes, my friend. What may I do for you?"

She laughed, soft and broken.

"You make it too easy," she said, and drew a breath, keeping her eyes on his.

"I would like to make love with you, little one."

He hesitated. She released his hand.

"I am maladroit," she said. "Please do not regard it."

"No, I *will* regard it," he said, taking her hand between both of his. "Only—to *make love*. I may not have the recipe. But, this I offer—that I value you, and would willingly share pleasure; give and receive comfort. Indeed, I have wished for it, but while we stood as teacher and student—"

"I see it," she said, offering a small smile, but a true one; "we are both fools."

"That is perhaps accurate. I propose that we now teach each other—I will learn to make love . . ."

"And I will learn to share pleasure. Agreed, but—"

She glanced about them, and he laughed.

"No; let us to my rooms; we may be private there."

"Yes," she said, and rose.

* * * ⬦ * * *

HIS ROOMS, at the top of the Institute . . . His rooms were neat, and modest; the bed under the eaves big enough for both, so long as she was careful of her head.

There was a window, which she learned later, after he had risen and left her in order to see to the day's first baking. It was marvelous, this window; one could oversee the entire City, even the Tower of Memories in the heart of the Old City.

Her City, that she loved; her City, that she served and protected.

There would be war; that was certain. A few days, perhaps, of quiet, while the Councilors gathered themselves, and made certain of those Watch Houses which were sworn to them. Benoit's patron was Gargon, of course. Fontaine's patron was Vertoi. It was not to be expected that she would stand shoulder to shoulder with Calvin in this, or with his sister, or any other of her comrades at Fontaine. No, this time, they would be set at each other, like dogs thrown into the pit, while the owners watched safely from above, and perhaps placed wagers on style, and form.

Her stomach cramped, and she turned away from the window, and the view of her City, to survey this place where her little one apparently spent all too few hours at rest.

There was a screen on a small table, under a bright light, a tidy pile of bills or letters placed to the right of the keyboard. Across the room from the bed stood an armoire so large it was certain that the room had been built around it. Beyond the armoire, an archway, through which more light streamed.

She stepped into a small kitchen. A teapot steamed gently on the table next to that sunny window, and the inevitable plate of breads; butter, cheese, and cold sausage. This window overlooked the river, a happy breakfast companion.

After she had eaten, and washed up, and refilled the teapot against his eventual return to his rooms, she showered in the tiny bathroom, and donned her armor, and stood looking down at the bed, recalling what had taken place there.

A sweet lad, indeed; generous and wise; and if he had not made love, then certainly he had given pleasure in full measure.

And Serana Benoit? Serana Benoit was a greater fool than even she had supposed herself to be. What precisely had been the purpose of bedding the child, when she knew he was preparing—as he must!—to flee to his safe future off-world, his small property, his dreamed-for bake-shop? She would miss him—she would have missed him, profoundly, without the sweetness they had shared. All she had accomplished was to make her own loss more poignant.

Yet . . . if she were to die, as it was probable that she would, and soon; she would have this memory in her when she stood to be judged before Camulus in the afterworld.

Mindful of the low ceiling, she bent and made the bed, smoothing the coverlet, catching the lingering perfume of their passion.

A deep breath, and she turned away, moving to the dark corner of the room, to the left, where she recalled the hall door had been.

A piece of paper was pinned to this portal, somewhat lower than her nose. She squinted at it, and found a neat, hand-drawn, map, guiding her to the nearest outside door. At the bottom of the map, was a note.

It is an interesting recipe, my friend. I would enjoy making more love with you. If you would also enjoy this, let us meet for wine at Paiser's this afternoon when our shifts are done.

She smiled, and tucked the note inside her armor, next to her heart.

. . .✧. . .

SHE BROUGHT HIM FLOWERS, of course. He was worth every rose in the City, and she would not stint him, though it *was* Paiser's and she would shortly be known as a besotted fool in every Watch House and bar in the city. No matter: there were things far worse than to be known as a doting lover.

He rose to take the bouquet from her, dark eyes wide with pleasure. She had exercised restraint, and the flowers did not, quite, overpower him, and in any case it *was* Paiser's and here was the waiter, murmuring that he would place them into a vase for *maysr* and most immediately bring them back.

"I ordered wine," Don Eyr said when they were both seated. "I did not know if you wished to dine, or . . . how you wish to proceed."

Proceed? She thought. She wished to proceed to his rooms—hers were too public for this affair—and undress him, slowly, running her hands over silky, golden skin . . .

Her imaginings were too vivid, and Don Eyr perceptive, as always.

"Perhaps not here?" he murmured, and she laughed.

"Perhaps not."

She paused at the return of the waiter, bearing a vase overfilled with roses, and a second, bearing a small stand. This was set at the side of their table in such way that the flowers formed a fragrant screen, shielding them somewhat from the rest of the room.

"*Maysr* has bespoken a bottle," the first waiter said. "Shall I bring it? With some cheeses, and fruit? A basket of bread, perhaps?"

"Serana?" Don Eyr asked and she smiled at him.

"All of it. Let us linger, and make plans."

He understood, and she was delighted to see a blush gild his cheeks with darker gold. She leaned toward him and lowered her voice.

"I have the night watch tomorrow," she murmured. "And you?"

His blush deepened, and his eyes sparkled.

"I," he said his voice low and sultry, "will ask Chauncey to lead the advanced seminar this evening."

• • •✧• • •

THE WAR was being fought in skirmishes, at the fringes of the city, and the few injuries sustained thus far were minor. Perhaps the Councilors were being discreet; perhaps they sensed a reluctance among their toy soldiers. They were positioning for advantage; feeling out the temper of the streets; searching for the flashpoint that would ignite violence.

Lots had been drawn at House Benoit, as at the other Watch Houses. Short straw placed you on the Council Watch, which had the duty to protect the City, and whose loyalty was to the Council. This was by necessity a short-term assignment, the Council not being plump in pocket, and was in any case a moot point.

Serana had drawn a long straw.

She did not tell him this. Of course not. There was no need to concern the child, who would be well out of everything in a matter of two weeks. Instead, she listened to him talk about his plans for this bake shop he would build on the world that was not Lutetia, far from the City, far from Serana, safe from the war brewing on the streets.

"Serana, only listen!" he said, looking up from his latest letter with eyes sparkling.

"I have kin on Ezhel'ti! My father's clan acknowledges the connection, and the delm has written to Mr. dea'Bon to say that they will give me a place as a Festival child among them, if I should wish it. Also—"

"*Do* you wish it?" she asked him, from her lazy slouch in his reading chair. She had pulled it over to the window—the window that looked over her City, and sat bathed in sunlight, her cotton shirt opened over her breasts, her hair blazing like living fire.

With difficulty, Don Eyr removed his attention from the picture she made there, and looked back to the letter, thinking about her question.

"I do not know," he admitted. "I am not accustomed to being in-clan. It would be a change, certainly; but it is all of it a change! And these people—my father's clan—they are long-time residents of Ezhel'ti, and in a very good place from which to introduce me . . ."

"Yes, so long as they are not scoundrels," she said; then wished the words back. Why blight his joy? And these people wanted him, which that wretched old man who had sent him away had never done, as she had heard in the spaces between the words in the tales he had told her of his childhood . . .

Don Eyr was smiling.

"You are suspicious, Watch Captain. You will therefore be pleased to know that Mr. dea'Bon is of a like turn of mind. He has put inquiries into motion, and assures me that there is no need to rush into an association until the facts are known. I may, he says, quite properly be busy with my own affairs for some time after my arrival."

"You are correct," she told him sincerely. "I am pleased, and relieved. Count me as an ardent admirer of Mr. dea'Bon."

"I will be jealous," he said lightly, and she laughed.

"An admirer *from afar*," she amended. "*Far* afar."

"I am soothed," he assured her, and tipped his head. "And now you are sad."

He was *far* too perceptive, she thought, and did not seek to lie to him.

"I will miss you," she said; "very much, Don Eyr."

"And I, you." He rose from the desk and crossed the room to kneel at her side and look up into her face.

"Serana," he said, softly—and she leaned forward to kiss him thoroughly, before he said the words that would bind them both.

He was made for fine things, her little one; for peace, which her own small researches had revealed was the general state of Ezhel'ti. No one knew what *she* had been born for. An orphan, she had been taken in by House Benoit, to be trained in arms and in violence.

His hands were on her breasts, strong fingers kneading. Good. She stood, bringing him with her to the bed, there to make such love between them that neither need utter a word.

* * * ❖ * * *

THEY WERE TO MEET AT PAISER'S mid-afternoon for a glass

of wine and a small luncheon. It was her free hour from patrol, and his, between test kitchen and seminar.

Serana arrived first, proceeding toward the outside tables, when she caught a movement from the side of her eye.

She continued her stroll, curving away from the cafe, now, finding two familiar faces on her left hand, moving toward her with precisely as much purpose as the two approaching from her right.

So, the Councilors had decided, she thought, calmly assessing the situation. And Serana Benoit was to be the flashpoint.

She continued to move away from Paiser's, toward the center of the small square, where there were fewer innocents to be caught in the action.

"Watch business!" she snapped at those few. "Move on, move away!"

She touched the weighted stick on her belt, but did not draw it. She did not need to draw it, one look at her face, and they moved, rushing away from danger.

There was a shout behind her, which she ignored. Jacques Blanchet could see her in hell. She supposed that she ought to be complimented, that the Councilors found her so provocative that her death would, with certainty, start a war.

Another shout. Serana smiled, grimly. Monique Sauvage could stand in line behind Blanchet.

She had reached the center of the square. She turned, quickly, the stick with its lead core coming up out of her belt, to slam into the extended right arm of Servais Tanguy. He screamed, and twisted aside, weapon falling from nerveless fingers. She spun to intercept Blanchet, kicking him in the knee with her reinforced boots. He was quick, however; the blow did not connect solidly, and here at last was Monique Sauvage, flying at her like the madwoman she was, knife dancing, while Simone Papin stood back, awaiting opportunity.

The world narrowed down to the work at hand. She managed to fell Sauvage with a blow of the stick to her temple, and there was Papin coming in, blade glittering; Tanguy rushing her off-side, shock grenade in hand, and she made the decision to let the armor take the knife-thrust—

Tanguy fell back, baiting her, and there was Blanchet spinning in from her other side. This time, the kick landed well, and she danced to one side as Tanguy triggered his toy, feeling the fizzing tingle as the armor dissipated the charge. She had broken his neck before the fizzing stopped, and turned at last to deal with Papin—

Who was lying on the stones, his neck at an unfortunate angle. From far away came the blare of an emergency wagon. Much closer stood a man in a white coat, knife in hand, point toward the cobbles. He raised his head and looked at her, dark eyes wide.

Serana took a breath.

"You fool!" she snapped.

"He was going to kill you!" Don Eyr snapped in return.

"*I* am wearing armor!" she shouted, and reached out to grab him by the shoulder. "*You* are wearing a baker's smock!"

"Serana," he began, his eyes filling. Her heart broke; she moved to embrace him—and looked up at the sound of boots pounding cobbles.

From the left came three of House Benoit. From the right, two of Fontaine.

Fontaine was nearer, the senior-most holding binders in such a way to make it clear she knew them for the insult they were.

"Serana Benoit," she said, her voice professional; her eyes sad. "You are under arrest."

She extended her hands to accept the insult, and glanced over her shoulder.

There were now two of House Benoit standing at ready, and Don Eyr was not in sight.

· · · ◇ · · ·

ONCE THE BINDERS WERE ON, and Fontaine's duty done, Benoit sued for Serana's release to the custody and discipline of her House.

The surprise was that Fontaine released her, in proper form, accepting House Benoit's honor as her bail.

The second surprise, when she emerged from her interview with Commander Mathilde Benoit, and went in search of *Grand-père* Filepe, to tell him with her own voice what had transpired—there was Don Eyr sitting in the sun on the back patio, listening with rapt attention to one of the old man's saltier tales.

She paused, her hand on the warm stone pillar. Don Eyr— someone of the house had given him shirt, vest, and trousers. He had rolled the shirt sleeves above his wrists, and left the top buttons open—in respect of the heat, which was considerable, in this little stone pocket that caught the sun even on rainy days.

Grand-père wore a shawl over thick, well-buttoned shirt and vest, for winter had gotten into his bones on a campaign outside the City when he was a young man, and had never melted away.

Or so he said.

He paused now, on the very edge of the story's bawdy denouement, raised his eyes and gave her a brief nod.

Don Eyr spun out of his chair and rushed to her, hands out, eyes on her face.

"Serana! Are you well?"

In truth, she was *not* well. As of this hour, she was a soldier without a House, in Lutetia, where war was about to erupt, and with her to blame, so far as the Councilors would tell it.

Those shames faded, however, to see him before her, unscathed, beautiful, and concerned for her well-being.

Wordless—for what could she say?—she opened her arms, and he stepped into her embrace.

Eventually, she recalled herself, and lifted her head to meet *Grand-père*'s eyes. He smiled, and nodded at the bench on his right side, where Don Eyr had been seated. A 'prentice came out of the cool, dark depths of the house, bearing a tray—wine so cold the carafe was frosty with sweat, cheese and small breads. This, she sat on the table by *Grand-père*'s hand, and departed, never once raising her head to see the disgraced soldier on the other side of the patio.

Don Eyr stirred in her arms. She stepped back and let him go, looking down into his face—a face ravaged, and why was that? Ah. She had shouted at him, and called his actions into doubt. Truly, she was a monster.

She caught his hand.

"*Petit . . .*" she began, but she had reckoned without *Grand-père* Filepe.

"Do not begin this on my porch, unless you intend a threesome!" he said, loudly enough to be heard in the house—or, indeed, at Paiser's.

Serana glared at him, but Don Eyr turned; and approached the bench, bringing her with him by their linked hand.

"Sir, we dare not," he said to the old man; "for certainly you will outstrip us."

A shout of laughter greeted this sally, even as *Grand-père* waved at the tray.

"Serana, child, serve us; then sit, so that we may plan together."

Plan? She thought, but did not ask. One did not ask *Grand-père*; one waited to be told.

She poured the wine, arranged the tray and table more conveniently for all, and settled onto the bench beside Don Eyr.

"So," *Grand-père* said, after they had savored the wine; "Mathilde has done her duty."

"She has," said Serana, matching his careless tone.

"Your lover, here, has explained how it is that he has had training of Benoit; and also how he was able to recognize and counter the particular killing strike Papin had prepared for you."

"The armor—" Serana began, and it was Don Eyr who interrupted her.

"No. Serana—that blade—it was curved. He was coming in low for a thrust and an upsweep . . ."

She stared at him in horror.

"*Under* the armor?"

"Yes," he said, and had recourse to his glass.

"But you—"

"I," he said with irony, "was a child wearing a baker's smock. I doubt he saw me, and if he did, he judged me no threat."

"And he would have been correct," *Grand-père* said, slapping his knee, "had you not learned that disarm so well, my friend! You make our House proud that you are one of our students."

Serana considered him carefully.

"Mathilde acknowledges this?"

"At first, she was inclined otherwise," *Grand-père* said airily. "She may have had hard words to say about bakers and civilians—" He bent a sympathetic eye upon Don Eyr. "You must not regard her, my friend; it was merely a release of her feelings, in order to free adequate room for thought."

"I understand," Don Eyr murmured. "And truly, it was an education."

Serana winced. The House Commander had a strong vocabulary, indeed. The rumor was that each commander logged every curse word in a massive book, kept under lock and key, and that adding to this book had been the sacred duty of Benoit Commanders for centuries.

"When it was put to her that having a half-trained citizen with a strong aversion to having his head stove in walking the street unsupervised was more of a danger to the City than producing a full-trained citizen, Mathilde did indeed rise to the occasion. A file was made, and a certificate produced. My friend here holds the rank of scholar-soldier in House Benoit."

"Scholar-soldier?" Serana repeated.

"There is such a rank," Don Eyr said beside her. "Sergeant Vauclelin would have me know that the last time it was awarded was nearly one hundred local years ago. But the rank was never removed from the lists."

"Indeed. And that rank will keep my young friend well, for the short time he remains on Lutetia. For yourself, Serana . . ."

"For myself," she said, tired now, despite the wine; "I must leave the City and establish myself elsewhere."

"That . . . was unavoidable," said *Grand-père*, sadness in his eyes. "It seems that I am doomed to lose you, child. And I would rather miss you than mourn you."

She stared at him for a moment before she recalled herself, and produced a grin which felt oddly tenuous on her mouth.

"I will miss you so very much, *Grand-père*."

He smiled at her.

"I know, child, but only think—you will never need mourn me, either."

It is true, thought Serana; I will never see him dead; he will therefore live forever.

"It would please me," Don Eyr said softly, "if you would consent to travel with me. Such a course would be all to my benefit, since I am insufficiently suspicious." He gave her a solemn look. "As has been pointed out."

She placed her hand on his knee and met his eyes.

"Little one, I would gladly come with you, but I will not be a burden to you. I have been turned out, with prejudice. To be crass, I have no money, and will have to make my way from the start . . ."

"As to that," said *Grand-père*, putting his glass aside and reaching into his vest. "I have been charged by the commander with an amount of money, which I am to give to my grandchild Serana. It is quite a considerable sum, which surprised me. I had privately considered Watch Captain Benoit something of a spendthrift. It pleases me to have been proved wrong."

He brought forth a fat wallet, and held it out to her.

Serana stared, first at the wallet, then into his eyes.

"Mathilde *agrees* to this?" she demanded.

"My child, Mathilde *proposed* this," *Grand-père* corrected, and smiled his particular, crooked smile. "She's coming along well, I think."

"So you see," said Don Eyr; "you need not be a burden, and, as you are well-funded, you may take your own decision, and not be . . . *beholden* to me."

She looked down into his eyes. His were grave.

"Serana, I would like you to come with me."

She took a breath.

"And I would like to do so," she said. "Do you think there is any possibility that I will be able to buy a berth on the ship you will be traveling on?"

"There is no need," Don Eyr said comfortably. "I hired a stateroom; there is room for both of us."

She blinked.

"You did this—when?"

"When I made my original reservations. All you need do is buy your passage."

Grand-père laughed, and rubbed his hands together.

"I like him, Serana! A man who knows what he wants, and pursues it, though others call him mad! I will miss *both* of you, in truth. And, now—"

The House bell rang—evening muster, that would be, thought Serana.

"Now," she said; "I must go."

"I fear so," said *Grand-père*. "Take the wallet, child. You will find a pack at the service gate—your clothes and other personal belongings. Take that, as well."

"Yes," she said, and rose, Don Eyr beside her.

She slipped the wallet into an inner pocket; bent and kissed the old man's cheek.

"Farewell, *Grand-père*; I will never forget you."

He patted her cheek, wordless for once. Serana stepped back— and Don Eyr went forward, bending to kiss the withered cheek in his turn.

"Farewell, *Grand-père*;" he said softly. "Thank you."

"Ah, child, would that we had longer, you and I! Take care of my Serana." A soft touch to the cheek, and a small shove against his shoulder.

"Go, now, both of you."

• • • ◇ • • •

SHE FITTED HERSELF HANDILY into his modest rooms, his quiet life. His associates in the school had long since become used to her occasional presence, and gave no sign that they noticed she was about more frequently these few last days.

She had some idea that she might assist him with his preparations, but there was not much to pack, and only a few things to give away. There was also a study-at-home kit that he dragged out of the bottom of the armoire, and stood for a moment, considering it ruefully.

"What is it?" Serana asked him.

"*The Liaden Code of Proper Conduct*," he answered, his eyes still on the kit. "My clan required that I make a study of it while I was being schooled here, as I would have done if I had remained at home."

"And did you study it?" she asked, eyeing the kit with new interest.

"Oh, yes; I passed every level. Then I put it away, and I fear that I have forgotten everything that I had Learned. There was no one to discuss it with, and I saw no need to continue after I had mastered the basics."

He threw a grin over his shoulder at her.

"Nor any need to make a review. My manner, I fear, cannot but offend."

"You have beautiful manners," Serana said, faintly shocked to hear this estimation. "And your presentation is pleasing."

"Thank you," he said, giving the box one last stare, and turning to face her.

"Will you bring it with you?" she asked, she having taken charge of such packing as there was to do.

"It is a resource, I suppose. Ezhel'ti is a composite world—Liaden and Terran. Were I Terran, I expect my ignorance would be excused. As I am Liaden, I fear I will be held to a higher standard." He sighed suddenly. "I will spend time on the journey, Learning Liaden. I have been speaking and thinking in Lutetian for twelve Standards, and I fear I've forgotten the modes entirely."

"We will practice together," said Serana; "I have ordered in a study pack for my own use, and a bundle of what purport to be *genuine melant'i plays*. Between it and your Code, we will be very busy. And here I had dreamed of a voyage spent almost entirely in bed . . ."

He laughed.

"We might study in bed, after all."

"Yes," she agreed, with a slow smile, "so we might."

It was pleasant, living thus; and the best part of the day occurred in the dark hours just before dawn, when he rose to start the day's baking.

She asked if she might accompany him—and succeeded in surprising him.

"There is nothing to see; only me, working."

"But I have never seen you, baking," Serana said, having discovered a desire in herself to observe him at every daily action. "I will be quiet and stand out of the way."

He was silent for so long that she knew the answer would be *no* when he spoke. But he in turn surprised her.

"There are stools, and tea," he told her, and added, perhaps to be clear, "Yes, you may come."

* * * ⟡ * * *

IT WAS A PLEASURE like none Serana had ever known, to sit quietly, and sip her tea, watching him at his work. He was calm, he was competent; he was unhurried and utterly concentrated. The universe held still and respectful while Don Eyr worked, and during this sacred time, no ill was permitted to intrude upon Lutetia.

She watched him for hours, and never once grew bored. It seemed to her that she might watch him for years, and be nothing other than content.

At the end of it, the sun up, and the kitchen nearly too warm, he would surrender his creations to the over-manager, and Serana would slip out to await him in the hall. They would go up to his rooms together, hand-in-hand, to make and eat their breakfast. Often, they would not care to break the silence, and she felt no lack for it.

This morning, however, the pattern varied.

An envelope had been shoved under the door while they were away. Don Eyr bent to retrieve it, and carried it into the kitchen, leaving it on the table as they put together a simple meal.

It was not until they were seated, tea poured and bread buttered, that he noticed it again—she saw him read the envelope—start— and read it again, more closely.

"Is there something wrong?" she asked.

"Nothing more than unusual," he said, picking the envelope up. "I have a letter from—from my delm."

The old man who hated the fact of him, who had sent him among strangers, careless of whether he might fail or thrive; more surely an orphan than she had ever been.

"Has he never written you before?"

"No, never," Don Eyr said, apparently finding nothing strange in this. "Mr. dea'Bon writes, and once, after I had first come here, Mrs. ban'Teli wrote. No one else."

If he found nothing strange, at least he found nothing dreadful, either. Serana lifted the teapot and refilled his cup.

Don Eyr slit the envelope open with a butter knife, and removed a single sheet of paper.

He stared at it, frowning, and she recalled his concern that he had forgotten his native tongue, having had so little use for it . . .

"I am—called home," Don Eyr said, sounding, for the first time in their acquaintance, uncertain. He looked up to meet her eyes. "Back to Liad, that is. I am to come immediately."

"Why such haste?"

"He does not say, merely to come at once; the clan has need of— oh."

She saw the blush mount his cheeks as his mouth tightened, and he raised his head again to meet her eyes.

"Oh?" she asked.

"Yes. I think I see. He has arranged a marriage for me—I can think of nothing else he might mean by *of use to the clan*."

"He has arranged a marriage?" Serana repeated. Her stomach ached, as if she had taken a punch. "But—would he not at least write you the name of your wife?"

"Not necessarily. In fact, it would be very like him to think it no concern of mine." He glanced back at the letter, mouth tight. He folded the single page, slid it into the envelope, and put the envelope on the table, address down.

He picked up his tea cup.

Serana carefully released the breath she had been holding. He was going to ignore this peremptory and rude summoning. Well, of course he was! What hold had the old man over him, now?

"I think," Don Eyr said slowly, "that we must change our plans, somewhat. You will go to Ezhel'ti, if you would, and see the house put to order, perhaps look about for a proper location for the *boulangerie*."

"Will I?" she said, watching him. "And where will you go, little one?"

He blinked at her.

"I? I will go to Liad, as my delm has ordered, and be of use to the clan. When the marriage is finished, I will join you on Ezhel'ti."

He said it so calmly, as if it made perfect sense. As if the scheming old man was his patron, and must, therefore, be obeyed!

"When do you expect that the marriage will be finished?" she asked, calm in her turn.

He moved his shoulders.

"If I recall my Code correctly, which is not very likely; a contract marriage lasts a Liaden year, on average. It ends when the child is born, and has been accepted into the receiving clan."

He sent her a shrewd glance.

"It is an alliance the delm wants. An alliance that would be good for the clan, else he would not pursue it, but not . . . grand enough to marry out the nadelm."

He was so certain about this marriage, she thought, as if there were no possibility of it going wrong. Well, she had promised to be suspicious for him, had she not?

"I will go with you," she said, nodding at the letter.

Don Eyr blinked at her.

"Serana, I do not think that you would . . . like . . ." he began, and she leaned forward to lay a finger across his lips.

"I would not like that you were bedding another woman? You are correct. However, we have not promised each other monogamy, and if you must marry to seal a good alliance for your clan; I believe I may accommodate that. It will be far better if I am with you, little one. You have lost the way of the homeworld, and will need someone on your off-side."

His lips bent into an ironic smile.

"I have undoubtedly forgotten much. But Serana, I have forgotten things you have never known!"

"Ah, but *I* do not need to know! I am a barbarian, as anyone can see by looking at me. In fact, I am your bodyguard, such being the custom of Lutetia."

She leaned forward, and put her hand over his, holding his eyes with hers.

"Don Eyr. *Petit*. Can you not ignore this . . . summons?"

He drew a breath.

"I think not—no."

"So, you will go to Liad, and accomplish this duty your delm demands of you?"

"Yes," he said, though not with any eagerness.

"Very well. If that is what you will do, then I will come with you." Silence.

Serana took a deep, quiet breath.

"If you do not want me, only say so, little one."

His free hand came to rest atop hers.

"But I *cannot* say so, Serana," he said. He leaned forward and brushed his lips across hers.

"Come, then," he murmured; "I want you."

THREE

Liad

THE *MELANT'I* playu that Serana had purchased had proved a valuable resource, giving insight into how the *Liaden Code of Proper Conduct* might—and might not—be used to one's own advantage.

For instance, the *Code* stated only that a child of the clan summoned home by the delm may enter the house by the front door, which would seem adamantine.

However, the *melant'i* plays illustrated the power of *may*.

May permitted choice, and thus Don Eyr paid off the taxi at the corner, and walked round to the servants' door, where, as a child, he had been accustomed to going and coming, so as not to risk affronting the *delm* with his presence.

Serana, in her guise as his bodyguard, walked half-a-step behind his left shoulder.

He found the small door in the wall, and pressed his palm against the plate. There came a small click, and he stepped inside, Serana ducking in behind him.

He made certain the door had sealed, then paused to take his bearings.

"The kitchen," he said, looking up at her, "is to the left."

She gave him a smile, and he started forward—and stopped as a woman stepped quickly out of the left-hand hallway.

She was a neat, elderly woman, her grey hair in a knot at the back of her head. She was wearing a house uniform of puce and green—Serat's colors.

"Who—" she began; and stopped, staring.

"Mrs. ban'Teli," he said, showing her his empty hands. "It is Don Eyr."

"So it ever was, Don Eyr," she said, coming forward to put her hands in his. "You look well, but—Child, whatever are you doing here?"

"The delm has called me home," he said, smiling at her.

"Has he?" This seemed to concern her; her fingers tensed on his. "Why?"

"He forgot to put down the reason in his letter," he said lightly, noting that she was trembling slightly, and also that the collar of her uniform was somewhat frayed, and her apron had been carefully mended with thread that did not quite match.

"You are a son of the House," Mrs. ban'Teli said then. "You should come in by the front door."

"Yes, and so I would have done," Don Eyr assured her, "save that I wished to see you first, and also to ask if you will give my poor Serana some tea in the kitchen, while I go to the delm."

He stepped slightly aside, and Serana came forward, offering a very nice bow.

"Madame," she said, gently, in her Letitian-accented Liaden. "I have heard much about you, and am pleased to meet you at last."

Mrs. ban'Teli performed a quick inventory, eyes bright, and bowed in her turn.

She looked back to Don Eyr.

"I will be pleased to bring your companion to the kitchen and see her comfortable," she said, which was also, he thought, a promise to ask many questions. That was expectable; he and Serana had agreed between them that all such questions would be met with truth. The kitchen staff did not bore the delm with the business of the kitchen.

"Come," said Mrs. ban'Teli, "both of you. We will see Lady Serana settled, and for you, sir, we will call Mr. pak'Epron, who will guide you properly to the delm. He is in his study with the papers, so it is likely that he would not have heard the bell in any case."

· · ·◇· · ·

SERAT SAT BEHIND A DESK covered in the racing papers. So much was unchanged from Don Eyr's memories of the delm. He looked up with considerable irritation when Mr. pak'Epron said quietly, "Master Don Eyr, sir."

"Go away," Serat said, and Mr. pak'Epron did so. Despite his inclinations, Don Eyr did not go away, but walked toward the desk and the two chairs set there. One was piled high with even more racing sheets, but the other was—

"Stop there!" snapped Serat. "I have not given you leave to approach!"

Don Eyr stopped, and stood, hands folded neatly before him. He took a deep breath, and waited for further instructions.

"Does your delm merit no bow?"

Ah, yes, thought Don Eyr; he was in violation of courtesy. No wonder the old man was testy.

He produced the required bow—clan member to delm—and straightened, murmuring, "Serat," in as neutral a tone as he could manage.

The old man glared at him.

"Why are you come?"

Don Eyr felt a tremble along his nerves. Had the old man forgotten? Could he, in fact, have merely ignored that peremptory letter and gone about his life?

Too late now to know the answers to those questions. Don Eyr inclined his head slightly, and said, quietly.

"You sent for me, sir."

There was a sniff.

"And you came. Remarkable. Your mother refused to come home when our delm sent for her. He froze her accounts, but she continued to disobey. Afraid, of course; she had already lost most of the clan's investments." He paused, looking Don Eyr up and down.

"You might have dressed to the delm's honor, but I suppose this is the best an impecunious student might do. Also, your accent is deplorable, which I suppose is expectable. However! I will have the proper mode from you, sirrah! That, at least, you will produce correctly. Arba is a stickler for such things and you will not give him insult! Am I plain?"

"No, sir," said Don Eyr, perhaps unwisely.

Papers crinkled as the old man's fingers closed on the sheets layering his desk.

"Are you defying me?"

"I do not see how I might do so, sir. Surely defiance may only follow comprehension," Don Eyr answered, keeping the mode in mind.

"Stupid, too," said Serat, and Don Eyr took a breath, thinking of Serana in the kitchen, sharing tea with Mrs. ban'Teli.

It was not, he told himself, unjust. He *had* been stupid, and Serana had been correct: He need not have come.

He thought then of the portions of the house he had seen on his way from the kitchens. It seemed that everything was shabby— worn, and that in at least one room there were signs that a rather large painting had been removed from the wall, and a piece of furniture, as well.

Serat needs this marriage, he thought then, not for alliance, but for money.

"What is it that I am required to do for the clan?" he asked, rather as if he were addressing a recalcitrant student than the delm of Serat.

The old man across the desk stared him up and down.

"You are required to go to Arba's house in the city and place yourself at his service. You are to say that you stand the payment of Serat's debt, which is now cleared."

"Am I to be married, then?" Don Eyr asked, his recent perusal of the Code having given him the very distinct notion that there were proprieties to be followed, papers to be filed . . .

"Married? No. Go away."

Serat was bent over his papers again; Don Eyr was already forgotten. Or perhaps not.

He bowed to the delm's honor, turned and let himself out of the study, closing the door quietly behind him.

He closed his eyes, took three deep breaths, opened his eyes and saw a figure hovering discreetly near the archway into the main hall.

"Mr. pak'Epron."

"Yes, Master Don Eyr."

"Is my cousin Vyk Tor in the house?"

"Yes, sir."

"Good," said Don Eyr. "Please take me to him."

* * * ✧ * * *

"COUSIN DON EYR."

Like his uncle, his cousin Vyk Tor was also found behind a desk smothered in paper—though these seemed to be business documents, and files, some on the letterhead of Mr. dea'Bon's office.

"May I give you a glass of wine?" his cousin asked, rising.

Don Eyr sighed.

"I hank you, a glass of wine would be most welcome," he said.

"You've been to see Father, then," said Vyk Tor, crossing the room to the wine table.

Don Eyr considered the small office, finding the same signs of shabbiness and deferred maintenance that were apparent elsewhere in the house.

His cousin turned from the table, glasses in hand, and moved toward the table and chairs set before the large window.

"Let us sit here," he said. "The prospect is slightly more pleasing than my desk."

Don Eyr joined him, took the offered glass, and sipped, automatically judging the vintage, and finding it—surprisingly—mundane.

He frowned slightly. His memory was that Serat had demanded expensive wines at table. A vintage such as this . . .

"The wine offends?"

He gave his cousin a frank look, remembering too late that to stare boldly into a man's face was to be rude.

"The wine—surprises," he said, and sank into the chair. His cousin stiffened, then relaxed and took his own chair.

"Understand," Don Eyr said, "I have spent the last dozen Standards learning wines and foods, in a culture that values wine and food . . . very much."

Vyk Tor tipped his head.

"I thought we had sent you to be a baker."

"That, too," Don Eyr said composedly. "One must certify for three specialties before one is permitted to graduate."

"I had not known the curriculum was so . . . rigorous," said his cousin, drinking deeply.

"The Lutetia *École de Cuisine* is a premier school. Their graduates go on to become chefs in the houses of queens, and in the great restaurants of the universe. Or," he raised his glass, "they found great restaurants."

"And you, have you founded your restaurant?"

"I was on my way to found a *boulangerie* on Ezhel'ti when Serat called me home. Now that I am here, I am bewildered. It seems I am not to marry for the advantage of the clan, but what I am meant to do eludes me."

Vyk Tor sighed.

"You must forgive Father," he began, and stopped at Don Eyr's sharp movement.

"No," he said, taking a deep breath against the growing anger; "I am not required to forgive Serat. Indeed, I begin to question whether I am required to obey him."

"Surely you are required to obey him!" his cousin said sharply. "He is the delm! The clan has brought you into adulthood; and seen you educated, and nourished!"

"So it has," said Don Eyr, dryly, and decided upon a change of topic.

"I missed a painting in the withdrawing room, when Mr. pak'Epron guided me to the delm; and it seemed also a divan had been removed. Is the house being remodeled?"

"The House," his cousin said, on the sharp edge of a sigh, "is foundering. I found by going through the clan's past finances that Father has always gambled. In fact, he lost his private fortune some years ago. That was when he began gambling with Serat's fortune."

Don Eyr stared at him.

"The *qe'andra* did not prevent him?"

"The *qe'andra* are in the clan's employ. Mr. dea'Bon withdrew himself, when it became apparent that Father would not abstain, but his heir . . . did not. We are not quite run off our legs, but we have had to embrace—" He raised his wine glass— "economies, as well as selling off certain items of value."

He drank, finishing the glass, and put it on the table.

"Thank the gods, we have not yet been required to sell our business interests."

Don Eyr put his glass on the table.

"Can you not curb him?"

His cousin looked at him with interest.

"How would you suggest I do that?"

This was familiar ground; many of the plays he and Serana had watched turned on points of honor between delm and nadelm.

"You are the nadelm. Surely, if the delm is not able—or endangers the clan . . ."

He stopped because his cousin was laughing.

"I have been able to move some of the businesses, and some of our stocks, into the nadelm's honor. I made a bolder throw, for all of our finances, and Father felt it necessary to tell me that he would declare me dead if I continued in my grasping ways."

He moved a hand—wearily, thought Don Eyr.

"Dead, I can do nothing. If I remain, at least I can do . . . something."

There was for the moment, silence. Don Eyr looked at his half-empty wine glass. Did not pick it up.

"In any case, that is where you come in, Cousin. Our funding is insufficient to pay off Arba's amount, but he agrees to accept one of Clan Serat to do such errands as might be assigned, at the compensation rate for unskilled labor, minus the costs of food and lodging, until such time as the debt has been balanced."

Don Eyr sat, feeling the blood roar in his ears, thinking of the house on Ezhel'ti; the clan of his father, which had been willing to acknowledge him.

Of Serana.

Gods, Serana.

"The delm has sold me to pay off his gambling debts," he said, his voice flat, and without mode.

"In a word," his cousin said; "yes."

. . . ✧ . . .

THEY WERE TAKEN in to Mr. dea'Bon without delay; the butler announcing them in soft, respectful tones.

"Lord Don Eyr fer'Gasta Clan Serat. Captain Serana Benoit."

The old man rose from behind his desk and bowed, to Serana's eye, with proper respect for her small one.

"Your Lordship," he said, and there was respect in the soft voice, too; a certain fondness in the gaze that she might have missed, had she not seen the *melant'i* plays.

Don Eyr raised a hand.

"Certainly, I am no lordship," he began, and the old gentleman raised a hand in turn.

"Certainly, you are; and I am delighted to be at your service. You're looking well, sir."

He might have argued, save his temper was already fully engaged, and the old gentlemen was in no way its target. Serana was informed; she had not previously been privileged to see Don Eyr *angry*. To know that he was not only capable of righteous rage, but remained its master—those things were good to know.

So, no argument, but a bow, less deep than the one he had received, because, so Serana deduced, the old gentleman would have it that way.

"I am pleased to see you again, sir; I only wish it might be under happier circumstances."

"Ah." The old gentleman looked wise. "You come to me from Serat."

He glanced at the butler, who remained in the doorway.

"Wine and a tray, if you will, Mr. ben'Darble. Lord Don Eyr and Captain Benoit are doubtless in need of refreshment after a trying afternoon."

"Sir." The butler bowed and was gone, closing the door silently behind him.

"I am remiss," her small one said then, and extended a hand to bring her forward. "This is Serana Benoit. You may speak to her as to myself."

It was a phrase from the plays. They had supposed, between them, that it had signaled a trust that went beyond mere clan connections, and thus seldom found favor with the delms of drama. Certainly, it meant something more than mere words to the old gentleman.

He was not so unsubtle as to raise even an eyebrow, but he considered her now with interest, rather than merely courtesy. She bowed, as would a Watch Captain to solid citizen.

"Sir."

"Captain Benoit; I am honored," he said, returning her bow precisely.

Straightening, he spoke again to Don Eyr.

"By your goodness, my lord—Captain—sit, take your ease. I know something of why you have come, I think. Be assured that my service is to you; not Serat, nor the nadelm. You may speak frankly to me. Everything you say will remain in this room, in the memory of we three; and recorded in my personal client files, which I share with no one, except on those same terms of confidentiality."

Don Eyr sighed; moved toward the chair at the right side of the old gentleman's desk, and paused to look to her.

She gave him a smile and a nod.

"I am well, here," she said, sliding into the too-small chair, and folding her legs expertly under her.

He smiled, faintly, and seated himself, whereupon the tray arrived and was disposed. The butler, assured that they could, indeed, look after themselves, left them, closing the door silently behind. The old gentleman poured wine; they sipped, Serana noting Don Eyr's shoulders softening somewhat as he tasted the vintage.

His glass set to one side, the old gentleman leaned back in his chair, looked to Don Eyr, and said, simply, "Tell me."

· · · ◇ · · ·

DON EYR wilted somewhat in his chair, weary with the telling. The old gentleman steepled his fingers, his gaze abstracted. Serana, not wishing to disturb a genius at his work, but unwilling to see her *petit* in need, rose, refreshed all three glasses, and placed two of the delicate sandwiches on the plate at Don Eyr's hand.

He smiled up at her.

"Thank you," he murmured in Lutetian.

"It is nothing; do not exhaust yourself before the battle."

She laid a hand on his shoulder, pressing for a moment before returning to her own chair and meeting the old gentleman's eyes.

He inclined his head gravely and turned to Don Eyr.

"Serat's actions are by Code. They are deplorable, but the Code does not disallow. The resources of the clan are for the delm to dispense. I will mention that this is the precise paragraph which Serat quotes . . . often . . . to justify his use of the clan's funds."

The old gentleman reached for his wine glass.

"Therefore, there is nothing for either the *qe'andra* nor the Council to take up."

Serana felt her own anger, well-banked against the hour when it would be useful to her—and to him—flicker and flare. In his chair, Don Eyr drew a breath, but said nothing.

The old gentleman inclined his head.

"We do, yes, have hope that the contract may be broken—not by you, but by Arba."

"You think that Delm Arba will not accept my service?" Don Eyr said, the accent of home gilding his mode. "I will be delighted to present myself in the worst possible light."

The old man smiled.

"Indeed, you must present yourself as you are—a lord in the delm's line, second only to the nadelm of Serat. You are an honorable man."

He sipped his wine, and set the glass aside.

"Arba, I fear, is *not* an honorable man. For proof, we have the record of his many fines paid to the Council for violations of Code. You must be vigilant. When he breaks with the Code, as he will do, you must relay this breach to me, so that I may act on your behalf."

"Is it so certain that he will violate the Code?" Don Eyr asked, brows drawn.

The old gentleman smiled.

"With Arba, it is as if the Code is an enemy he must strike at again and again. He is no more able to help himself than Serat can refrain from placing wagers. All you need do is wait, and be vigilant."

Serana stirred. Don Eyr and Mr. dea'Bon turned to her.

"Is he dangerous, this man?" she asked.

"One of the fines Arba paid was to the Guild of *Qe'andra*, for the death of an apprentice. The child had found a second set of books, and was, as required by the protocols of his house and those of the Guild, in the process of documenting the incident. Arba ordered him to stop; the child stated that he was not able to do so. Arba struck him . . ."

There was a small pause; the old gentleman extended a hand to toy with his glass.

". . . and killed him. Arba paid the life-price without protest, which I think is telling in itself."

"Yes," said Serana. "I have known such men. Thank you."

"Of course."

Don Eyr had gathered himself once more, sitting alert in his chair.

"Thank you, sir. I am grateful for your time and insights. I ask."

"By all means, sir. I will answer to the best of my ability."

"I am long away from the Code, alas, but it is my understanding that I may become dead to the clan. I wish this to occur as speedily as possible."

"Ah."

The old gentleman's smile was edged with regret.

"The only person who may declare a clan member dead is the

delm. In this case, I think we may agree that Serat will do no such thing. Also, having obeyed the summons to return, you are now in the position of having accepted the Delm's Word. If you should simply leave, after having been instructed in your duty by the delm, you will be pursued, arrested, and brought back."

He paused, and spread his palms.

"The Council has much precedent for this, I fear."

Silence, before Don Eyr bowed his head and gathered himself to rise. Serana ached to hold him; the busy mind had produced the best solution for this absurd situation—and it had been checked and blocked. Don Eyr was not accustomed to losing, Serana realized abruptly. The relative modesty of his goals had kept this aspect of his nature hidden, until now.

"I think your lordship was not given his suite at Serat's clanhouse for the night?" said Mr. dea'Bon delicately.

Don Eyr tipped his head to one side.

"I was not. Apparently, Arba is to provide all things for me."

"Yet, as little as Arba values virtue, he does value courtesy, though neither so much as his own comfort. If you will allow me to advise you once more, I would suggest that you send a note around by one of my house's staff, stating that you will wait upon Delm Arba tomorrow in the early afternoon. This will insure he is not wakened too early in the day, which may lead to bad temper. Also, if you wish, you and Captain Benoit may partake of the hospitality of *this* House, where you may rest easy tonight."

Don Eyr bowed, abruptly. Serana thought it might have been done to hide an excess of emotion.

"You are far too good to us, sir."

"That would be difficult. Now, if you please, I will call Mr. ben'Darble to show the way to your . . ."

He paused, delicately, and Don Eyr murmured.

"Room, if you please, sir."

"Indeed. Mr. ben'Darble will show you to your suite. I very much hope that you will join us for the prime meal, but if you prefer, it will be brought to you."

He stood and bowed.

"Please," he said, and Serana felt tears prick her eyelids. "Be welcome in our House."

• • •◇• • •

IF ARBA'S HOUSE was too fine for the street it graced, Arba was too fine for the house. Or, Serana thought darkly, so he wished to appear. Certainly, he dressed well, with many small jewels glittering about his person, and rings on his fingers. His hair was pale brown, extravagantly curled, and perfumed. His face was long, his mouth cruel, and his chin weak. At the moment, he was . . . amused; coolly so. It must seem to him, Serana thought, that Don Eyr was the merest sweet morsel, which he must be careful not to consume too quickly.

"Now, it seems to me that Serat and I had agreed that I would accept the service of Telma fer'Gasta's by-blow in payment for his debt. I do not recall mention of a . . . *pet*, and I can assure you that I will neither feed it nor pay it."

Don Eyr remained calm in the face of these insults, which were of course meant to touch him and try him. It was well, Serana thought, that he did so, though it would only mean that Arba would strike harder, next time.

"Sir," she said, stepping forward, and speaking as if she had much less of the language than she did. "I am Serana Benoit. I am Lord Don Eyr's bodyguard, and I have been paid, sir, with the money upfront, for a contract of seven years. There are yet five years remaining on this contract, and so I am here."

He stared at her, the cruel mouth thin with distaste. Serana returned his regard, mildly, until at last, he turned away and spoke to Don Eyr.

"A bodyguard?"

Don Eyr bowed.

"All high-ranking Lutetian persons employ a bodyguard."

"I was told you were a baker."

Don Eyr said nothing.

"I repeat that I will not feed it," Arba said after a moment.

"You need not feed me, sir," said Serana. "I account my expenses, and my lord pays them. It is in the contract. Perhaps sir would like to see it?"

Arba drew a hard breath, but did not turn his head. Once more, he addressed Don Eyr. "You will instruct it not to speak to me."

Don Eyr bowed, briefly, and Serana thought she saw the flicker of a knife in that gesture.

"Serana," he said, turning to face her, and speaking in the mode known as Comrade. "You are relieved of the burden of his lordship's conversation. Please do not speak to him directly, as it agitates his *melant'i*."

He turned back to Arba, and met his eyes.

"His lordship will naturally refrain from addressing you," he continued, "as I am certain that doing so must also distress him extremely."

Arba's eyes were cold, his beringed fingers were tight on the arm of his chair. He inclined his head gracefully, however.

"We come now to the matter of your domestic arrangements. As you are my servant, a room has been set aside for you in the servant's wing."

He paused, perhaps to savor an anticipated protest, as this was, Serana saw, yet another insult.

Don Eyr inclined his head slightly, face attentive.

"You will take your meals with the servants," Arba continued after a moment, his cruel mouth tight.

"As I am your servant," Don Eyr murmured. "Exactly so."

That was perhaps an error, to have shown so much spirit. Arba's eyes gleamed, and he gave a curt nod.

"You are dismissed. I will be going out this evening you will wait upon me. I will summon you when I am ready to leave."

With that, he turned his back on them, pretending to busy himself at his screen.

Don Eyr bowed, turned and let them out, closing the door very quietly behind them.

"Now the question becomes," he said softly in Lutetian, "which is more amusing, to have us caught as thieves in his house, or showing all the world his new possession?"

"Surely," Serana answered, "he will go for the long game, that man."

"Indeed. Now—ah."

He stepped quickly to a small side hall, and looked inside. The woman who had let them in stood there, impassive, but clearly interested.

"Good day to you," Don Eyr said easily in the mode between comrades. "I am new in his lordship's employ. He has graciously granted me and my household a room in the servant's wing. Will you teach me how to arrive there?"

The butler stirred slightly, and Serana saw her weighing which course would anger her master more—to aid the newcomer or to allow him to wander the house. Commonsense decided the day, or a realization of proper duty. In any case, she offered a small nod.

"I will show you," she said.

* * * ✦ * * *

IT WAS A SMALL ROOM, though not nearly as rude as he had prepared himself to entertain. It was not, however, kind to Serana's proportions.

"Well," she said, good-naturedly, "at least here I may lose myself entirely in passion."

He considered her.

"How so?"

"Why, I will not have to constantly be aware of the eaves, and their proximity to my head. Only think how we may soar, now that my attention will not be divided."

"Of course," he said, politely. "But, consider, Serana, the size of this room, not only of the bed. It is not a hovel, but I would not see you here. We shall ask Mr. dea'Bon to find you a more fitting apartment . . ."

"If this place fits you, it fits me," Serana interrupted him. She leaned forward and touched his cheek. "Little one, accept that I will not leave you alone in that man's hand. He does not want a servant; he wants a whipping boy. It will please him to taunt you. Already he insults your birth."

"No," said Don Eyr; "he is nothing more than factual. I was not born from a proper contract, nor was I caught at Festival. I am the product of an affair of pleasure, whom my mother decided to regularize."

"In fact, you were born of love," said Serana.

He smiled.

"In fact, you are a woman of Lutetia," he answered her. "And, indeed—it is Arba's error, that he attempts to diminish my *melant'i*. As the plays teach us—we each know the value of our own *melant'i*."

He took a breath.

"I am not, however, certain of my answer, the next time he insults *you*."

"But he will not insult me again! I have been instructed not to speak to him, and he has been instructed not to speak to me."

"He takes my instruction exactly so much as you do," he said, sounding bitter in his own ears. "Serana, this . . . this *gallimaufry* is nothing of yours. I would not see you waste your life. You are made for—for bold ventures, and fair. This is . . . drab and dreary, and—wholly unworthy of you."

She smiled at him, and he knew he would not win this argument. Oh, he could send her away. All he needed do was tell her that he did not want her and she would remove herself immediately. The words settled on the edge of his tongue. He would tell her—*Serana, I do not want you*. She would leave him to pursue her own life, free of this stupid circumstance he had brought her to . . .

And, yet . . . he could not bring the lie to his lips.

"Come," she said cheerfully, "let us find the kitchen, and see what arrangements might be made."

"Arrangements?" he asked, his heart aching.

"Indeed. You have not had your luncheon, and if that man is feeding you, he can begin now."

• • • ◆ • • •

THE KITCHEN they found easily enough by following their noses. Don Eyr paused on the threshold, Serana at his back, and surveyed the area, pleased to find it clean and well-appointed, with proper stations, staffed appropriately.

He felt some of the tension leave him, soothed by this display of orderly busyness.

"May I help you . . . sir?"

The grizzled over-chef was approaching, wiping his hands on a towel, looking from him to Serana. Plainly, he had not been told about the new servant and his bodyguard, Don Eyr thought. And, plainly, it suited the master's whim to make the assimilation of the new servant into his household as difficult as possible.

"I am Don Eyr fer'Gasta," he said, bowing to the chef's honor; "newly arrived to serve Delm Arba. This is my companion, Serana Benoit. One was told that the house would feed me, and I have come to speak with you regarding the necessities of the kitchen, so that I do not impede your work."

The over-chef was . . . puzzled, but gracious.

"I had not been informed of your arrival," he said. "The house is sometimes not so forthcoming with the kitchen as one would wish. We are preparing Prime, but surely there is food at the staff table. I will show you. My name is Mae Nir vas'Urbil."

"It was Arba's word," Serana said as they crossed the busy kitchen toward a window at the back, "that he will not feed me, as I am not employed by the house, but am here on Don Eyr's account."

Chef vas'Urbil frowned.

"I recall now," he said, looking closely at Don Eyr's face. "You're the lad Serat lost at cards."

Don Eyr bowed gently, not slackening his pace.

"Here. We keep this area stocked for staff; you may eat at any hour that duty does not claim you." He glanced at Serana. "*Both* of you. Arba has not given me any instructions regarding new servants in the house, and this kitchen can feed two more as easily as one."

"You are kind," Don Eyr murmured.

Chef vas'Urbil moved a hand.

"I am efficient, and I keep within budget. That is what Arba cares about. Now—"

A lamentation rose from a far corner of the kitchen.

"The bread!" cried a voice. "Ah, the bread!"

Don Eyr was moving before he recalled that this was not his kitchen to oversee, and by then, he had arrived at the ovens, and the lamenting under-baker there.

"What is the difficulty?" asked the chef, who had arrived at Don Eyr's shoulder.

"The bread, sir; it did not rise. And there is no time to begin again. I—"

"When is Prime?" asked Don Eyr.

"In two hours," said Chef vas'Urbil.

"May I assist?" Don Eyr asked. "I do not wish to disorder your kitchen. This, however, is my work; I am trained in bread."

"Who trained you?"

"I have graduated from *École de Cuisine* at Lutetia."

Chef vas'Urbil blinked.

Then, he waved a hand.

"If you know what to do, Baker, by all means, do it. I have a kitchen to oversee."

"Yes," said Don Eyr and turned to the weeping under-baker, feeling very much in his element, even to the point of calming an overwrought student.

"What we shall do is make *petit pain*," he told her. She stared at him.

"Sir?"

"Small breads," he said briskly. "They rise once, and bake quickly. We have time enough; and they will arrive pleasingly hot at the table."

"I do not—"

"I will demonstrate," he told her moving around the station, and plucking an apron from a hook.

"What is your name?"

"Zelli, sir."

"Well, Zelli, my name is Don Eyr. I have done this many times before, and can assure you that we are in no danger of failing. Is the mixer clean and ready?"

"Yes, sir."

"Good. Now attend me . . ."

* * * ⟡ * * *

SERANA STARTED UP from the chair where she had been reading.

"Tell me he did not do this."

Don Eyr sat on the edge of the bed. His face hurt, and his pride, though he had not been struck in public. He was not accustomed to being struck. Worse, it had taken every ounce of his will, not to strike back.

"Of course, he did it," he said now to Serana. "It is his right, is it not? The Code and the plays teach us that a delm may do what the delm pleases to all members of the clan, including taking their lives. My delm gave me into Arba's care."

"He will not live to strike you again," Serana said calmly.

He looked up sharply.

"Go," he said, his voice harsh. "Leave me now."

Shock etched her face.

"Don Eyr—"

He held up a hand.

"I will not be the instrument of your ruin! I will not see you tarnish yourself. I will not—"

His voice broke, and to his own horror, he began to cry.

Serana turned abruptly, and left the room, the door closing behind her.

Don Eyr gasped.

"Good," he said raggedly, and bent over until his forehead rested on his knees. He tried to regulate his breathing, to master the tears, to—

Serana was gone. He was alone. It was well; he ought to send to Mr. dea'Bon, to be certain that she had passage wherever she wished to go. The house on Ezhel'ti was hers, he would make it so, if she wished to establish herself there, or to—

The door cycled. Gentle hands were on his shoulders.

"Sit up, *petit*; allow me to examine this bruise. Here. Here is ice, and I have also some salve which is recommended to me by the night cook. A tray will be brought, wine, cheese, and fruits. We shall make a merry feast, eh?"

He jerked under the soft pressure of her fingers.

"He did not withhold himself, I see. First, the ice, then the salve . . ."

The cold stung, then numbed.

"Serana—you must go."

"Indeed, little one; I must not. You have the right of it; to kill this man would not be at all clever. I give you my word that I will not kill him. May I remain?"

He reached out, half-blind with weeping, and touched her lips.

"I am weak. Yes, Serana. Please stay."

• • •✧• • •

FOR THE FIRST *relumma* of service, Arba was content to take Don Eyr on his evening rounds of pleasure, explaining to everyone he met who his servant was and how he had come into Arba's service. This generated much gossip, which Arba was certain would discommode his new toy, especially the betting pool regarding the exact day and time when Serat crumbled under the weight of its own debts and was written out of the Book of Clans, and the rumors regarding Don Eyr's mother.

After that sport had worn thin, Don Eyr was given various menial tasks that took him to the borders of Low and Mid-Port, Arba having ownership of many of the most disreputable houses on that border. He was always glad to have Serana with him, but especially so on these errands, where he felt her long, competent presence was everything that prevented him being robbed.

There were periods when he was "on-call"—constrained to remain in the house and await the master's word. These might have lain heavier on him had there not been the kitchen, and the beginning of a friendship between himself and Mae Nir vas'Urbil. He was welcome in the kitchen at any time, to teach, or to create whatever pleased him. Those creations went to the staff room, and thus he won the goodwill, if not the friendship, of his fellow servants.

On the occasions when they both had an hour free, Don Eyr and Mae Nir would sit at study, the over-chef having produced a book of recipes from the *Lutetia École de Cuisine*, translated into Liaden from Lutetian. Serana gathered that the translation was inadequate to the utmost, and Don Eyr spent much time explaining—and occasionally demonstrating—certain techniques which had not translated *at all*.

For her part, Serana taught those of the staff who wished to learn disengages, and feints. It seemed Arba's guests were not always of impeccable *melant'i*, and sometimes went so far as to touch that which was not theirs. It would not do to provide lasting harm to Arba's guests, so Serana told her students; however, no one could possibly object to receiving a small lesson.

In this manner, two *relumma* passed, and Arba had not yet, in their sight, done one bit of violence to the Code.

On the morning of the first day of his third *relumma* of service, Arba called Don Eyr to his office.

"I have acquired a piece of land in Low Port, at the corner of Offal Court and Pudding Lane. Before it can be put to use, it needs to be cleared of debris. See to it."

FOUR

Low Port

THE ENFORCERS WERE COMING. That was the word on the street.

Arba's enforcers.

He had put the most able on the outer walls, the least able inside walls. There was a risk there, that those inside would be easy meat, once he had fallen. He had thought to send them away. If there had been any place safer than this place that he had made, he *would have* sent them away.

But, this was Low Port. There was no safety in Low Port, save being stronger than everyone else.

There were bolt holes from the inner room—tunnels too small for an adult to use. They would be able to get away, when—if—away. Out into Low Port, where they would be prey.

And he would be forsworn.

"Here they come," he heard someone say as feet hurried past his huddling place.

Jax Ton peered carefully around the edge of the wall, his cheek rubbing the gritty old stone.

Yes, here they were, just coming 'round the corner. Not Low Porters, you could tell by the clothes, and by the walk. Up Porters, they walked firm, like they could take anything on the street. A lot of them, they didn't look, and that got them in trouble. These two, though . . .

These two walked alert, and he'd seen them, he realized. Both of them, together, just like now. A dark-haired man, walking light and watchful; at his back a giantess, with cropped red hair, who walked even lighter, her eyes sweeping the street like beacons.

They were coming this way. Of course, they were coming this way.

Jax Ton made sure of his grip, and said, in a piercing whisper. "*Now.*"

· · · ⟡ · · ·

LOW PORT was where the clanless, the criminal, and the mad collected. There was no place for them in Mid-Port, and certainly not in High Port. Rats strolled the broken streets at their leisure; buildings sagged, and occasionally fell down, from lack of care. The people were hungry, and shabby, and, most of them, hopeless. There were predators on every street, and a man might be murdered for a good pair of boots.

That had been Don Eyr's judgment of Low Port from his previous visits on Arba's behalf. He realized now that he had not seen the worst of it.

Pudding Lane was lined with basic shelters, from ragged tents and sagging inflatables, to huts built from scavenged bits of plastic, stone, and cardboard.

In fact, there was one building on the entire street—a stone pile that would likely survive a meteor strike.

Arba's property.

"Are we to bulldoze the walls," he asked Serana, "or merely pick up the trash?"

In fact, there was remarkably little trash around the walls, unlike the rest of the street. There were also remarkably few pedestrians, though Don Eyr could feel the pressure of eyes watching from those tattered shelters. No one challenged them, which happened often on the . . . better streets of Low Port, a circumstance that made his nerves tingle.

"Softly, little one," said Serana. "There is a door. Let us approach from either side, so that we do not tempt anyone into an indiscretion."

"Yes," he said and swung to the right, as Serana went to the left—

Directly into a hail of stones, and sticks.

He hit the ground, rolling on a shoulder, and rising to one knee, arms over his head to protect it.

Serana . . .

Serana had continued forward as if the missiles were made of whipped cream. She went down on her knees some distance from the doorway, and held her hands up, palms showing.

"Peace," he heard her say, in a calm, carrying voice. "Child, stand down. We are not here to hurt you."

. . . ⬧ . . .

IT WAS A TERRIBLE TALE the lad, Jax Ton, told them—starting with his own family's ruin and destruction—a small clan, a small business located on the edge of Mid-Port and Low, in the section known as Twilight. To throw suspicion off of themselves, a neighbor had given information against them for smuggling and human trafficking. It wasn't true, Jax Ton said hotly; his delm would never have stood for it, but the Port Authority didn't care to hear the truth, so long as they put the fear of retribution into guilty and innocent alike. The clan was broken; the elders arrested, and Jax Ton—Jax Ton had fled. Into Low Port. Growing up in the Twilight, he had friends in Low Port, or so he thought, until his friends tried to sell him and he ran again, not to Mid-Port, where the proctors waited, but deeper into Low Port, where he found two children, starving, and spent his last coins to feed them.

Over time—Jax Ton wasn't entirely clear on how much time— three *relumma*? A year?—more children had gathered to him, usually an elder child with a younger in their care. They were eight, now, and Jax Ton; they had needed a safe place, a place that they, that was—

"Defensible," Serana said with a nod, looking 'round at the ring of tense faces. "You have done well. These walls will stand against a siege engine."

In fact, Don Eyr thought, looking at those same tense faces, they had done well, indeed. The faces were grubby, perhaps, but not distressingly so, and while they were dressed in a motley of garments, those were, by local standards, clean. Thin, yes, but not desperately so. Wary, but not feral. Or not quite feral. No doubt, the elder ones were accomplished thieves.

There was nothing here that he had not seen before. Lutetia had its poor, after all, and the Institute, sitting in the shadow of the Old City, saw them often.

"As much as this place meets your needs . . ." he said now, speaking softly so as not to startle any of them, but Jax Ton, particularly. It was Jax Ton they must win to trust. The others would follow him.

"I regret, but you cannot stay here. The man who owns this building is both acquisitive and cruel. Best for all to relocate. Is there another place, perhaps not quite so well arranged, where you might go?"

Jax Ton frowned, and one of the older children leaned forward.

"There's the Rooms," she said, speaking to Jax Ton.

"Need money for the Rooms," another child protested.

Don Eyr held up a hand.

"Money need not concern you at the moment. Is it a place where you might keep together and in safety?"

Jax Ton looked at him, eyes wide.

"Money no concern?" he repeated. "Will *you* pay for us?"

Plainly, he disbelieved it, and Don Eyr could not blame him.

"Indeed, I will pay for you. More, we will escort you to this place, and see you settled and provisioned."

The boy was wary of a trap. Of course he was. Don Eyr waited.

"My friend, you cannot stay here," Serana said. "What my partner has told you is true. If we turn a blind eye and report this property clear, Arba will learn soon enough that we lied. Aside from what may be done to Don Eyr for such transgression, you will again be exposed and in danger. Best to retreat in good order, and establish a base elsewhere."

Jax Ton took a hard breath, looked around at his band of eight, wordlessly gathering their input. His gaze moved to Don Eyr, to Serana, and he inclined his head, jerkily, as if the gesture were not much used.

"Yes," he said. "We will go with you."

* * * ✧ * * *

THE ROOMS was a rambling and ramshackle building that had, Don Eyr thought, once been half-a-dozen buildings, now connected by catwalks, ladders, and impromptu lifts. It looked a veritable fire-trap, and the manager was no better than she ought to be. Still, she showed them a suite of rooms on the top floor, accessible by a stair, a woven rope walkway, and a catwalk connecting them to the next building.

Jax Ton inspected it, and Serana did, Don Eyr standing with the manager at the door.

"That's a twelfth-cantra for a *relumma*," she said. "No business done up here, though if they wanna work, I can put 'em in touch."

Don Eyr feared he did not misunderstand her, which did nothing to reconcile him to this place. To leave children here? And, yet, they were capable children, and they had been surviving very well, snug inside their rock walls. This . . . he looked around—plasboard walls, plasboard floor, plasboard ceiling with discolorations, here and there, which hinted that the rain came through.

"Yes," said Jax Ton, arriving with Serana. Don Eyr looked at her over the boy's head, saw doubtful eyes in a grim face.

"That is well, then," he said to Jax Ton. "Go and bring the others up."

"My money, sir," the manager said.

He turned. Perhaps he moved too quickly; perhaps something of his thoughts showed on his face. In any case, she stepped back.

"Your money," he repeated moderately. "Of course. Let us go to your office and settle the account."

* * * ✧ * * *

THE RENT WAS PAID for two *relumma*, and it did occur to Don

Eyr that it was perhaps not quite wise to have exposed himself as a man who had so very much coin in his pocket. Still, it was done, while Serana stood aside with Jax Ton, handing over a card, and speaking with him most earnestly.

The boy slipped the card into some inner pocket, and made sober reply, then extended both hands to catch Serana's.

"Thank you," Don Eyr heard him say as he left the manager's office. "I am—grateful."

"Be wary, and take care," Serana told him. "That is our thanks. And remember—if there is trouble you cannot turn aside, send or come to that address. I will help you."

It was on the tip of his tongue to correct that, but, there, Serana, as ever, had the right of it. *He* could not promise *we*. His life was ordered at the whim of Arba, who would surely do his utmost to thwart any assistance Don Eyr might offer.

"Sir, thank you." The boy grasped Don Eyr's hand, his grip strong, and perhaps, a little, desperate.

"You are welcome," he said, smiling into the worried eyes. "Be well, Jax Ton."

The boy left, climbing the swaying stairs like a squirrel. He and Serana walked out to the street, and turned their steps toward Mid-Port.

They walked a block, and those pedestrians they encountered did very little to set his mind at ease regarding the fate of those eight children.

Don Eyr stopped, and looked up at Serana.

"They cannot be left there," he said. "Capable as they are, they are too soft, too easy. There are too many against them. That woman—offered to guide them to a brothel, in case any wished to work."

"I agree," Serana said softly. "They are too vulnerable. I will return, and guard them. You, with your twisty mind, will consider how we may do better for them. Come, I will escort you to safer streets, and—"

"I need no escort," Don Eyr said, recalling the last group they had passed on this street.

"Go back to them, now, Serana. I will . . . think of something."

She gazed into his face, hers showing wonder and no little irony. At last, she raised a hand and touched his cheek.

"I will see them safe, *petit*. Guard yourself close."

And with that, she turned and left him on the street.

* * * ✧ * * *

"CHILDREN IN THE LOW PORT, my friend?" Chef vas'Urbil looked doubtful. "What would you have me do?"

"Advise me," Don Eyr said. "Surely, there must be some safe place to which we can deliver them, where they can receive an education other than how to survive on the streets."

"As I understand it, that is the highest class available in Low Port," returned the chef. He moved a hand. "Understand me, I am not unsympathetic; children ought not to be in danger, and yet, Low Port . . . you will not find many in Mid-Port or High who will care to discuss Low Port. It is widely held that those who live there deserve no better, else they would not have fallen so far. There is no . . . agency . . . to support them." He paused to sip his tea, and looked at Don Eyr with curiosity.

"Was it not thus at Lutetia?"

"At Lutetia there were slums, surely, and the poor. But the city and the citizens provided some support. Orphanages, clinics, schools."

The chef looked aside.

"We on Liad are not so kindly. The clan is all and everything, as you have found. What recourse is there for you, ceded to Arba to cover your delm's markers?"

"None that I am aware of," Don Eyr said, and considered his friend with weary amusement. "Is my delm an idiot?"

"That and more!" the chef said heatedly. "He might have paid off Arba and gained income for the clan. Only, he would have had to find investors for a restaurant, which would have been easy enough, with an *École de Cuisine* chef to manage it, not to say provide the breads and desserts!"

He looked thoughtful.

"Of course, investors would demand that the profits be safe from Serat, which he would not like, at all. And, yet, this! It is to throw you, and every hope of Serat ever coming about into the wind!" He blow out a hard breath.

"Fool and son of a fool."

Don Eyr raised his eyebrows.

"Did you know my grandfather?"

"I am older than you, though not so old as that. No, it was a tale to amaze all of Liad, that Serat chose to send his daughter outworld—"

"I have heard the tale," said Don Eyr, and the chef threw him a wise look.

"You have heard the gossip, I'll warrant, and the most malicious of it, at that. Serat's daughter was sound; the son was a fool, but the son had not defied the father, nor called his judgment into question. For those crimes, she was sent to mind the clan's faltering fortunes off-world, since she was wiser than her delm in finance. The boy— your delm, now—grew up with the fixed notion that any competition for the ring was dangerous, and his intellect has plainly deteriorated from there." He drank off what was left of his tea.

"Forgive me if I offend," he added.

Don Eyr laughed.

"Yes, well. Returning to your children in the Low Port . . . I cannot advise you, save to say, walk away. Life is cheap in the Low Port, and children's lives cheaper than most. Rabbits among wolves, if they are without a clan or a . . . a group of some kind."

"And would you walk away from children in need? Children in danger?"

His friend moved his shoulders, turning empty palms up.

"Gods grant it never comes to me, because, in truth, I do not know what I would do."

• • •◇• • •

IT HAD BEEN DON EYR'S INTENTION to return to Low Port within a day—two at the most—though his vaunted twisty brain had not yet produced a solution for the children. Surely, there must be something . . . and Serana . . .

Serana was a warrior; she was cautious, and canny, and fully capable.

But Low Port was a killer, and he did not intend to leave her there without backup . . .

It was Arba's genius to know precisely how best to do harm. For the next twelve-day, he kept Don Eyr busy from dawn to dawn, with errands all about the city and the port, and then to stand as his trained monkey, trailing him from party to gaming table to an assignation.

At the latter, the lady considered him with interest.

"Does it perform?"

"One supposes so," Arba said, voice languid and eyes glinting. "Will you try it?"

"Perhaps I will—unless you do not care for competition?"

Arba raised his head at that, and there was a look in his eye that did not bode well for the lady, should she persist in this vein. She ignored him, or perhaps she did not see. Instead, she crossed the room to Don Eyr standing where he had been left, near the bureau. He lowered his eyes, and recruited himself to stillness.

"I believe he is shy," said the lady, and he felt her stroke his hair. "Serat's sister's child, you say?"

"It is what Serat says, in any case," said Arba, carelessly. "Will you have him?"

"While you watch?"

"I fear so, as I own him, and must therefore be certain that he comes to no harm."

The lady snorted delicately.

"Surely, the Code forbids slavery," she said, trailing a slim hand down Don Eyr's arm, and raising his hand to her lips.

He stiffened as she blew lightly across his knuckles—before releasing him to toy again with his hair.

"But this is not slavery; it is the payment of a rather considerable debt. In essence, I own him until such time as he has worked out the amount Serat owes me. Which, given the leisurely pace at which he pursues his duties, will be some years into his second lifetime."

"You might call the debt paid," said the lady.

"Now, why would I do that?"

"Ah, of course; I forget myself," said the lady, and slid her hand under Don Eyr's chin.

"Look at me, little one," she murmured.

His temper flared, and he raised his head, meeting her eyes, which widened slightly, eyebrows rising, as she tipped her head to one side, as if considering his merits.

"Insipid," she said after a moment, and turned away.

"Come, Har Per, send the child home, and let us continue our explorations."

"Perhaps he needs an education, if he is as insipid as you say?"

"I am not a school," the lady said tartly. "Nor do I desire an audience this evening."

"But perhaps on some other evening? I tremble with anticipation," Arba said, placing his hand over his heart.

"Yes, very likely. Perhaps you would care to leave, also?"

Arba stiffened, and Don Eyr feared for the lady, who, perhaps did not know the limits of her power.

. . . or perhaps she did. Outrage melted into something else, and Arba raised a hand to cup the lady's cheek. He bent as if to kiss her—and paused in the act to look over her head.

"Go home," he snarled. "Tomorrow is rent day. Mind you find tal'Qechee in his office. I want no missed payments."

Don Eyr bowed, and turned, finding the door opening before him, and the lady's butler there to guide him away.

* * * ✧ * * *

TAL'QECHEE'S office was not in Low Port. Not *quite* in Low Port, though it danced with the boundary. His business interests were definitely based on the other side of the line, and the persons he employed were questionable at best. He was also difficult to find in his office, as Don Eyr had discovered on the previous occasions when he had been sent to collect tal'Qechee's "rent." The best hour to find him was early—*very* early—in the morning, when he was counting his own receipts from the night before.

Don Eyr therefore arrived early.

Night Port had not quite given over to Day; dawn teased the horizon, but had not yet committed to a fuller embrace. The streets were damp, it having rained somewhat in the night time. The gambling hells, bars, and other night side entertainment would be calling *last bid, last drink, last start*, and Mr. tal'Qechee would surely be in his office, now or very soon, in order to receive the couriers bearing the night's gleanings.

His reasoning was correct, though his arrival did not please Mr. tal'Qechee, who required him to tarry until all of the night's receipts were in and counted, so he was later than he wished to be, leaving for his next errand, which was much on his mind as he finally departed, his inside pocket heavy with cash.

The second errand was not so difficult as Mr. tal'Qechee, who made difficulty an art, but it would require some finesse to extract the "rent" when he was so far beyond his appointed hour. The second appointment pretended to grandeur, and a missed appointment was an affront worthy of a duel.

Still, he managed the thing, ruthlessly sacrificing Mr. tal'Qechee's character in the process, so that they both had a common boor to deplore, and left the office with a hurried step. If he went quickly, he might arrive at his third destination very nearly at the proper time.

Hurry and distraction almost saw him murdered.

As it was, he glimpsed the attacker from the corner of his eye in time to duck, and kick, feeling a kneecap go under his boot, even as he spun to engage the second, who had a cudgel . . .

* * * ⟡ * * *

"NOT BROKEN," said his friend the chef. "Mind you, it *ought* to be broken. You have the Dragon's own luck, Don Eyr."

"I was stupid," Don Eyr protested, wincing as Zelli wrapped an icy towel around his shoulder. "He should never have touched me."

"And he?" asked the chef.

"One has a shattered kneecap; the other—the one with the stick—I think I broke his wrist."

"You think." The chef stared.

"I was distracted," Don Eyr told him. "Happily, I kept hold of Arba's rent money, or I would be hurt, indeed."

"I will tend this, Zelli—see to the small breads," the chef said, and looked closely into Don Eyr's face.

"He strikes you? Arba, I speak of."

"When he feels able," said Don Eyr. "After all, he owns me; why should he restrain himself?"

"He may *say* that he owns you, my friend, but that is not the truth. I grant that the difference is subtle, but Serat did not *sell* you. He contracted with Arba for one of his to work off his debt. Serat might beat you, all by the Code and proper. But *you are not* Arba's; and he ought to be careful—very careful, I might say—with Serat's asset."

Don Eyr stared at him, took a breath. This—Arba's lover had said much the same; giving him a hint that he had been too ignorant to take up.

"I wish to send a note around to Mr. dea'Bon," he said abruptly. "Can you spare someone to take it? I would do so myself, but I'm to wait on him tonight."

"Cho Lin will carry your note, as soon as you write it. You are in no condition to go anywhere tonight, save bed, after a good meal, and wine."

"If I do not go, I will break faith with the contract."

"Surely, the contract does not say that you will accompany him when you are ill, or injured."

"It says that I am his to command in all things," Don Eyr said. "Is he likely to cede me an evening?"

The chef was silent, and Don Eyr sighed.

"Yes, far more likely that he will derive a good deal of pleasure from dragging me here and there until dawn, and explaining to all and sundry how I happened to be clumsier than usual this evening."

"My friend, this is not a life for you."

"I agree," Don Eyr said. "Of your kindness; may I have a pen and a blank page?"

* * * ⋄ * * *

THE NOTE was dispatched.

At the chef's insistence, Don Eyr had spent a half-hour with his shoulder in the grip of the kitchen's first aid kit, which did little more than administer an analgesic, and a therapeutic massage. Had the bone been broken, it might have done more; bruises, though, had to take their own time.

He showered, and changed his clothes, and was sitting down to a bowl of soup, cheese, and a small bread—Zelli had become proficient with small breads—when there came a clamor at the delivery door, which Vessa scrambled to answer.

"Don Eyr? There's a . . . young person wanting to speak with you."

A young person?

He shoved back his stool and all but ran to the back door.

The child—not Jax Ton, but one of the older children. To his shame, he had not learned their names. He had not thought it would be needful.

"Forgive me—you are?"

"Ashti, sir." She bobbed her head, and swallowed. "Jax Ton sends that Serana had been injured."

. . . ⋄ . . .

ARBA BE DAMNED; and Serat, and their soulless, legal contract, too.

"You have not seen me," he told his friend the chef. "You have no idea where I am."

"He will not ask; but yes—if he does so, that is my tale."

Don Eyr bundled Ashti into a taxi, got out when the driver balked at going any further, and fair ran along the broken streets.

He followed the child up the rattling stairs to the ramshackle suite at the top of the building. She paused at the landing, and a shadow stepped out of darker shadows—Jax Ton, holding his pipe at ready.

"He came," Ashti said, and Jax Ton looked beyond her, to his face, his own pale and worried.

"Go in," he said, and stepped aside.

Don Eyr inclined his head, and paused a moment to steady his breathing. Serana was injured; he must not come to her in disorder.

Calmer, if not calm, he opened the door, and stepped through.

The first room was crowded with solemn-faced children, who stepped aside to let him through, to the back room, bathed in the uncertain light of emergency dims. There was a long form stretched out on what might easily have been a bed or a table, and another, sitting on the stool beside.

That figure rose at his entrance, and moved forward, to the place where the light was strongest. She was whip-thin, and dark, wearing the usual Low Port motley, with a soldier's jacket over all. There were two deliberate, diagonal scars down her right cheek.

She bowed.

"I am Fireyn, sir. The medic."

A medic. Of course. Serana was wounded. Jax Ton was a sensible lad; he would have called for a medic. Though it made his blood run cold, that she had needed one.

"How badly . . ." he began, but at that point, the bed spoke.

"A scratch only, *petit*; I swear it to you. And my own fault, to add to the sting."

"You cannot see around corners," Fireyn the medic said, in a comfortable, mild way, as if she and Serana were long known to each other. "And it is rather more than a scratch, my friend, though not nearly as bad as it could have been."

She stepped aside, and moved a hand, waving him to the bed and the stool.

"Please—you are Don Eyr, are you not?"

"Yes. Forgive me. I am remiss."

"You are, I expect, worried. Satisfy yourself, I beg. I will be outside, with Jax Ton."

The medic left. Don Eyr sank down to the stool she had vacated.

"So," he said, his voice shaking, despite an effort to sound appropriately stern. "This scratch of yours."

"I was careless, and met paz'Kormit at the corner. He took offense more quickly than I could mount a defense." She sighed.

"But as Fireyn says, it is not so bad as it could have been—he was thrusting for the gut, and I made very sure to break his arm."

"Serana . . ."

"Hush, small one; it is done, and already I am mending. Fireyn was trained as a field medic; she is very good."

"Where did she come from?"

Serana smiled at him.

"Where should she come from, save Low Port? And now it is your turn."

"My turn?" He blinked at her.

"Yes, your shoulder; there is some stiffness there; I marked it when you came in."

His shoulder, gods; it seemed a hundred years ago.

"It is a day to be careless, I suppose. I went to collect the rent today—"

"Alone!"

"Of course, alone," he said gently. "In any case, I went early to Mr. tal'Qechee, who was annoyed by my impertinence, and made me wait until all of last night's winnings had been counted out to pay me. So that he did not have to open the safe, you see."

Serana muttered something in Lutetian under her breath.

"I object, as it casts curs in a bad light. But, yes; I was therefore late for my second appointment, and was in addition required to soothe ruffled emotions, before I could collect what was owed. Leaving that appointment, I saw that I might almost be on time for the third, if only I hurried . . ."

"So you hurried, and you did not look."

"Exactly. Two in Mr. tal'Qechee's employ sought to recover the rent, plus a bonus. I disabled the first, but the second had a stick. He was almost too quick."

"Almost," said Serana, with satisfaction.

"I believe that he has a broken wrist. In any case, I had the stick until I threw it away in Mid-Port."

"And your shoulder. Broken?"

"Merely deeply insulted."

She smiled in the dimness.

"It seems obvious to me, little one, that we each do better when we have the other nearby."

"I have also reached this conclusion."

He raised his hands; lowered them.

"Serana, forgive me. I had not meant to leave you alone so long, but Arba has kept me busy every hour since I returned."

"It is fortunate that he did not require you tonight," she said.

"He did," Don Eyr said. "But your need was greater."

She drew a hard breath.

"I am flattered, but he will hurt you, little one."

"No," said Don Eyr. "He will not. I am done with this sham. And I will not leave you, Serana. Not again."

"Peace." She placed a hand on his knee. "The children, Don Eyr . . ."

"I have no notion about the children; my famously twisty mind has failed me."

"Then it is fortunate that I have had a notion," she said. "What is wrong, Don Eyr, with Low Port?"

"Aside from being lawless and blighted by poverty and ignorance?"

"You put it so succinctly! Yes, exactly. We can, with these children—we can make a beginning."

"A beginning of what?"

"We may establish a Watch house, in the grand tradition of Lutetia. I may teach; and you may. We shall gather to us also a handful of senior officers . . ."

"From whence will these senior officers come?" he wondered.

"As Fireyn, they will come from Low Port. There are those who were abandoned, as she was, by her merc unit, and others, who are not naturally lawless, and who resist a devolution into brutes. They are intermittently forces of law, order, and protection, but they perhaps lack motivation, or opportunity to do more."

"And we offer them motivation—the children?"

"Indeed, little one. What master does not wish for an apprentice to carry her work on when it is come time for her to sit on the back porch, drink wine, and tell bawdy stories?"

He smiled.

"And you—I have seen how you leap to teach, who rejected the role of a teacher at the Institute. Would it not please you, to teach, as well as to nourish?"

"You paint a picture," he said slowly. "But, Serana—in Low Port?"

"In fact. Fireyn knows of a place—an old barracks, not far from here; perhaps a block nearer the Mid-Port. There is, she tells me, a kitchen, with ovens. She not being a baker or a cook, she cannot tell me if they would meet your needs. In front, there is what had been a recruiting office, which may be well for a bakery. It is tentative; I have not seen it. Indeed, I was on my way to meet her so that I might inspect it today when I fell into error. It is how she came upon me so quickly."

"Serana . . ."

"A scratch, I swear it to you. I will be perfectly fine on the morrow."

"More lives than a cat," he said softly, putting his hand over hers.

"Just so."

"What will happen, now that you have broken Serat's agreement?" Serana asked after a time.

"I think . . . nothing," he said, slowly, the other events of the evening beginning to return to him. "I must, tomorrow, leave you—for a few hours. I sent 'round to Mr. dea'Bon; it is possible that Arba has broken Code, or at least defied the terms of the contract, on the occasions when he struck me. I have had it pointed out to me that he is not my delm, who may kill me as the whim takes him, and nothing in the contract cedes a delm's authority over me to Arba."

"So," said Serana with satisfaction.

"It may not suffice; my word against his—"

"And mine," she said, fiercely.

"And yours. But, tomorrow, I must go. Also . . ." he hesitated, unwilling to raise hope prematurely.

"Tell me."

"I may have found a way to release myself from Serat, at least in part."

She stirred.

"What has Don Eyr's twisty mind produced this time?" she wondered softly.

"Do you remember the play—*Degrees of Separation*?"

There was a pause before Serana laughed softly.

"Do you think it will suffice, the clever nadelm's scheme?"

"I think that I will lay it before Mr. dea'Bon and allow him to determine that."

He leaned forward suddenly.

"Do you, indeed, wish to remain here, to establish a Watch, and raise these children to the tradition?"

"I do. We cannot abandon them; therefore, we must teach them.

They will then teach others, and so it will spread, wider with each new generation of teachers."

"A long goal, Serana."

"But worthy."

"As you say."

Silence fell; he may have dozed, for he waked to her pulling on his hand.

"Come and lie down by me. I have missed sleeping with you, *petit*."

He needed no more persuasion than that, and so they arranged themselves, careful of their injuries, and fell asleep in each other's arms.

• • • ◇ • • •

HIS ACCOUNT as an honorable man, with Law Officer Serana Benoit corroborating, was, indeed, enough.

"You need not return to him, my lord," Mr. dea'Bon said, with stern authority. "While this matter is under examination by the Accountant's Guild, you may return to the safety of your clanhouse."

"Ah," said Don Eyr; "you anticipate my next topic. But, first, if I may—how much could I expect to realize from the sale of my property on Ezhel'ti?"

"As it happens, I have an offer on my desk, from your father's clan. Their offer, so my colleague on Ezhel'ti tells, me is low, though not insultingly so. We may be able to negotiate upwards somewhat. Have you instructions?"

"Yes," Don Eyr said, "sell it for as good a price as you can reasonably get. Do not endanger the sale by attempting to wring every bit from the buyer. My need is cash, in the very near future."

Mr. dea'Bon made a note on his pad.

"I will see it done, my Lord." He looked up. "I remind that you have complete control over the account which is fed by your rents. If your need exceeds those funds, I am prepared, personally, to advance you a portion of the money you will certainly realize from the sale of your property."

"Thank you; that may be necessary, but for the moment, let it remain a possibility."

"Yes, my lord."

"Excellent; we now address the likelihood of my return to the supposed safety of my clanhouse. Under no circumstances will I do so. My intention is set up my own establishment. I will remain on-planet, for I think that may be required, but I wish to file an Intention to Separate, immediately."

Mr. dea'Bon raised his eyebrows.

"That is . . . quite old."

"Is it disallowed?"

"Disallowed? Oh, no. No, not at all. I will have to do some research, but there is nothing to prevent you from filing such an Intention. However, you must, if memory serves me, set forth the conditions by which you would return to the arms of your clan."

"Yes. I will gladly return if and when Serat agrees to accommodate my household. Which at this moment includes Captain Benoit, nine children, and a calico kitten. I anticipate the household will grow, as we establish our base. Also, I insist that the monies belonging to my household shall be kept separate from the clan's accounts, and the delm shall be specifically barred from access."

Mr. dea'Bon had a dreamy look on his face. Very nearly, he was seen to smile. He made a brisk series of notes on his pad, and looked up once more.

"I believe I may work with this. May I ask, when we have achieved a successful outcome, that I be allowed to share the work with my colleagues? An Intention of Separation is rare enough, but these terms . . ."

He blinked and emerged somewhat from his dream state.

"You do understand, my lord? You must be prepared to return to Serat's care, if your terms are met."

"I understand," said Don Eyr.

"Excellent. There is one more detail. While the investigation into Arba's breach of contract is taking place, by Code your delm may freeze your quartershare, and your personal accounts." He paused.

"I advise that, in this case, Serat long ago emptied your accounts. The monies you received while you were attending school were from the rent of your house on Ezhel'ti."

He glanced once more at his note pad.

"Is there any other way in which I might serve you, my lord?"

"I think—yes. There is an old barracks at Crakle and Toom in the Low Port. Can you find for me who owns it, and how I may acquire it?"

Another note.

"Yes. Is there a comm code I may have, in order to report my progress?"

"I will have it for you . . . tomorrow, sir. For today, we are wanted in our household."

"I understand, sir."

The old gentleman rose, and bowed.

"Until soon, my lord. Captain Benoit."

FIVE

Some Years Later

THE MORNING RUSH WAS OVER, and Don Eyr stepped out onto the porch to bask in the mid-morning sunshine. The porch faced the exercise yard, and there was a self-defense lesson in progress. Cisco and Ail Den were pushing the older children hard, and they were rising to the challenge.

The younger children were at their ethics lesson, taught by Serana. Later, he would meet them in the kitchen, and they would collaborate on making the mid-day meal for the household. A household that had expanded, from the original nine children, to a dozen, guarded and educated by five very capable adults, supported by a veritable army of cats, fierce mousers, and interested companions.

There was more—a small neighborhood had grown up around them; an area of relative peace, in which the neighbors assisted, and kept watch for, each other. The bakery provided bread, and sweets, and a gathering place, and the children of other households often attended lessons with the children of the bake house.

Don Eyr sighed, and stretched, and, hearing the step behind him, turned into Serana's embrace.

"Is it well, little one?" she asked softly.

He laughed softly.

"It is well, Serana. Very well, indeed."

Une Petite Liste de Mots Étranges
A small list of strange words

chouquettes	(f): cream puffs
commis	(f): junior chef
dacquoise	(f): almond and butternut meringue cake
delm	(l): the head of a clan
École de Cuisine	(f): School of Cooking
grand-père	(f): grandfather
Lutetia	(g): . . . in our timeline, Lutetia was the capital city of the Parisii, a Gallic tribe. It was renamed Paris back a few years ago— Wikipedia says 360 AD.
masyr	(l): monsieur
melant'i	(l): who one is, in whole or in part, depending upon circumstances
merde	(f): damn. More or less.
nadelm	(l): the heir to the delm
on-dits	(f): "they say" aka gossip
boulangerie	(f): bakery
petit	(f): small
qe'andra	(l): a person of business; sort of an accountant-lawyer
relumma	(l): one-quarter of a Liaden year

✧✧✧

Key:
f: French
g: Gallic
l: Liaden

✦ Excerpts from Two Lives ✦

A LIADEN STORY that's been waiting to be written for a long time from the Terran side of things, "Excerpts from Two Lives" is based on a song mentioned in our third novel, Carpe Diem. We'd known from the song that a tragedy was involved, but exactly how that unfolded we didn't know until this story—requested by Baen editors Christopher Roucchio and Tony Daniel for their anthology Star Destroyers—was finished.

✦✦✦

Averil 21, 407 Confederation Standard Year

"Beam Banks One and Two, go live as leads. We have identified and targeted a threat. Prepare to fire on my command, on radar's central target. This is not a drill, you will go to full combat power. Saturate the disc at all wavelengths."

Proper quiet, proper response. The ship's routine went on but the air circulators changed speed, and life-support panels grew angry red as combat-power overrides initiated. Small bells echoed the necessities of combat: hatches, airlocks, and pressure doors sealed.

"Combat power up." Nerves in that voice, but it didn't squeak.

"Lead banks, we'll need three consecutive full-power bursts from each—lock that in! Bank Three, slave to Bank One, two point seven

275

five second delay, wide angle. Bank Four, slave to Bank Three, ultrawide angle. Banks Five through Twelve, go to high alert. Missilery Section, watch for bulk breakaway going in-system, target at will. Section leaders, you will particularly react to bulk breakaway coming our way."

The crew shared glances. They'd deviated, on captain's orders, from what was to be a calm and peaceful direct rendezvous with the RosaRing.

Meteor shields went live automatically. The target was a little over a tenth of a light-second away, so energetic debris wasn't an immediate threat.

The captain said nothing, watching this crew's first live-fire action. The sub-captain was sweating: His experience on this system was simulations. His battle experience had been on ships whose entire beam output was negligible compared to any single projector in any of the battleship's twenty multibeam projector banks. There was a reason these beams were called planet busters, as they were about to prove.

Radar showed the target, distance and rotation. Like many planets, there was ice at the poles. Like many planets there was atmosphere. Like many planets, one might target the broadside equator, where rotational stress assisted the destructive effects of incoming beams.

The captain and the sub-captain had spent several sessions in the captain's cabin perfecting this plan. The crew thought it merely the third drill, but the target *was* a danger to Trikandle; the sub-captain had done the math the captain required.

The sub-captain's orders from the captain: develop an attack sequence, prepare the crew through drills, and then give the deck commands required for the kill, on the captain's signal. The captain required excellence from those who served under him.

In return, in those sessions, he displayed excellence. He'd shared the words and codes of exigency—the ship's self-destruct sequence, the code of relinquishing command, the codes for . . . all of them. Smit had taught him, and he passed the ship's necessities on.

The captain listened to the deck, the radar, the hum of power that underlay the deck, the stars beyond, just as he'd seen Admiral Smit listen. The form was Admiral Smit's axiom: Effective command radiates power; those under command bask in the rays of their orders.

Watching the screens, feeling the universe flow around him, the captain radiated command, looking firmly at the sub-captain and saying "*Ni faris*," into the mic that reached only the sub-captain's headset.

A startle there, a so brief pause. The sub-captain's glance fled from the captain's face to his command screen, and he echoed the captain to his crew. "We commit! Fire!"

The deck thrummed and the power was an audible rasp ending in a noise that was . . .

"Zap!"

The sotto voce comment by a crewman unseen barely beat the squeal of discharge that thrummed the entire fabric of the battleship. On screens crew throughout the ship saw what happens when a bank of planet-buster projectors hurls the forces of chaos.

The captain blinked. Some teaching moments have more impact than others. When he'd accepted this mission on that Day of Changes, when he'd last held Verita in their own bed, he hadn't expected to train a crew so raw, nor to have orders on file permitting such a mission. Things were going well, seventeen days in system.

Change Year Day, Sumtap 01, 404 CSY

They'd begun that Day of Changes knowing there *would be* changes.

This was not their first Day of Changes; they'd learned the meaning of it together as child scholars, learned the joy of festive food and guessing games, learned later of the small pains that might come from the day, then, the larger ones as schoolmates and first crushes were pared away by the necessities of more adult pursuits.

Eventually they'd pled their cases one to another for more than stolen kisses and learned to trust in each other's hard-driving ambition. They turned to each other rather than others, asking "How do we solve this?" or, admitting being at wit's end: "Solve this!" They wore matching bands of custom Triluxian in honor of their plans.

His ambition led him to the fleet, in search of opportunity as it recovered from the debacle of the Battle of Azren Clouds. He'd risen quickly, leading several raiding missions and rescues before being attached to Admiral Smit and *Implacable*.

She, drawn to research, joined the efforts to extract the most dangerous secrets of the Ligonier Library, where her skills at academic infighting were as recognized as her scientific insights. Nor had Verita shared all her solvings with the academic community, reserving for herself and Kiland the news that she'd moved from theory to actual practice several strains of those life-constructions thought lost in the collapsed universe their foremothers had fled.

While the old guard flailed at the changes wrought by dusty carbon clouds invading their trade lanes, Kiland and Verita shone as beacons for the future. Let the failures retire or suicide—they dealt only in power and success.

On that memorable Day of Change, they played before the clock buzzed them officially into the dawn. Verita began by nipping his ear and spooning him, her hands busy, mouth full of kisses and words; promises, teases—and *more*, her potent arms pulling his shoulder, aiming his willing mouth and . . .

After, they sat in their atrium, cheered by their nakedness as ocean breezes brought them spring's promise of more than mere renewal. What sprang from this year would crown their lives.

By tradition, they arrived at dusk, he from the south, she from the north, at their own front door. Flowers and gifts they each carried in profusion, the promise of change strong in their hands while their faces were a little secret, the mouths a little sad under the smiles.

"I will be your slave tonight, my love," said Verita, as they exchanged delicate fragrant bouquets on their threshold. "And you will solve my passion.

"Unless," she added, as she followed him into their home, "unless you demand I solve for you, in which case I will take tomorrow."

"Slave or solve." He laughed. "I'll savor either."

He trembled with lust, though they were still dressed, and his eyes darkened his smile. But her smile, too, was near fled, dancing on the tip of her tongue.

"Is it well, *Katido Volupto*?" he whispered, and shed his burdens as she shed hers, the hall table not large enough for the wealth of gifts they had brought.

"It is," she said. "It is so well it is nearly perfect. The project goes forward . . . yes. But until it is announced, I can hardly tell you more. And for you?"

"Yes, it is nearly perfect. Next week, I return to space!"

She laughed, and was relieved, nearly knocking him down as she wrapped herself about him, filling his eyes with her kisses and his ears with her demand, "Tell me, tell me that you will not be lonely. Next week I go to space, as well!"

Averil 04, 407 CSY

Implacable in a hurry was a sight to be seen, which was good, since there was no way of hiding the fearsome output of its antique power units. The mighty timonium plasma sets spewed neutrons and neutrinos alike while powering the last ship of the line from any of the Cloudgate armed forces. She left behind an elemental thermal signature that might cloud an astronomer's view of the cosmos for centuries, but the chance of there being such, here, was negligible.

Ship of the line was a misnomer when applied to *Implacable*, for most ships of its type fielded two centuries ago were gone. Of that generation of *batalsipo grandas*—a dozen dozen ships more powerful than entire modern star fleets—only *Implacable* held air. The others were victims of their wars or, as often, dismantled for resources.

Verita watched the secret news of *Implacable*'s arrival. Station Ops was slow in this; her own equipment better tuned—she'd had budget for new installs while Ops was stuck with original equipment. So much of the mission was on scant budget, including using the mighty *Implacable* as a towboat! However, the calculations had worked well for the incoming trip, with the transit from Jump point to Trikandle's one-hundred-day orbit a mere twelve days. This time *Implacable* was too awkwardly placed for such a quick run, she knew.

Kiland's Change Day news had placed him back aboard the vessel that had made him one of the most powerful men in the reformed Confederation. The same Change Day saw Verita leap to her life-long goal—science leader of an expedition that could return the Confederation to greatness.

As principal investigator she was technically second-in-command of the RosaRing, an agricultural lab repurposed into a self-sufficient xenoplanet research laboratory. The administrator's position was higher in the flow charts, but Prenla Verita was the reason the RosaRing had been dispatched.

Among the last messages from *Implacable* as it departed the system had been several for her, under admiral's seal—sent by Kiland, with Admiral Smit's approval. Each was more full of promise than the last, and the final promising what they'd suspected: Smit was retiring, and he favored as commander of *Implacable* none but Kiland.

Now orbiting the fecund planet Trikandle, the real mission of the RosaRing was daunting: hurry Trikandle through an evolution toward the oxygenated photosynthetic atmosphere required to add it as a populated Confederation world. This was hands-on work—with satellites, imaging systems, drones, rovers, and observer craft.

The Confederation's directors had risked much in mounting the expedition at all, and they'd cast for glory over stability, rushing their claim on the Trikandle system by making the station a permanent fixture.

The atmosphere on Trikandle was an unbreathable amalgam: storms of methane mixing with unstable compounds, leaving odd pools of multilayered liquids . . . including water. Measurable pockets of oxygen enriched the atmosphere in deep valleys and craters. It was now oxygen rich for a world where free oxygen had hitherto been bound to rocks or was a trace gas high in the atmosphere.

On Trikandle life roiled, it flittered, it rolled; it gathered itself into mats of color and motion, it launched itself against barriers of other life with potent chemistry of acid and base. It grew through ceaseless life cycles of solution and dissolution. As it writhed into toxic tentacles, grew sniffer stalks and eye puddles, it fed a future Verita was struggling to direct.

Verita was supported by the work she'd done since graduate school, fed by secrets pilfered in the great war more than a century gone by, when *Implacable*'s weapons led the attack on Quadraterra's defenses and stood guard over the looting of the Ligonier Library.

Some of that looted knowledge had been useless; the physics of a closed and finite universe did not translate perfectly to this one. But in the end times of the old universe, there'd been clones and all manner of living abominations shaped by the unknowable minds of the Great Enemy, *Sherikas*. That there were detailed instructions of the building of such pseudolife was a secret Verita held close.

Scientists at Ligonier Library had plotted their control of the new universe, using the tools that had won the old. They'd been pushed to unleash at-will terraforming, wild cellular advances—and much of their knowledge had come to Verita's hands.

Verita's ambition supported Kiland's. They were a good team politically and would carry their bloodlines to the top of the Confederation's hierarchy. Well-placed by birth and education, they would easily live two centuries or more. Their Confederation would sweep aside the remnants of the old Terran Empire, the Liaden, and even the Yxtrang.

In Verita's display screens *Implacable*'s thrust sparkled across many bands, infernos created by in-system engines that were no longer welcome in most habited systems.

The Confederation's pride and joy . . . well, once there was a new source of accessible wealth under their control, a whole new planet to be used, followed by many more to be farmed at will—then, *Implacable* could be a regal exemplar of their might!

Kiland's parting message going out she knew by heart, and believed it still:

"I live to serve your needs and solve your problems, my Verita. Our next Change Day together we shall reprise and surmount all our dreams and fantasies."

And now—*Implacable* was back, and all of their future beckoned.

• • •✧• • •

IT WAS THE SIXTH HUNDREDTH DAY since the special pair of rovers was unleashed.

Today, Verita studied the area called Quozmo. The implication of the new, bolder streaking on ground and air was clear to her, though she really wished to be sure it was not yet clear to Admin Desler. Admin was only a few days returned from her course of enforced rest. In other days her episode might have been called "nervous exhaustion." Admin's work had become more difficult with the several suicides among the staff overworked with aging equipment and shredded schedules. Desler, a tenured academic appointed to the post to remove her from a politically sensitive position, was unequal to the increased stress.

It had taken time for the crew psychologist to understand the situation and by then, Admin Desler had been in a precarious state. She was taken under care, some of her work redistributed to Verita and to Desler's assistant.

The right corner of the screen showed a notification—ground side ops. She gestured and took the voice call.

"Investigator, I've a message from Quozmo Ob2. They've lost relay from the Debae and Dabbie rover pair again and they're down to four drones, three of them lightweights. Do we want the drones all back now?"

Verita pushed back at her hair—if Kiland didn't prefer it long enough to brush and caress she'd have cut it short.

"Condense the last of the valley images and send them to me. Begin reacquisition interrogation on the rovers. Work on that, priority!"

The rover teams . . . the rover teams acted like they were sentient. They weren't, of course, Verita never quite dared bringing both parts of the legacy together. Though for this, she had considered it.

The rovers *were* semi-autonomous. They could go for years without input—collecting, analyzing, reporting when queried. The pair's self-selected braided trail method was working so well she'd asked the next units be programmed to emulate it. The lead rovers were encountering pods and accumulations of . . . things. Life. New life. Life chosen and sown by her will, growing in a wilderness of chaos.

The valley the rovers roamed was a tectonic artifact, more a long gash than a crater. The upthrust of plateau at the far end looked to be impact residue, but her studies confirmed the heights as cooling volcanic plumes, recent. Those plumes generated thermal activity in the valley, a rich source of energy and minerals. Minerals including timonium, platinum, gold.

The valley was geologically active, with three rivers rushing into it. The hydrocarbons were interesting, but one of those rivers ran seasonally as water, as it did now, sometimes sharing the riverbeds, sometimes competing. Within the last year, spongy mats of winter vegetation had begun catching against the cliffsides, and the oxygen levels were notably higher.

"Yes," Verita said to ground ops, "recover the drones, as long as they haven't been below the pressure threshold."

"Altitude threshold, right, not height threshold? We've been pushing, as you requested. There's been wind and updrafts around the mount—we've been using that to keep the glidefoils active beyond normal duration."

Verita closed her eyes, considering. Yes, she'd approved that. There shouldn't have been any problem there, surely . . .

"Show me the flight paths. Show me recent weather, too."

As those screens came up, simultaneously there was a shout from somewhere down the hall and a chime.

The admin's voice rang out throughout the RosaRing.

"Attention, all staff. We have a distant Jump arrival confirmed and are awaiting ID. Scan Security, please man your stations. Timing is appropriate for our Year Three Rendezvous."

Verita grinned, even though she'd known. She had so much to share with Kiland, doubtless he for her.

In the meantime, she had a decision to make.

She leaned back, sniffing at the flight paths now on screen as if she could scent a hint of ammonia, or of the crystalline precipitate which sometimes wafted to the gravel beds left behind after the flush of spring floods.

The pressure gradients were in flux. The stronger of the atmospheric currents had tunneled through the flat current they called the mesostream, which sometimes held considerable water vapor. The visualization showed a convective dance then, as if ramped high into the sky by the volcanic uplands, high into the stratopause.

Technically, the drones were not to fly as low as the stratopause, where the temperatures neared the freezing point of water. In such conditions microbes might be found on normal worlds.

Verita made her decision.

"Call them home."

Averil 04, 407 CSY

"What's the measure on that? Are we even at the right star? Where's the gassers?"

Kiland's sarcasm was inappropriate if nearly inaudible.

Automatics admitted that yes, *Implacable* had come to the right place despite her recalcitrant Struven units and the haste of their departure. The gas giants rolled in their orbits, the companion brown dwarf continued its distant, lonely journey three quarters of a light-year away among rocky clouds of debris. *He* read them that quickly, but his crew . . .

His crew checked their instruments, followed protocol, eventually they nodded at him.

He signaled the traditional arrival announcement. It went out without the usual time-to-dock though, and he . . . did the math himself, signaling the sub-captain to do the same.

"Shield at basic," he said, but the automatics were seeing to that, the junior officers chasing behind, just in case.

"Weapons checks, threats?"

There were no threats.

At full in-system power it would take them days just to overcome the fractional errors; right now they were moving at significant velocity *away* from their target. The revamped crew was still learning the ship—Admiral Smit's veteran crew would never have arrived so far off the mark, or so unsure of the recover.

"Attention, *Implacable*, we are arrived and making our way to the RosaRing. This will not be a twelve-day jaunt; expect full maintenance routines. Deck officers set duty cycles. Acceleration alerts within the hour."

Kiland looked to the sub-captain.

"Three channels, in the clear, Captain. The time signals are there, but no space weather roundups. The orbital elements are automatic, but the star observation reports ought to be continuous."

"Record what's there, get us synced, ask for what's missing. Send captain's regards to the RosaRing's Trikandle Expedition. Tell them we're bringing treasures from home. Once comm schedules are established, send and request the archives. In the meanwhile, let us compare projected courses, shall we? We have work to do."

Averil 05, 407 CSY

From Principal Investigator via RosaRing Secure COMM 7 for Captain's Eyes Only

Point A: My joy and strength, the investigation has moved rapidly beyond experiment and is well into proof. The rover pair are the perfect delivery system—I utilize testing systems on board to recreate the binary delivery methods outlined in the records we inherited. These are superior organisms, they continue to multiply not only in the track of the vehicles, as I'd intended, but well beyond. I expect great things, and find myself limited by materials and conditions on station. I expect you may solve many of my minor problems.

Point B: I remain your devoted slave at all times.

PI Verita

Averil 07, 407 CSY

From Captain, *Implacable*, to RosaRing Secure COMM 7 for Principal Investigator Only

My Beauty Beyond All, you astound me with your progress, which is prodigious and worthy. You exceed our original goals for so early a date. My progress is less pleasing, our dreams delayed by both orbital mechanics and politics.

Admiral Smit's retirement was received with much division. His ascension to council head was contested and defeated; he demurred taking vice chair. My position is at risk; the opposition demanded the immediate dismantling of *Implacable* as a threat to border peace. This failed, but our military mission has been de-emphasized, and my term on the Fleet Council, which is statutory as *Implacable*'s commander, may end after this voyage.

My crew is far less than full strength. Many retirements and cost-balancings have gone into effect. Review the appended, please. Many experienced officers and crew were replaced by fresh graduates, as if I head a training squad!

Implacable's whole mission is a bargaining point between the parties, as a support ship for the RosaRing. We shall move forward. Your success is paramount to our success.

I am, as always, willing to command such an eager supplicant. Remember that in restriction is liberation.

Captain Kiland

· · ·◇· · ·

THEY had in the course of their bed-talk discussed much that was secret and that stood her in good stead now. The charts, spreadsheets, and projections revealed Kiland as an optimist. Ship's provisioning had suffered. Even a five-year mission was perilous. Weaponry updates were off the budget, savings were achieved by replacing seasoned staff with new graduates, positions left empty, and militia called up for training. Ship's company included too few experienced pilots, and too many untested crew.

Alone in her suite, Verita suffered for Kiland. His setback made her success ever more important. Re-energized by his necessity, she applied herself more fully to duties at hand.

Averil 14, 407 CSY

From Principal Investigator via RosaRing Secure COMM 7 for Captain's Eyes Only

My Strength and Direction, one is desolate to be less than perfect in all things for you. I must request technical aid as well as spiritual solving. So often your lessons bring me clarity.

In the face of Station Admin's orders to conserve fuel can *Implacable* offer assistance until the fuel and drones you carry are delivered? Might a more militant drone-recovery protocol be employed? Can you read signals and plot better courses? Assure me—assure the station!—with your guidance.

I suggest and cannot demand; my Strength reflects yours at all times.

Your latest lesson assists my considerations and will be recalled as often as possible until we are joined again in the harmony of a Perfected Evening.

PI Verita

• • •✧• • •

KILAND'S tactical officers enjoyed the challenge of the long-distance scan and solve; they caught the orders as a frolic, as if they were back at school. He had them look for ways to improve the drone's routes, to search for threats in the system, and all threats to the RosaRing. They daily requested more information from the ring. They worked with energy, concentration, amusement.

He was less amused than concerned. The ship's skills depended far more on the practicing of things his staff recalled only from school than they ought.

As captain he deserved a crew capable of supporting his—and the ship's—necessities. Therefore he would push the boundaries of these youngsters. They would become the crew *Implacable* deserved. Each order would be carried out with dedication and devotion. Each solution would be born of submission to the necessity of mission. They would learn. The sub-captain in particular needed growth if he were to serve as a proper second.

Averil 17, 407 CSY

From Captain, *Implacable*, to RosaRing Secure COMM 7 for Principal Investigator Only

Sweet Touch of A Giving Noon, the crew relishes drone tracking. We thank you for the opportunity. The more experienced appear reticent to enjoy our adoption of a Joint Mission. The brightest see that dedication to Mission is all they want.

Your administrator professes surprise at *Implacable*'s ability to compute simple math and solve minor problems in interception. Yes, we can access the telemetry channels of your drones; we pick up signals from your rovers as well. Confederation leaders at many levels lack understanding of what this ship is and what it can do, as they lack an understanding of the RosaRing's potential. We will show them all; we will demonstrate that, together, we can transform planets.

Your administrator embraces details? Perhaps you may offer her more to deal with, so that she may be fully involved in details. She need not be overly concerned with flight planning now that the RosaRing is again in *Implacable*'s shadow.

The tender's co-pilot is a former naval officer; he ought have none of the finicky training the head pilot admires. I append a flight plan for the tender—discussed at mess among the more forward of my sub-officers—which may permit the tender to better retrieve your drones as well as utilize the gravity well to regain lost energy.

I have engaged the co-pilot in a radio correspondence; we discuss a campaign long past in which a ship not unlike the tender was able to overperform simple guidelines designed for ordinary pilots. I, of course, have no orders to give about what must be pilot's choice, nor you; we may simply discuss, suggest, and request.

I remain devoted to the Delicate Delights and such arts you perfect through me, I admonish you to please yourself and please me in all you do.

Captain Kiland

Averil 18, 407 CSY

The pilot's message was not quoted in full; it was apparent that Kiland's suggestions had been acted upon. Alas, the pilot and co-pilot were barely on speaking terms. She? She was unnerved by information that there were now stains on the skin of the tender, where it had driven deeper into the atmosphere than ever before, bringing with it all of the drones. It was a daring mission, no doubt.

The pilot had been on sleep shift when the dive sequence began and went to the administrator straight away after they'd returned to the RosaRing. The tender pilot . . .

The tender pilot was not a biologist.

The tender pilot was not a chemist.

The pilot was a pilot. Stains on her ship offended her; and she found them a clear sign that pilot and co-pilot needed a break, each from the other.

There were also stains on the drones, which the pilot cared about not one whit. That was someone else's job. Drones were tended by their own staff, their samples double-checked in the lab.

Verita grimaced. She'd been enjoying a crew amused by the understanding that the *Implacable*'s captain and their own prime investigator were a link-couple. Now she needed to become again the firm scientist and see the entirety of the crew reminded of the necessity for proper isolation technique and contamination control sequences.

Cha-bling, went the annunciator. The administrator's direct line shattered the usual screen image, followed by an image of the administrator herself, chewing her lips, staring at the screen still blank on her end.

Verita composed herself with a deep breath and a straightening of her lab coat; she moved three empty otim cups from screen range. Another centering breath and she was ready to be distantly polite. . . .

"Your comm fails to display, Verita. If you are present, reply so I don't have to send a messenger. This is rather important!"

She composed her expression to what she hoped was a look of general, unalarmed interest, then finished her reach to activate the visual display on her end.

"Important, Administrator?"

"Yes, important! There's an outer-belt asteroid on a collision course with Trikandle. The captain has sent me a secure message! A strike on the planet is within the margin of error, he tells me."

Verita felt her pleasant expression vanish—

"Our mission!"

The administrator offered a grim little smile, apparently pleased with this reaction.

"Yes, our mission, indeed, yes. Also, our station. I gather this 'pass' as he calls it is not immediate but needs be dealt with. There is some factor of resonances and such still being determined. I am not informing the crew, wishing not to spread alarm."

The administrator pursed her lips, her visage taking on the near rictus she assumed when issuing commands not to be denied.

"You shall not tell the crew, do you understand? I *will* direct the captain to inform you of the technical details, and I shall decide what needs be done. I have promised a reply within two shifts, so hold yourself ready for consultation."

With that the screen went back to ordinary.

· · ·✧· · ·

THE CREW took direction well; they'd even taken to the maintenance-plus-pursuit staffing. Given that they were technically shorthanded, with entire Fleet Operations sections of dozens reduced to shifts of pairs, this was a fine way to return the ship to the spit-and-polish days of Smit.

The sub-captain in particular seemed to relish his extra duties. While he'd commanded a small vessel in recent peacetime, his service had not been properly recognized. Passed over several times for political reasons, he, like Kiland, was a volunteer to the *Implacable*. A man with ambition made a good ally.

The sub-captain's shifts responded for him as well as they did for the captain, and he had enough camaraderie with crew to have a mathematician come forward with the threat the asteroid posed several orbits out—which was to say, eleven hundred and seventy-two Standard Years, away. They would chase that asteroid down now. It was the duty of a captain to remove known space hazards.

Reward? The crew would see and taste their own power. For the moment they worked harder and fell into the proper crew-spirit.

Averil 22, 407 CSY

From Principal Investigator via RosaRing Secure COMM 7 for Captain's Eyes Only

My full heart, my hot blood, surely you have outdone yourself! The destruction of that menace delights. It was good that the event could be shared, though some, like the administrator, were shaken by it. In fact, the administrator, speaking confidentially, considers she might order passage on *Implacable* rather than attempt another three years. She asks that I hold updates on my work for the moment.

I have agreed that I could share burden of a Joint Command with her second, and on the other side I have spoken with the Second, who is willing to have promotion sooner. She has been consulting with the physicians to that end.

Admin's oversight of operations has been recently uneven; meals have been late due to minor problems with the energy systems, the air circulators are changed to manual on some shifts as they are affected by a glitch in the attitude controls as we maintain our synchronous orbit above the prime research zone. It is vexing, but to be expected with the staff waiting for decisions easily made. It will be solved soon, I am certain.

On the practical side, the chief tender pilot placed herself on sick leave. The tender's new pilot has been dropping off-the-record radiosondes along with the regular drones. These drop parallel to the rovers; they are wonderfully useful. I see exponential expansion to the limits of the habitat boundaries. We should see blossoming that will change Trikandle sooner rather than later.

My work consumes me nearly as much as my desire to offer myself up to you.

PI Verita

• • • ✧ • • •

THE CAPTAIN was pleased. The crew was brazen in their newfound self-esteem. They'd done something violent and powerful, they'd destroyed—down to gas, plasma, gravel, and powder—a worldlet. The ship might have landed there, the crew might have walked suited in the ravines, collected water from the ice packs. It had been *a place*, and by their action it was gone. They were ready, eager, proven. They searched for more threats, they honed their skills at drills to battle station.

The captain let them strut for themselves; he was willing to admire them, their newfound ambition. They were no longer in awe of the ship—now they were in awe of themselves! Someone had even slipped him a recording of a new song sung on the ship. Made by the same mischievous mathematician who discovered it, the song celebrated *Implacable* and her captain and described the obliteration of the asteroid. The old Fleet might be gone but the urge of youth to bathe in the glory of power had not died!

Averil 24, 407 CSY

From Captain, *Implacable*, to RosaRing Secure COMM 7 for Principal Investigator Only

My Second Heart, I do so desire to share your tremble. Your work engages my crew; we study Trikandle with our sensors and shall share our findings with you. Particularly involved are crew in meteorology and mathematics. I am informed that some regions we'd imaged last trip have changed drastically in these three years. There are streaks of new color evident on the continent you concentrate upon. Also dots of that new color are seen where the rivers flow, around shore lines, ridges, elsewhere. Are the currents and winds so strong? Do the tender flights and the drones work so hard? I shall return to the High Command with evidence of your success.

As always, thoughts of your touch and tone beguile me to sleep; I seek your ministrations.

Captain Kiland

Averil 26, 407 CSY

From Principal Investigator via RosaRing Secure COMM 7 for Captain's Eyes Only

My Partner in Sense and Sensation, I quiver at your approach. The administrator may now opt for very early transfer to *Implacable*, as she is finding sleep and concentration difficult. Several of the lab crew are reporting such issues as well—I ascribe it to general excitement over the approach of your ship.

The changes you report outside the river valleys we've studied amaze. I am not so much sleepless as vibrating with energy and anticipation. I hope the cargo shifts will allow the new drones among the first items available; the old ones have become unreliable. We lost one to weather, an upper current overwhelmed it. A second drone found it crash-landed outside of our prime valley with a large burden of unexpended biotic canisters.

Do tell me you have new challenges and rewards for me, I seek to please you soonest.

PI Verita

Averil 27, 407 CSY

From Captain, *Implacable*, to RosaRing Secure COMM 7 for Principal Investigator Only

Your burden is mine; you will find my requirements a pleasure.

I have requests from your station administrator asking of arrangements for a ceremony of arrival; I hesitate to authorize an on-docking event out of hand. She mentions the possibility of a transfer; paradoxically she requests it and can order it and seems overmatched by her position, indeed. My staff must prompt hers for ordinary transmissions and data sharing, she runs an unprofessional operation, I am afraid.

Can it be that there is a weather wave spreading your new biotics? Is it a chemical reaction catalyzed by the increase in oxygen? Our observers report a surge of color changes on planet; the spectra show unusual mixtures, the temperature sensors show wild variations. Have you science you can share on this?

Supplies will be offloaded by pod and bin, we have become a cargo vessel and are not suited to it! The sub-captain reports basic supplies in the first rounds, and then laboratory items, by necessity of the pod mounts. The pattern is preset.

Do not doubt that I will be firm with you, very soon. I long to hear you whispering.

Captain Kiland

Averil 29, 407 CSY

Glaring at the screen in front of her, Verita rotated the troth ring on her third finger without looking at it. The weight and the repetition were comforting. As much as she twisted it, she couldn't change the fact that docking with *Implacable* was just sixteen hours away, and things were getting worse instead of better.

This latest news from the lab sections was not good. Four of seven biology technicians in the drone research area were on sick call and both of the service mechanics.

She clicked off the message; the staff knew their work. She'd get to them later with a pep talk about yesterday's results. Now, she needed to concentrate . . .

This was not how she'd intended to display a well-controlled station! The mechanics complained of different maladies—one of skin rashes leaving behind a kind of scar, the other of dizziness with headache. All complained of strange odors and odd tastes; she'd not visited the hangar for days to avoid the sneezes that had become common there. Her own tests . . . well, she was not a medical doctor. It just seemed wise to be cautious and remain in her offices and suite.

It was unfortunate that replacement drones could not be brought to bear sooner. He should have known that chasing the asteroid would add delay . . . but no, nothing about this was *his* fault. Nothing.

· · ·✧· · ·

VERITA opened her eyes, realizing that she'd been swimming in the half-sleep she'd become prone to. A chime in the halls had woken her, one of the administrator's many notes to maintenance.

She was in her own chair, office door locked, so no one saw her start to wakefulness. She was sleeping short shift as she tried to keep up. The returned rovers reported astounding amounts of local free oxygen in the long midafternoon of the planet's forty-hour day. Not an atmosphere breathable by humans, by any means, but one promising explorers might walk the world, extracting the oxygen they needed directly, within a century, perhaps even a decade. She wanted to see it sooner, she wanted to make it happen in a rush of . . .

A chime woke her; the screen was filled by the administrator, her face blotchy and busy with tension.

"Investigator? The tender is under my direct control. Understand me? Until I leave! The pilot's under doctor's care for exhaustion. The backup pilot is nearing the same point. People are ill all around you because you push too hard. You push everyone too hard, Verita."

. . . ✧ . . .

KILAND suppressed the yawn by force of will as he went over routine schedules on the bridge. Smit had always done his paper work on the bridge, too—it was good for the crew to see the leader at work. Lunch was only moments away . . .

"Captain?" The sub-captain's voice was firm. "I don't have any incident reports from the station on this—would you like to take a look on the main screen? I was having some of the crew practice long-range visual ID and we were getting mismatches—"

At high magnification the RosaRing spun in space, filling the screen. The station silhouette was clear but the alternating angled white and blue stripes, clear on large parts of the hull, were smudged and blotchy, as if overlain by a layer of greenish rust around the protruding docking bay on the lower reaches.

"I don't think I've ever seen anything like this, sir."

Kiland's boredom fell away, memory jostling his concentration, trying to come to the front of the mind.

He pointed at a second screen.

"I'ul some samples from our outbound recorded images there, Sub-Captain, close as you can to a match. Ask Station Operations if they've suffered any gas leakage or maintenance issues they haven't passed on? Get as good an image as you can for them. . . . And ask Ops . . . no, ask the administrator's office to share results of the routine tests they've run on our docking ports and loading locks. Also, request current readings on the inner docks."

"Sir!"

The sub-captain issued commands, brought the bridge to alert, used the keypad to search images and bring them live on screen, ran a match, adjusted sizes.

The ordinary sounds on the bridge fell away; watch partners messaged quick notes or whispered.

The captain hand-signaled the sub-captain, who approached, bowing slightly to hear the captain's order.

Instead, the captain asked, "Were you on academy on the mount, or on the islands?"

The sub-captain, caught by what seemed a non-sequitur, hesitated and said "Why, like you, the islands, sir."

The captain nodded, then nodded toward the images on the main screen.

"So you are familiar with the Citadel's wind walls? Perhaps along Chespick Beach, or the tidal falls at Injridge?"

The sub-captain's features showed remembrance, a touch of a smile for some assignation late night at oceanside, where the waves and wind conspired to produce a lovely romantic place overseen by ancient star-bleached walls smudged at base and higher with the greens, browns, and even reds of algal scums.

Recognition blossomed and . . .

"There's nothing to grow, there's nothing to grow on if there was . . ."

The sub-captain quieted, perplexity wrinkling his youthful visage in much the way passion might.

Kiland nodded and sighed. "Not an oxy world yet, is it? Who knows what's a balmy seaside for what's already growing down there?"

. . . . ✧ . . .

"STATION OPS—sir, I'm afraid we woke them up. Our contact is somewhat unfamiliar with standard comm protocols and has 'gone off to find someone' in charge—"

The air quotes were audible.

"—who's apparently dealing with an engineering issue. There seems to be some confusion . . . the administrator hasn't answered a direct call, sir. The automatic transmissions have become sporadic."

"Is anyone talking to us at lower levels?"

The sub-captain queried his consoles.

"Engineering reports they had a contact yesterday, asking for suggestions on dealing with a sluggish stability ring. . . . We sent them updates and a testing program."

Kiland stared at the images, pristine and stained. This could go wrong . . .

"Try again for the administrator and send lunch to my office. If the administrator's office does not respond within five minutes, connect me with the principal investigator. I'm declaring a System Alert; chief pilots should sim-up on irregular rendezvous and docking."

Averil 30, 407 CSY
"Prime Investigator, sir."

Verita heard the connection go through, and looked up. He was handsome, stern. It was good to see him, her own . . .

"Captain Kiland," she said, "I'm informed that the administrator's second is escorting her to the tender, as she is planning to transfer before *Implacable* docks. If both leave this station at the same time, I will be in charge."

There was no privacy, of course—the sub-captain was monitoring the line—so she said no more than the immediate information, waiting for his voice, his support . . .

"We've no flight plan filing on that, Investigator; I'll alert my staff to the potential, though if the stability of the ring is in question they ought not plan on launching."

"There have been some irregularities in the spin, Captain, I think as a result of preparation for docking. There is some issue . . ."

"Are you aware, Investigator, of the buildup on the ring's external surfaces?"

Kiland's face was calm, his voice too neutral to be glad of. Beside his face were video images of the RosaRing looking disreputable, like an out-of-use parts dump.

"I am not—"

"We must have clarity about these stains, Investigator. If they are involved with your stability issues they must surely be solved before we can begin docking. We must have the test results for our docking pilots."

Verita floundered. Her expertise was in living things, not in mundane issues of habitat upkeep. She . . .

"My staff is stretched thin, Captain," she told him, reaching for time to think. . . . "And I am not yet in charge. I will have to study this to . . ."

His expression went bland and she saw him sigh. Then his face went gentle, and she became frightened.

"We cannot enter into final docking procedures until we're sure of the docking mechanisms. Have you access to the records? Surely the dock integrity tests have been done! We cannot query your computer directly without permissions and I cannot risk docking until we have updated information. You must act so that we may properly arrive!"

. . . . ◇ . . .

THE SUB-CAPTAIN took the orders without blinking. If the crew blinked, they did so with face bent over screens, following their orders. In a few hours they would be well away from the RosaRing, orbiting the planet and pacing the station at a distance, any docking approach awaiting developments.

The captain did what a captain does: he let his crew work. It was possible that he could have stepped into any one of the work streams, but they were becoming teams and he would have unbalanced them. The sub-captain directs the crew, the captain directs the sub-captain, and has the big picture.

The tactical crew studied the images; some savant had their computers going over accidental information drawn from the drone reports they'd intercepted. There were more images to be studied for change over time, and possible insight into the stability issues, if engineering could be roused to take a look . . .

Engineering—only a few of the current crew had been on the mission which had brought the station here! Engineering was studying the feasibility of a cold-latch using the very pod mounts they'd used to ferry it here in the first place.

The pod transfer systems. . . . If the standard docking system was compromised, the cargo transshipment would be a logistical terror.

"Captain, Station Ops has someone with experience holding down the deck now, sir. We've got one clear line, and they're asking if we can get some medical advice for them in a hurry. They have a lot of sick people, sir, and she says the administrator's locked in the tender bay, refusing to come out. There's unrest."

Kiland stared into the reflection of deck lights in his troth ring for a half a second.

To the sub-captain: "Add me to the listen list, get a medic online, take any information you can about the physical plant situation. Try to patch through to the line I was on with the principal investigator last shift, open to the command chairs only."

"Sir," was the response, and then he listened.

"And this is?"

The image came from RosaRing's medics; he shared it back across space and waited.

Verita winced when she saw it, her indrawn breath loud between them.

"There is this as well, and this, all isolated within the last hours. Tell me about them!"

Captain to subordinate, the last demand. Verita nodded and began.

"The last image is a fairly common nanopump; it is available for use on restricted crops on many worlds. It biodegrades over time; that one is close to the end of utility. I use them in my work.

"The second image appears to be a blood platelet from an oxygen breather. I'm assuming it is human, and it is malformed— perhaps it has been paired with a nanopump and become separated.

"The first image is an anomaly. We see two of these cell structures, intertwined, one with a cell nucleus being—let us say examined or read—and one with a variant cell in, let us say, production. It uses an alternate chirality to induce evolutionary opportunity."

He said nothing for a moment, shared a list of symptoms . . .

"And this . . ."

"Is not surprising."

"This is native to Trikandle, and it is infecting humans through some strange happenstance?"

Verita glanced at the screen, which made it look to Kiland that she'd been avoiding looking at him.

"No, it is not natural to the world. It is not natural anywhere. We brought it. I introduced it. It is of the *Sherikas*."

She looked at him as if he were in the room with her.

"It ought not to have been able to do this, I swear."

• • • ✧ • • •

"THE ENTIRE MISSION is in grave danger, Sub-Captain; nothing medical personnel on board the station have tried have been more than palliative; the filtration approach has failed entirely. We must act quickly and responsibly . . ."

Captain Kiland piloted the captain's gig alone; he'd done so as a young officer and had had the ceremonial honor of piloting Admiral Smit's farewell flight from the *Implacable*. Going over the log books he'd long ago discovered that he had more hours on board than any other and now . . . and now he was the best able to bring the tiny vessel to the scene of the crisis.

They'd jury-rigged infection monitors once it was apparent that the kitchens had been infested, or the air filters or . . . and so maybe it *was* true that the only person on board the RosaRing free of the mutagenic was the principal investigator. He carried two of the touch-free monitors and eight of the *Implacable*'s biohazard suits, while he wore a standard spacesuit he could shed in an outer lock. The gig could use the smaller connects and emergency ports, and he had a target, a hatch well away from the crew quarters where the sick were lying where they fell, or hiding in the darkness as systems went offline.

The sub-captain was overseeing refitting a wing of half-empty crew quarters into an isolation ward, though by now there was word of deaths among the ill, and odd behaviors among the living. They'd gotten some hope, though, from a few stalwarts who switched to back-up air supplies early . . .

It was a largely silent voyage. Several hours for the gig, a considered lifetime for Kiland. They'd mapped out as best they could the ports where the stains were, and clearly the hub ends were both affected. The tender's failed launch made that port inaccessible as well.

His targets were the several ports in the area of the labs, ports largely unused since the station was first provisioned by massive temporary dry docks long before the mission to Trikandle. The station was visible to naked eye against space, strobes pointing to the parts he didn't want to visit—he was avoiding the central hubs in favor of the outer ring, the lower quarter of the outer ring once he'd got oriented. The thing was huge—of course it was, that's why it had taken the *Implacable* to move it!

"Kiland? They gave me this as a direct channel."

He froze. There was too much to say now, and most of it said or shared before. He needed to concentrate. And . . .

"Verita. Yes, I am here. Approaching. Be calm. I'm cruising along the hull, watching section numbers go by. Yours will be soon, Verita."

The contact was voice alone, so he watched the structure go by as he corrected for spin. He doubted that he wobbled, and he waited, glad that she could not see his face.

"Kiland, we have always been honest, so I will be honest. I am not well. It is not mere tension—you know that I know tension. I— I fell and bloodied my nose, Kiland, and it stopped instantly. But, I have tools. I am good at my work.

"My blood shows changes, too, Kiland. Please, fly on by, Kiland. Fly on by!"

* * * ◇ * * *

SHE WAS AWAY from the microphone some moments but he heard and said· "It is too late for me to fly by, Verita. We are committed. I must see and report for myself.

"Tell me your exact location. I will find the port closest to you. I will . . ."

He was under the bulk of the thing, with white and blue and white and blue and white and blue blurring before his eyes to white. . . . Then blue. He matched velocity until the surface below him barely crawled and then, numbers and letters.

"Forty-four AGAAGF/FE," he said out loud as the gig answered his touch sweetly, approaching hatches auxiliary collars could link to. A hatch outlined, as if sketched over from within, by a collar of red and green crystals around the more prosaic ceramics meant to guard the ship close, even in the no-space that was Jump. His cameras surely transmitted that to the *Implacable*, surely the sub-captain saw the signs . . .

"Yes," Verita said, "that will be several doors down. I can go there, Kiland."

"There is a wobble," he said, which was true of the ring's motion and not his own.

"The next hatch will provide a better attachment angle. I will check that."

The little vessel let the ring slide on by, and in a moment he heard a sound that might have been a cry or a cough and . . .

"Kiland, I am not well. It will take me some minutes to get to the next airlock."

"No matter, the time," he said, "*Implacable* awaits my order."

"Yes, but I should move while I can, you see . . ."

"I have seen what I need to see, Verita. I shall return to the port where you are now. We shall be together very soon."

The gig bumped very slightly against the stain edging the port. "*Implacable*, I am docking. We have blue, blue, blue. Without doubt, we have blue, blue, blue."

"Kiland, tell me where to move?"

"Stay there, Verita. I will come to you. I am solving this."

* * * ◇ * * *

"BEAM BANKS One and Two, go live as leads. The captain has declared a lethal threat situation. We have identified and targeted a threat.

"Prepare to fire on my command, on radar's current target T02. This is not a drill, you will now go to full combat power. Your target should be oversaturated at all wavelengths until plasma. Repeat, until plasma. Await my command."

"Beam Banks Three and Four. Your targets are any rapidly vectoring objects showing planetary escape velocity. Your targets should be oversaturated at all wavelengths until plasma. Repeat, until plasma. Await my command."

"Beam Banks Five through Twenty, your planetary grids are pretargeted and programmed. You will fire until plasma. Repeat, you will fire until plasma. Await my command."

A decisive moment, the image from the gig, showing an empty pilot's seat and board. The forward cams show a fringe of strange color around the docking collar, growing.

"All fire," says the man. "All fire, all fire."

Somewhere, a singer is sobbing quietly at her terminal. The ship trembles. And trembles again, the ship's rotation bringing all the beam projectors to bear, one after another, a rotational broadside searing the ether.

There is silence, and then, loud in the silence of tense breathlessness there is the news of solving:

"Zap."

✧ Revolutionists ✧

FROM THE FIRST BOOK the Liaden Universe® has dealt with the often necessary conflict between progress and stability. Here, in a story requested for The Razor's Edge, *an anthology all about revolution, we looked at what can happen when that conflict hits the inexperienced, the naive, and the privileged young of an out of the way space station.*

✧✧✧✧

"Arin's Envidaria, *as instituted for the Seventeen Worlds by Arin Gobelyn's son Jethri Gobelyn and overseen by the Carrassens-Denobli, established an egalitarian trade network meant to be self-supporting during the disruptive incursion of Rostov's Dust into the lesser galactic sub-arm.*

"Jethri Gobelyn, a peripatetic traveler and trader, left his mark in many ways; his genes are said to be widely dispersed in and around the Seventeen World trading nexus. Due to divergent local institutional traditions the Seventeen Worlds Network experienced a period of instability following the end of the dust-dark and the reestablishment of regular trading with the wider Terran-Liaden trading web."

—*Gehrling's Middle History of the Inhabited Galactic Sub-Plane, Third Terran edition*

GERAL WAS ALONE, as he often was. This time was different because he was doing squad work solo instead of with the whole squad. Famy Binwa'd called him sudden.

"We got a big meeting for only Full Staff and Seniors, no cits allowed. Secret, too, you can't mention it. You're covering for Security. Get to it!"

Another drill, he'd figured, but once his ID read as present in Service Squad's corridor, Binwa'd said, "Not a drill this time, Geral. You're mobile structure security! Watch yourself, there's been trouble!"

So he went careful. The logs did show trouble—odd trouble. Bar fights gone to flash-riots, followed by attempts to enter Admin without permission. Sabotaged cameras. Yeah, the cits weren't pleased with Admin changing anything—heck, people would argue and fight if their old veeds disappeared and no chance to stuff 'em into personal holdings, much less work shortages and menus gone thin.

Down here in the inner structure, though, he ought to be fine, no real chance of riot or change to threaten him. Binwa'd sounded tense, like Geral might not be up to the job.

It didn't help Geral that he'd been raised like he was fragile, him being a good birth in a bad Standard Year. In fact, him and Luchee being the only pair born across three hundred and ten days—and before-hand some doubts he'd be born at all.

Once he *was* born they were careful of him—after him there were three years in a row with no births, period. They said it was the famine that did it, but then the cheese planets got back in gear after their little civil war and things got back to regular. Kids was born station-side again—they used fertility drugs and had a bunch of twins and triplets—so there were always a pack of youngers that he didn't quite fit in with.

The Seniors, it was known, kept him in reserve as a special case, 'cause he had good blood, since it was the 'fusions that let them get to their proper ages and the 'fusions that kept them safe during the thin-food. They'd been so close-knit that cousins were sisters and little brothers nephews. They tested him and never tapped him, but they kept his mother close. She had the blood and had survived his birth sturdy, even in those bad times.

His mother—he hadn't seen her for almost a Standard Year; she'd gone up deck and was living in Senior Pod, where the Seniors had their own medico and kept their own shifts. The last time he'd seen her, he'd been on 'cide clean-up. She'd been in a hurry elsewhere and had stopped when she saw him, nodding a greeting.

"Looking good, Geral Jethri. Don't join no rowdies, and don't think you need a way out," here she'd gestured to the 'cide site, "'cause you're set. I'm good for years and you—you're in the right orbit. You got the blood, so they'll hold on to you like they hold on to me. The Seniors need you! I'll see you about, I bet."

That orbit had brought him here, after all, with him having not spoken to her again.

He patted the metal turnwheel at the master seal between open corridors and the utility tunnels. He tested the seal with a gas sniffer. He looked for little hidden messages. His comm unit was on channel, so he spoke to it.

"Seal three checks out, Binwa, got the veed. No hosties, no notes."

No reply for the moment, but Famy Binwa was always a tad slow in the Control room, more afraid of making a mistake than—

Mud, ought to use the correct form, shouldn't he? Things were spelled out proper on Security Detail, especially for Binwa, who was a boss because his ma was and not so much 'cause he knew what he was doing.

Silence went on. Binwa got touchy, but not like he was a bad sort—they'd talked many times about how things might change now that the curl of the dust the system'd been stuck in for three hundred Standards was drifting out. Lately Binwa was always on duty when Geral was, like they were going to be paired on the low shift forever, like kids being left to deal while the adults did something for adults.

"Please repeat, Squad," Binwa finally insisted.

Geral translated this time, from the start, his voice sounding odd in his own ears, which meant Binwa'd just turned the recorders on and his mic was live.

"Attention Internal Control. Squad Forty Security Update. Seal Three is tight. No hostiles. No anomalies."

"Squad Forty, we confirm your voice match, we confirm your

location, we confirm no hostiles, we confirm Seal Three is secure, we confirm there are no service reminder notes. Please move to next station. Veed feed as time permits."

He hadn't found any hostiles so far. Hostiles in his early training had always meant Yxtrang invaders, but that was a scare tactic to help kids keep serious. His whole life, born and bred here, he'd never heard of an actual Yxtrang station invasion. So far as he'd ever seen, a hostie was a Security full-timer slurping toot or half asleep over a streaming 'venture veed.

These days the threat was supposed to be Revolutionists, a secret group trying to change the way things on Spadoni Station worked and who was in charge. He'd never met any of them outright, though some of the tougher hanger-abouts might could be. They'd complain that things needed changing—that it used to be you was free to work at what you wanted or what you could, but now they were being sent to the cheese planets on contract, want to or no! Somehow it was Admin doing things wrong, or the Seniors who needed replacing to make things right.

The Revolutionist talk had gained a lot of energy in the last quarter, what with Odd Things happening Out There. Out There being other sectors, sectors they were hearing more and more about because the dust was thinning so rapidly. Outside hadn't been important growing up, except that it made the Seventeen Worlds allies because of the *Envidaria*.

He'd read the *Envidaria* a bunch of times, and you could say he believed in it. To stop one world being the top spot like Liad tried to do, the *Envidaria*'d kept the sides even . . . and that meant worlds shouldn't own all the ships, all the stations, all the commerce. Spadoni was 'sposed to be independent, her people free to work at what they could, while the trade org belonged to the planet system and most of the ships came from Outside. The *Envidaria* was supposed to make that work.

He'd also read a bunch of the couldies about *Envidaria*, the idea. They were made-up things like *The Secret of Lord Jethri*, *The Clouds of Spite*, and yes, even a buncha the mances like *Three on A Ship* and *The Master Firegemster*. It was kind of funny seeing the images of

Jethri on this very same station back when it was fresh-built, and knowing he, Geral, carried part of that name, and that he really did, if you squinted, look like Jethri. Stars in his blood, courtesy of his multi-great-grandma's bunking with the man with the plan.

* * * ◇ * * *

GERAL LINGERED in Corridor Nine, feeling a little homesick.

He'd brought Luchee to the 9-9 storeroom for a kiss and some touches back when he was just Deck Plus, and even showed her Vent 77, the inactive space that was technically just a Three Seal since it had been a part of the temporary build-in docks meant for short term storage. Him and Luchee'd been of an age, and 'bout as poor, both born to mothers on station base pay. The mothers lived cubbywall to cubbywall, shared corridor frontspace, and on slowdown weeks they sat out front with everyone else, passing sips while the kids hunted stuff to turn in for credits at the recycle, being too young to trade blood for points. Once he'd been born and was proof her line was clean, that was the start, and after he hit puberty they knew he didn't break his bones just by standing, or bleed forever, nor any of the other problems that had come along to stationers in the rough times a couple hundred Standards goneby.

Him and Luchee, they'd got in a fight once, a fierce thing where they wasted some of that precious blood arguing about if it was *good* to trade blood in.

"Points are good and you know it. Have to save a little extra," he'd told her.

She'd squinched her face up, looked those grey eyes straight at him. "You do it more than once and it'll go on your records. And then you'll get stuck, just like your ma. She can't go higher, 'cause Admin keeps her like she's a crop down in 'ponics!

"I see my own ma just waiting for the points to rack up and I'm not gonna live like that and neither should you.

"I could just shake you sometimes for not paying attention!"

Well, she did shake him, and he shook her back, and somehow they hit a gravity well frustrated with each other. And there was the blood, and needing to clean it up before someone called a safety on them for creating a hazmat situation.

In the end they'd patched it up and kept hanging together. They promised each other they'd keep their blood and use all that extra energy to study. They even did some joint Informatics until their skills didn't match any more. Luchee was good with maths, and she'd been set to student status, 'cept all the classes were always full of the C and B deck folks and no room for her, no matter how high her test scores were.

Him, the one Luchee was always getting out of scrapes—*he'd* been free to study how he wanted—station stuff, and the *Envidaria*—always interested as much in how the station worked as in how far he could go updecks in life. So, turned out, *he* could make a living doing what he wanted, and *she* couldn't even go to school, nor get anything better than hour-work.

Luchee and him had thrilled a couple times in the vent space in Corridor Nine but he gave it up after he'd stopped by to find her there not very dressed and with an older guy from up Admin Deck just as sweaty and calling her name like he was hurting, which still made him twitch to think about even if it was a few years back.

She might have warned him, anyhow . . . but she hadn't, and they'd got all disconnected over it, with her saying things was too complicated for her to talk about with him anymore, and levels he had no business to know—him being in the Service Squad and his ma still transfusing.

She wouldn't know him, then, and he got busy with his doin's, so he forgot to miss her, 'til he heard she'd connected with a visiting spacer, and gone off as side-crew with no notice to no one. He figured that was luck for her and he did miss her, though by then he had a crew-grade sleep-unit, and didn't need the cubby, anyway.

"Squad Forty, this is Green Office." Binwa's voice in his ear jerked him out from remembering. "We have inbound ships and I have to check-mark all the security stations. No one's covering the armory. I have keyed your unit in; I need you to go there and sit at the boards, it's supposed to be occupied when ships approach."

"Green Office, Squad Forty is just one of me, and that's supposed to be a three-crew location, according to training. I . . ."

"*This* is also a three-crew location and there's one of me, Squad Forty. We are in security lockdown mode because of that meeting. Go, lock yourself in, report. The hatch is set to your ID."

"I'm on my way. Does route matter?"

"Squad Forty . . . call it a hurry, and I don't care how you get there long's you do it quick."

"Confirmed, this is a hurry and I'm on free route. Going."

• • •✧• • •

THE ARMORY had opened to him, as Binwa'd told him it would. Geral rushed into the control area and was in front of the screen, helmet and gloves off, still sweating—and only part of that from the path he'd followed. He looked at the controls, familiar only from sim, and worried, thought of Luchee getting stuff right off and figured he could remember what he had to here.

He was trying to get his balance back on account of the tween-deck utility shafts he'd run as fast as he could. The places where you could be caught in gravity errors where you got pulled in two or three directions from overlapping grav fields or where weak fields might let you dive down a metal tunnel for meters on end.

"Squad Forty! Check that hatch!"

Geral twisted his head.

"Closed." It had made a muffled thrum when he'd pushed it across hard.

"Not showing good here!"

He rose carefully, left leg and knee a trifle sore from a missed gravity slip. It hadn't been there last time he was through . . . but that happened these days as the fabric of the station strained against its age. It should have been refitted before he was born, but there'd been the Troubles, after all.

He twisted the handle and slid the hatch open an arm's length. He hadn't tested the pressure gauges and now his helmet sat at the second seat, with all his readouts . . .

He pulled, sullenly, and yelled across the room as it slammed . . .

"Now?" He forgot his formal again, but then so did Binwa, who was sounding strained.

"Not sealed!"

Geral pulled his weight against the handle, yanked it open, staring into the hatch mechanicals.

"Mud and wind twists!"

There were four pressure latches meant to grab and seat when the handle was rotated. One close to his hip level was fine and bright, and the one just above chest height was, too. The top and bottom latches though, looked like they had something in the way of that final click-seal, something printed in a very thin flex-sheet that fell into place after the hatch was cycled once.

"What was that, Squad Forty?" Now Binwa sounded *really* worried.

Fingers quick on the sharp metal hatch edge, Geral pulled hard, and out came the bottom strip, unfolding to near half his arm length. He stared, shoved it into a storage pocket on the duty-suit, reached to pull the other while . . .

"Problem spot, *hold comm,*" he managed, and emphasizing that helped him pull the tattered top strip down to shove it, too, into his pocket.

"Jonimo!" He slammed the hatch hard, and this time the click sounded like a solid thunk, all right, and . . .

"Jonimo?" came the worried voice and then: "That's got it!"

He sat heavily at the console, pulling a frayed yellow strip from his suit.

"Is that code, Squad Forty?"

Geral gasped a short laugh, wiping sweat from his forehead.

"Kind of is, Binwa. Haven't you ever done a suit-walk? *Jonimo* is what you say when you jump off the station, to tell your squad you're free in space."

"Never been off-station. Never been on a ship, either," Binwa admitted.

"Anyhow, looks like the hatch was blocked from tight seal. I mean on purpose—I've sent you veed of it!"

"Yes. I should have expected this. This is part of it all, I'm afraid."

"Part of what?"

"Things happening. Comm channels I can't get to, and ships incoming but no one's talking to me. There's a Conference going on and I can't get feed on that, either. Security's tampered with, locking me out! I don't think they trust me, Geral, I see what they're up to!"

He sat; the board demanded ID.

"Binwa, you have to approve my biometrics, it says."

"Yes. They left me alone here and now I invoked Catastrophe Ops. I'll confirm you as Security, Acting Squad Leader. I got the key. Heck, I'll just make you Shift Security Leader. Sensors on!"

Geral paused, the sound of *Catastrophe Ops* bouncing around his thoughts, making him a little worried.

"I'm looking into the camera, straight-face, and got my left hand on the pad."

"I see this, Squad. Takes a moment—give me your full ID, number, and names."

He did the numbers and letters first, then said "Geral Jethri Quai-Hwang."

"Moment, Squad."

The screens lit up, followed by a shockingly loud click as something mechanical thunked in the walls near the hatch.

"You are live, Security Leader. Right now, there's you and me, and then there's the rest of the station. You're Security Lead. You can do almost anything. Wait, I need to take care of something. It may be a few minutes."

Probably has to go pee, Geral figured, *he's like that when he's nervous.*

Geral was used to waiting, but not to having this much information in front of him, open to him, with the time going from one minute to many.

But yes, he *did* see, there on one screen all the pressure points on the station, on a zoomable map-grid, and there, on another, the status of the doors, the pressure variations, water and fluid flow, the gravity variations. Also, *all* the reports, everyone's shift status, security stations, medical alerts, a blinking yellow triangle showing a guard status—

Two names he knew quite well, under guard in the hospital, on pregnancy watch. Tifney and Pettipi! Both of them? Both of the twins under guard? Both due multi-births?

He rolled the idea around in his head, remembering how they'd corralled him on First Orbit's Eve, the pair full of energy and inviting him to a quiet shindig, offering up a touch of *vya* and, after the *vya*, a long night on a bed full of them and them alone. The following shift-month they'd collected him individually a time or two—and then the Admin shifts changed and his moved to match Famy Binwa's. He'd wondered what happened.

The blood. They'd wanted his blood, that was what. And when they'd tested pregnant . . .

There was dread in his gut and he couldn't quite swallow it away.

• • •✧• • •

BINWA DIDN'T TELL HIM what took a few minutes, but Geral knew it was far longer than that. He'd drilled down, peeking into private records, including the two women in hospital expecting multiple births. He found his own record, eventually, full of notations like "loner, no strong friendships, tractable if left to his own pursuits," but the cross-references to Senior Resource and Admin Alert made him worried, and the multiple notes over time— *Transfuse only to Seniors and Blood Resource*—worried him more.

Other areas didn't open to him—but yes, the Seniors had their own shifts and apparently they'd added his mother to their number, for her records were all behind a security wall he couldn't breach.

He'd closed that file, tried to understand the rest of the boards in front of him, including the 3D station situation board.

"I am back," Binwa said, sounding winded. "What do you see?"

"Three ships," Geral said once he figured out what he was looking at. "Three ships closing this says."

There was a curse then, and an ugly sound, like muffled warning horns over and over, and then distant shivers in the fabric of the station. Inside the armory, panels flashed, lights dimmed, the status board showed blue blocks on the station map—every pressure door and hatch was sealed or sealing. The words GENERAL SECURITY LOCKDOWN were prominent.

Under that status a series of images flashed onto the screens, security cameras showing rotating views of corridors. The red lights showed—

"Where's Security? If this is a general lockdown, where's the rest of Security?" Geral tried the corridor cameras, finding nothing. The meeting rooms, though, were crowded.

"Never mind them, Geral, *you're* Security, because I can depend on you, and *they're* conspirators. All of them. The rest are . . . offline. They'll have to back down, now."

"Who?"

"There's a revolt, Geral. The Seniors are trying to sell the station to the cheesers and that's not in the Crew Compact. The station and all of us, they want to trade us so they can live forever. You and me and . . . the Seniors are locked in a room, and Admin, too. They were having their meeting, so I had to act. The Seniors made me do it! I've put out a call-in for the rest of the Service Squad to take over Security, but you're the only one's come to me, Geral. My mother's on their side, she says the *Envidaria* is over, done. Who believes that?"

Geral thought about it. There hadn't been an end date on the *Envidaria*, the arrangement. It was how they'd lived for hundreds of Standards. It was what made Jethri and Arin so important, and helped guide millions of lives . . .

"Control, Green Office. I mean—I don't think the *Envidaria* is over, Binwa. I don't! What should I do, then?"

"There's a loyalty oath on the screen, Geral. Accept it. Then we'll open the armory weapons bay, so you can repel boarders."

• • •✧• • •

GERAL WAS, according to Famy, fully second in command now. The Seniors, the Security Squad, everyone had to listen to Binwa until this got fixed. Binwa had a copy of *The Crew Compact* open and was reading it out across the channels to them. Geral could hear him in the background, droning on, then emphasizing random words.

Geral'd left the anteroom, secured it so it would only open to him or on order from Binwa. He'd rushed to the inner armory and now, in the weapons bay, he was bathed in brightness.

The full-suits were there. All of them were there, including three brand-news that had Full test Green labels everywhere—new and never worn.

He hurried, stripped to basics, grabbed up one with a green tag showing shoulder and hip to toe ratios that ought to do, and squiggled his way in, knowing that the wrong that was happening was *really* wrong—all the suits here ought already to be on someone, all of them ought to be in position, *all* of them. Comes to worst, might be someone expecting this suit might come through the seal any minute—

But they weren't roused, were they? All the external packs were on the wall, weren't they, *and* all the guns?

Seemed strange that they wouldn't have grabbed the guns for a revolt. Seemed strange they could have grabbed the Bloodlines—that would be Ma, among others!—without bothering other services. But the alert was out and they weren't here, the regular crew, nor his.

"Squad Forty," he said to the mic even before his gloves clicked on seal, "this is Lead on Squad Forty, back-up not suited yet," he said, knowing that someone in Control ought to have a veed feed and see him standing alone and know what he meant. If someone was back-up to Squad Forty they were going to have to show soon, else . . .

"Squad Forty, confirmed. Watching for you to get under pressure. Pack M and L are assigned yours. If crew shows with my code, make them double up on extras."

But there *wasn't* anybody else. It would be him and Binwa, wouldn't it? Pack M was the full mobility unit with projectiles as well as lasers. It was a leader's unit—had some range on the jets, had some firepower he'd never tried, but supposed to be automatic. The suit should fit itself in when he got there, and the unit ought to heed him . . .

"Sealed," he said when he was, again seeing the squad room that ought to have sixteen people, empty but for him. The heads-up display came live, bringing almost too much information: local internal and external pressure and atmospheres, state of the connections and network, ammunition count, loitering time, battery state, and . . . empty slots where Squad Leader ought to have a squad.

"Control? Squad Forty prepped for EVA, grabbing packs."

Not much more to be said, with no one talking back and no one yet coming to be his backup.

He slapped the plate and walked through, lights coming up as he did. Earnestly wishing there was motion behind him, knowing there wasn't, he only quarter-turned to the plate on this side, where the pre-packs waited, patient as death, for their missions.

That slap was bordering wistful; the angled sliver of view showed the stark white of the two closest suits, hanging empty, before the scissors of the closing door left him even more alone.

"Two seals, Control. Mounting up."

"You are authorized to open to vacuum and deploy. You are authorized to use force; your weapons are live."

There were two hatches, one with pack rails and one without, and the packs sat there waiting. The hatch could take five at a time if need be—

Geral backed into Pack M, reaching overhead to pull himself up onto that slight saddle, his elbows and forearms resting on the U of the equipment, his legs on the stirrups. Quick motions clicked the umbilical on each side into the power systems and into the pack's extended environmental units.

"Pack M systems attached to Leader," a quiet voice told him. "Accept, please."

He did that, and Pack M let him know that Pack L was attaching to hard points, which he felt, and he took a deep breath. Now the view was augmented even further and all those points there on the left side were weapons far more powerful than a pistol. He shuddered with knowing he'd not armed things yet, and knowing he had too much power, anyway, for someone whose leading had mostly been to a spot at the bar and then open a door for bed and a roll, if he was lucky.

"Geral, we need you to occupy Bay Four. The other docks are under control from here, so they're secure . . . and I got Traffic's radio feeds locked up tight so they can't be involved—but if that ship gets to the dock, I can't stop them here—none of the other service units are responding. Security has gone over, they're on strike, too. They're all Revolutionists and we got to stop them. Hold Bay Four!"

"Confirm, Control. Hold Bay Four."

• • •✧• • •

HE BARELY NOTICED SPACE, space being what there was mostly except for the reality of the station and the need to be at a hard-to-reach location. His suit was quiet around him, but he heard his own breathing, kept reminding himself to follow the color-coded dots, to follow the easy-to-read blinking lights . . . but no, he shouldn't!

Resisting the urge to talk to himself about it, he said, "Control, you might want to turn off traffic control lighting. I can see where I'm going without."

"Will do. Might need to go silent so they can't monitor . . . I'm releasing all suit control to you, Geral. You're autonomous now."

Many of the flashing lights went away. The numbers on the side of the station's hull didn't, but the details of a docking collar would be harder to see with the station rotating into darkness, especially if there was someone between you and getting close enough to use ship lights to illuminate it.

Guidance. He could use some guidance here . . .

"Control?"

Silence.

Out there, suddenly, there was blackness as the local star was eclipsed, and then again, the light making him a shadow.

They'd never warned him about this kind of stuff, that he'd be a sharp spot on the hull, that resisting invasion gave the advantage to the people out there who wanted to take . . .

"Test, circuit open. Spadoni, please reply. Please initiate routine docking. . . . There's my echoes, Spadoni, you can hear me.

"Spadoni, we are coming to dock. Please turn guidance on. This is Carrassens *Anna V* on a scheduled shipment. I am Pilot In Charge Luchinda Eerik of the—"

Luchinda? His Luchee? It sounded just like her, it did, even across the years and, yeah, she was quick and sharp. A pilot? But there was trouble now . . .

Also, Control was on silence and had locked down Traffic's radio.

"This is Squad Forty. There's been riots and Revolutionists. We can't let you dock until there's an all-clear ordered. We may use any means to hold this docking bay. We have been authorized to use force, if required."

"If you fire on my ship I will return fire, Squad Forty."

"I know you will, Luchee," he said, "Just like you busted my nose, thank you."

A pause, not caused by the slow crawl of radio waves. He used it to maneuver his unit to one of the hard points. The dull red triangle glowed in outline on the left and he speared the arms-length metal pipe protecting the cabling into it, feeling the snap as it tightened, followed by inserting the cable into the blue circle on the right with a similar mechanical snap. Pack M and Pack L oriented themselves as the hardpoint locked; he was essentially an external gun turret now.

He should have heard confirmation from Control on that, but inside the suit everything matched up. Autonomous.

Through his faceplate he could see another eclipsed star, and then augments hit and he had targeting information on a ship coming nearly straight at him. The bad news was that they must have him now, as well, know that he was not speaking from a station defense battery, he was merely a stud locked upright on a bright hull, casting a shadow to infinity.

"Squad Forty, we are not looking for a fight. We're not Revolutionists, we're a trade ship. And I'm getting counter information from another source claiming that you have been misrouted and misinformed and are to be ignored. If you're Geral, you're a braver fool than I ever realized, facing down a ship with a suit!"

He heard that, breathed a curse that was loud in his own ears even if not broadcast.

"Control? What status? What support?"

He was clicking between comm broadcast channels furiously, the head's up display showing him active bands.

After a long pause, Binwa broke silence.

"I still hold Control. Security won't help. They want to give the station away, the whole station, Geral! Why's there three ships? At least one of those ships are what they've been waiting on. They want to send us all to Fromage Two. They're going to occupy the station . . . you got to stop them from getting in."

"Squad?" came Luchee's drawl.

"*AnnaV*, I'm sorry. My orders remain."

"Dammit, Geral, you're alone in a spacesuit and there's three ships out here."

"I'm on lockpoint," he managed. "I've got war units, Luchee. Are you in a battleship?"

"Can't discuss it, Squad Forty. You're going to have to move away from that dock. I hope you'll do it soon; my shift is due to end but I'm not allowed to leave docking incidents unresolved. I'm lighting up for rendezvous."

The faceplate showed two ghostly outlines now, the M unit's sensors showing where the approaching ships were, where . . .

There! A blot took shape exactly where the faceplate put it, stars going away, and then the blot took color and shape as brilliant points of light, some blinking to varying pulses and others just there.

Training recall came to him, the five blue lights circling the nose of the ship meaning *AnnaV* was headed right at him, the slow blinking red lights ringing the blue were the pods-heads, the apparent bright ring between the blue and the red was where *AnnaV*'s hull swelled to the pod points. More light now, and he was awash in it, the faceplate barely shielding him from the full intensity. The approaching ship slowed, loomed . . .

From the station channels:

"Squad Forty, you must stand down and return your aux-packs to the armory. Your training mission is over. Famy Binwa has been relieved of all command. Your loyalty oath is noted. You must return to the armory . . ."

Geral shivered. It was Famy's ma!

"Don't listen! They've breached this line, but we resist the revolution. Civilians cannot understand the dangers—"

"This is Vice Administrator Binwa. My son has been relieved of shift and staff command and is being removed from the control room. You are now under my direct orders, Geral Jethri. Return to station, place yourself under Security's protection. You will be escorted to upgraded quarters and this incident will be purged from your file."

There was a short pause before she spoke again, sharply.

"Geral Jethri?"

He swallowed, the promise of upgrades making his stomach clench, as he thought of the twins, both pregnant. His kids. His blood . . .

There came sounds of heavy breathing, and pounding, through the earset, then Famy Binwa's voice, loud.

"I'm loyal to the *Envidaria*. This is a breach—I will resist, I will eject, I will—"

Beneath Geral, the station lurched, vibration traveling through the taut cables locking him and his packs to the surface, shaking him and his suit against the strapping.

"Geral Jethri? Let me make your choice plain. Return to station and receive an upgrade. Continue this revolt and we will be rid of you."

Geral was still trying to understand. Famy. The Revolutionists. Forced labor on the cheese worlds. The—

"I am," he whispered, "under the command of Famy Binwa."

There was another lurch; this one smaller and more personal.

"Control?" Geral demanded, wondering if some unknown ship had managed a violent latch-dock out of his view. "Squad Forty reporting anomaly—"

His faceplate showed him a flashing: UNLOCK ALERT UNLOCK ALERT UNLOCK ALERT UNLOCK at the same time it showed a potential target not much bigger than him drifting away from the station, a tumbling figure, a . . .

His faceplate flashed a warning—power issues for the lockpoint.

A KLUNG shook him; distantly a station thruster showed power and the station twisted. Or he did.

Jettisoned. He'd been jettisoned!

Below him the station rolled and the faceplate echoed that, and now it showed him the station as a target, receding slowly.

Everyone he knew in the universe was out there, targets. Targets, if he was willing.

· · ·✦· · ·

HE'D TRIED THREE AIRLOCKS, chasing them as the station rotated. It was as if he didn't exist. His suit showed station comm circuits locked against him, and the last effort to close with the station had been met by a round of attitude jets, almost taunting him.

Working his suit kept him calm; he had to think hard about it, but it was a new suit and getting easier to use every minute.

Eventually, one of the ships disappeared beyond the bulk of the station; he could see portions of it as it docked, but wasn't in comm circuit.

The other two ships now rode in orbit between him and the station. One was, he knew, the *AnnaV*. The other he didn't know—

"Spacer Geral Jethri, this is *AnnaV*, offering to connect you with a recovery ship."

Luchee's voice was calm and quiet in his ear.

"Spacer? I'm a stationer. I can't . . ."

"You are a distressed spacer, discovered free-floating in an orbit you are unable to recover from under your own power. I can certify that. We can do that for you, Geral Jethri."

"But the station! I'm Service Squad, I'm supposed to . . ."

"They abandoned you, Geral Jethri. You're locked out."

He fought with himself. He had forty hours of air. Enough firepower, though, to . . .

Famy Binwa had trusted him. Famy had fooled him. Famy . . . had ejected without a suit . . .

Luchee took a breath.

"Either you're a distressed spacer or you're dead," she said flatly.

"I don't have anything . . ." He stuttered to a stop.

She didn't argue that point. His air showed thirty-eight-point-seven hours now.

"Geral, I'm going off-duty. My shift is ending. Be smart. I can arrange for pick-up, while I'm Pilot In Charge. That's all I can do. You need to make the choice.

"You need to save yourself."

Geral stared beyond the lurking ships, beyond the station's

disorienting rotation against the background of a distant three-mooned planet.

There was silence for a while. When Luchee spoke again, it was like she'd woken him up from a drowse.

"Geral, we're docking next. We can't pick you up; if you're on-board when we dock, Spadoni will arrest you. They'll lock you up and take your blood and you won't even get points for it! You'll never be free!"

The station rotated under him.

"The other ship with us is not docking, Geral. Will you let them pick you up? She . . . they believe in the *Envidaria*. They live by it. They're free! They want to talk to you, Geral. I trust them. Remember, we said we weren't going to give blood to the Seniors. You promised me, Geral! We'll be in radio shadow now, be smart!"

The station's rotation was patient, unforgiving. *AnnaV*, in pursuit of a docking bay, slid into the bright side while he and his suit were in the darkness.

Geral was alone, as he often was. But . . .

He had a choice. He could be desperate for what wasn't going to happen, like Famy Binwa, or he could be like Jethri and Arin had been and make something happen. He could let the Seniors own him or he could . . .

"This is Spacer Geral Jethri Quai-Hwang What ship?"

He asked as if he knew ships, which he didn't; as if the name mattered. He'd been prepared to fire upon them, an hour gone, and now . . .

A pleasant female voice filled the ether, carried by a strong, directional signal.

"This is Ship *Disian*. Geral Jethri, may we match velocity with you and bring you aboard? Please, call me *Disian*.

"Also," came the pleasant voice, with no sense of irony, "it would be good if you would turn off targeting mode and safe your weapons. We can rendezvous in ten minutes."

Geral flinched, shook his head at himself, and safed the weapons. The oxygen read-out on his faceplate said thirty-six-point-seven hours and he was free to watch it count down, if he really wanted to. Maybe the station would pull him in, right before the last. Maybe they'd decide they needed his blood too bad to let him go.

Or, maybe they wouldn't.

A deep breath then, and he used his jets, turning to admire the view, and the ship, approaching.

The oxygen countdown had begun to bore him and he realized that, despite it all, he was getting hungry.

"Yes, Ship *Disian*," he said eventually. "Thank you. Please come for me. This distressed spacer accepts your offer of aid."